The
THE INITIATION AND THE CAPTIVE PART I
SECRET CIRCLE

VOLUME 1

L.J. SMITH

Hodder
Children's
Books

A division of Hachette Children's Books

Secret Circle © 1992 by Lisa Smith and Daniel Weiss Associates

Secret Circle – The Initiation/The Captive first published in the USA in 2008 by HarperTeen, an imprint of Harper Collins Publishers.

A bind-up edition first published 2010 by Hodder Children's Books

This TV tie-in edition published in Great Britain in 2011 by Hodder Children's Books

1

A catalogue record for this book is available from the British Library

ISBN: 978 1 444 90792 6

Typeset in Meridien Roman by Avon DataSet Ltd, Bidford-on-Avon, Warwickshire

Printed and bound by CPI Group (UK) Ltd, Croydon, CR0 4YY

The paper and board used in this paperback by Hodder Children's Books are natural reyclable products made from wood grown in sustainable forests. The manufacturing processes conform to the environmental regulations of the country of origin.

Hodder Children's Books
a division of Hachette Children's Books
338 Euston Road, London NW1 3BH
An Hachette UK company
www.hachette.co.uk

For my mother, as patient and loving as Mother Earth
For my father, the parfit gentil knight

PROLOGUE

That night Cassie had a dream – or perhaps it wasn't a dream. She dreamed that her mother and grandmother came into the room, moving noiselessly, almost gliding over the floor. In her dream she was aware of them, but she couldn't move as they lifted her from the chair and undressed her and put her to bed. Then they stood over the bed, looking down at her. Her mother's eyes were strange and dark and unfathomable.

'Little Cassie,' her grandmother said with a sigh. 'At last. But what a pity—'

'Sh!' her mother said sharply. 'She'll wake up.'

Her grandmother sighed again. 'But you can see that it's the only way...'

'Yes,' her mother said, her voice empty and resigned. 'I can see that you can't escape destiny. I shouldn't have tried.'

That's just what I thought, Cassie realized as the dream faded. You can't escape destiny. Vaguely she could see her mother and grandmother moving towards the door, and she could hear the whisper of their voices. She couldn't make out any words, though, until one sibilant hiss came through.

'...sacrifice...'

She wasn't sure which of the women had said it, but it echoes over and ove rin her mind. Even as darkness covered her, she kept hearing it. *Sacrifice . . . sacrifice . . . sacrifice . . .*

THE
INITIATION

CHAPTER

1

It wasn't supposed to be this hot and humid on Cape Cod. Cassie had seen it in the guidebook; everything was supposed to be perfect here, like Camelot.

Except, the guidebook added absently, for the poison ivy, and ticks, and green flies, and toxic shellfish, and undercurrents in seemingly peaceful water.

The book had also warned against hiking out on narrow peninsulas because high tide could come along and strand you. But just at this moment Cassie would have given anything to be stranded on some peninsula jutting far out into the Atlantic Ocean – as long as Portia Bainbridge was on the other side.

Cassie had never been so miserable in her life.

'...and my other brother, the one on the MIT debate team, the one who went to the World Debate Tournament in Scotland two years ago...' Portia was saying. Cassie felt her eyes glaze over again and slipped back into her wretched trance. Both of Portia's brothers went to MIT and were frighteningly accomplished, not only at intellectual pursuits but also at athletics. Portia was frighteningly accomplished herself, even though she was only going to be a junior in high school this year, like Cassie. And since Portia's favourite subject was Portia, she'd spent most of the last month telling Cassie all about it.

'...and then after I placed fifth in extemporaneous speaking at the National Forensic League Championship last year, my boyfriend said, "Well, of course you'll go All-American..."'

Just one more week, Cassie told herself. Just one more week and I can go home. The very thought filled her with a longing so sharp that tears came to her eyes. Home, where her friends were. Where she didn't feel like a stranger, and unaccomplished, and boring, and stupid just because she didn't know what a quahog was. Where she could laugh about all this: her wonderful vacation on the eastern seaboard.

'...so my father said, "Why don't I just *buy* it for you?" But I said, "No – well, maybe..."'

Cassie stared out at the sea.

It wasn't that the Cape wasn't beautiful. The little cedar-shingled cottages, with white picket fences covered with roses and wicker rocking chairs on the porch and geraniums hanging from the rafters, were pretty as picture postcards. And the village greens and tall-steepled churches and old-fashioned schoolhouses made Cassie feel as if she'd stepped into a different time.

But every day there was Portia to deal with. And even though every night Cassie thought of some devastatingly witty remark to make to Portia, somehow she never got around to actually making any of them. And far worse than anything Portia could do was the plain raw feeling of *not belonging*. Of being a stranger here, stranded on the wrong coast, completely out of her own element.

The tiny duplex back in California had started to seem like heaven to Cassie.

One more week, she thought. You've just got to stand it for one more week.

And then there was Mom, so pale lately and so quiet... A worried twinge went through Cassie, and she quickly pushed it away. Mom is fine, she told herself fiercely. She's probably just miserable here, the same way you are, even though this is her native state. She's probably counting the days until we can go home, just like you are.

Of course that was it, and that was why her mother looked so unhappy when Cassie talked about being homesick. Her mother felt guilty for bringing Cassie here, for making this place sound like a vacation paradise. Everything would be all right when they got back home, for both of them.

'Cassie! Are you listening to me? Or are you day-dreaming again?'

'Oh, listening,' Cassie said quickly.

'What did I just say?'

Cassie floundered. Boyfriends, she thought desperately, the debate team, college, the National Forensic League... People had sometimes called her a dreamer, but never as much as around here.

'I was *saying* they shouldn't let people like that on the beach,' Portia said. 'Especially not with dogs. I mean, I know this isn't Oyster Harbors, but at least it's clean. And now look.' Cassie looked, following the direction of Portia's gaze. All she could see was some guy walking down the beach. She looked back at Portia uncertainly.

'He works on a *fishing* boat,' Portia said, her nostrils flared as if she smelled something bad. 'I saw him this morning on the fish pier, unloading. I don't think he's even changed his *clothes*. How unutterably scuzzy and vomitous.'

He didn't look all that scuzzy to Cassie. He had dark red hair, and he was tall, and even at this distance she could see that he was smiling. There was a dog at his heels.

'We never talk to guys from the fishing boats. We don't even look at them,' Portia said. And Cassie could see it was true. There were maybe a dozen other girls on the beach, in groups of two or three, a few with guys, most not. As the tall boy passed, the girls would look away, turning their heads to stare in the opposite direction. It wasn't a flirtatious sort of looking-away-and-then-back-and-giggling. It was disdainful rejection. As the guy got closer to her, Cassie could see that his smile was turning grim.

The two girls closest to Cassie and Portia were looking away now, almost sniffing. Cassie saw the boy shrug slightly, as if it were no more than he expected. She still didn't see anything so disgusting about him. He was wearing ragged cut-off shorts and a T-shirt that had seen better days, but lots of guys looked like that. And his dog trotted right behind him, tail waving, friendly and alert. It wasn't bothering anybody. Cassie glanced up at the boy's face, curious to see his eyes.

'Look *down*,' Portia whispered. The guy was passing right in front of them. Cassie hastily looked down, obeying automatically, although she felt a surge of rebellion in her heart. It seemed cheap and nasty and unnecessary and cruel. She was ashamed to be a part of it, but she couldn't help doing what Portia said.

She stared at her fingers trailing into the sand. She could see every granule in the bright sunlight. From far away the sand looked white, but up close it was shimmering with colours: specks of black-and-green mica, pastel shell fragments, chips of red quartz like tiny garnets. Unfair, she thought to the boy, who of course couldn't hear her. I'm sorry; this just isn't fair. I wish I could do something, but I can't.

A wet nose thrust under her hand.

The suddenness of it made her gasp, and a giggle caught in her throat. The dog pushed at her hand again, not asking; demanding. Cassie petted it, scratching at the short, silky-bristly hairs on its nose. It was a German shepherd, or mostly, a big, handsome dog with liquid, intelligent brown eyes and a laughing mouth. Cassie felt the stiff, embarrassed mask she'd been wearing break, and she laughed back at it.

Then she glanced up at the dog's owner, quickly, unable to help herself. She met his eyes directly.

Later, Cassie would think of that moment, the moment when she looked up at him and he looked down at her. His eyes were blue-grey, like the sea at its most mysterious. His face was odd; not conventionally handsome, but arresting and intriguing, with high cheekbones and a determined mouth. Proud and independent and humorous and sensitive all at once. As he looked down at her his grim smile lightened and something sparkled in those blue-grey eyes, like sun glinting off the waves.

Normally Cassie was shy around guys, especially guys she didn't know, but this was only some poor worker from the fishing boats, and she felt sorry for him, and she wanted to be nice, and besides she couldn't help it. And so when she felt herself start to sparkle back at him, her laughter bubbling up in response to his smile, she let it happen. In that instant it was as if they were sharing a secret, something nobody else on the beach could understand. The dog wiggled ecstatically, as if he were in on it too.

'*Cassie*,' came Portia's fuming hiss.

Cassie felt herself turn red, and she tore her eyes away from the guy's face. Portia was looking apoplectic.

'Raj!' the boy said, not laughing any more. 'Heel!'

With apparent reluctance, the dog backed away from Cassie, tail still wagging. Then, in a spray of sand, he bounded towards his master. It isn't fair, Cassie thought again. The boy's voice startled her.

'*Life* isn't fair,' he said.

Shocked, her eyes flew up to his face.

His own eyes were as dark as the sea in a storm. She saw that clearly, and for a moment she was almost frightened, as if she had glimpsed something forbidden, something beyond her comprehension. But powerful. Something powerful and strange.

And then he was walking away, the dog frisking behind him. He didn't look back.

Cassie stared after him, astounded. She hadn't spoken aloud; she was sure she hadn't spoken aloud. But then how could he have heard her?

Her thoughts were shattered by a hiss at her side. Cassie cringed, knowing exactly what Portia was going to say. That dog probably had mange and fleas and worms and scrofula. Cassie's towel was probably crawling with parasites right this minute.

But Portia didn't say it. She too was staring after the retreating figures of the boy and dog as they went up a dune, then turned along a little path in the beach grass. And although she was clearly disgusted, there was something in her face – a sort of dark speculation and suspicion that Cassie had never seen before.

'What's the matter, Portia?'

Portia's eyes had narrowed. 'I think,' she said slowly, through tight lips, 'that I've seen him before.'

'You already said so. You saw him on the fish pier.'

Portia shook her head impatiently. 'Not *that*. Shut up and let me think.'

Stunned, Cassie shut up.

Portia continued to stare, and after a few moments she began nodding, little nods to confirm something to herself. Her face was flushed blotchily, and not with sunburn.

Abruptly, still nodding, she muttered something and stood up. She was breathing quickly now.

'Portia?'

'I've got to do something,' Portia said, waving a hand at Cassie without looking at her. 'You stay here.'

'What's going *on*?'

'Nothing!' Portia glanced at her sharply. 'Nothing's going on. Just forget all about it. I'll see you later.' She walked off, moving quickly, heading up the dunes towards the cottage her family owned.

Ten minutes ago, Cassie would have said she'd be deliriously happy just to have Portia leave her alone, for any reason. But now she found she couldn't enjoy it. Her mind was all churned up, like the choppy blue-grey water before a gale. She felt agitated and distressed and almost frightened.

The strangest thing was what Portia had muttered before getting up. It had been under her breath, and Cassie didn't think she could have heard it right. It must have been something else, like 'snitch', or 'bitch', or 'rich'.

She *must* have heard it wrong. You couldn't call a *guy* a witch, for God's sake.

Calm down, she told herself. Don't worry, be happy. You're alone at last.

But for some reason she couldn't relax. She stood and picked up her towel. Then, wrapping it around her, she started down the beach the way the guy had gone.

CHAPTER 2

When Cassie got to the place where the boy had turned, she walked up the dunes between the pitiful little clumps of scraggly beach grass. At the top she looked around, but there was nothing to be seen but pitch pines and scrub oak trees. No boy. No dog. Silence.

She was hot.

All right; fine. She turned back towards the sea, ignoring the twinge of disappointment, the strange emptiness she felt suddenly. She'd go get wet and cool off. Portia's problem was Portia's business. As for the red-haired guy – well, she'd probably never see him again, and he wasn't her business either.

A little inside shiver went through her; not the kind that shows, but the kind that makes you wonder if you're sick. I must be *too* hot, she decided; hot enough that it starts to feel cold. I need a dip in the water.

The water was cool, because this was the open-Atlantic side of the Cape. She waded in up to her knees and then continued walking down the beach.

When she reached a dock, she splashed out of the water

and climbed up to it. Only three boats were tied there: two rowboats and a powerboat. It was deserted.

It was just what Cassie needed.

She unhooked the thick, frayed rope meant to keep people like her off the dock and walked onto it. She walked far out, the weather-beaten wood creaking beneath her feet, the water stretching out on either side of her. When she looked back at the beach, she saw she'd left the other sunbathers far behind. A little breeze blew in her face, stirring her hair and making her wet legs tingle. Suddenly she felt – she couldn't explain it. Like a balloon being caught by the wind and lifted. She felt light, she felt expanded. She felt free.

She wanted to hold her arms out to the breeze and the ocean, but she didn't quite dare. She wasn't as free as all *that*. But she smiled as she got to the end of the dock.

The sky and the ocean were exactly the same deep jewel-blue, except that the sky lightened down at the horizon where they met. Cassie thought that she could see the curve of the earth, but it might have been her imagination. Terns and herring gulls wheeled above.

I should write a poem, she thought. She had a notebook full of scribbled poems at home under her bed. She hardly ever showed them to anyone, but she looked at them at night. Right now, though, she couldn't think of any words.

Still, it was lovely just to be here, smelling the salt sea-smell and feeling the warm planks beneath her and hearing the soft plashing of the water against the wooden piers.

It was a hypnotic sound, rhythmic as a giant heartbeat or the breathing of the planet, and strangely familiar. She sat and gazed and listened, and as she did she felt her own breathing slow. For the first time since she'd come to New England, she felt she belonged. She was a part of the vastness of sky and earth and sea; a tiny part in all the immensity, but a part just the same.

And slowly it came to her that her part might not be so small. She had been immersed in the rhythm of the earth, but now it seemed to her almost as if she controlled that rhythm. As if the elements were one with her, and under her command. She could feel the pulse of life in the planet, in herself, strong and deep and vibrant. The beat slowly rising in tension and expectancy, as if waiting for... something.

For what?

Staring out to sea, she felt words come to her. Just a little jingle, like something you'd teach a child, but a poem nonetheless.

Sky and sea, keep harm from me.

The strange thing was that it didn't feel like something she'd made up. It felt more like something she'd read – or heard – a long time ago. She had a brief flash of an image: being held in someone's arms, and looking at the ocean. Being held up high and hearing words.

Sky and sea, keep harm from me. Earth and fire, bring...
No.

Cassie's entire skin was tingling. She could sense, in a way she never had before, the arch of the sky and the granite solidity of the earth and the immeasurable span of the ocean, wave after wave after wave, to the horizon and beyond. And it was as if they were all waiting, watching, listening to her.

Don't finish it, she thought. Don't say any more. A sudden irrational conviction had taken hold of her. As long as she didn't find the last words of the poem, she was safe. Everything would be as it always had been; she would go home and live out her quiet, ordinary life in peace. As long as she could keep from saying the words, she'd be all right.

But the poem was running through her mind, like the tinkling of icy music far away, and the last words fell into place. She couldn't stop them.

Sky and sea, keep harm from me. Earth and fire, bring... *my desire.*

Yes.

Oh, what have I *done*?

It was like a string snapping. Cassie found herself on her feet, staring wildly out at the ocean. Something had happened; she had felt it, and now she could feel the elements receding from her, their connection broken.

She no longer felt light and free, but jangled and out of tune and full of static electricity. Suddenly the ocean looked more vast than ever and not necessarily friendly. Turning sharply, she headed back towards the shore.

Idiot, she thought as she neared the white sand of the beach again and the frightened feeling slipped away. What were you afraid of? That the sky and the sea were really listening to you? That those words were actually going to *do* something?

She could almost laugh at it now, and she was embarrassed and annoyed with herself. Talk about an overactive imagination. She was still safe, and the world was still ordinary. Words were only words.

But when a movement caught her eye then, she would always remember that deep down she had not been surprised.

Something *was* happening. There was motion on the shore.

It was the red-haired guy. He'd burst out between the

pitch pines and was running down the slope of a dune. Suddenly inexplicably calm, Cassie hurried the rest of the way down the dock, to meet him as he reached the sand.

The dog beside him was loping easily, looking up at the guy's face as if to say this was a great game, and what next? But from the boy's expression and the way he was running, Cassie could tell it wasn't a game.

He looked up and down the deserted beach. A hundred yards to the left a headland jutted out, so you couldn't see what was beyond. He glanced at Cassie and their eyes met. Then, turning abruptly, he started towards the headland.

Cassie's heart was beating hard.

'Wait!' she called urgently.

He turned back, scanning her quickly with his blue-grey eyes.

'Who's after you?' she said, though she thought she knew.

His voice was crisp, his words concise. 'Two guys who look like linebackers for the New York Giants.'

Cassie nodded, feeling the thump of her heart accelerate. But her voice was still calm. 'Their names are Jordan and Logan Bainbridge.'

'It figures.'

'You've heard of them?'

'No. But it figures they'd be named something like that.'

Cassie almost laughed. She liked the way he looked, so windblown and alert, scarcely out of breath even though he'd been running hard. And she liked the daredevil sparkle in his eyes and the way he joked even though he was in trouble.

'Raj and I could take them, but they've got a

couple of friends with them,' he said, turning again. Walking backwards, he added, 'You'd better go the other way – you don't want to run into them. And it would be nice if you could pretend you hadn't seen me.'

'Wait!' cried Cassie.

Whatever was going on wasn't her business... but she found herself speaking without hesitation. There was something about this guy; something that made her want to help him.

'That way's a dead end – around the headland you'll run into rocks. You'll be trapped.'

'But the other way's too straight. I'd still be in sight when they got here. They weren't far behind me.'

Cassie's thoughts were flying, and then suddenly she knew. 'Hide in the boat.'

'What?'

'In the *boat*. In the powerboat. On the dock.' She gestured at it. 'You can get in the cabin and they won't see you.'

His eyes followed hers, but he shook his head. 'I'd really be trapped if they found me there. And Raj doesn't like to swim.'

'They won't find you,' Cassie said. 'They won't go near it. I'll tell them you went down the beach that way.'

He stared at her, the smile dying out of his eyes. 'You don't understand,' he said quietly. 'Those guys are trouble.'

'I don't *care*,' Cassie said, and she almost pushed him towards the dock. Hurry, hurry, hurry, something in her brain was urging. Her shyness had vanished. All that mattered was that he got out of sight. 'What are they going to do to me, beat me up? I'm an innocent bystander,' she said.

'But—'

'Oh, *please*. Don't argue. Just do it!'

He stared at her one last instant, then turned, slapping his thigh for the dog. 'C'mon, boy!' He ran down the dock and jumped easily into the powerboat, disappearing as he ducked into the cabin. The dog followed him in one powerful spring and barked.

Sh! thought Cassie. The two in the boat were hidden now, but if anyone went up the dock, they would be plainly visible. She hooked the loop of frayed rope over the top of the last pier, screening off the dock.

Then she cast a frantic glance around and headed for the water, splashing in. Bending down, she dug up a handful of wet sand and shells. She let the water wash the sand out of the loose cage of her fingers and held on to the two or three small shells that remained. She reached for another handful.

She heard shouting from the dunes.

I'm gathering shells, I'm only gathering shells, she thought. I don't need to look up yet. I'm not concerned.

'Hey!'

Cassie looked up.

There were four of them, and the two in front were Portia's brothers. Jordan was the one on the debate team and Logan was the one in the Pistol Club. Or was it the other way around?

'Hey, did you see a guy come running this way?' Jordan asked. They were looking in all directions, excited like dogs on a scent, and suddenly another line of poetry came to Cassie. *Four lean hounds crouched low and smiling*. Except that these guys weren't lean; they were brawny and sweaty. And out of breath, Cassie noticed, vaguely contemptuous.

'It's Portia's friend – Cathy,' said Logan. 'Hey, Cathy, did a guy just go running down here?'

Cassie walked towards him slowly, her fists full of shells. Her heart was knocking against her ribs so hard she was sure they could see it, and her tongue was frozen.

'Can't you talk? What're you doing here?'

Mutely, Cassie held out her hands, opening them.

They exchanged glances and snorts, and Cassie realised how she must look to these college-age guys – a slight girl with unremarkable brown hair and ordinary blue eyes. Just a little high-school ditz from California whose idea of a good time was picking up worthless shells.

'Did you see somebody go *past* here?' Jordan said, impatient but slow, as if she might be hard of hearing.

Dry-mouthed, Cassie nodded, and looked down the beach towards the headland. Jordan was wearing an open windbreaker over his T-shirt, which seemed odd in such warm weather. What was even odder was the bulge beneath it, but when he turned, Cassie saw the glint of metal.

A *gun*?

Jordan must be the one in the Pistol Club, she thought irrelevantly.

Now that she saw something really to be scared about, she found her voice again and said huskily, 'A guy and a dog went that way a few minutes ago.'

'We've got him! He'll be stuck on the rocks!' Logan said. He and the two guys Cassie didn't know started down the beach, but Jordan turned back to Cassie.

'Are you sure?'

Startled, she looked up at him. Why was he asking? She deliberately widened her eyes and tried to look as childish and stupid as possible. 'Yes...'

'Because it's *important*.' And suddenly he was holding her wrist. Cassie looked down at it in amazement, her shells scattering, too surprised at being grabbed to say anything. 'It's very important,' Jordan said, and she could feel the tension running through his body, could smell the acridity of his sweat. A wave of revulsion swept through her, and she struggled to keep her face blank and wide-eyed. She was afraid he was going to pull her up against him, but he just twisted her wrist.

She didn't mean to cry out, but she couldn't help it. It was partly pain and partly a reaction to something she saw in his eyes, something fanatical and ugly and hot like fire. She found herself gasping, more afraid than she could remember being since she was a child.

'Yes, I'm sure,' she said, breathless, staring into that ugliness without letting herself look away. 'He went down there and around the headland.'

'Come on, Jordan, leave her alone!' Logan shouted. 'She's just a kid. Let's go!'

Jordan hesitated. He knows I'm lying, Cassie thought, with a curious fascination. He knows, but he's afraid to trust what he knows because he doesn't know *how* he knows it.

Believe me, she thought, gazing straight back at him, willing him to do it. Believe me and go away. Believe me. *Believe me.*

He let go of her wrist.

'Sorry,' he muttered ungraciously, and he turned and loped off with the others.

'Sure,' Cassie whispered, standing very still.

Tingling, she watched them jog across the wet sand, elbows and knees pumping, Jordan's windbreaker flapping loose behind him. The weakness spread from her stomach to her legs, and her knees suddenly felt like Silly Putty.

She was aware, all at once, of the sound of the ocean again. A comforting sound that seemed to enfold her. When the four running figures turned the corner and disappeared from her sight, she turned back to the dock, meaning to tell the red-haired guy that he could come out now.

He already had.

Slowly, she made her jellied legs carry her to the dock. He was just standing there, and the look on his face made her feel strange.

'You'd better get out of here – or maybe hide again,' she said hesitantly. 'They might come right back...'

'I don't think so.'

'Well...' Cassie faltered, looking at him, feeling almost frightened. 'Your dog was very good,' she offered uncertainly, at last. 'I mean, not barking or anything.'

'He knows better.'

'Oh.' Cassie looked down the beach, trying to think of something else to say. His voice was gentle, not harsh, but that keen look never left his eyes and his mouth was grim. 'I guess they really are gone now,' she said.

'Thanks to you,' he said. He turned to her, and their eyes met. 'I don't know *how* to thank you,' he added, 'for putting up with that for me. You don't even know me.'

Cassie felt even stranger. Looking up at him made her almost dizzy, but she couldn't take her eyes from his. There was no sparkle now; they looked like blue-grey steel. Compelling – hypnotic. Drawing her closer, drawing her in.

But I do know you, she thought. In that instant a strange image flashed through her mind. It was as if she were floating outside herself and she could see the two of them, standing there on the beach. She could see the sun shining on his hair and her face tilted up to him. And they

17

were connected by a silver cord that hummed and sang with power.

A band of energy, linking them. It was so real she could almost reach out and touch it. It bound them heart to heart, and it was trying to draw them closer.

A thought came to her, as if some small voice from deep inside her was speaking. *The silver cord can never be broken. Your lives are linked. You can't escape each other any more than you can escape destiny.*

Suddenly, as quickly as it had come, the picture and the voice vanished. Cassie blinked and shook her head, trying to wrench her mind back. He was still looking at her, waiting for an answer to his question.

'I was glad to help you,' she said, feeling how lame and inadequate the words were. 'And I didn't mind – what happened.' His eyes dropped to her wrist, and there was a flash from them almost like silver.

'I *did*,' he said. 'I should have come out earlier.'

Cassie shook her head again. The last thing she'd wanted was for him to be caught and hurt. 'I just wanted to help you,' she repeated softly, confused. Then she said, 'Why were they chasing you?'

He looked away, drawing in a deep breath. Cassie had the sense of trespassing. 'That's all right. I shouldn't have asked—' she began.

'No.' He looked back at her and smiled, his wry one-sided smile. 'If anybody has a right to ask, you do. But it's a little difficult to explain. I'm... off my turf here. Back home, they wouldn't dare come after me. They wouldn't dare *look* at me cross-eyed. But here I'm fair game.'

She still didn't understand. 'They don't like people who are – different,' he said, his voice quiet again. 'And I'm different from them. I'm very, very different.'

Yes, she thought. Whatever he was, he wasn't

like Jordan or Logan. He wasn't like anyone she had ever met.

'I'm sorry. That's not much of an explanation, I know,' he said. 'Especially after what you did. You helped me, and I won't forget about it.' He glanced down at himself and laughed shortly. 'Of course, it doesn't look like there's much *I* can do for *you*, does it? Not here. Although...' He paused. 'Wait a minute.'

He reached in his pocket, fingers groping for something. All in an instant Cassie's dizziness overwhelmed her, blood rushing to her face. Was he looking for money? Did he think he could *pay* her for helping him? She was humiliated, and more stricken than when Jordan had grabbed her wrist, and she couldn't help the tears flooding her eyes.

But what he pulled out of his pocket was a stone, a rock like something you might pick up on the ocean floor. At least that was what it looked like at first. One side was rough and grey, embedded with tiny black spirals like little shells. But then he turned it over, and the other side was grey swirled with pale blue, crystallised, sparkling in the sunlight as if it were overlaid with rock candy. It was beautiful.

He pressed it into her palm, closing her fingers around it. As it touched her she felt a jolt like electricity that ran through her hand and up her arm. The stone felt *alive* in some way she couldn't explain. Through the pounding in her ears she heard him speaking, quickly and in a low voice.

'This is chalcedony. It's a – good-luck piece. If you're ever in trouble or danger or anything like that, if there's ever a time when you feel all alone and no one else can help you, hold on to it tight – *tight*' – his fingers squeezed hers – 'and think of me.'

She stared up at him, mesmerised. She was hardly breathing, and her chest felt too full. He was so close to her; she could see his eyes, the same colour as the crystal, and she could feel his breath on her skin and the warmth of his body reflecting the sun's heat. His hair wasn't just red, but all sorts of colours, some strands so dark they were almost purple, others like burgundy wine, others gold.

Different, she thought again; he was different from any guy she'd ever known. A sweet hot current was running through her, a feeling of wildness and possibility. She was trembling and she could feel a heartbeat in her fingers, but she couldn't tell if it was hers or his. He had seemed to hear her thoughts before; now she felt almost as if he were in her mind. He was so close and he was looking down at her...

'And what happens then?' she whispered.

'And then – maybe your luck will change.' Abruptly he stepped back, as if he'd just remembered something, and his tone altered. The moment was over. 'It's worth a try, don't you think?' he said lightly.

Unable to speak, she nodded. He was teasing now. But he hadn't been before.

'I've got to go. I shouldn't have stayed this long,' he said.

Cassie swallowed. 'You'd better be careful. I think Jordan had a gun—'

'Wouldn't surprise me.' He brushed it off, stopping her from saying anything further. 'Don't worry; I'm leaving the Cape. For now, anyway. I'll be back; maybe I'll see you then.' He started to turn. Then he paused one last moment and took her hand again. Cassie was too startled at the feeling of his skin against hers to do anything about it. He turned her hand over and looked at the red marks on her wrist, then brushed them lightly with his fingertips. The steely light was back in his eyes when he looked up. 'And believe me,' he whispered, 'he'll pay for this some day. I guarantee it.'

And then he did something that shocked Cassie more than anything else had during that whole shocking day. He lifted her wounded hand to his lips and kissed it. It was the gentlest, the lightest of touches, and it went through Cassie like fire. She stared at him, dazed and unbelieving, utterly speechless. She could neither move nor think; she could only stand there and *feel*.

And then he was leaving, whistling for the dog, which romped around Cassie in circles before finally breaking away. She was alone, gazing after him, her fingers clenched tightly on the small rough stone in her palm.

It was only then she realised she'd never asked him his name.

CHAPTER
3

An instant later Cassie came out of her daze. She'd better get moving; Logan and Jordan might be coming back any second. And if they realised she'd deliberately lied to them...

Cassie winced as she scrambled up the sloping dune. The world around her seemed ordinary again, no longer full of magic and mystery. It was as if she'd been moving in a dream, and now she'd woken up. What had she been thinking? Some nonsense about silver cords and destiny and a guy who wasn't like any other guy. But that was all ridiculous. The stone in her hand was just a stone. And words were just words. Even that boy... Of course there was no way he could have heard her thoughts. No one could do that; there had to be a rational explanation...

She tightened her grip on the little piece of rock in her palm. Her hand was still tingling where he'd held it, and the skin he'd touched with his fingertips *felt* different from any other part of her body. She thought that no matter what happened to her in the future, she would always feel his touch.

Once inside the summer cottage she and her mother

rented, she locked the front door behind her. Then she paused. She could hear her mother's voice from the kitchen, and from the sound of it she could tell something was wrong.

Mrs Blake was on the phone, her back to the doorway, her head slightly bowed as she clutched the receiver to her ear. As always, Cassie was struck by the willow slimness of her mother's figure. With that and the fall of long, dark hair worn simply clasped at the back of her neck, Mrs Blake could have been a teenager herself. It made Cassie feel protective towards her. In fact, sometimes she almost felt as if she were the mother and her mother the child.

And just now it made her decide not to interrupt her mother's conversation. Mrs Blake was upset, and at intervals she said 'Yes' or 'I know' into the mouthpiece in a voice full of strain.

Cassie turned and went to her bedroom.

She wandered over to the window and looked out, wondering vaguely what was going on with her mother. But she couldn't keep her mind on anything but the boy on the beach.

Even if Portia knew his name, she would never tell, Cassie was sure of that. But without his name, how would Cassie ever find him again?

She wouldn't. That was the brutal truth, and she might as well face it right now. Even if she *did* find out his name, she wasn't the sort to chase after a boy. She wouldn't know how.

'And in one week I'm going home,' she whispered. For the first time these words didn't bring a surge of comfort and hope. She put the rough little piece of chalcedony down on the nightstand, with a sort of final clink.

'Cassie? Did you say something?'

Cassie turned quickly to see her mother in the doorway.

'Mom! I didn't know you were off the phone.' When her mother continued to look at her inquiringly, she added, 'I was just thinking out loud. I was saying that we'll be going home next week.'

An odd expression crossed her mother's face, like a flash of repressed pain. Her large black eyes had dark circles under them and wandered nervously around the room.

'Mom, what's wrong?' said Cassie.

'I was just talking with your grandmother. You remember how I was planning for us to drive up and see her sometime next week?'

Cassie remembered very well. She'd told Portia she and her mother were going to drive up the coast, and Portia had snapped that it wasn't called the coast here. From Boston down to the Cape it was the south shore, and from Boston up to New Hampshire it was the north shore, and if you were going to Maine it was down east, and anyway, where did her grandmother live? And Cassie hadn't been able to answer because her mother had never told her the name of the town.

'Yes,' she said. 'I remember.'

'I just got off the phone with her. She's old, Cassie, and she's not doing very well. It's worse than I realised.'

'Oh, Mom. I'm sorry.' Cassie had never met her grandmother, never even seen a picture of her, but she still felt awful. Her mother and grandmother had been estranged for years, since Cassie had been born. It was something about her mother leaving home, but that was all her mother would ever say about it. In the past few years, though, there had been some letters exchanged, and Cassie thought that underneath they still loved each other. She *hoped* they did, anyway, and she'd been looking forward to seeing her grandmother for the first time. 'I'm really sorry, Mom,' she said now. 'Is she going to be okay?'

'I don't know. She's all by herself in that big house and she's lonely... and now with this phlebitis it's hard for her to get around some days.' The sunshine fell in strips of light and shadow across her mother's face. She spoke quietly but almost stiltedly, as if she were holding some strong emotion back with difficulty.

'Cassie, your grandmother and I have had our problems, but we're still family, and she hasn't got anyone else. It's time we buried our differences.'

Her mother had never spoken so freely about the estrangement before. 'What was it all about, Mom?'

'It doesn't matter now. She wanted me to – follow a path I didn't want to follow. She thought she was doing the right thing... and now she's all alone and she needs help.'

Dismay whispered through Cassie. Concern for the grandmother she'd never met – and something else. A trickle of alarm started by the look on her mother's face, which was that of someone about to deliver bad news and having a hard time finding the words.

'Cassie, I've thought a lot about this, and there's only one thing for us to do. And I'm sorry, because it will mean such a disruption of your life, and it will be so hard on you... but you're young. You'll adapt. I know you will.'

A twinge of panic shot through Cassie. 'Mom, it's all right,' she said quickly. 'You stay here and do what you need to. I can get ready for school by myself. It'll be easy; Beth and Mrs Freeman will help me—' Cassie's mother was shaking her head, and suddenly Cassie felt she had to go on, to cover everything in a rush of words. 'I don't need that many new school clothes...'

'Cassie, I'm so sorry. I need you to try and

understand, sweetheart, and to be adult about this. I know you'll miss your friends. But we've both got to try to make the best of things.' Her mother's eyes were fixed on the window, as if she couldn't bear to look at Cassie.

Cassie went very still. 'Mom, what are you trying to say?'

'I'm saying we're not going home, or at least not back to Reseda. We're going to *my* home, to move in with your grandmother. She needs us. We're going to stay here.'

Cassie felt nothing but a dazed numbness. She could only say stupidly, as if this were what mattered, 'Where's "here"? Where does Grandma live?'

For the first time her mother turned from the window. Her eyes seemed bigger and darker than Cassie had ever seen them before.

'New Salem,' she said quietly. 'The town is called New Salem.'

Hours later, Cassie was still sitting by the window, staring blankly. Her mind was running in helpless, useless circles.

To *stay* here... to stay in New England...

An electric shock ran through her. *Him. I knew we'd see him again*, something inside her proclaimed, and it was glad. But it was only one voice and there were many others, all speaking at once.

To stay. Not going home. And what difference does it make if the guy is here in Massachusetts somewhere? You don't know his name or where he lives. You'll never find him again.

But there's a chance, she thought desperately. And the voice deepest inside, the one that had been glad before, whispered: *More than a chance. It's your fate.*

Fate! the other voices scoffed. Don't be ridiculous! It's

your fate to spend your junior year in New England, that's all. Where you don't know anyone. Where you'll be alone.

Alone, alone, alone, all the other voices agreed.

The deep voice was crushed and disappeared. Cassie felt any hope of seeing the red-haired boy again slip away from her. What she was left with was despair.

I won't even get to say good-bye to my friends at home, she thought. She'd begged her mother for the chance to go back, just to say good-bye. But Mrs Blake had said there was no money and no time. Their airline tickets would be cashed in. All their things would be shipped to Cassie's grandmother's house by a friend of her mother's.

'If you went back,' her mother had said gently, 'you'd only feel worse about leaving again. This way at least it will be a clean break. And you can see your friends next summer.'

Next summer? Next summer was a hundred years away. Cassie thought of her friends: good-natured Beth and quiet Clover, and Miriam the class wit. Add to that shy and dreamy Cassie and you had their group. So maybe they weren't the in-crowd, but they had fun and they'd stuck together since elementary school. How would she get along without them until next summer?

But her mother's voice had been so soft and distracted, and her eyes had wandered around the room in such a vague, preoccupied way, that Cassie hadn't had the heart to rant and rave the way she would have liked.

In fact, for an instant Cassie had wanted to go to her mother and throw her arms around her and tell her everything would be all right. But she couldn't. The small, hot coal of resentment burning in her chest wouldn't let her. However worried her mother might be, she didn't have to face the prospect of going to a strange new school in a state three thousand miles from where she belonged.

Cassie did. New hallways, new lockers, new classrooms, new desks, she thought. New faces instead of the friends she'd known since junior high. Oh, it couldn't be true.

Cassie hadn't screamed at her mother this afternoon, and she hadn't hugged her, either. She had just silently turned away to the window, and this was where she'd been sitting ever since, while the light slowly faded and the sky turned first salmon pink and then violet and then black.

It was a long time before she went to bed. And it was only then that she realised she'd forgotten all about the chalcedony lucky piece. She reached out and took it from the nightstand and slipped it under her pillow.

Portia stopped by as Cassie and her mother were loading the rental car.

'Going home?' she said.

Cassie gave her tote bag a final push to squeeze it into the trunk. She had just realised she didn't want Portia to find out she was staying in New England. She couldn't stand to have Portia know of her unhappiness; it would give Portia a kind of triumph over her.

When she looked up, she had her best attempt at a pleasant smile in place. 'Yes,' she said, and flicked a quick glance over to where her mother was leaning in the driver's-side door, arranging things in the back seat.

'I thought you were staying until the end of next week.'

'We changed our minds.' She looked into Portia's hazel eyes and was startled by the coldness there. 'Not that I didn't have a good time. It's been fun,'

Cassie added, hastily and foolishly.

Portia shook straw-coloured hair off her forehead. 'Maybe you'd better stay out west from now on,' she said. 'Around here, we don't like liars.'

Cassie opened her mouth and then shut it again, cheeks flaming. So they did know about her deception on the beach. This was the time for one of those devastatingly witty remarks that she thought of at night to say to Portia – and, of course, she couldn't summon up a word. She pressed her lips together.

'Have a nice trip,' Portia concluded, and with one last cold glance, she turned away.

'Portia!' Cassie's stomach was in a knot of tension, embarrassment, and anger, but she couldn't let this chance go. 'Before I leave, will you just tell me one thing?'

'What?'

'It can't make any difference now – and I just wanted to know... I just wondered... if you knew his name.'

'Whose name?'

Cassie felt a new wave of blood in her cheeks, but she went on doggedly. '*His* name. The red-haired guy. The one on the beach.'

Those hazel eyes didn't waver. They went on staring straight into Cassie's, the pupils contracted to mean little dots. Looking into those eyes, Cassie knew there was no hope.

She was right.

'What red-haired guy on the beach?' Portia said distinctly and levelly, and then she turned on her heel again and left. This time Cassie let her go.

Green. That's what Cassie noticed on the drive north from the Cape. There was a *forest* growing on either side of the highway. In California you had to go to a national park to see trees this tall...

'Those are sugar maples,' her mother said with forced cheerfulness as Cassie turned her head slightly to follow a stand of particularly graceful trees. 'And those shorter ones are red maple. They'll turn red in the fall – a beautiful glowing, sunset red. Just wait until you see them.'

Cassie didn't answer. She didn't want to see the trees in the fall because she didn't want to *be* here.

They passed through Boston and drove up the coast – up the *north shore*, Cassie corrected herself fiercely – and Cassie watched quaint little towns and wharves and rocky beaches slip by. She suspected they were taking the scenic route, and she felt resentment boil up in her chest. Why couldn't they just get there and get it over with?

'Isn't there a faster way?' she said, opening the glove compartment and pulling out a map supplied by the car rental company. 'Why don't we take Route 1? Or Interstate 95?'

Her mother kept her eyes on the road. 'It's been a long time since I drove up here, Cassie. This is the way I know.'

'But if you cut over here at Salem...' Cassie watched the exit go by. 'Okay, don't,' she said. Of all places in Massachusetts, Salem was the only one she could think of that she wanted to see. Its macabre history appealed to her mood right now. 'That's where they burned the witches, isn't it?' she said. 'Is New Salem named for it? Did they burn witches there, too?'

'They didn't burn anyone; they hanged them. And they weren't witches. Just innocent people who happened to be disliked by their neighbours.' Her mother's voice was tired and patient. 'And Salem was a common name in colonial times; it comes from "Jerusalem".'

The map was blurring before Cassie's eyes. 'Where *is* this town, anyway? It's not even listed,' she said.

There was a brief silence before her mother replied. 'It's a small town; quite often it's not shown on maps. But as a matter of fact, it's on an island.'

'An *island*?'

'Don't worry. There's a bridge to the mainland.'

But all Cassie could think was, An *island*. I'm going to live on an island. In a town that isn't even on the map.

The road was unmarked. Mrs Blake turned down it and the car crossed the bridge, and then they were on the island. Cassie had expected it to be tiny, and her spirits lifted a little when she saw that it wasn't. There were regular stores, not just tourist shops, clustered together in what must be the centre of town. There was a Dunkin' Donuts and an International House of Pancakes with a banner proclaiming GRAND OPENING. In front of it there was someone dressed up like a giant pancake, dancing.

Cassie felt the knot in her stomach loosen. Any town with a dancing pancake couldn't be all bad, could it?

But then her mother turned onto another road that rose and got lonelier and lonelier as the town fell behind.

They must be going to the ultimate point of the headland, Cassie realised. She could see it, the sun glinting red off the windows on a group of houses at the top of a bluff. She watched them get closer, at first uneasily, then anxiously, and finally with sick dismay.

Because they were *old*. Terrifyingly old, not just quaint or gracefully aged, but *ancient*. And although some were in good repair, others looked as if they might fall over in a crash of splintering timbers any minute.

Please let it be that one, Cassie thought, fixing her eyes on a pretty yellow house with several towers and bay windows. But her mother drove by it without slowing. And by the next and the next.

And then there was only one house left, the last house on the bluff, and the car was heading towards it. Heartsick, Cassie stared at it as they approached. It was shaped like a thick upside-down T, with one wing facing the road and one wing sticking straight out the back. As they came around the side Cassie could see that the back wing looked nothing like the front. It had a steeply sloping roof and small, irregularly placed windows made of tiny, diamond-shaped panes of glass. It wasn't even painted, just covered with weathered grey clapboard siding.

The front wing had been painted... once. Now what was left was peeling off in strips. The two chimneys looked crumbling and unstable, and the entire slate roof seemed to sag. The windows were regularly placed across the front, but most looked as if they hadn't been washed in ages.

Cassie stared wordlessly. She had never seen a more depressing house in her life. This *couldn't* be the one.

'Well,' said her mother, in that tone of forced cheerfulness, as she turned into a gravel driveway, 'this is it, the house I grew up in. We're home.'

Cassie couldn't speak. The bubble of horror and fury and resentment inside her was swelling bigger and bigger until she thought it would explode.

CHAPTER
4

Her mother was still talking in that falsely bright way, but Cassie could only hear snatches of the words. "... original wing actually Pre-revolutionary, one-and-a-half stories... front wing is Post-revolutionary Georgian...'

It went on and on. Cassie clawed open the car door, getting an unobstructed view of the house at last. The more she saw of it, the worse it looked.

Her mother was saying something about a transom over the front door, her voice rapid and breathless. '... rectangular, not like the arched fanlights that came later—'

'*I hate it!*' Cassie cried, interrupting, her voice too loud in the quiet air, startlingly loud. She didn't mean the transom, whatever a transom was. 'I *hate* it!' she cried again passionately. There was silence from her mother behind her, but Cassie didn't turn to look; she was staring at the house, at the rows of unwashed windows and the sagging eaves and the sheer monstrous bulk and flatness and horribleness of it, and she was shaking. 'It's the ugliest thing I've ever seen, and I *hate* it. I want to go home. I want to go home!'

She turned to see her mother's white face and stricken eyes, and burst into tears.

'Oh, Cassie.' Mrs Blake reached across the vinyl top of the car towards her. 'Cassie, sweetheart.' There were tears in her own eyes, and when she looked up at the house, Cassie was astounded at her expression. It was a look of hatred and fear as great as anything Cassie felt.

'Cassie, sweetheart, listen to me,' she said. 'If you really don't want to stay—'

She stopped. Cassie was still crying, but she heard the noise behind her. Turning, she saw that the door to the house had opened. An old woman with grey hair was standing in the doorway, leaning on a cane.

Cassie turned back. 'Mom?' she said pleadingly.

But her mother was gazing at the door. And slowly, a look of dull resignation settled over her. When she turned to Cassie, the brittle, falsely cheery tone was back in her voice.

'That's your grandmother, dear,' she said. 'Let's not keep her waiting.'

'Mom...' Cassie whispered. It was a despairing entreaty. But her mother's eyes had gone blank, opaque.

'Come on, Cassie,' she said.

Cassie had the wild idea of throwing herself into the car, locking herself in, until someone came to rescue her. But then the same heavy exhaustion that had descended over her mother seemed to wrap around her as well. They were here. There was nothing to be done about it. She pushed the car door shut and silently followed her mother to the house.

The woman standing in the doorway was ancient. Old enough to be her great-grandmother, at least. Cassie tried to detect some resemblance to her mother, but she could find none.

'Cassie, this is your Grandma Howard.'

Cassie managed to mutter something. The old woman with the cane stepped forward, fixing her deep-set eyes on Cassie's face. In that instant a bizarre thought flashed into Cassie's mind: *She's going to put me in the oven.* But then she felt arms around her, a surprisingly firm hug. Mechanically she lifted her own arms in a gesture of response.

Her grandmother pulled back to look at her. 'Cassie! At last. After all these years.' To Cassie's discomfiture she went on looking, staring at Cassie with what seemed like a mixture of fierce worry and anxious hope. 'At last,' she whispered again, as if speaking to herself.

'It's good to see you, Mother,' Cassie's mother said then, quiet and formal, and the fierce old eyes turned away from Cassie.

'Alexandra. Oh, my dear, it's been too long.' The two women embraced, but an indefinable air of tension remained between them.

'But we're all standing here outside. Come in, come in, both of you,' her grandmother said, wiping her eyes. 'I'm afraid the old place is rather shabby, but I've picked the best of the rooms for you. Let's take Cassie to hers.'

In the fading red light of the sunset the interior seemed cavernous and dark. And everything did look shabby, from the worn upholstery on the chairs to the faded oriental carpet on the pine-board floors.

They went up a flight of stairs – slowly, with Cassie's grandmother leaning on the banister – and down a long passage. The boards creaked under Cassie's Reeboks and the lamps high on the walls flickered uneasily as they passed. One of us ought to be holding a candelabra, Cassie thought. Any minute now she expected to see Lurch or Cousin It coming down the hall towards them.

'These lamps – it's your grandfather's wiring,' her grandmother apologised. 'He insisted on doing so much of it himself. Here's your room, Cassie. I hope you like pink.'

Cassie felt her eyes widen as her grandmother opened the door. It was like a bedroom setting in a museum. There was a four-poster bed with hangings cascading from the head and foot and a canopy, all made of the same dusty-rose flowered fabric. There were chairs with high carved backs upholstered in a matching rose damask. On a fireplace with a high mantel rested a pewter candlestick and a china clock, and there were several pieces of massive, richly glowing furniture. The whole thing was beautiful, but so grand...

'You can put your clothes here – this chest is solid mahogany,' Cassie's grandmother was saying. 'The design is called bombé, and it was made right here in Massachusetts – this is the only area in all the colonies that produced it.'

The colonies? Cassie thought wildly, staring at the decorative scroll top of the chest.

'And this is your dressing table and your wardrobe... Have you looked out the windows? I thought you might like a corner room because you can see both south and east.'

Cassie looked. Through one window she could see the road. The other faced the ocean. Just now it was a sullen lead grey under the darkening sky, exactly matching Cassie's mood.

'I'll leave you here to get settled in,' Cassie's grandmother said. 'Alexandra, I've given you the green room at the opposite end of the hallway...'

Cassie's mother gave her shoulder a quick, almost timid squeeze. And then Cassie was alone. Alone with the massive ruddy furniture and the cold fireplace and the heavy draperies. She sat gingerly on a chair because she was afraid of the bed.

She thought about her bedroom at home, with her white pressed-wood furniture and her *Phantom of the Opera* posters and the new CD player she'd bought with her baby-sitting money. She'd painted the bookcase pale blue to show off her unicorn collection. She collected every kind of unicorn there was – stuffed, blown glass, ceramic, pewter. Back home, Clover had said once that Cassie was like a unicorn herself: blue eyed, shy, and different from everyone else. All that seemed to belong to a former life now.

She didn't know how long she sat there, but sometime later she found the piece of chalcedony in her hand. She must have taken it out of her pocket, and now she was clinging to it.

If you're ever in trouble or danger, she thought, and a wave of longing swept over her. It was followed by a wave of fury. Don't be stupid, she told herself sharply. You're not in danger. And no *rock* is going to help you. She had an impulse to throw it away, but instead she just rubbed it against her cheek, feeling the cool, jagged smoothness of the crystals. It made her remember his touch – how gentle it had been, the way it had pierced her to the soul. Daringly, she rubbed the crystal over her lips and felt a sudden throb from all the places on her skin he had touched. The hand he had held – she could still feel his fingers printed on her palm. Her wrist – she felt the light brush of cool fingertips raising the hairs there. And the back of it... She shut her eyes and her breath caught as she remembered that kiss. What would it have felt like, she wondered, if his lips had touched where the crystal touched now? She let her head fall back, drawing the cool stone from her own lips down her throat to rest in the hollow where her pulse beat. She could almost feel him kissing her, as no boy ever had; she could almost imagine that it really was his lips there. I would let you, she thought, even though I wouldn't let anyone else... I would trust you...

But he'd left her. Suddenly, with a shock, she remembered that. He'd left her and gone away, just as the other most important man in Cassie's life had.

Cassie seldom thought about her father. She seldom allowed herself to. He'd gone away when she was only a little girl, left her mother and her alone to take care of themselves. Cassie's mother told people he had died, but to Cassie she admitted the truth: he'd simply left. Maybe he was dead by now, or maybe he was somewhere else, with another family, another daughter. She and her mother would never know. And although her mother never spoke about him unless someone asked, Cassie knew that he'd broken her mother's heart.

Men always leave, Cassie thought, her throat aching. They both left me. And now I'm alone... here. If only I had somebody else to talk to... a sister, somebody...

Eyes still shut, she let the hand with the crystal trail down and fall into her lap. She was so exhausted with emotion that she couldn't even get up to go to the bed. She simply sat there, drifting in the lonely dimness until her breathing slowed and she fell asleep.

That night Cassie had a dream – or perhaps it wasn't a dream. She dreamed that her mother and grandmother came into the room, moving noiselessly, almost gliding over the floor. In her dream she was aware of them, but she couldn't move as they lifted her from the chair and undressed her and put her to bed. Then they stood over the bed, looking down at her. Her mother's eyes were strange and dark and unfathomable.

'Little Cassie,' her grandmother said with a sigh. 'At last. But what a pity—'

'Sh!' her mother said sharply. 'She'll wake up.'

Her grandmother sighed again. 'But you can see that it's the only way...'

'Yes,' her mother said, her voice empty and resigned. 'I can see that you can't escape destiny. I shouldn't have tried.'

That's just what I thought, Cassie realised as the dream faded. You can't escape destiny. Vaguely she could see her mother and grandmother moving towards the door, and she could hear the whisper of their voices. She couldn't make out any words, though, until one sibilant hiss came through.

'...*sacrifice*...'

She wasn't sure which of the women had said it, but it echoed over and over in her mind. Even as darkness covered her, she kept hearing it. *Sacrifice... sacrifice... sacrifice...*

It was morning. She was lying in the four-poster bed and sunlight was streaming in the eastern window. It made the pink room look like a rose petal held up to the light. Sort of warm and shining. Somewhere outside a bird was singing.

Cassie sat up. She had a confused memory of some kind of a dream, but it was dim and vague. Her nose was stuffed up – probably from crying – and she felt a little lightheaded but not really bad. She felt the way you do after being very sick or very upset and then getting some deep, restful sleep: strangely spacey and peaceful. The quiet after the storm.

She got dressed. Just as she was about to leave the room, she noticed the chalcedony lucky piece on the floor and slipped it in her pocket.

No one else seemed to be awake. Even in the daytime the long passage was dark and cool, lit only by the windows at opposite ends. Cassie found herself shivering as she walked down the hall, and the dim bulbs of the wall lamps flickered as if in sympathy.

Downstairs was lighter. But there were so many rooms that when she tried to explore, she quickly got lost. Finally, she ended up in the front hallway and decided to go outside.

She wasn't even thinking about why – she guessed she wanted to see the neighbourhood. Her steps took her down the long, narrow country road, past house after house. It was so early, no one else was outside. And eventually she ended up at the pretty yellow house with the towers.

High in one tower, the window was sparkling.

Cassie was staring at it, wondering why, when she noticed motion in a ground-floor window much closer to her. It was a library or study, and standing inside was a girl. The girl was tall and slender, with an incredibly long cascade of hair that obscured her face as she bent over something on the desk in front of the window. That hair – Cassie couldn't take her eyes off it. It was like moonlight and sunlight woven together – and it was natural. No dark roots. Cassie had never seen anything so beautiful.

They were so close – Cassie standing just behind the

neat hedge outside the window, and the girl standing just inside, facing her, but looking down. Cassie watched, fascinated, at what the girl was doing at the desk. The girl's hands moved gracefully, grinding something up with a mortar and pestle. Spices? Whatever it was, the girl's movements were quick and deft and her hands slender and pretty.

And Cassie had the oddest feeling... If the girl would only look *up*, she thought. Just look outside her own window. Once she did, then... something would happen. Cassie didn't know what, but her skin had broken out in gooseflesh. She had such a sense of connection, of... *kinship*. If the girl would just look up...

Yell. Throw a stone at the window. Cassie was actually looking for a stone when she saw movement again. The girl with the shining hair was turning, as if responding to someone inside the house calling her. Cassie had a glimpse of a lovely, dewy face – but only for the briefest instant. Then the girl had turned and was hurrying away, hair flying like silk behind her.

Cassie let out her breath.

It would have been stupid anyway, she told herself as she walked back home. Fine way to introduce yourself to your neighbours – throwing rocks at them. But the sense of crushing disappointment remained. She felt that somehow she'd never have another chance – she'd never get up the courage to introduce herself to that girl. Anyone that beautiful undoubtedly had plenty of friends without Cassie. Undoubtedly went with a crowd far beyond Cassie's orbit.

Her grandmother's flat, square house looked even worse after the sunny Victorian one. Disconsolately, Cassie drifted over to the bluff, to look down at the ocean.

Blue. A colour so intense she didn't know how to

describe it. She watched the water washing around a dark rock and felt a strange thrill. The wind blew her hair back, and she stared out at the morning sun glittering on the waves. She felt... kinship again. As if something were speaking to her blood, to something deep inside her. What *was* it about this place – about that girl? She felt she could almost grasp it...

'Cassie!'

Startled, Cassie looked around. Her grandmother was calling from the doorway of the old wing of the house.

'Are you all right? For heaven's sake, get away from the edge!'

Cassie looked down and immediately felt a wave of vertigo. Her toes were almost off the bluff. 'I didn't realise I was that close,' she said, stepping back.

Her grandmother stared at her, then nodded. 'Well, come away now and I'll get you some breakfast,' she said. 'Do you like pancakes?'

Feeling a little shy, Cassie nodded. She had some vague memory about a dream that made her uncomfortable, but she definitely felt better this morning than she had yesterday. She followed her grandmother through the door, which was much thicker and heavier than a modern one.

'The front door of the original house,' her grandmother explained. She didn't seem to be having much trouble with her leg today, Cassie noticed. 'Strange to have it lead directly into the kitchen, isn't it? But that was how they did things in those days. Sit down, why don't you, while I make the pancakes.'

But Cassie was staring in amazement. The kitchen was like no kitchen she'd ever seen before. There was a gas range and a refrigerator – even a microwave shoved back on a wooden counter – but the rest of it was like something out of a movie set. Dominating the room was an enormous open fireplace as big as a walk-in closet, and although there was no fire now, the thick layer of ashes at the bottom showed that it was sometimes used. Inside, an iron pot hung on an iron crossbar. Over the fireplace were sprays of dried flowers and plants, which gave off a pleasant fragrance.

And as for the woman in front of the hearth...

Grandmothers were supposed to be pink and cosy, with soft laps and large bank accounts. This woman looked stooped and coarse, with her grizzled hair and the prominent mole on her cheek. Cassie kept half expecting her to go over to the iron pot and stir it while muttering, 'Double, double, toil and trouble...'

Immediately after she thought this, she felt ashamed. That's your *grandmother*, she told herself fiercely. Your only living relative besides your mother. It's not her fault she's old and ugly. So don't just sit here. Say something nice.

'Oh, thanks,' she said, as her grandmother placed a plate of steaming pancakes in front of her. Then she added, 'Uh, are those dried flowers over the fireplace? They smell good.'

'Lavender and hyssop,' her grandmother said. 'When you're done eating, I'll show you my garden, if you like.'

'I'd love it,' Cassie said, truthfully.

But when her grandmother led her outside after she'd finished eating, the scene was far different than Cassie had expected. There were *some* flowers, but for the most part the 'garden' just looked like weeds and bushes – row after row of overgrown, uncared-for weeds and bushes.

'Oh – how nice,' Cassie said. Maybe the old lady was senile after all. 'What unusual – plants.'

Her grandmother shot her a shrewd, amused glance. 'They're herbs,' she said. 'Here, this is lemon balm. Smell.'

Cassie took the heart-shaped leaf, wrinkled like a mint leaf but a little bigger, and sniffed. It had the scent of freshly peeled lemon. 'That *is* nice,' she said, surprised.

'And this is French sorrel – taste.'

Cassie gingerly took the small, rounded leaf and nibbled at the end. The taste was sharp and refreshing. 'It's good – like sour grass!' she said, looking up at her grandmother, who smiled. 'What are those?' Cassie said, nibbling again as she pointed to some bright yellow buttons of flowers.

'That's tansy. The ones that look like white daisies are feverfew. Feverfew leaves are good in salads.'

Cassie was intrigued. 'What about those?' She pointed to some creamy white flowers that twined up other bushes.

'Honeysuckle. I keep it just because it smells good. The bees love it, and the butterflies. In spring it's like Grand Central Station around here.'

Cassie reached out to snap off a fragrant stem of delicate flower buds, then stopped. 'Could I – I thought I'd take some up for my room. If you don't mind, I mean.'

'Oh, good heavens, take as many as you want. That's what they're here for.'

She's not really old and ugly at all, Cassie thought, snapping off stems of the creamy flowers. She's just – different. Different doesn't necessarily mean bad.

'Thanks – Grandma,' she said as they went back into the house. Then she opened her mouth again, to ask about the yellow house, and who lived there.

But her grandmother was picking up something from beside the microwave.

'Here, Cassie. This came in the mail for you yesterday.'

She handed Cassie two booklets bound in construction paper, one red and one white.

New Salem High School Student and Parent Handbook, one read. The other read, *New Salem High School Programme of Studies*.

Oh, my God, Cassie thought. School.

New hallways, new lockers, new classrooms, new faces. There was a slip of paper between the booklets, with *Schedule of Classes* printed boldly at the top. And under that, her name, with her address listed as Number Twelve Crowhaven Road, New Salem.

Her grandmother might not be as bad as she'd thought; even the house might turn out to be not so awful. But what about school? How could she ever face school here in New Salem?

CHAPTER
5

The grey cashmere sweater or the blue-and-white Fair Isle cardigan, that was the question. Cassie stood in front of the gilt-framed mirror, holding first one and then the other in front of her. The blue cardigan, she decided; blue was her favourite colour, and it brought out the blue of her eyes. The plump cherubs on top of the old-fashioned looking glass seemed to agree, smiling at her approvingly.

Now that the first day of school had actually come, Cassie found that she was excited. Of course, she was nervous too, but it wasn't the stark and hopeless dread she'd expected to feel. There was something interesting about beginning school in a new place. It was like starting her life over. Maybe she'd adopt a whole new personality. Back home, her friends would probably describe her as 'nice, but shy' or 'fun, but kind of quiet'. But no one here knew that. Maybe this year she'd be Cassie the Extrovert or even Cassie the Party Girl. Maybe she'd even be good enough for the girl with the shining hair. Cassie's heart beat more quickly at the thought.

It all depended on first impressions. It was vital she get off to a good start. Cassie pulled on the blue sweater and anxiously checked her reflection again in the mirror.

She wished there were something more to do with her own hair. It was soft and it waved slightly, with pretty highlights, but she wished she could do something more dramatic with it. Like the girl in this ad – she glanced at the magazine open on the dressing table. She'd bought it specially when she'd driven into town last week so she could see the back-to-school fashions. She'd never gotten the courage to walk up to the yellow Victorian house again, although she'd cruised by it slowly in her grandmother's Volks-wagen Rabbit, hoping vainly to bump into the girl 'accidentally'.

Yes, tomorrow she'd pull her hair back like the model in the ad, she decided.

Just as she was about to step away, something on the opposite page of the magazine caught her eye. A horoscope column. Her birth sign, Cancer, seemed to be staring out at her. Automatically her eyes followed the words after it.

That daggy insecure feeling has got you again. It's time for positive thinking! If that doesn't work, remember that nothing lasts forever. Try not to make waves in your personal relationship this month. You've got enough to cope with already.

Horoscopes are such garbage, Cassie thought, closing the magazine with a slap. Her mother had always said so, and it was true. 'That daggy insecure feeling' – just telling someone they felt insecure was enough to make them feel it! There was nothing supernatural about that.

But if she didn't believe in the supernatural, what was the chalcedony lucky piece doing in the zipper compartment of her backpack? Setting her jaw, she took it out and put it in her jewellery box, then went downstairs to say good-bye.

The school was an impressive three-storey red brick building. So impressive that after Cassie had parked the Rabbit, she was almost afraid to go any closer. There were several narrow paths that led up the hill, and she finally nerved herself to take one. At the top her throat closed and she simply stared.

God, it looked like a *college* or something. Like a historical landmark. The bold stone facing on the front read NEW SALEM HIGH SCHOOL, and below was a sort of crest with the words *Town of New Salem, Incorporated 1693*. Was that how old this town was? Three hundred *years*? Back in Reseda, the oldest buildings around had been there for maybe fifty years.

I am not shy, Cassie told herself, forcing herself to walk forward. I am Cassie the Confident.

An incredibly loud roar made her head jerk around, and sheer instinct sent her jumping to the side just in time to avoid being run over. Heart pounding, she stood and gawked at what had almost hit her. It was a motorcycle on the bike path. But even more astonishing was its rider – a girl. She was wearing tight black jeans and a motorcycle jacket, and her trim, athletic body looked tough. But when she turned around after parking the motorcycle by a bike rack, Cassie saw that her face was ravishingly pretty. It was small and feminine, framed by tumbling dark curls, and marred only by a sullen, belligerent expression.

'What are you staring at?' the girl demanded suddenly.

Cassie started. She supposed she had been staring. The girl took a step forward and Cassie found herself stepping back.

'I'm sorry – I didn't mean to—' She tried to tear her eyes away, but it was hard. The girl was wearing a skimpy black midriff top under the jacket, and Cassie glimpsed what looked like a small tattoo just above the material. A tattoo of a crescent moon. 'I'm sorry,' Cassie said again, helplessly.

'You better be. You keep out of my face, get it?'

You were the one who almost ran *me* over, Cassie thought. But she nodded hastily, and to her vast relief the girl turned away.

God, what a horrible way to start the first day of school, Cassie thought, hurrying towards the entrance. What a horrible *person* to be the first one you spoke to. Well, at least after a beginning like that, things could only get better.

All around her teenagers were greeting one another, shouting hello; the girls giggling and hugging, the boys horsing around. It was an excited bustle, and everybody seemed to know everybody else.

Except Cassie. She stood looking at the fresh haircuts of the guys, the brand-new clothes of the girls, smelling the scents of too much perfume and unnecessary aftershave and feeling more alone than she ever had in her life.

Keep moving, she told herself sternly. Don't stand around looking for that girl – find your first class. Maybe you'll see somebody there who's alone, and you can talk to them. You've got to *look* extroverted if you want people to think you are.

Her first class was writing for publication, an English elective, and Cassie was glad she had it. She liked creative writing, and the *Programme of Studies* had said that the class would offer opportunities for publication in the school literary magazine and newspaper. She'd worked on the newspaper in her old school; maybe she could here, too.

Of course, the *Programme* also said you had to sign up for writing for publication the previous spring, and Cassie still couldn't quite understand how her grandmother had gotten her enrolled just before school started. Maybe her grandmother had special pull with the administration or something.

She found the class without much trouble and took an inconspicuous desk near the back. The room was filling up, and everyone seemed to have someone to talk to. Nobody took the slightest notice of Cassie.

She began doodling ferociously on the front of her notebook, trying to look totally involved in it, trying to look as if she weren't the only one in class sitting alone.

'You're new, aren't you?'

The boy in front of her had turned around. His smile was genuinely friendly, but it was also dazzling, and she had a feeling he knew exactly how dazzling it was. His hair was auburn and curly, and it was clear that when he stood, he'd be very tall.

'You're new,' he said again.

'Yes,' said Cassie, and was furious to hear her voice shake. But this guy was so good-looking... 'I'm Cassie Blake. I just moved here from California.'

'I'm Jeffrey Lovejoy,' he said.

'Oh,' Cassie said, trying to make it sound as if she'd heard of him before, since this seemed to be what he expected.

'Centre on the basketball team,' he said. 'Also captain.'

'Oh, how great.' Oh, how *stupid*. She had to do better than this. She sounded brainless. 'I mean – that must be really interesting.'

'Are you interested in basketball? Maybe we could talk

about it sometime.' Suddenly Cassie felt very grateful to him. He was ignoring her blundering, her lameness. Okay, so maybe he liked to be admired, but what difference did that make? He was nice, and it would definitely improve her status to be seen around the campus with him.

'That would be great,' she said, wishing she could think of another adjective. 'Maybe – maybe at lunch...'

A shadow fell over her. Or at least that was how it felt. In any case, she was aware, all at once, of a *presence* at her side, a presence that made her voice trail off blankly as she looked up, wide-eyed.

A girl was standing there, the most striking girl Cassie had ever seen. A big, beautiful girl, both tall and voluptuous. She had a mane of pitch-black hair and her pale skin was touched with the glow of confidence and power.

'Hello, Jeffrey,' she said. Her voice was low for a girl's; vibrant and almost husky.

'Faye.' Jeffrey's voice, by contrast, was noticeably unenthusiastic. He looked tense. 'Hi.'

The girl leaned over him, one hand on the back of his chair, and Cassie caught the scent of some heady perfume. 'I didn't see much of you over summer vacation,' she said. 'Where've you been?'

'Around,' Jeffrey said lightly. But his smile was forced, and his entire body was taut now.

'You shouldn't keep yourself hidden away like that. Naughty boy.' Faye leaned in closer yet. She was wearing an off-the-shoulder top – completely off both shoulders. It left a great deal of skin exposed just at Jeffrey's eye level. But it was her face Cassie couldn't help staring at. She had a sensuous, sulky mouth and extraordinary honey-coloured eyes. They seemed almost to glow with a strange golden light. 'You know, there's a new horror movie at the Capri this week,' she said. 'I like horror movies, Jeffrey.'

'I can take them or leave them myself,' Jeffrey said.

Faye chuckled, a rich, disturbing sound. 'Maybe you just haven't seen them with the right girl,' she murmured. 'Under the proper circumstances, I think they can be very... stimulating.'

Cassie felt embarrassed blood rise to her cheeks, though she scarcely knew why. Jeffrey wet his lips, looking fascinated in spite of himself, but also scared. Like a rabbit in a trap.

'I was going to takc Sally down to Gloucester this weekend—' he began, voice strained.

'Well, you'll just have to tell Sally that... something came up,' Faye said, raking him with her eyes. 'You can come get me Saturday night at seven.'

'Faye, I—'

'Oh, and *don't* be late, all right? I hate it when boys are late.'

All this time, the black-haired girl had not even glanced at Cassie. But now, as she straightened up to leave, she did. The look she turned on Cassie was sly and secretive, as if she were perfectly aware that Cassie had been listening, and she liked it. Then she turned back to Jeffrey.

'Oh, and by the way,' she said, lifting one hand in a languid gesture that showed off her long red nails, *'she's* from Crowhaven Road too.'

Jeffrey's jaw dropped. He stared at Cassie a moment with an expression of shock and distaste, and then he quickly turned around to face the front of the room. Faye was chuckling as she walked away to take a seat at the very back.

What is going *on*? Cassie thought wildly. What difference did it make where she lived? The only thing she could see now of Jeffrey-of-the-dazzling-smile was his rigid back.

She had no time to think anything more, because the

teacher was talking. He was a mild-looking man with a greying beard and glasses. He introduced himself as Mr Humphries.

'And since you've all had a chance to talk during your summer vacation, now I'll give you a chance to write,' he said. 'I want each of you to write a poem, right now, spontaneously. We'll read some of them aloud afterwards. The poem can be about anything, but if you have trouble thinking of a subject, write about your dreams.'

There were groans from the class, which gradually died into silence and pen chewing. But Cassie bent over her notebook with her heart beating rapidly. A vague memory of her dream of last week intruded, the one where her mother and grandmother had stood over her. But she didn't want to write about that. She wanted to write about *him*.

After a few minutes she scribbled down a line. When Mr Humphries announced that the time was up, she had a poem, and reading it over she felt a thin chill of excitement. It was good – or at least *she* thought so.

What if the teacher called on her to read it out loud? She didn't want him to, of course, but what if he *made* her, and what if somebody else in class thought it was good and wanted to talk to her afterwards Maybe they'd ask her about the guy in the poem, and then she could tell them the mysterious and romantic story about him. Maybe she'd get a reputation for being kind of mysterious and romantic herself. Maybe the girl in the Victorian house would hear about her...

Mr Humphries was calling for volunteers. Predictably, no hands were raised... until one went up in the back.

The teacher hesitated. Cassie turned to see that the raised hand had long red nails.

'Faye Chamberlain,' Mr Humphries said at last.

He sat on the edge of his desk as the tall, striking girl came to stand beside him, but Cassie had the oddest feeling that he would have moved away if he could. An almost palpable air of tension had filled the room, and all eyes were on Faye.

She tossed her glorious mane of black hair back and shrugged, causing her off-the-shoulder top to slip down a little lower. Tilting her head back, she smiled slowly at the class and held up a piece of paper.

'This is my poem,' she said in her lazy, husky voice. 'It's about fire.'

Shocked, Cassie looked down at the poem on her own desk. Then Faye's voice caught her attention.

I dream about fire—
Tongues of flame licking me.
My hair burns like a torch;
My body burns for you.
Touch my skin and your fingers will stick—
You'll blacken like a cinder.
But you'll die smiling;
Then you'll be part of the fire too.

As the entire class watched, riveted, Faye produced a match and somehow – Cassie didn't quite see how – managed to light it. She touched it to the paper and the paper caught fire. Then, walking slowly, she moved to stand directly in front of Jeffrey Lovejoy, waving the burning paper gently before his eyes.

Howls, whistles, and desk banging from the audience. Many of them looked scared, but most of the guys looked excited, too. Some of the girls looked as if they wished *they* dared to do something like that.

Voices called out, 'See, Jeffrey, that's what you get for

being so cute!' 'Go for it, man!' 'Watch out, Jeff, Sally's gonna hear about this!'

Jeffrey just sat there, the back of his neck slowly flushing dull red.

As the paper was about to burn her fingers, Faye sashayed away from Jeffrey again and dropped it in the metal wastebasket by the teacher's desk. Mr Humphries didn't flinch when something in the wastebasket flared up, and Cassie admired him for that.

'Thank you, Faye,' he said evenly. 'Class, I think we can call what we've just seen an example of... concrete poetry. Tomorrow we'll study some more traditional methods. Class dismissed.'

Faye walked out the door. There was an instant's pause; then, as if everyone had been released by a spring, a sudden mass exodus. Jeffrey grabbed his notebook and was gone.

Cassie looked at her own poem. Fire. She and Faye had both written about the same thing...

Suddenly she tore the sheet out and, crumpling it into a ball, thrust it into her backpack. So much for her dreams of being romantic and mysterious. With a girl like *that* around, who was ever going to notice Cassie?

And yet they all seemed almost afraid of her, she thought. Even the teacher. Why didn't he give her a detention or something? Or is lighting fires in trash cans normal in New Salem?

And why did Jeffrey let her hit on him that way? And why did he care where I *live*, for God's sake?

In the hall, she nerved herself to stop someone and ask where room C310 was.

'It's on the third floor,' the girl said. 'All the maths classes are. Go up that stairway—'

'Yo! Look out! Heads up, everybody!' a shouting

voice interrupted. Something was whizzing down the hall, scattering students right and left from its path. Two somethings. Dumb-founded, Cassie saw that it was two guys on roller blades, laughing and bellowing as they tore through the crowd. Cassie had a glimpse of dishevelled shoulder-length blond hair and almond-shaped, slightly tilted blue-green eyes as one passed – and then she saw it all again as the second one streaked by. The boys were identical, except that one was wearing a Megadeth T-shirt and the other's said Mötley Crüe.

They were creating chaos as they went, knocking books out of people's arms and grabbing at girls' clothes. As they reached the end of the hallway, one of them caught a pretty redhead's miniskirt and deftly flipped it up to waist level. The girl shrieked and dropped her backpack to push it down.

'Why doesn't somebody *do* something?' Cassie blurted out. Was everybody in this school crazy? 'Why doesn't somebody stop them – or report them – or *something*...'

'Are you kidding? Those are the Henderson brothers,' the girl said, and she walked away, joining another girl. Cassie heard a fragment of a sentence float back: '...doesn't even know about the Club...' and both girls glanced back at her, then walked on.

What Club? That girl had said it as if it had capital letters. What did a club have to do with breaking school rules? What kind of place *was* this?

Another bell rang, and Cassie realised that she was now late for class. She slung her backpack over her shoulder and ran for the stairs.

By lunchtime, she still hadn't exchanged more than a 'hi' or 'hello' with anyone, no matter how she tried. And she hadn't seen the girl with the shining hair anywhere – not that that was really surprising, considering the many floors and corridors of this school. In her present state of insecurity, Cassie wouldn't have dared to approach the girl if she *had* seen her. A leaden, miserable feeling had settled in her stomach.

And one glance at the glass-walled cafeteria teeming with laughing students made her knees go weak.

She couldn't face it. She just didn't have the nerve.

Arms wrapped around herself, she walked away and kept walking. She walked right through the main entrance and out the door. She didn't know where she was going – maybe she was going home. But then she saw the lush green grass of the hill.

No, she decided; I'll just eat here. Partway down the hill there were several craggy outcrops of natural rock, and she found she could sit comfortably in a little hollow below one, shaded by a tree. She was shielded by the rock from the school; it was almost as if the school didn't exist. She could look down a flight of meandering steps to the bottom of the hill and the road beyond, but no one from above could see her.

As she sat, looking at the dandelions dotting the grass, the tension gradually drained out of her. So what if the morning hadn't been the greatest? Things would be better this afternoon. The clear blue sky seemed to tell her that.

And the rock at her back – the famous red granite of New England – gave her a feeling of security. It was strange, but she almost felt she could hear a buzzing in the rock, like a heartbeat tremendously speeded up. A buzzing of *life*. If I put my cheek to it, I wonder what would happen? she thought with a curious excitement.

Voices distracted her. Dismayed, Cassie knelt up to look over the top of the rock – and tensed.

It was that girl, Faye. There were two other girls with her, and one of them was the biker who'd nearly run Cassie over that morning. The other was a strawberry blonde with a tiny waist and the most well-developed chest Cassie had ever seen on a teenager. They were laughing and sauntering down the steps – right towards Cassie.

I'll just stand up and say hi, Cassie thought, but she didn't. The memory of those disturbing honey-coloured eyes was still with her. She kept quiet and hoped they'd pass her by, go all the way down the hill and off campus.

Instead they stopped on the landing just above Cassie, sitting with their feet on the steps below and pulling out paper lunch bags.

They were so close that Cassie could see the red stone blazing at Faye's throat. Although she was in shadow now, if she moved they wouldn't be able to miss her. She was trapped.

'Did anybody follow us, Deborah?' Faye asked lazily as she rummaged through her backpack.

The biker girl snorted. 'Nobody's stupid enough to try.'

'Good. Because this is top secret. I don't want you-know-who to hear anything about it,' Faye said. She took out a stenographer's notebook with a red cover and laid it on her knee. 'Now let me see, what shall we do to start this year off? I feel like something really wicked.'

CHAPTER
6

'Well, there's Jeffrey...' the strawberry blonde said.

'Already begun,' Faye said, smiling. 'I work fast, Suzan.'

Suzan laughed. When she did, her extraordinary chest jiggled in a way that made Cassie certain she wasn't wearing anything underneath her apricot-coloured sweater.

'I still don't see the point of Jeffrey Lovejoy,' the biker girl said, scowling.

'You don't see the point of any guy, Deborah; that's your problem,' said Suzan.

'And your problem is that you can't see the point of anything else,' Deborah retorted. 'But Jeffrey's worse than most. He's got more teeth than brain cells.'

'It isn't his teeth I'm interested in,' said Faye thoughtfully. 'Who are you going to start with, Suzan?'

'Oh, I don't know. It's so hard to decide. There's Mark Flemming and Brant Hegerwood and David Downey – he's in my remedial English class, and he's developed this killer body over the summer. And then there's always Nick...'

Deborah hooted. 'Our Nick? The only way he'd look at you is if you had four wheels and a clutch.'

'And besides, he's taken,' Faye said, and her smile reminded Cassie of a crouching jungle cat.

'You just said you wanted Jeffrey—'

'They both have their uses. Get this straight, Suzan. Nick and I have an ... arrangement. So you just back off and pick yourself a nice outsider, all right?'

There was a moment of tension, and then the strawberry blonde shrugged. 'Okay, I'll take David Downey. I didn't really want Nick anyway. He's an iguana.'

Deborah looked up. 'He's my cousin!'

'He's still an iguana. He kissed me at the junior prom, and it was like kissing a reptile.'

'*Can* we get back to business?' Faye said. 'Who's on the hate list?'

'Sally Waltman,' Suzan said immediately. 'She already thinks because she's class president she can stand up to us, and if you take Jeffrey, she's going to be really mad.'

'Sally...' Fay mused. 'Yes, we'll have to come up with something truly special for dear old Sally... What's wrong, Deborah?'

Deborah had stiffened, looking up the hill towards the school entrance. 'Intruder alert,' she said. 'In fact, it looks like a whole delegation.'

Cassie had seen it too, a group of guys and girls coming through the main entrance down the hill. She felt a surge of hope. Maybe while Faye and the other two were occupied with them, she herself could slip away unnoticed. Heart beating quickly, she watched the new group approach.

A broad-shouldered boy in front, who seemed to be the leader, spoke up.

'Look, Faye, the cafeteria's crowded. So we're

going to eat out here – okay?' His voice started out belligerent, but it wavered towards the end, becoming more of a question than a statement.

Faye looked up at him without haste, then smiled her slow, beautiful smile. 'No,' she said, briefly and sweetly. 'It isn't okay.' Then she turned back to her lunch.

'How come?' the boy burst out, still trying to sound tough. 'You didn't stop us last year.'

'Last year,' Faye said, 'we were only *juniors*. This year we're seniors – and we're wicked. As wicked as we wanna be.'

Deborah and Suzan smiled.

Frustrated, Cassie shifted her weight. So far there had never been a moment when all three of the girls were looking away. Come on, turn *around*, she thought pleadingly.

The group of guys and girls went on standing there for a minute or two, exchanging angry glances. But finally they turned and walked back towards the school building – all except one.

'Uh, Faye? Did you mean I had to go too?' she said. She was a pretty, flushed girl, and young. Probably a sophomore, Cassie guessed. Cassie expected her to get packed off like the others, but to her surprise Faye raised her eyebrows and then patted the landing invitingly.

'Why, Kori,' she said, 'of course you can stay. We just imagined you'd be eating in the cafeteria with the Princess of Purity and the rest of the goody-goodies.'

Kori sat down. 'Too much goodness can get boring,' she said.

Faye tilted her head and smiled. 'And there I thought you were a namby-pamby little Puritan. Silly me,' she said. 'Well, you know you're always welcome here. You're *almost* one of us, aren't you?'

Kori ducked her head. 'I'll be fifteen in two weeks.'

'There, you see,' Faye said to the others. 'She's almost eligible. Now what *were* we talking about? That new slasher movie, wasn't it?'

'That's right,' Deborah said, showing her teeth. 'The one where the guy chops people up and makes them into condiments at his salad bar.'

Suzan was unwrapping a Twinkie. 'Oh, Deborah, don't. You're making me sick.'

'Well, you makc *me* sick with those things,' Deborah said. 'You never stop eating them. That's what those are, you know,' she told Kori, pointing at Suzan's chest. 'Two giant Twinkies. If Hostess went out of business, she'd be wearing a double A.'

Faye laughed her sleepy, throaty laugh, and even Suzan giggled. Kori was smiling too, but looking uncomfortable.

'Kori! We're not *embarrassing* you, are we?' Faye exclaimed, opening her golden eyes wide.

'Don't be silly. I don't embarrass easily,' Kori said.

'Well, with brothers like yours, I should think not. Still,' Faye went on, 'you seem so young, you know; almost... virginal. But that's probably just a false impression, right?'

Kori was blushing now. All three senior girls were looking at her with insinuating smiles.

'Well, sure – I mean, it is a false impression – I'm not all *that* young...' Kori swallowed, looking confused. 'I went out with Jimmy Clark all last summer,' she ended defensively.

'Why don't you tell us all about it?' Faye murmured. Kori looked more confused.

'I – well – I think I'd better get going. I've got gym next period, and I have to get all the way over to E-wing. I'll see you guys.' She got up quickly and disappeared.

'Strange, she left her lunch,' Faye mused, frowning gently. 'Oh, well.' She extracted a package of cupcakes from Kori's lunch sack and tossed them to Suzan, who giggled.

Deborah, though, was frowning. 'That was stupid, Faye. We're going to need her later – like in two weeks. One empty space, one candidate, you know?'

'True,' Faye said. 'Oh, well, I'll make it up to her. Don't worry; when the time comes, she'll be on our side.'

'I suppose *we'd* better get moving too,' Suzan said, and behind her rock, Cassie shut her eyes in relief. 'I've got to climb all the way to the third floor for algebra.'

'Which could take hours,' Deborah said maliciously. 'But don't strain yourself just yet. There's more company coming.'

Faye sighed in exasperation, without turning. 'Who *now*? What do we have to do to get a little peace around here?'

'It's Madame Class President herself. Sally. And there's *steam* coming out of her ears.'

Faye's expression of annoyance vanished, dissolving into something more beautiful and infinitely more dangerous. Still sitting with her back to the school, she smiled and worked her long, red-tipped fingers like a cat exercising its claws. 'And I thought today was going to be boring,' she murmured, clucking her tongue. 'It just shows you can never tell. Well, *hello*, Sally,' she said aloud, standing and turning in one smooth motion. 'What a lovely surprise. How was your summer?'

'Save it, Faye,' said the girl who'd just marched down the steps. She was a good head shorter than Faye, and slighter of build, but her arms and legs had a wiry look and her fists were clenched as if she were prepared to do physical battle. 'I didn't come out here to chat.'

'But we haven't had a good talk in so long... Did you do something to your hair? It's so – interesting.'

Cassie looked at Sally's hair. It had a rusty cast to it, and looked frizzled and overpermed. As the girl raised a defensive hand to her head Cassie could almost have giggled – if it all hadn't been so horrible.

'I didn't come to talk about my hair, either!' snapped Sally. She had a strident voice that was climbing higher with every sentence. 'I came to talk about Jeffrey. You leave him alone!'

Faye smiled, very slowly. 'Why?' she murmured, and in contrast to Sally's voice hers seemed even lower and more sensual. 'Afraid of what he'll do if you're not there to hold his hand?'

'He's not interested in you!'

'Is that what he told you? Hmm. He seemed very interested this morning. He's taking me out Saturday night.'

'Because you're *making* him.'

'Making him? Are you suggesting a big boy like Jeffrey can't say no when he wants to?' Faye shook her head. 'And why isn't he here now to speak for himself? I'll tell you something, Sally,' she added, her voice dropping confidentially. 'He didn't fight hard this morning. He didn't fight hard at all.'

Sally's hand drew back as if she wanted to hit the bigger girl, but she didn't. 'You think you can do anything, Faye – you and the rest of the Club! Well, it's time somebody showed you that you can't. There are more of us – lots more – and we're getting tired of being pushed around. It's time somebody took a stand.'

'Is that what you're planning to do?' Faye said pleasantly. Sally had been circling her like a bulldog looking for an opening, and now the wiry girl had ended on the edge of the landing with her back to the steps leading down.

'Yes!' Sally cried defiantly.

'Funny,' murmured Faye, 'because it's going to be hard to do that flat on your back.' With the last words she flicked her long red fingernails in Sally's face.

She never actually touched Sally's skin. Cassie, who had been watching intently, desperately waiting for an opportunity to flee, felt sure of that.

But it was as if something *hit* Sally. Something invisible. And heavy. The wiry girl's entire body jerked back and she tried frantically to regain her footing on the edge of the landing. Arms flailing, she teetered for an endless instant and then fell backwards.

Cassie could never remember what happened then. One minute she was behind her rock, crouching and safe, and the next she had flung herself out across the falling girl's path, knocking her sideways onto the grass. For a heartbeat Cassie thought they were both going to roll all the way down the hill, but somehow or other they didn't. They ended up in a heap, with Cassie underneath.

'Let go! You ripped my *shirt*,' a strident voice exclaimed, and an unkind fist planted itself in Cassie's midriff as Sally pushed herself to her feet. Cassie stared up at her, open-mouthed. Talk about gratitude...

'And as for you, Faye Chamberlain – you tried to *kill* me! But you'll get yours, you wait and see!'

'I'll get yours too, Sally,' Faye promised, smiling, but the sleepiness in her smile wasn't genuine any more. She looked as if underneath she were grinding her teeth.

'You just wait,' Sally repeated vehemently. 'Someday they may find *you* at the bottom of those stairs with a broken neck.' With that, she marched to the landing and up the steps, bringing her foot down on each as if she were stamping on Faye's face. She didn't even look back or acknowledge Cassie's existence.

Cassie slowly got up and glanced down the long, winding flight of stairs that led to the foot of the hill. She couldn't have done anything differently, she realised. Sally would have been lucky to break nothing more than her neck before she reached bottom. But now...

She turned to face the three senior girls above her.

They were still standing with careless, unstudied elegance, but underneath their easy demeanour was violence. Cassie saw it in the sullen darkness of Deborah's eyes, and in the spiteful curve of Suzan's lips. But most of all she saw it in Faye.

It occurred to her, quite incidentally, that these were probably the three most beautiful girls she'd ever seen. It wasn't just that each had perfect skin, free of the slightest trace of teenage blemishes. It wasn't their gorgeous hair: Deborah's dark disordered curls, Faye's pitch-black mane, and Suzan's cloud of reddish gold. It wasn't even the way they set each other off, each one's distinctive type enhancing the others' instead of detracting from them. It was something else, something that came from within. A kind of confidence and self-possession that no girl at sixteen or seventeen should have. An inner strength, an energy. A *power*.

It terrified her.

'Well, now, what do we have here?' Faye said in a throaty voice. 'A spy? Or a little white mouse?'

Run, Cassie thought. But her legs wouldn't move.

'I saw her this morning,' Deborah said. 'She was hanging out in front of the bike rack, staring at me.'

'Oh, I've seen her before *that*, Debby,' Faye replied. 'I saw her last week at Number Twelve. She's a neighbour.'

'You mean *she's*—' Suzan broke off.

'Yes.'

'Whatever else she is, she's dead meat now,' Deborah said. Her petite face was twisted in a scowl.

'Let's not be hasty,' Faye murmured. 'Even mice may have their uses. By the way, how long were you hiding there?'

There was only one answer to this, and Cassie fought not to say it. This was no time to come up with a devastatingly witty remark. But at last she gave in, because it was the truth, and because she couldn't think of anything else.

'Long enough,' she said, and shut her eyes in misery.

Faye descended slowly to stand in front of her. 'Do you always spy on other people's private conversations?'

'I was here before you came,' Cassie said, with as much spirit as she could manage. If only Faye would stop *staring* at her like that. Those honey-coloured eyes seemed to glow with an eerie, supernatural light. It was focussed on Cassie like a laser beam, draining away her will, causing the strength to flow out of her. It was as if Faye wanted her to do something – or wanted something *from* her. It made her feel so disoriented – so off balance and weak...

And then she felt a sudden surge of strength that seemed to come up from her feet. Or, rather, from the ground beneath them, from the red New England granite that she'd felt buzzing with life earlier. It steadied her, sweeping up and straightening her spine, so that she lifted her chin and looked into those golden eyes without flinching.

'I was here first,' she said defiantly.

'Very good,' murmured Faye, and there was an odd look in her eyes. Then she turned her head. 'Anything interesting in her backpack?'

Cassie saw, to her outrage, that Deborah was going through her backpack, throwing things out one by one. 'Not much,' the biker said, tossing it on the ground so the rest of its contents scattered down the hillside.

'All right.' Faye was smiling again, a particularly unpleasant smile that made her red lips look cruel. 'I think you were right the first time, Deborah. She's dead meat.' She looked at Cassie. 'You're new here, so you probably don't understand what kind of mistake you've made. And I don't have time to stand here and tell you. But you'll find out. You'll find out – Cassie.'

She reached out and caught Cassie's chin with long, red-tipped fingers. Cassie wanted to pull away, but her muscles were locked. She felt the strength in those fingers and the hardness of the long, slightly curving nails. Like talons, she thought. The talons of a bird of prey.

For the first time she noticed that the red stone Fay wore at her throat had a star in it, like a star sapphire. It winked in the sunlight, and Cassie found she couldn't take her eyes off it.

Laughing suddenly, Faye released her.

'Come on,' she said to the other two girls. The three of them turned and went up the steps.

The air exploded from Cassie's lungs as if she were a balloon that had just been pricked. She was shaking inside. That had been... That had been absolutely...

Get a grip on yourself!

She's only a teenage gang leader, she told herself. At least the mystery of the Club is solved. They're a gang. You've heard of gangs before, even if you never went to a school with one. As long as you leave them alone and don't cross them from now on, you'll be okay.

But the reassurance rang hollow in her mind. Faye's last words had sounded like a threat. But a threat of what?

When Cassie got back to the house that afternoon, her mother didn't seem to be downstairs. Finally, as she wandered from room to room calling, her grandmother appeared on the staircase. The look on her face made Cassie's stomach lurch.

'What's wrong? Where's Mom?'

'She's upstairs, in her room. She hasn't been feeling very well. Now, there's no need for you to get worried...'

Cassie hurried up the creaking old steps to the green room. Her mother was lying in a grand four-poster bed. Her eyes were shut, her face pale and lightly perspiring.

'Mom?'

The large black eyes opened. Her mother swallowed and smiled painfully. 'Just a touch of the flu, I think,' she said, and her voice was weak and distant, a voice to go with the pallor of her face. 'I'll be fine in a day or two, sweetheart. How was school?'

Cassie's better nature battled with her desire to spread her own misery around as much as possible. Her mother took a little breath and shut her eyes as if the light hurt her.

Better nature won. Cassie dug her nails into her palms and spoke evenly. 'Oh, fine,' she said.

'Did you meet anyone interesting?'

'Oh, you could say that.'

She didn't want to worry her grandmother, either. But during dinner, when her grandmother asked why she was so quiet, the words just seemed to come out by themselves.

'There was this girl at school – her name's Faye, and she's awful. A female Attila the Hun. And on my very first day I ended up making her hate me...' She told the whole story. At the end of it, her grandmother looked into the fireplace as if preoccupied.

'It will get better, Cassie,' she said.

But what if it *doesn't*? Cassie thought. 'Oh, I'm sure it will,' she said.

Then her grandmother did something surprising. She looked around as if somebody might be listening and then leaned forward. 'No, I mean that, Cassie. I know. You see, you have – a special advantage. Something very special...' Her voice dropped to a whisper.

Cassie leaned forward in turn. 'What?'

Her grandmother opened her mouth, then her eyes shifted away. There was a pop from the fire, and she got up to poke the wood there.

'Grandma, what?'

'You'll find out.'

Cassie felt a shock. It was the second time today she'd heard those words. 'Grandma—'

'You've got good sense, for one thing,' her grandmother said, a new, brisk tone in her voice. 'And two good legs, for another. Here, take this broth up to your mother. She hasn't eaten anything all day.'

That night, Cassie couldn't sleep. Either her dread kept her awake so that she noticed more of the creaking, rattling, old-house sounds than she had before, or there were more of the sounds to notice. She didn't know which, and it didn't matter: she kept falling asleep and then jerking back to awareness. Every so often she reached under her pillow to touch the chalcedony piece. If only she could really sleep... so she could dream about *him*...

She sat bolt upright in bed.

Then she got up, bare feet pattering on the hardwood

floor, and went over to unzip her backpack. She took the things she'd re-collected from the hillside out one by one, pencil by pencil, book by book. At last she looked at the array on the bedspread.

She was right. She hadn't noticed it at the time; she'd been too worried about Faye's threat. But the poem she'd written that morning and then crumpled up in anger was missing.

CHAPTER
7

The first person Cassie saw at school the next morning was Faye. The tall girl was standing with a group in front of a side entrance that Cassie had been taking to be inconspicuous.

Deborah, the biker, and Suzan, the pneumatic strawberry blonde, were in the group. So were the two blond guys who had been roller blading through the halls yesterday. And there were two other guys. One was a short boy with a hesitant, slinking look and a furtive smile. The second was tall, with dark hair and a handsome, cold face. He was wearing a T-shirt with rolled-up sleeves and black jeans like Deborah's, and he was smoking a cigarette. Nick? thought Cassie, remembering the girls' conversation yesterday. The reptile?

Cassie flattened herself against the red brick wall and retreated as quickly and quietly as possible. She went in the main entrance, then hurried to her English class.

Almost guiltily, she reached down to pat her hip pocket. It was stupid to have brought it, but the little piece of chalcedony *did* make her feel better. And of course it was ridiculous to believe that it could bring her luck – but then again, she'd gotten to school this morning without running into Faye, hadn't she?

She found an empty desk in a back corner of the classroom on the opposite side from where Faye had sat yesterday. She didn't want Faye near her – or behind her. Here, she was shielded by a whole cluster of people.

But strangely, soon after she sat down, there was a sort of shuffling around her. She looked up to see a couple of girls moving forward. The guy beside her was moving too.

For a moment she sat quite still, not even breathing.

Don't be paranoid.

Just because people move doesn't mean it has anything to do with you. But she couldn't help notice that there was now a wide expanse of empty desks all around her.

Faye breezed in, talking to a stiff Jeffrey Lovejoy. Cassie got a glimpse of her and then quickly looked away.

She couldn't keep her mind on Mr Humphries's lecture. How could she *think* with so much space around her? It had to be only a coincidence, but it shook her just the same.

At the end of class, when Cassie stood up, she felt eyes on her. She turned to see Faye looking at her and smiling.

Slowly, Faye closed one eye in a wink.

Once out of the room Cassie headed for her locker. As she twirled the combination dial she saw someone standing nearby, and with a jolt recognised the short, slinking boy who'd been with Faye that morning.

His locker was open, and she could see several ads from what looked like Soloflex brochures taped inside the door. He was grinning at her. His belt buckle was silver with shiny, mirrorlike stones in it, and it was engraved *Sean*.

Cassie gave him the unimpressed look she reserved for little boys she baby-sat back home and pulled open her locker.

And screamed.

It was more of a choked, strangled cry, actually, because her throat closed up on her. Dangling from the top of her locker by a piece of twine around its neck was a doll. The doll's head lolled grotesquely to one side – it had been pulled out of the socket. One blue glass eye was open; the other was stuck gruesomely halfway shut.

It seemed to be *winking* at her.

The short boy was gazing at her with a strange, eager expression. As if he were drinking in her horror. As if it intoxicated him.

'Aren't you going to report that? Shouldn't you go to the principal's office?' he said. His voice was high and excited.

Cassie just stared at him, her breath coming quickly.

Then: 'Yes, I *am*,' she said. She grabbed the doll and jerked it and the twine came free. Slamming the locker shut, she headed for the stairs.

The principal's office was on the second floor. Cassie thought she'd have to wait, but to her surprise the secretary ushered her in as soon as she gave her name.

'Can I help you?' The principal was tall, with an austere, forbidding face. His office had a fireplace, Cassie noted distractedly, and he stood in front of it with his hands clasped behind his back.

'Yes,' she said. Her voice was shaking. And now that she'd gotten here, she wasn't at all sure that this was a good idea. 'I'm new at school; my name is Cassie Blake—'

'I'm aware of who you are.' His voice was clipped and brusque.

'Well...' Cassie faltered. 'I just wanted to report... Yesterday, I saw this girl having a fight with another girl, and she pushed her...' What was she *talking* about? She was babbling. 'And I saw it, and so she threatened me. She's in this club – but the point is, she threatened me. And I wasn't going to do anything about it, but then today I found *this* in my locker.'

He took the doll, holding it by the back of the dress with two fingers. He looked at it as if she'd handed him something the dog had dug up in the yard. His lip was curled in a way that reminded Cassie somehow of Portia.

'Very amusing,' he said. 'How apt.'

Cassie had no idea what that was supposed to mean. Apt meant appropriate, didn't it? It was appropriate that somebody was hanging dolls in her locker?

'It was Faye Chamberlain,' she said.

'Oh, no doubt,' he said. 'I'm quite aware of the problems Miss Chamberlain has in interacting with other students. I've even had a report about this incident yesterday, about how you tried to push Sally Waltman down the stairs—'

Cassie stared, then blurted out, 'I *what*? Who told you that?'

'I believe it was Suzan Whittier.'

'It isn't true! I never—'

'Be that as it may,' the principal interrupted, 'I really think you'd better learn to solve these problems among yourselves, don't you? Instead of relying on – outside help.'

Cassie just went on staring, speechless.

'That's all.' The principal tossed the doll in the

wastebasket, where it hit with a resounding plastic clunk.

Cassie realised she was dismissed. There was nothing to do but turn around and walk out.

She was late for her next class. As she walked in the door all eyes turned to her, and for an instant she felt a flash of paranoia. But at least no one got up and left when she took a desk.

She was watching the teacher do an example on the board when her backpack moved.

It was lying on the floor beside her, and out of the corner of her eye she saw the dark blue nylon hump up. She *thought* she saw it. When she turned to stare at it, it was still.

Imagination...

As soon as she faced the board, it happened again.

Turn and stare. It was still. Look at the board. It humped up. As if something were *wriggling* inside it.

It must be waves of hot air, or something wrong with her eyes.

Very slowly and carefully, Cassie edged her foot over to the backpack. She stared at the blackboard as she lifted her foot and then brought it down suddenly on the 'hump'.

All she felt was the flatness of her French book.

She hadn't realised she was holding her breath until she sighed out. Her eyes shut in helpless relief...

And then something beneath her foot writhed. She *felt* it under her Reebok.

With a piercing shriek, she leaped to her feet.

'*What* is the matter?' the teacher cried. Now everyone really was staring at her.

'There's something – something in my backpack. It *moved*.' Cassie had a hard time not clutching at the teacher's arm. 'No, don't – don't reach in there...'

Shaking her off, the teacher held the backpack open. Then she plunged her hand inside and pulled out a long rubber snake.

Rubber.

'Is this supposed to be funny?' the teacher demanded.

'It's not mine,' Cassie said stupidly. 'I didn't put it there.'

She was gazing, mesmerised, at the flopping, bobbing rubber head and the painted black rubber tongue. It looked real, but it wasn't. It was unalive. Dead meat?

'It did move,' she whispered. 'I felt it move... I thought. It must have just been my foot shifting.'

The class was watching silently. Looking up, Cassie thought she saw a flash of something like pity on the teacher's face, but the next moment it was gone.

'All right, everybody. Let's get back to work,' the teacher said, dropping the snake on her desk and returning to the blackboard. Cassie spent the rest of the period with her eyes locked on those of the rubber snake. It never moved again.

Cassie looked through the glass at the cafeteria full of laughing, talking students. French class had passed in a blur. And the paranoia, the feeling that people were looking at her and then deliberately turning their backs, kept growing.

I should go outside, she thought, but of course that was ridiculous. Look where going outside had gotten her yesterday. No, she would do today what she should have done then: walk up and ask somebody if she could sit next to them.

All right. Do it. It would have been easier if she hadn't been feeling so giddy. Lack of sleep, she thought.

She stopped, with her filled tray, beside two girls eating

at a square table built for four. They looked nice, and more important, they looked like sophomores. They should be glad to have a junior sit with them.

'Hi,' she heard her own voice saying, disembodied but polite. 'Can I sit here?'

They looked at each other. Cassie could almost see the frantic telegraphing. Then one spoke up.

'Sure... but we were just leaving. Help yourself.' She picked up her tray and made for the garbage can. The other girl looked dismayed an instant, gazing down at her own tray. Then she followed.

Cassie stood as if she'd taken root in the floor.

Okay, that was too bad – you picked somebody who was just leaving, all right. But that's no reason to be upset...

Even though their lunches were only half eaten?

With a supreme effort, she made herself walk over to another table. A round one this time, seating six. There was one seat empty.

Don't ask, she thought. Just sit. She put her tray down at the empty place, shrugged her backpack off her shoulder, and sat. She kept her eyes glued to her tray, concentrating on one piece of pepperoni in her slice of pizza. She didn't want to seem to be *asking* permission of anyone.

All around her, conversation died. Then she heard the scraping of chairs.

Oh my God I don't believe this I don't believe this is happening it's not true...

But it was. Her worst nightmare. Something so much worse than dead dolls or rubber snakes.

In a daze of unreality she looked up to see every other occupant of the table rising. They were picking up their lunches; they were leaving. But unlike the two nice sophomore girls, they weren't heading for the garbage cans. They were just moving to other tables, one here, another there, anywhere they could fit in.

Away from her. Anywhere so long as it was away from her.

'Mom...?' She looked down at the shut eyes with their thick black lashes, the pale face.

She didn't know how she'd made it through the rest of school today, and when she came home, her grandmother said her mom had been doing worse. Not a *lot* worse, nothing to be *worried* about, but worse. She needed peace and quiet. She'd taken some sleeping medicine.

Cassie stared at the dark circles under the shut eyes. Her mother looked sick. And more than that, fragile. Vulnerable. So *young*.

'Mom...' Her voice was pleading but hollow. Her mother stirred, a twinge of pain crossing her face. Then she was still again.

Cassie felt the numbness sink in a little deeper. There was nobody to help her here.

She turned and left the room.

In her own bedroom, she put the chalcedony piece in her jewellery box and didn't touch it again. So much for luck.

The creaking and rattling of the house kept her up that night, too.

On Thursday morning, there was a bird in her locker. A stuffed owl. It stared at her with shining round yellow eyes. A custodian happened to be passing by, and she pointed it out to him mutely, her hand shaking. He took it away.

That afternoon, it was a dead goldfish. She made a funnel of a sheet of paper and scooped it out. She didn't go near her locker for the rest of the day.

She didn't go near the cafeteria, either. And she spent lunch in the farthest corner of the library.

It was there that she saw the girl again.

The girl with the shining hair, the girl she'd given up on ever meeting. It was hardly surprising that Cassie hadn't seen her at school before this moment. These days Cassie slunk around like a shadow, walking through the halls with her eyes on the ground, speaking to no one. She didn't know why she was at school at all, except that there was nowhere else to go. And if she *had* seen the girl, she'd probably have run the other way. The thought of being rejected by *her* as Cassie was rejected by everyone else at school was unbearable.

But now Cassie looked up from her table at the back of the library and saw a brightness like sunlight.

That hair. It was just as Cassie remembered, impossibly long, an impossible colour. The girl was facing the circulation desk, smiling and talking to the librarian. Cassie could *feel* the radiance of her presence from across the room.

She had the wildest urge to leap up and run to the girl. And then... *what*? She didn't know. But the urge was almost beyond her control. Her throat ached, and tears filled her eyes. She realised she was on her feet. She would run to the girl, and then – and then... Images flooded Cassie's mind, of her mother hugging her when she was young, cleaning out a skinned knee, kissing it better. Comfort. Rescue. Love.

'Diana!'

Another girl was hurrying up to the circulation desk. 'Diana, don't you know what time it is? Hurry up!'

She was pulling the girl with the shining hair away, laughing and waving at the librarian. They were at the door; they were gone.

Cassie was left standing alone. The girl had never even glanced her way.

On Friday morning Cassie stopped in front of her locker. She didn't want to open it. But it exerted a bizarre fascination over her. She couldn't stand *feeling* it there, wondering what was in it and not knowing.

She dialled the combination slowly, everything too bright.

The locker door opened.

This time she couldn't even scream. She felt her eyes opening, straining as wide as the stuffed owl's. Her mouth opened in a soundless gasp. Her stomach heaved. The smell...

Her locker was full of hamburger. Raw and red like flesh with the skin torn off, darkening to purple where it was going bad from lack of refrigeration. Pounds and pounds of it. It smelled like...

Like meat. Dead meat.

Cassie slammed the locker shut, but it bounced off some of the hamburger that was oozing out the bottom. She whirled and stumbled away, her vision hazing over.

A hand grabbed her. For an instant she thought it was an offer of support. Then she felt her backpack being pulled off her shoulder.

She turned and saw a pretty, sullen face. Malicious dark eyes. A motorcycle jacket. Deborah tossed the backpack past Cassie, and automatically Cassie whirled, following it.

On the other side she saw shoulder-length blond hair. Slanted, slightly mad blue-green eyes. A laughing mouth. It was one of the roller-blade guys – the Henderson brothers.

'Welcome to the jungle,' he sang. He threw the backpack

to Deborah, who caught it, singing another line.

Cassie couldn't help turning around and around between them, like a cat chasing a fur mouse on a string.

Tears flooded her eyes. The laughter and singing rang in her ears, louder and louder.

Suddenly a brown arm thrust into her field of vision. A hand caught the backpack in midair. The laughter died.

She turned to see through a blur of tears the cold, handsome face of the dark-haired guy who had stood with Faye that morning two days ago ... could it really be only two days ago? He was wearing another T-shirt with rolled-up sleeves and the same worn-in black jeans.

'Aw, Nick,' the Henderson brother complained. 'You're wrecking our game.'

'Get out of here,' Nick said.

'You get out,' Deborah snarled from behind Cassie. 'Doug and me were just—'

'Yeah, we were only—'

'Shut up.' Nick glanced at Cassie's locker, with globs of meat still seeping out of it. Then he thrust the backpack at her. '*You* get out,' he said.

Cassie looked into his eyes. They were dark brown, the colour of her grandmother's mahogany furniture. And like the furniture, they seemed to reflect the overhead lights back at her. They weren't unfriendly, exactly. Just – unimpassioned. As if nothing much touched this guy.

'Thank you,' she said, blinking back the tears.

Something flickered in those mahogany-dark eyes. 'It's not much to thank me for,' he said. His voice was like a cold wind, but Cassie didn't care. Clutching the backpack to her, she fled.

It was in physics class that she got the note.

A girl named Tina dropped it on her desk, casually, trying to look as if she were doing nothing of the sort. She went right on walking and took a seat on the other side of the room. Cassie looked at the square of folded paper as if it might burn her if she touched it. Her name was written across the front in handwriting that managed to look pompous and prim at the same time.

Slowly, she unfolded the paper.

Cassie, it read. *Meet me in the old science building, second floor, after school. I think we can help each other. A friend.*

Cassie stared at it until the writing doubled. After class she cornered Tina.

'Who gave you this to give to me?'

The girl looked at the note disowningly. 'What are you talking about? I didn't...'

'Yes, you did. Who gave it to you?'

Tina cast a hunted look around. Then she whispered, 'Sally Waltman, all right? But she told me not to tell anybody. I have to go now.'

Cassie blocked her. 'Where's the old science building?'

'Look—'

'Where is it?'

Tina hissed, 'On the other side of E-wing. In back of the parking lot. Now let me go!' She broke away from Cassie and hurried off.

A friend, Cassie thought sarcastically. If Sally were really a friend, she'd talk to Cassie in public. If she were really a friend, she'd have stayed that day on the steps, instead of leaving Cassie alone with Faye. She'd have said, 'Thanks for saving my life.'

But maybe she was sorry now.

The old science building didn't look as if it had been used for a while; there was a padlock on the door, but that had been sprung. Cassie pushed on the door and it swung away from her.

Inside, it was dim. She couldn't make out any details

with her light-dazzled eyes. But she could see a stairway. She climbed it, one hand on the wall to guide herself.

It was when she reached the top of the stairway that she noticed something strange. Her fingers were touching something... soft. Almost furry. She moved them in front of her face, peering at them. Soot?

Something moved in the room in front of her.

'Sally?' She took a hesitant step forward. Why wasn't more light coming in the windows? she wondered. She could see only glowing white cracks here and there. She took another shuffling step, and another, and another.

'Sally?'

Even as she said it, realisation finally dawned on her exhausted brain. Not Sally. Whoever, whatever was out there, it wasn't Sally.

Turn around, idiot. Get out of here. *Now*.

She whirled, clumsily, straining her dark-adapting eyes, looking for the deeper blackness of the stairwell—

And light shone suddenly, streaming into her face, blinding her. There was a creaking, wrenching noise and more light burst into the room. Through a window that had been boarded up, Cassie realised. Someone was standing in front of it now, holding a piece of wood.

She turned towards the stairway again. But someone was standing there, too. Enough light shone into the room now that she could see features as the girl stepped forward.

'Hello, Cassie,' said Faye. 'I'm afraid Sally couldn't make it. But maybe you and I can help each other instead.'

CHAPTER

8

'**Y**ou sent the note,' Cassie said flatly.

Faye smiled her slow, terrible smile. 'Somehow I didn't think you'd come if I used my own name,' she said.

And I fell for it, Cassie thought. She must have coached that girl Tina on what to say – and I swallowed it.

'How do you like the little presents you've been finding?'

Tears came to Cassie's eyes. She couldn't answer. She felt so drained, so helpless – if only she could *think*.

'Haven't you been sleeping well?' Faye continued, her throaty voice innocent. 'You look awful. Or maybe your *dreams* have been keeping you awake.'

Cassie turned to cast a quick look behind her. There was an exit there, but Suzan was in front of it.

'Oh, you can't go yet,' Faye said. 'I wouldn't *dream* of letting you.'

Cassie stared at her. 'Faye, just leave me alone...'

'*Dream* on,' said Deborah, and she laughed nastily.

Cassie could make no sense out of this. But then she saw that Faye was holding a sheet of paper. It was smoothed flat, but it had once been tightly crumpled.

Her poem.

Anger blazed through her exhaustion. Blazed so bright that for an instant she was full of energy, lifted by it. She lunged at Faye crying, 'That's *mine*!'

It took Faye by surprise. She reeled back, dodging, holding the poem high out of Cassie's reach.

Then something caught Cassie's arms from behind, pinning them.

'Thank you, Deborah,' Faye said, slightly breathless. She looked at Cassie. 'I suppose even a little white mouse will turn. We'll have to remember that. But just now,' she continued, 'we're going to have an impromptu poetry reading. I'm sorry the atmosphere isn't more – appropriate – but what can you do? This used to be the science building, but nobody comes here much any more. Not since Doug and Chris Henderson made a little mistake in a chemistry experiment. You've probably seen the Henderson brothers – they're hard to miss. Nice guys, but a little irresponsible. They accidentally made a bomb.'

Now that Cassie's eyes had adjusted again, she could see that the room was burned out. The walls were black with soot.

'Of course, some people think it's unsafe here,' Faye continued, 'so they keep it locked. But we've never let a little thing like that stop us. It is *private*, though. We can make all the noise we want and nobody will hear us.'

Deborah's grip on Cassie's arms was painful. But Cassie started to struggle again as Faye cleared her throat and held up the paper.

'Let me see ... "My Dreams", by Cassie Blake. Imaginative title, by the way.'

'You don't have any *right*—' Cassie began, but Faye ignored her. She began reading in a theatrical, melodramatic voice:

'Each night I lie and dream about the one—'

'It's *private*!' Cassie cried.

'Who kissed me and awakened my desire—'

'Let me *go*!'

'I spent a single hour with him alone—'

'It isn't *fair*—'

'And since that hour, my days are laced with fire.' Faye looked up. 'That's it. What do you think, Deborah?'

'It stinks,' Deborah said, then gave a little wrench to Cassie's arms as Cassie tried to tear away. 'It's stupid.'

'Oh, I don't know. I liked some of the imagery. About fire, for instance. Do you like fire, Cassie?'

Cassie went still. That lazy, husky voice had a new note in it, a note she recognised instinctively. Danger.

'Do you *think* about fire, Cassie? Do you dream about it?'

Dry-mouthed, Cassie stared at Faye. Those honey-coloured eyes were warm, glowing. Excited.

'Would you like to see a fire trick?'

Cassie shook her head. There were things worse than humiliation, she was realising. For the first time this week she was afraid, not for her pride, but for her life.

Faye snapped the piece of paper in her hand, forming it into a loose cone. Flame burst out of one corner at the top.

'Why don't you tell us who the poem is about, Cassie? This boy who *awakened* you – who is he?'

Cassie leaned away, trying to escape the blazing paper in front of her face.

'Careful,' Deborah said mockingly from behind her. 'Don't get too close to her hair.'

'What, you mean *this* close?' said Faye. 'Or *this* close?'

Cassie had to twist her neck to evade the flame. Little

glowing bits of paper were flying off in every direction. The brightness left an after-image, and she could feel heat on her skin.

'Oops, that *was* close. I think her eyelashes are too long anyway, Deborah, don't you?'

Cassie was fighting now, but Deborah was astonishingly strong. And the more Cassie struggled, the more the grip hurt.

'Let go of me—' she gasped out.

'But I thought you liked fire, Cassie. Look into the fire. What do you see?'

Cassie didn't want to obey, but she couldn't help it. Surely the paper should have burned up by now. But it was still blazing. Yellow, she thought. Fire is yellow and orange. Not red like they say.

All her senses were fixed on the flame. Its heat brought a dry tingle to her cheeks. She could hear the crumple of paper as it was consumed; she could smell the burning. And she could see nothing else.

Grey ash and yellow flame. Blue at the bottom like a gas burner. The fire changed shape every second, its radiance streaming endlessly upward. Pouring out its energy...

Energy.

Fire is power, she thought. She could almost feel the charge of the golden flame. It wasn't the vast quietness of sky and sea, or the waiting solidity of rock. It was active. Power there for the taking...

'Yes,' Faye whispered.

The sound shocked Cassie out of her trance. Don't be *crazy*, she told herself. Her fantasy about the flame collapsed. This was what happened when you didn't get any sleep. When the stress became unbearable and you got to the end of your resources. She was going insane.

Tears flooded her eyes, fell down her cheeks.

'Oh, she's just a baby after all,' Faye said, and there was savage disgust in her voice. Disgust and something like disappointment. 'Come on, baby, can't you cry any harder than that? If you cry hard enough, maybe you can put it out.'

Still sobbing, Cassie tossed her head back and forth as the blazing paper stabbed closer. So close that tears fell on it and sizzled. Cassie was no longer thinking; she was simply terrified. Like a trapped animal, a desperate, pathetic trapped animal.

Dead meat dead meat dead meat dead meat ...

'What are you *doing*? Let go of her – now!'

The voice came out of nowhere, and for an instant Cassie didn't even attempt to locate it. Her whole being was focussed on the fire. It flared up suddenly, dissolving almost instantaneously into soft grey ash. Faye was left holding only a stump of charred paper cone.

'I said let her *go*!' Something bright came at Deborah. But not bright like fire. Bright like sunlight. Or moonlight, when the moon is full and so dazzling you can read by it.

It was *her*.

The girl, the girl from the yellow house, the girl with the shining hair. Utterly dumbfounded, Cassie stared as if seeing her for the first time.

She was almost as tall as Faye, but unlike Faye in every other respect. Where Faye was voluptuous, she was slender; where Faye was dressed in red, she was dressed in white. Instead of a wild black mane like Faye's, her hair was long and straight and shimmering – the colour of the light streaming in the window.

And of course she was beautiful, even more beautiful this close than she had been at a distance. But it was a beauty so different from Faye's it was hard to think

89

of it as the same thing. Faye's beauty was stunning but scary. Her strange golden eyes were fascinating, but they also made you want to run away.

This girl looked like something from a stained-glass window. For the first time Cassie saw her eyes, and they were green and clear, brilliant, as if light were behind them. Her cheeks were faintly flushed with rose, but it was natural colour, not make-up.

Her breast was heaving with indignation, and her voice, though clear and musical, was filled with anger.

'When Tina told me she'd delivered that note for you, I knew there was something going on,' she said. 'But this is unbelievable. For the last time, Deborah, let her go!'

Slowly, reluctantly, the grip on Cassie's arms loosened.

'Look at this ... you could have *hurt* her,' the fair-haired girl raged on. She had a Kleenex out and was wiping ash – and tears – off Cassie's cheeks. 'Are you all right?' she asked, her tone gentling.

Cassie could only look at her. The shining girl had come to rescue her. It was like something out of a dream.

'She's frightened to death,' the girl said, turning on Faye. 'How *could* you, Faye? How could you be so cruel?'

'It just comes naturally,' Faye murmured. Her eyes were hooded, sullen. As sullen as Deborah's face.

'And you, Suzan – I'm surprised at you. Don't you see how wrong it is?'

Suzan mumbled something, looking away.

'And *why* would you want to hurt her? Who is she?' She had a protective arm around Cassie now as she looked from one of the senior girls to another. None of them answered.

'I'm Cassie,' Cassie said. Her voice wobbled at the end, and she tried to steady it. All she could feel was the girl's arm around her shoulder. 'Cassie Blake,' she managed to finish. 'I just moved here a couple of weeks ago. Mrs Howard is my grandmother.'

The girl looked startled. 'Mrs Howard? At Number Twelve? And you're living with her?'

Fear darted through Cassie. She remembered Jeffrey's reaction to hearing where she lived. She would die if this girl responded the same way. Wretchedly, she nodded.

The fair-haired girl whirled back on Faye. 'Then she's one of us! A *neighbour*,' she added sharply as Faye's eyebrows shot up.

'Oh, hardly,' Faye said.

'She's only half—' Suzan began.

'Shut up!' said Deborah.

'She's a neighbour,' the fair-haired girl repeated stubbornly. She looked at Cassie. 'I'm sorry; I didn't know you'd moved in. If I *had*' – she threw an angry glance at Faye – 'I'd have stopped by. I live down at the bottom of Crowhaven Road, Number One.' She gave Cassie another protective squeeze. 'Come on. If you want, I'll take you home now.'

Cassie nodded. She would have happily followed if the girl had told her to jump out a window.

'I forgot to introduce myself,' the girl said, stopping on the way to the stairs. 'My name's Diana.'

'I know.'

Diana had a blue Acura Integra. She stopped in front of it and asked Cassie if she wanted to get anything from her locker.

With a shudder, Cassie shook her head.

'Why not?'

Cassie hesitated. Then told her. Everything.

Diana listened, arms folded, toe tapping with increasing

speed as the story went on. Her green eyes were beginning to shine with an almost incandescent fury.

'Don't worry about it,' was all she said at the end. 'I'll call and have the custodian clean out the locker. For now, we need to get you out of here.'

She drove, telling Cassie to leave the Rabbit. 'We'll take care of it later.' And Cassie believed her. If Diana said it would be taken care of, it would be taken care of.

In the car, all Cassie could do was stare at a strand of long, shining hair falling over the emergency brake. It was like sunlight-coloured silk. Or sunlight-and-moonlight coloured, rather. For an instant, in the back of Cassie's mind, a thought popped up about someone else who had hair that was more than one colour, but when she grasped after it, it was gone.

She didn't quite dare to touch the strand of hair, although she wanted to see if it felt like silk too. Instead she tried to listen to what Diana was saying.

'. . . and I don't know what gets into Faye sometimes. She just doesn't *think*. She doesn't realise what she's doing.'

Cassie's eyes slid cautiously up to Diana's face. In her opinion, Faye knew exactly what she was doing. But she didn't say anything – they were pulling up to the pretty Victorian house.

'Come on,' Diana said, jumping out. 'Let's get you cleaned up before you go home.'

Cleaned up? Cassie found out what she meant when Diana led her into an old-fashioned bathroom on the second floor. Soot stained her grey sweater, her hands, her jeans. Her hair was a mess. Her face was smudged with black and striped with tears. She looked like a war orphan.

'I'll lend you some clothes while we get yours

clean. And *you* can get clean in this.' Diana was bustling around, running hot water into a claw-footed bathtub, adding something that smelled sweet and bubbled. She put out towels, soap, shampoo, all with a speed that bewildered Cassie.

'Throw your clothes outside when you get undressed. And you can put this on afterwards,' she said, hanging a fluffy white bathrobe on a hook on the door. 'Okay, you're set.'

She disappeared, and Cassie was left staring at the shut door. She looked at the slightly steamy mirror, then at the bathtub. She felt cold and achy inside. Her muscles were trembling from tension. The hot, sweet-scented water looked perfect, and when she climbed in and it rose around her, she let out an involuntary sigh of bliss.

Oh, it was lovely. Just right. She lay and basked for a while, letting the heat soak into her bones and the light, flowery smell fill her lungs. It seemed to clear the last tired cobwebs from her head and refresh her.

She took a washcloth and scrubbed the grime off her face and body. The shampoo smelled sweet too. When she finally got out of the tub and wrapped herself in the big white terrycloth robe, she was clean, and warm, and more relaxed than she could remember being in weeks. She still could scarcely believe this was happening, but she felt filled with light.

The bathroom *was* old-fashioned, but not in an ugly way, she decided. Pretty towels and jars of coloured bath salts and what looked like potpourri made it nice.

She slipped on the soft white slippers Diana had left and padded into the hall.

The door opposite was ajar. Hesitantly she knocked, pushed it open. Then she stopped on the threshold.

Diana was sitting on a window seat, head bent over

Cassie's grey sweater on her lap. Above her, in the window, prisms were hanging. The sun was striking them so that little triangles of rainbow fell in the room: bands of violet and green and orangey-red. They were sliding across the walls, dancing on the floor, on Diana's arms and hair. It was as if she were sitting in the middle of a kaleidoscope. No wonder the window had sparkled, Cassie thought.

Diana looked up and smiled.

'Come in. I was just getting the soot out of your sweater.'

'Oh. It's cashmere—'

'I know. It'll be all right.' Diana took some book that had been open on the window seat and put it into a large cabinet that stood against one wall. Cassie noticed she locked the cabinet afterwards. Then she went out with the sweater.

Cassie looked at the window seat curiously. She didn't see any spot remover. Only a packet of potpourri and what looked like part of somebody's rock collection.

The room itself was lovely. It managed to combine pretty, antique-looking furniture with modern things, as if the past and the present existed side by side in harmony here.

The hangings on the bed were pale blue with a delicate trailing-vine design, light and airy. On the walls, instead of movie posters or pin-ups, there were some kind of art prints. The whole place looked – classy. Elegant and artistic, but comfortable, too.

'Do you like those? The prints?'

Cassie turned to find that Diana had noiselessly entered the room again. She nodded, wishing she could think of something intelligent to say to this girl who seemed so far above her. 'Who's in them?' she asked, hoping that wasn't something she ought to know already.

'They're Greek gods. Or Greek goddesses, actually. This one's Aphrodite, the goddess of love. See the cherubs and doves around her?'

Cassie gazed at the woman in the picture, who was reclining on a sort of couch, looking beautiful and indolent. Something about the pose – or maybe it was the exposed bosom – reminded her of Suzan.

'And this is Artemis.' Diana moved to another print. 'She was goddess of the hunt. She never married, and if any man saw her bathing, she had him ripped to pieces by her dogs.'

The girl in this picture was slim and lithe, with toned-looking arms and legs. She was kneeling, aiming a bow. Her dark hair fell in tumbled waves down her back, and her face was intense, challenging. Deborah sometimes looked like that, Cassie thought. Then she glanced at the next print and started.

'Who's that?'

'That's Hera, queen of the gods. She could be – jealous.'

Cassie bet she could. The young woman was tall and proud, with an imperious set to her chin. But it was her eyes that held Cassie. They seemed almost to blaze from the print, full of passion and will and danger. Like a crouching jungle cat...

Shuddering uncontrollably, Cassie turned away.

'Are you all right?' Diana asked. Cassie nodded, gulping. Now that she was safe, it was all coming back. Not only the events of the last day, but of the entire last week. All the hurt, all the humiliation. The hanged doll in her locker, the scene in the cafeteria. The rubber snake. The game of keep away with her backpack...

'Cassie?' A hand touched her shoulder.

It was too much. Cassie turned around and flung herself into Diana's arms, bursting into tears.

'It's okay. It'll all be okay, really. Don't worry...' Diana held her and patted her back. All the tears Cassie hadn't been able to release in front of her mother or grandmother were flooding out now. She clung to Diana and sobbed like a little child.

And it was just like the images she'd had in the library. As if she were seven years old and her mother was comforting her. Somehow, Diana made Cassie feel that everything *was* going to be all right.

Eventually, she slowed to hiccups and sniffles. Finally she lifted her head.

'Tell you what,' Diana said, handing a Kleenex to Cassie. 'Why don't you stay here for dinner? My dad won't be back until late tonight – he's a lawyer. I can call a couple of friends and we can order a pizza. How does that sound?'

'Oh – great,' Cassie said, biting her lip. 'Really great.'

'You can put on these clothes until yours dry – they'll be a little big, but not too bad. Come downstairs when you're ready.' Diana paused, her emerald-green eyes on Cassie's face. 'Is something wrong?'

'No... not really, but...' Cassie floundered, then shook her head angrily. 'It's only... it's just... why are you being so *nice* to me?' she burst out. It all still seemed like a dream.

Diana stared at her a minute, then she smiled with her eyes, although her lips remained grave. 'I don't know... I guess I think *you're* nice and you deserve it. I can work on trying to be rotten if you want.'

Cassie shook her head again, but not angrily this time. She felt her own lips twitch.

'And...' Diana was looking off into space now,

her clear green eyes distant. 'We're all sisters, you know.'

Cassie caught her breath. 'Are we?' she whispered.

'Yes,' Diana said firmly, still looking far away. 'Yes, we are. In spite of everything.' Then her face changed, and she looked at Cassie. 'You can call your mom from this line,' she said, indicating a phone. 'I'll go down and order the pizza.' And just like that, she was gone.

CHAPTER 9

The girls who came over were named Laurel and Melanie. Laurel was the girl Cassie had seen in the library with Diana. Up close she was very slim, with light-brown hair almost as long as Diana's and a pretty, pixieish face. She was wearing a floral dress and pink hightops.

'It's veggie pizza, isn't it?' she said, kicking the door shut behind her because she was carrying a stack of Tupperware containers in her arms. 'You didn't order any patriarchal pepperoni, did you?'

'No meat,' Diana assured her, opening the door again to reveal another girl standing there patiently.

'Oops – sorry!' Laurel shouted on her way to the kitchen. 'I've got stuff here for a salad.'

Diana and the new girl turned as one to shout, *No tofu!*

'It's just veggies and greens,' Laurel's voice floated back. Diana and the new girl exchanged looks of relief.

Cassie was fighting shyness. The new girl was definitely a senior, tall and beautiful in a sophisticated way. Her smooth cap of chestnut hair was pulled back with an Alice band, and under it her grey eyes were cool and assessing.

She was the only person Cassie had ever seen who looked as if she were wearing glasses when she wasn't.

'This is Melanie,' Diana said. 'She lives on this same road at Number Four. Melanie, this is Cassie Blake – she just moved into Number Twelve. Mrs Howard's her grandmother.'

The thoughtful grey eyes were turned on Cassie, then Melanie nodded. 'Hi.'

'Hi,' Cassie said, glad she'd had a bath and hoping Diana's clothes didn't look too silly on her.

'Melanie's our brain,' Diana said fondly. 'She's devastatingly smart. And she knows everything there is to know about computers.'

'Not everything,' Melanie said without smiling. 'Sometimes I think not anything.' She looked at Diana. 'You know, I overheard some whispers about a Cassie, and something to do with Faye, but nobody would tell me more.'

'I know. I only found out about it today. Maybe I'm out of touch with what's really going on in school – but *you* should have told me you'd heard something, at least.'

'You can't fight everybody's battles, Diana.'

Diana just looked at her, then shook her head slightly. 'Cassie, why don't you go in and help Laurel with the salad? You'll like Laurel; she's a junior like you.'

In the kitchen Laurel was standing in front of a counter full of vegetables, chopping away.

'Diana said I should help you.'

Laurel turned. 'Good! You can wash that shepherd's purse over there – it's fresh, so it's probably got some native wildlife crawling on it.'

Shepherd's purse? Cassie looked at several piles of greenery doubtfully. Was this something she ought to know?

'Uh … this?' she said, picking up a dark green triangular leaf with a mealy white underside.

'No, that's wild spinach.' Laurel gestured with her elbow to a pile of long, slender leaves with ragged edges. 'That's the shepherd's purse. But you can wash them both.'

'Do you ever use – uh, feverfew – in salads?' Cassie asked hesitantly as she washed. She was glad to have something to contribute. These girls were so smart, so competent, so *together*; she desperately wanted to make a good impression.

Laurel smiled and nodded. 'Yes, but you have to be careful not to eat too much; you can get a rash. Feverfew's good for other things, too; it makes a good wash for insect bites and a great love—' Laurel broke off suddenly and went into a flurry of chopping. 'There, this burnet is ready. It's good to get these greens fresh, you know,' she added quickly, 'because they taste better and they're still full of life from Mother Earth.'

Cassie glanced at her warily. Maybe this girl wasn't so together after all. Full of life from Mother Earth? But then, suddenly, she recalled that day when she had leaned against the red granite and felt a buzzing deep inside it. When she'd imagined she'd felt that, rather. Yes, she could see how you might think that fresh plants were full of that life.

'Okay, this is done. You can tell Di and Melanie it's ready; I'll get some plates,' Laurel said.

Cassie went back into the spacious front room. Melanie and Diana were absorbed in conversation, and neither of them saw her come up behind them.

'…picking her up like a puppy off the street. You're always doing that,' Melanie was saying earnestly, and

Diana was listening with her arms folded. 'But what's going to happen later—?'

She broke off as Diana saw Cassie and touched her forearm.

'It's ready,' Cassie said, feeling awkward. Had they been talking about her? Calling her a puppy off the street? But it hadn't been Diana saying that; only Melanie. She told herself that she didn't care what Melanie thought.

The cool grey eyes weren't unfriendly, though, as Melanie looked at her while they ate the salad. Only – thoughtful. And when the pizza came, Cassie had to admire the ease with which the other three girls laughed and talked with the college-age delivery guy. He got so interested in Melanie that he practically invited himself inside, but Diana, laughing, shut the door on him.

Afterward, Melanie told several amusing stories about her trip to Canada over the summer, and Cassie almost forgot about the remark. It was so good just to be surrounded by easy, friendly talk; not to feel shut out. And to be here by Diana's invitation, to see Diana smiling at her... she still could scarcely believe it.

When she was getting ready to leave, though, she got a shock. Diana handed her a neat pile of clothes – the grey sweater showed no trace of soot now – and said, 'I'll take you home. Don't worry about your grandma's car. If you give me the keys, I'll have Chris Henderson drive it to your place.'

Cassie froze in the act of handing over the keys. 'Henderson? You mean – you don't mean one of the Henderson brothers.'

Diana smiled as she unlocked the Integra. 'So you've heard of them. Chris is nice, really, just a little wild. Don't worry.'

As they drove off, Cassie remembered that the one

playing keep away with her backpack had been called Doug, not Chris. But she still couldn't help feeling alarmed.

'We all know each other out here on Crowhaven Road,' Diana explained in a comforting tone. 'See, there's Laurel's house, and the next one is Faye's. The kids who grew up here sort of stick together. It'll be okay.'

'Stick together?' Cassie had a sudden, disturbing idea.

'Yes.' Diana's voice was deliberately light. 'We've got a sort of club...'

'The Club?' Cassie was so appalled she interrupted. 'You mean – you're in it too? You and Laurel and Melanie?'

'Mm,' Diana said. 'Well, here's your house. I'll call you tomorrow – maybe I could come over. And we can carpool to school on Monday...' She stopped at the expression on Cassie's face. 'What is it, Cassie?' she said gently.

Cassie was shaking her head. 'I don't know... yes, I *do* know. I told you how I heard Faye and Suzan and Deborah talking the first day of school – that was how all the trouble started. I heard the kind of things they said, and I know they're in the Club. And it was so awful... I don't see how *you* could be in a club like that, with them.'

'It isn't what you think...' Diana's gentle voice trailed off. 'And I can't really explain. But I'll tell you this – don't judge the Club by Faye. Although there's a lot of good in Faye too, if you look for it.'

Cassie thought you would have to look with a scanning electron microscope to find it. After a moment, she said so.

Diana laughed. 'No, really. I've known her since we were babies. We've all known each other that long out here.'

'But...' Cassie looked at her worriedly. 'Aren't you

afraid of her? Don't you think she might try to do something terrible to you?'

'No,' Diana said. 'I don't think so. For one thing, she's – made a sort of promise not to. And for another' – she looked at Cassie almost apologetically, although a smile was tugging at the corner of her lips – 'well, don't hate me, but Faye happens to be my first cousin.'

Cassie gaped.

'We're mostly cousins up here,' Diana said softly. 'Sometimes second and third, and all that, but lots even closer. Here's some herb tea Laurel made up for me over the summer,' she added, putting something in Cassie's hand. 'Drink some tonight if you've been having trouble sleeping. It ought to help. I'll see you tomorrow morning.'

When Diana appeared at the door, her hair was pulled back in one long, exquisite French braid. It hung down like a silk tassel. She had a packet of good-smelling dried leaves wrapped in cheesecloth in one hand.

'You said your mom had the flu, so I brought some tea for her. It's good for coughs and chills. Did you try that tea I gave you last night?'

Cassie nodded. 'I couldn't believe it. I went right to sleep and woke up this morning feeling great. What was in it?'

'Well, for one thing, ground-up catnip,' Diana said, and then smiled at Cassie's reaction. 'Don't worry; it doesn't have the same effect on humans as on cats. It's just relaxing.'

Was that what Diana had been doing that first morning Cassie had seen her? Making some kind of tea? Cassie didn't quite dare to admit she'd been spying that day, but she was pleased when Diana said she'd like to make the tea and give it to Cassie's mother personally.

'It's a simple herb and gem elixir for chills,' she said quietly to Mrs Blake, and there was something reassuring about her voice. Cassie's mother hesitated a moment, then reached for the cup. She tasted it, and then looked up and smiled at Diana. Cassie felt warm all over.

Even Cassie's grandmother's seamed old face broke into a smile at the sight of Diana as she passed the two girls walking down the hall to Cassie's room.

'It must be great to have a grandmother like that,' Diana said. 'She must be full of old stories.'

Cassie was relieved. She'd been afraid that Diana wouldn't be able to see past the mole and the stooped back and the coarse, grizzled hair. 'She is pretty great,' she said, marvelling at how much her own attitude had changed since that first day when she'd seen the figure in the doorway. 'And it's nice to finally get to know her, since she's the only relative I have left. All my other grandparents are dead.'

'So are mine,' Diana said. 'And my mom, too. It's sad, because I always wanted a little sister, but my mother died the same year I was born, and my dad never remarried, so there never was any chance.'

'I've wished for a sister too,' Cassie murmured.

There was a silence. Then Diana said, 'This is a beautiful room.'

'I know,' Cassie said, looking around at the massive, shining furniture and the formal draperies and the stiff chairs. 'It's beautiful, but it's like a museum. That's all my stuff that got shipped from home.' She pointed to a pile of belongings in the corner. 'I tried to spread it around, but I was afraid of scratching something or breaking something.'

Diana laughed. 'I wouldn't worry. These things have made it through the last three hundred years; they'll hold out a little longer. You just need to arrange the room so your stuff fits in with them. We could try it next weekend – I'm sure Laurel and Melanie would help too. It would be fun.'

Cassie thought of Diana's bright, airy, harmonious room and felt a surge of hope. If her bedroom could look just *half* as good as that, she'd be happy.

'You're just too nice to me,' she blurted out, then winced and put a hand to her forehead. 'I know how incredibly stupid that sounds,' she said helplessly, 'but it's true. I mean, you're doing all this for me, and you're not getting anything back. And – I just can't understand why you'd *want* to.'

Diana was looking out the window at the ocean. It rolled and sparkled, reflecting a clear, radiantly blue September sky. 'I told you,' she said, and smiled. 'I think *you're* nice. You were good to help Sally the way you did, and it was brave to stand up to Faye. I admire that. And besides,' she added, shrugging, 'I *like* being friendly to people. It doesn't feel like I'm getting nothing back. I'm always wondering why people are so nice to *me*.'

Cassie threw a look at her, sitting there by the window with sunlight spilling over her, haloing her in brightness. Her fair hair seemed literally to glow, and her profile was perfect, like a delicately carved cameo. Could Diana really not know?

'Well, I guess the fact that you always seem to try and find the good in everybody could be part of it,' Cassie said. 'People probably can't resist that. And the fact that you're not vain and you're really interested in what other people have to say... and I guess the fact that you're the most beautiful person I've ever seen in my entire life doesn't hurt,' she added finally.

Diana burst out laughing. 'I'm sorry you grew up around such ugly people,' she said. Then she sobered, looking out the window again and playing with the drapery cord. 'But you know...' she said, and her voice was almost shy. Then she turned to Cassie, her eyes so brilliantly green that it took Cassie's breath away.

'You know, it's funny about us both wishing for sisters, and neither of us having one,' she said. 'And ever since I saw you in the science building... well, I've *felt* almost as if you were my little sister. It sounds strange, but it's true.'

It didn't seem strange to Cassie. Ever since she'd seen Diana, she'd felt as if they were connected in some way.

'And – I don't know; I feel I can *talk* to you, somehow. Even more than to Melanie and Laurel, even though we just met. I feel that somehow you understand me and that... I can trust you.'

'You can,' Cassie said quietly, but with a passion that surprised even her. 'I don't know why either, but you *can* trust me, no matter what.'

'So if you wanted...' Diana was frowning slightly, chewing her lip, still looking down as she pleated the curtain material. 'Well... I was thinking maybe we could sort of be foster sisters to each other. Sort of adopt each other. Then I'd have a little sister and you'd have a big one. But only if you want to,' she added quickly, looking up again.

Want to? Cassie's problem was that she didn't know what to do – throw her arms around Diana, dance around the room, burst into laughter, or burst into tears.

'That would be okay,' she managed to say after a minute. Then, heart singing, she smiled at Diana, shyly, but meeting her eyes directly. 'No, that'd be – great.'

* * *

'You're looking better this morning, Mom,' Cassie said. Her mother, sitting on the edge of her bed, smiled at her.

'It was a bad flu, but I *am* better now,' she said. 'And you – you're looking happier, sweetheart.'

'I am,' Cassie said, dropping a quick kiss on her mother's cheek. You'll never know how much, she thought.

This morning was almost like the first day of school in excitement and anticipation. I don't care if everyone else in the entire school hates me, Cassie thought. Diana will be there. Just thinking about that will make the rest not matter.

Diana was looking particularly beautiful that day, wearing a green suede jacket lined with blue silk over jeans faded almost white. At her throat hung a simple pendant with a single stone in it, a milky stone with a blue-white shimmer. Cassie was proud just to walk beside her at school.

And in the halls, she noticed something strange. It was hard to walk three steps without getting stopped by someone.

'Oh, hi, Diana – have you got a minute?' 'Diana! I'm so glad to see you...' 'Diana, it's killing me. Won't you just *think* about this weekend?' (This from a guy.) Practically everybody they passed wanted to talk with Diana, and those who didn't have something to say hung around the edges just listening.

Cassie watched Diana speak to each of them. The guys begging for dates were the only ones she dismissed, smiling. Some of the people shot nervous glances at Cassie, but none of them backed away or said anything nasty. Apparently Diana had the power to counteract even Faye.

Finally, a few minutes before the bell, Diana pulled away from the crowd and walked Cassie to her English class. She not only came inside but sat down at a desk beside Cassie's and chatted with her, ignoring everyone who was looking at them.

'We'll have to have another pizza party this week,' she said in a clear, carrying voice. 'And Laurel and I were talking about ways to redecorate your room if you still want to. Laurel's very artistic. And I really think you ought to transfer into my AP history class if you can. It's last period, and the teacher, Ms Lanning, is great...'

She went on talking, seeming utterly oblivious to the rest of the class. But Cassie could feel something bubbling up inside her like the carbonation in a bottle of soda. Girls who had actually turned their backs and scuttled away from her last week were now listening avidly to Diana's monologue, nodding as if they were part of the conversation.

'Well, I guess I'd better go – I'll meet you at eleven fifteen for lunch,' Diana said.

'Where?' Cassie asked, almost panicking as Diana got up. She had just realised she'd never seen Diana – or Laurel or Melanie either – at lunch.

'Oh, in the cafeteria – the part in the rear. Behind the glass door. We call it the back room. You'll see it,' Diana said. The girls around Cassie were exchanging looks of astonishment. As Diana walked away one of them spoke.

'You get to eat in the back room?' she asked enviously.

'I guess so,' Cassie said absently, watching Diana.

'But...' Another look passed between the girls. 'Are you in the Club?' one of them finished.

Cassie felt uncomfortable. 'No... not really. I'm just friends with Diana.'

A pause. Then the girls settled back, looking bewildered but impressed.

Cassie scarcely noticed. She was watching the door, and the girl who'd walked in just as Diana reached it to walk out.

Faye was looking particularly beautiful this morning too. Her black hair was wild and lustrous, her pale skin glowing. Her lips looked more sensuous than ever, emphasised by some new shade of berry-red lipstick. She was wearing a red sweater that clung to every curve.

She stopped in the doorway, blocking it, and she and Diana looked at each other.

It was a long, measuring glance, hooded golden eyes locked with green. Neither of them said anything, but the air between them almost crackled with electricity. Cassie could almost *feel* the two strong wills fighting for dominance there. Finally, it was Faye who moved aside, but she gestured Diana through the door with an ironic flourish that seemed more like contempt than courtesy. And as Diana passed by, Faye spoke over her shoulder, without turning to look.

'What did she say?' one of the girls asked Cassie.

'I couldn't hear it,' Cassie said.

But that was a lie. She had heard. She just didn't understand. Faye had said, 'Win a battle; lose the war.'

At lunch, Cassie wondered how she hadn't seen the back room of the cafeteria before. She understood, though, how Diana and her friends hadn't seen *her* – the entrance to the back room was swamped with people. People standing around, people hoping to be invited in, or people just hanging out on the fringes. They blocked any view those seated inside might have of the cafeteria proper.

It was easy to see why this room was the favourite

gathering place. There was a TV mounted on one wall, although it was too noisy to hear it. There was even a microwave and a Veryfine juice machine. Cassie was aware of stares on her back as she went in and sat down beside Diana, but today they were stares of envy.

Melanie and Laurel were there. So was Sean, the little slinking boy who'd urged her to go to the principal. So was a guy with dishevelled blond hair and slightly tilted blue-green eyes – oh, God, one of the Henderson brothers. Cassie tried not to give him a look of alarm as Diana nodded at him and said, 'That's Christopher Henderson – Chris, say hi; this is Cassie. You moved her white Rabbit.'

The blond guy turned and stared defensively. 'I never touched it. I didn't even see it, okay? I was somewhere else.'

Diana and Melanie exchanged a patient look. 'Chris,' Diana said, 'what are you talking about?'

'This chick's rabbit. I didn't take it. I'm not into little furry animals. We're all brothers, okay?'

Diana stared at him a moment, then shook her head. 'Go back to your lunch, Chris. Forget it.'

Chris frowned, shrugged, then turned back to Sean. 'So there's this new group, Cholera, right, and they've got this new album...'

'Somebody did move my car,' Cassie offered tentatively.

'He did it,' Laurel said. 'He just doesn't have a very good memory for reality. He knows a lot about music, though.'

Sean, Cassie noticed, was a different boy in here than he'd been by the lockers. He was excessively polite, seeming eager to please, and frequently offering to get things for the girls. They treated him like a slightly annoying little brother. He and Laurel were the only juniors besides Cassie.

They'd been eating just a few minutes when a strawberry-blonde head appeared in the doorway. Suzan looked cross.

'Deborah's got a lunch detention and Faye's off doing something, so I'm eating in here,' she announced.

Diana looked up. 'Fine,' she said evenly, then added, 'This is my friend Cassie, Suzan. Cassie, this is Suzan Whittier.'

'Hi,' Cassie said, trying to sound casual.

There was a moment of tension. Then Suzan rolled her china-blue eyes. 'Hi,' she said finally, and immediately sat down and began removing things from her lunch sack.

Cassie looked at Suzan unloading her lunch, then threw a quick glance over at Laurel. Then she looked at Diana and raised her eyebrows questioningly.

She heard the crinkle of plastic as Suzan produced the last item from her bag; then a piercing shriek from Laurel.

'Oh, my God – you're *not* still eating those! Do you know what's in those things, Suzan? Beef fat, lard, palm oil – and it's about fifty per cent white sugar...'

Diana was biting her lip and Cassie was shaking silently, trying to keep a straight face. Finally it was too much, and she had to let the giggles escape. As soon as she did Diana burst into laughter too.

Everyone else looked at them, baffled.

Cassie smiled down at her tuna sandwich. After so many weeks of loneliness, she had found where she belonged. She was Diana's friend, Diana's adopted sister. Her place was here beside Diana.

CHAPTER
10

That Friday, Kori came to the back room for lunch. She seemed in awe of the older girls and was even absently respectful of Cassie, which was nice. Certainly Suzan and Deborah had no such respect. The strawberry blonde seemed unaware of Cassie's existence unless she wanted something passed to her or picked up, and the biker fixed Cassie with a surly glare whenever they passed in the hall. Deborah and Doug – the other Henderson brother – had appeared in the back room only once since Cassie started eating there, and they had spent the entire time arguing furiously about some heavy-metal band.

Neither Faye nor Nick, the dark, coldly handsome boy who'd rescued Cassie's backpack, showed up at all that week.

But Kori Henderson was nice. Now that Cassie knew, she could see the resemblance to Chris and Doug – the blonde hair and the blue-green eyes that Kori emphasised by wearing a turquoise necklace and ring all the time. Kori wasn't as wild as her brothers, though. She seemed just an ordinary, friendly, going-on-fifteen girl.

'I've been waiting so long for it, I can't believe it's

finally here,' she was saying at the end of lunch. 'I mean, just think, next Tuesday's the day! And Dad says we can have the party down on the beach – or at least he didn't say we *couldn't* – and I want to make it really special, because of it being a holiday, too...' She trailed off suddenly. Cassie, following her gaze, saw that Diana had her lip caught between her teeth and was almost imperceptibly shaking her head.

What was Kori saying wrong? Cassie wondered. And then it struck her: this was the first she'd heard about a party, although it clearly wasn't news to the others. Was she not invited?

'So, uh, do you think Adam will be back in time for – for – I mean, when do you think Adam will be back?' Kori stuttered.

'I don't really know. I hope it's soon, but...' Diana gave a little shrug. 'Who can tell? Who can ever tell?'

'Who's Adam?' Cassie said, determined to show she didn't care about the party.

'You mean she hasn't told you about Adam yet? Diana, there's such a thing as carrying modesty too far,' Melanie said, her cool grey eyes disbelieving.

The colour had come to Diana's cheeks. 'There just hasn't been time—' she began, and Laurel and Melanie hooted.

Cassie was surprised. She'd never seen Diana react this way. 'No, but really,' she said. 'Who is he? Is he your boyfriend?'

'Only since childhood,' Laurel said. 'They've been together forever.'

'But *where* is he? Is he in college? What's he like?'

'No, he's just – visiting some people,' Diana said. 'He's a senior, but he's been away so far this year. And as for what he's like... well, he's nice. I think you'll like him.' She smiled.

Cassie looked towards Laurel for more information. Laurel waved a zucchini stick in the air. 'Adam's...'

Kori said, 'Yes, he's...'

Even Melanie couldn't seem to find the right words. 'You'll have to meet him,' she said.

Cassie was intrigued. 'Do you have a picture of him?' she asked Diana.

'As a matter of fact, I don't,' Diana said. Seeing Cassie's disappointment she went on, 'You see, around here people have a sort of silly superstition about photographs – they don't like them. So lots of us don't get pictures taken.'

Cassie tried to pretend this wasn't as bizarre as she thought it was. Like aboriginals, she thought in amazement. Thinking the camera will steal their souls. How can anybody in the twentieth century think that?

'He's cute, though,' Kori was saying fervently.

Suzan, who had been absorbed in eating, looked up from her lunch to proclaim in feeling tones: 'That *bod*.'

'Those *eyes*,' Laurel said.

'You'd better go easy,' Melanie said, smiling. 'You're going to drive Diana crazy before he gets back.'

'Crazy enough to give somebody else a chance, maybe?' Sean piped up. Looks of forbearance passed between the girls.

'Maybe, Sean – sometime in the next millennium,' Laurel said. But being a kind girl, she didn't say it very loudly.

Looking amused, Melanie explained to Cassie, 'Adam and Diana don't even *see* anyone of the opposite sex except each other. For years Adam thought the rest of us were boys.'

'Which in Suzan's case took quite a lot of imagination,' Laurel put in.

Suzan sniffed and glanced at Laurel's flat chest.

'And in some people's case took no imagination at all.'

'What about you, Cassie?' Diana interrupted before an argument could begin. 'Did you leave a boyfriend back home?'

'Not really,' Cassie said. 'There was one guy, though, this summer. He was...' She stopped. She didn't want to tell the story in front of Suzan. 'He was sort of... all right. So, anyway, how did Faye's date with Jeffrey go?' she asked Suzan abruptly.

Suzan's look said she wasn't fooled by the sudden change of subject, but she couldn't resist answering. 'The fish got hooked,' she said with a smirk. 'Now all she has to do is reel him in.'

The bell rang then, and there was no further conversation about boyfriends or dates. But Cassie noticed a look about Diana's eyes – a tender, wistful dreaminess – that lingered for the rest of the day.

After school, Diana and Cassie drove back to Crowhaven Road together. As they drove by the Henderson house – one of those in the worst repair – Cassie noticed Diana biting her lip. It was a sure sign the older girl was worried about something.

Cassie thought she knew what. 'I don't mind about Kori's party,' she offered quietly, and Diana looked at her, surprised. 'I don't,' Cassie insisted. 'I don't even know Kori, really. The only time I saw her before was when she was out with Faye on the steps. What's wrong?' she added as Diana looked even more surprised.

'Kori was eating with Faye and the others that day you overheard them talking?'

'Yes – well, she came when they were almost finished eating. There was a whole group of kids, but she was the only one Faye would let stay. Faye said...'

'Faye said what?' Diana sounded resigned.

'She said, "I thought you'd be eating in the cafeteria with the rest of the goody-goodies."' Cassie left out the Princess of Purity part.

'Hm. And what did Kori say to that?'

Cassie felt uncomfortable. 'She said something about too much goodness being boring. She didn't stay with them long, though. I think Faye and Suzan were trying to embarrass her.'

'Mm,' said Diana. She was biting her lip again.

'Anyway,' Cassie went on, 'I *don't* mind not being invited to her party, but do you think... well, do you think there's a chance that someday I could be in the Club too?'

Diana's green eyes had widened fractionally. 'Oh, Cassie. But you don't *want* to,' she said.

'I know I said things last week that sounded that way. But you told me not to judge the Club by Faye, and I'm not, now. And I like you and Melanie and Laurel and Kori – and Suzan's sort of okay. Even Chris Henderson is. So I thought, maybe...' She let her sentence trail off delicately. She could feel her heart beating faster.

'That's not what I meant,' Diana replied. 'I meant you don't want to because you want to go back home, to California, whenever you can. That's the truth, isn't it? You said you were planning to go to college there.'

'Well, yes, eventually, but...' Cassie *had* said that, that first night at Diana's house. Now she was no longer so sure, but she didn't quite know how to explain this. 'What has that got to do with it?' she said. 'I mean, joining doesn't mean staying here the rest of your life, does it?'

Diana's eyes were on the road. 'It's hard to explain.' Then she said softly, 'And in any case – well, I'm afraid membership is sort of limited.'

Abruptly Cassie remembered Deborah's words after Kori had left that day. *One empty space, one candidate, you know?* And Kori was part of the neighbourhood. She'd grown up here. Chris and Doug were her brothers. She wasn't a stranger taken in just because Diana insisted, a puppy picked up off the street.

'I understand,' Cassie said. She tried to sound as if it were all okay, as if it didn't matter. But it did. It did, terribly.

'No, you don't,' Diana murmured. 'But I think that's better. It really is, Cassie, believe me.'

'Oh, no,' Diana said. 'I don't have the Scotch tape. It must have rolled under the car seat. You stay here; there's no reason for us both to go back.' She turned and hurried towards the parking lot.

They were early that morning. Diana had a banner that she and Laurel had painted, saying 'Happy Birthday, Kori'. She was going to hang it above the main entrance of the school, and Cassie had offered to help. Cassie thought that was a particularly noble and unselfish gesture, considering she still wasn't invited to Kori's party. It also showed how much she didn't really mind.

Now she looked up at the main entrance of the school building that had scared her to death two weeks ago.

Two weeks. The first week she had spent as a pariah, an outcast, someone too dangerous to speak to because it might bring down the wrath of Faye on the speaker's head. But the second week...

Diana, she mused, didn't influence people by frightening them. She did it much more subtly, with love. It sounded impossibly stupid and Hallmark card-ish, but it was true. Everyone loved Diana – girls as well as boys – and most of them would walk over hot coals for her. As Diana's adopted 'little sister' Cassie had instantly gained status far beyond anything she could have ever achieved on her own. She now went around with the coolest crowd in school – and if she wasn't completely a part of it, only the real insiders knew.

You're *almost* one of us. She heard Faye's words to Kori in her mind again. Well, today was Kori's birthday, and today Kori *would* be one of them. Today Kori would join the Club.

And Cassie never would.

Cassie hunched her shoulders, trying to shrug the thought off, but a shiver caught her midway through. She wrapped her arms around herself, clasping her elbows. It was colder than she was used to for late September. Laurel and Melanie had been talking over the weekend about the fall equinox, which was today too. Melanie had explained that it was the day when the hours of daylight and darkness were of equal length, which meant the start of fall. Cassie supposed it had a right to be cold. Everyone said the leaves would be turning soon.

Melanie and Laurel had really gotten into that discussion of the equinox. It had seemed terribly important to them, although Cassie couldn't exactly see why. It was another of the little mysteries about New Salemers that were starting to drive Cassie crazy.

She shivered again and began to pace, rubbing her arms.

The hill spread out beneath her. She walked to the top of the stairs and stood bouncing on her toes. It was a clear, crisp day, and mixed in with the luxuriant green all around her she could see a tinge of fall colours here and there. The shrubs across the road – what had Laurel called them? Sumac. The sumac across the road was already red. And some of the sugar maples were turning golden yellow, and there was more red at the bottom of the hill...

Cassie frowned and forgot to rub her arms. She took a step or two down and leaned forward, looking again. The red at the bottom of the hill was almost *too* red, too bright. She'd never known foliage could turn that colour. It wasn't natural.

A violent shiver went through her. God, it was cold. Whatever was down there was half hidden by the underbrush, but it wasn't a bush itself, she decided. It looked more like a sweater somebody had discarded.

It'll get ruined, lying on the damp ground like that, Cassie thought. Whoever owns it is going to be unhappy.

She took another step down. Of course, it's probably ruined already – or maybe it's just a scrap somebody's thrown out.

But it didn't look like a scrap. It had a *shape* – she could see what looked like the sweater's arm. In fact, it looked like a whole bundle of clothes. See, there was something like jeans lying below it...

Suddenly Cassie couldn't breathe.

That's funny – that's really funny, because it looks almost like a person. But that would be so stupid – it's cold and wet on the ground. Anybody lying down there would freeze—

She was moving down the steps quickly now.

Stupid – but it really *does* look a lot like somebody. See, there's legs. That yellow could be hair. They must be asleep – but who would go to sleep like that? Right beside the road. Of course, the weeds and stuff screen them—

She was very close now, and everything had gone

into slow motion – everything but her whirling, reeling thoughts.

Oh, thank God – it isn't a person after all; it's just a dummy. Like one of those stuffed scarecrow things they put out at Halloween to scare people. See, it's all floppy in the middle... no *person* could bend that way... the neck looks like the neck of that doll in my locker. Like somebody pulled the head out...

Cassie's own body was reacting strangely. Her chest was heaving and her muscles were shaking. Her knees were trembling so hard she could scarcely remain standing. And her vision was sparkling at the edges as if she were going to faint.

Thank God, it's not a person – but oh, my God, is that a *hand*? Dummies don't have hands like that... not hands with little pink fingers... and dummies don't wear rings, turquoise rings...

Where had she seen a ring like that before?

Look at it closer; no, don't look, don't look—

But she had seen. The hand, stiff as a claw, was human. And the ring was Kori's.

Cassie didn't realise that she was screaming until she was halfway up the hill. Her legs, which had been trembling so badly, were taking her up in leaps and surges. And she was screaming over and over again: 'Help, help, help.' Only they were such thin, pathetic little shrieks – it was no wonder no one heard her. It was like one of those nightmares where your vocal cords are paralysed.

But someone had heard. As she reached the top of the hill Diana appeared, running. She caught Cassie by the shoulders.

'What is it?'

'Kori!' Cassie gasped in a strangled voice. She could hardly speak. 'Diana – help Kori! She's hurt. Something's wrong—' She knew it was more than something wrong, but she couldn't bring herself to say the words. 'Help her, please—'

'Where?' Diana cut in sharply.

'The bottom. Bottom of the hill. But don't go down there,' Cassie gasped illogically. Oh, God, she was completely falling apart. She couldn't cope – but she couldn't let Diana go down there alone, either.

Diana was flying down the stairs. Stiff-legged, Cassie followed. She saw Diana reach the bottom and hesitate, then swiftly kneel and bend forward.

'Is she—?' Cassie's hands were clenched.

Diana straightened up. Cassie saw the answer in the set of her shoulders. 'She's cold. She's dead.'

Then Diana turned around. Her face was white, her green eyes burning. Something in her expression gave Cassie strength, and she stumbled down the last two steps and flung her arms around her.

She could feel Diana shaking, clinging to her. Kori had been Diana's friend, not hers.

'It'll be okay. It'll be okay,' she gasped, illogical again. There was no way for this to be okay, ever. And over and over in Cassie's mind other words were echoing.

Someday they may find you at the bottom of those stairs with a broken neck. Someday they may find you ...

Kori's neck was broken.

That was what the police doctor said. After Cassie and Diana went back up the stairs, everything that day seemed like a dream. Adults came and took over. School officials, the police, the doctor. They asked questions. They made notes in their notebooks. Throughout it all the kids in the school stood aside and watched. They weren't part of the adults' process. They had questions of their own.

'What are we waiting for? Why don't we just *get* her?' Deborah was saying as Cassie came into the back room. It wasn't her lunch period, but all the rules seemed to have been suspended that day.

'We all heard her say it,' Deborah was continuing. 'Suzan, Faye, and me – even *she* heard it.' She gestured at Cassie, who was numbly trying to get a can of juice out of the machine. 'That bitch said she was going to do it, and she did it. So what are we waiting for?'

'For the truth,' Melanie said quietly and coldly.

'From *them*? Outsiders? You can't be serious. They'll never admit Sally did it. The police are saying it was an accident. An accident! No sign of a struggle, they're saying. She slipped on a wet step. And you know what the kids are saying? They're saying it was one of *us*!'

Laurel looked up from the hot water she was pouring over some dried leaves in a mug. The end of her nose was pink. 'Maybe it *was* one of us,' she said.

'Like who?' Deborah blazed back.

'Like somebody who didn't want her in the Club. Somebody who was afraid she'd come in on the wrong side,' said Laurel.

'And we all know which side would be afraid,' said a new voice, and Cassie jerked around, nearly dropping her juice.

It was Faye. Cassie had never seen her in the back room before, but she was here now, her honey-coloured eyes hooded and smouldering.

'Well, Diana's side certainly had nothing to be afraid of,' Laurel said. 'Kori idolised Diana.'

'Did she? Then why did she spend the last week having lunch with *me*?' Faye said in her slow, husky voice.

Laurel stared, looking uncertain. Then her face cleared

and she shook her head. 'I don't care what you say; you're never going to make me believe Diana would hurt Kori.'

'She's right,' Suzan put in, to Cassie's surprise. 'Diana wouldn't.'

'Besides, we already know who *would*,' Deborah said sharply. 'It was Sally – or maybe that moron boyfriend of hers. I say we get them – now!'

'She's right,' said Sean.

Laurel looked at him, then at Deborah, then at Faye. 'What do you think, Melanie?' she said finally.

Melanie's voice was still quiet, detached. 'I think we need to have a meeting,' she said.

Sean bobbed his head. '*She's* right,' he said.

Just then Diana came in. The Henderson brothers were behind her. They both looked ravaged – and bewildered. As if they couldn't understand how this could happen to them. Chris's eyes were red-rimmed.

Everyone sobered at the sight of the brothers. There was silence as they sat down at the table.

Then Faye turned to Diana. Her golden eyes were like two golden flames. 'Sit down,' she said flatly. 'We need to talk.'

'Yes,' said Diana.

She sat down, and so did Faye. Laurel, after putting two cups of hot liquid in front of the Henderson brothers, did the same. Deborah jerked out a chair and threw herself into it. Suzan and Melanie had already been seated.

Everyone turned to look at Cassie.

Their faces were strange. Alien. Laurel's normally elfin face was closed. Melanie's cool grey eyes were more remote than ever; Suzan's pouting lips were compressed tightly; Deborah's fierceness was barely kept in check. Even Sean's usually furtive expression had an unprecedented dignity. Diana was pale and stern.

The glass door swung open and Nick came in. His face was like a cold and handsome stone, revealing nothing, but he sat down at the table beside Doug.

Cassie was the only one in the room left standing. She looked at them, the members of the Club, and they looked at her. No one needed to say anything. She turned around and left the room.

CHAPTER

11

Cassie didn't know where she was going. The school was trying to hold classes, even though there were probably more kids outside the classrooms than inside. They were in the halls, on the stairs, hanging around the main entrance. Cassie looked dazedly at a clock and then went to her science class, conceptual physics. She could probably call her mom and just go home if she liked, but she didn't want to face her mother right now. She just wanted to try and pretend to be normal.

As she sat taking meaningless notes, she could feel eyes on her. She had the odd feeling that she'd been transported back in time and that it was two weeks ago, when Faye had blackballed her. But after class she saw the difference. People kept coming up to her and murmuring, 'Are you okay?' and 'How're you doing?' They looked ill at ease – as if they didn't *want* to be talking to her but felt they'd better. After her last class there were more little visits: people coming in groups of two or three to say, 'Sorry' or 'Just want you to know we'll miss her too.'

The truth of it struck her suddenly, and she almost

laughed at the irony. They were condolence calls! Cassie was standing in for the Club. All of these *outsiders* were coming to her, not realising that she was as much outside as any of them.

When a cheerleader came and said, 'Oh, this must be *so* hard for you,' Cassie lost it.

'I didn't even know her!' she burst out. 'I only spoke to her once in my life!'

The cheerleader backed off hastily. After that the condolence calls stopped.

Ms Lanning, the history teacher, drove Cassie home. She sidestepped her mother's worried questioning – apparently the school had called to explain what had happened – and went outside. She climbed down the steep bluff to the beach below her grandmother's house.

The ocean had never looked bleaker. It was a heavy, shining silver colour – like the mercury in a thermometer. The day, which had started out so bright, had turned overcast, and it got darker and darker as Cassie paced.

And paced. This beach had been one of the good things about living here – but what good was it now? She was walking on it alone.

Her chest was bursting. It was as if all the terrible events of the day were locked inside her, struggling to get out. But there was no release.

She'd thought being an outcast at school was the worst thing that could happen to her. But it was worse to *almost* belong, and to know inside that you didn't, and never would. She knew it was selfish to care about herself after what had happened to Kori, but she couldn't help it. With all the rage of confusion and pain inside her, she almost *envied* Kori. Kori was dead, but she still belonged. She had a place.

Cassie, on the other hand, had never felt so lonely.

The sky was dark grey. The ocean stretched out endlessly beneath it, even darker. Looking at it, Cassie felt a strange and terrible fascination. If she just started walking towards it and kept on going...

Stop that! she thought savagely. Get hold of yourself.

But it would be so easy...

Yes, and then you'd really be alone. Alone forever, in the dark. Sounds good, doesn't it, Cassie?

Shivering violently, she wrenched herself away from the whispering grey waters. Her feet were numb and cold and her fingers felt like ice. She stumbled as she climbed up the narrow, rocky path.

That night, she pulled all the curtains shut in her room so she wouldn't have to see the ocean or the darkness outside. Chest aching, she opened her jewellery box and took out the piece of chalcedony.

I haven't touched your gift in a while. But I've thought about you. Whatever I'm doing, wherever I am, you're somewhere in my mind. And oh, how I wish...

Her hand shook as she shut her eyes and put the stone to her lips. She felt the familiar crystalline roughness, the coolness of it warming to her warmth. Her breath came more quickly and tears started to her eyes. Oh, someday, someday, she thought...

Then her mouth twisted in pain. A surge of something like lava welled up in her chest, and she threw the stone as hard as she could across the room. It hit the wall with a sharp sound and fell, clattering, to the floor.

Someday nothing! the cruel voice inside her cried. Stop fooling yourself! You'll never see *him* again.

She lay in bed staring with sore eyes into the dimness, lit by a small night-light on the far wall. She couldn't cry. All her tears had been scorched away. But her heart felt as if it had been torn open.

Cassie was dreaming of the ocean – the dark and endless ocean. The ship was in trouble – she could hear the timbers creaking beneath her. They were going aground. And something was lost... lost...

She came awake all at once, sucking in her breath. Was that a noise?

Body tense, she listened. Silence. Her eyes struggled to pierce the darkness. The night-light had gone out.

Why hadn't it occurred to her to be afraid earlier? What had been wrong with her this evening? She'd gone out there on the beach alone, never even wondering if the person who'd killed Kori might be watching, waiting...

Accident, she thought, every sense alert and straining. They said it was probably an accident. But her heart was thundering dizzily. She seemed to see scintillating lights in the darkness. And she could *feel*...

A presence. Like a shadow in front of her. Oh, God, she *could* feel it. She sensed it like a pressure on her skin, like a radiation of cold. There was something in her bedroom.

Her eyes were staring into the utter blackness, her body trembling with tension. Insane as it was, she had the wild thought that if she didn't move, didn't make a sound, it couldn't find her.

But she was wrong.

She heard a shuffling noise, a stealthy advancing. Then the unmistakable creak of a floorboard.

It was coming towards her.

Suddenly she could move. She drew in breath for a scream – and there was a rush in the darkness and something clapped over her mouth.

Instantly, everything changed. Before, all had been

stillness, now all was dizzy motion. She was fighting. It didn't do any good; her arms were being caught and held. Something else had her feet.

She was being rolled over and over. Wrapped in the sheet. She couldn't move. Her arms were trapped in the material. She was trying to kick, but her feet were trapped too.

She felt herself being lifted. She couldn't scream; she was choking. Something was over her head, suffocating her. And the most terrible thing was the silence, the utter, continuing silence. Whatever had her was as noiseless as a ghost.

As a ghost... and she herself was now wrapped in a shroud. Wild thoughts careened in Cassie's head.

It was taking her out of her bedroom. Taking her downstairs – out of the house. It was taking her outside to bury her.

She had envied Kori – now she was going to join her. It was going to put her in the ground – or in the sea. Frantic, she tried to thrash, but the restraining material was too tight.

She had never been so frightened.

In time, though, the violence of her first panic exhausted itself. It was like fighting against a straitjacket; her struggles only served to tire her out. And overheat her. She was smothering and she was so hot... if only she could breathe...

Panting, Cassie felt her body go limp. For the next few minutes all her concentration was devoted to getting enough air. Then, slowly, she began to think again.

She was being carried by more than one person. That was certain. Her arms and legs were being restrained not only by the winding material of the sheet, but by hands.

Human hands? Or... images flooded her mind. Images out of horror movies. Skeletal hands barely covered by withered flesh. Dusky hands with nail beds the cyanotic blue of death. Mutilated hands, hands from the grave...

Oh, God, please... I'll lose my mind. Please make it stop or I'll die. I'll die of terror. Nobody can be this frightened and live.

But it wasn't so easy just to die after all. It didn't stop, and she went on living. It was like a nightmare, but Cassie knew she was not asleep. She could pray all she wanted, but she wouldn't wake up.

Then everything stopped.

She was no longer being carried; she was being held. Then tilted... her legs kicked and touched ground. She was being set on her feet. The sheet was unwinding; she felt a breeze on her legs, and her nightgown hem flapping against them. Her arms were free.

Weakly she grabbed out, and her wrists were caught and held behind her. She still couldn't see. Something was over her head, some kind of hood. It was hot inside, and she was breathing her own carbon dioxide. She swayed, wanting to kick, to fight again, and knowing she didn't have the strength.

Then, from directly behind her, she heard a sound that changed everything.

It was a chuckle.

Slow and rich. Amused. But with a grim edge to it.

Unmistakable.

Faye.

Cassie thought she had been frightened before. She'd imagined ghosts, the living dead come to drag her back into the ground with them. But all those wild and supernatural fears were nothing compared to the sheer terror she felt now.

In one blinding instant she put it all together. Faye had killed Kori. The way she was going to kill Cassie now.

'Walk,' Faye said, and Cassie felt a push in the centre of her back. Her hands had been tied together behind her. She staggered and then took a step. 'Straight ahead,' Faye said.

Cassie staggered another step, and an arm steadied her. It came from the side. Faye wasn't alone, then. Well, of course not; she couldn't have carried Cassie by herself.

Cassie had never realised how important it was to see. It was terrifying to be made to walk like this, on and on into nothingness. For all she knew Faye might be marching her straight off a cliff.

No, not off a cliff. They weren't on a bluff; they were on the beach. Although she couldn't see, now that she was no longer wrapped in the sheet her other senses were functioning. From her left came the slow, rhythmic roar of waves. Very close. Under her feet she could feel crumbling, slightly damp sand. The breeze that lifted her nightgown around her calves was cold and fresh. It smelled of salt and seaweed.

'Stop.'

Cassie obeyed automatically. She tried to swallow and found the inside of her mouth was like glue.

'Faye—' she managed to get out.

'Be quiet!' The voice was sharp, no laziness now. Like a cat with its claws unsheathed. A sudden pressure at her neck made Cassie stiffen – someone had grabbed the bottom of the hood and was tightening it warningly. 'Don't talk unless you're asked a question. Don't move unless you're told. Do you understand?'

Numbly, Cassie nodded.

'Now take one step forwards. Turn to your left. Stop.

Stay right there. Don't make a sound.'

Hands moved at the back of Cassie's neck. Then there was a glorious rush of cool air as the hood was lifted away. Light burst in on her, and Cassie stared in astonishment at the fantastic scene before her eyes.

Black and white, that was her first thought. Everything was stark black and white, like a scene from the surface of the moon.

But there was the moon in front of her. Pure white, just risen, it formed a perfect crescent over the ocean. The ocean was as black as the sky, except for the ghostly white foam on the waves. And in front of it stood a figure that seemed to shine with a pale light.

Diana?

She was wearing a thin white shift that left her arms bare. Clasped around one upper arm was a wide cuff of silver with strange engraving on it. On her forehead was a sort of diadem with a crescent moon, the horns pointing upwards. Her long hair, hanging loose beneath it, seemed to be woven of moonlight.

In her hand was a dagger.

With terrifying sharpness Cassie now remembered the dream she'd had of her mother and grandmother in her room. Sacrifice, one of them had said. Was that what she was here for now? Sacrifice?

Mesmerised, she stared at the blade of the dagger, at the moonlight shimmering on it. Then she looked at Diana's face.

I would never have believed it – no, I wouldn't have believed that you would help Faye do this. But you're here, with a knife. I'm seeing it. How can I not believe my own eyes?

'Turn around,' a voice said.

Cassie felt her body turn.

A circle was drawn in the sand, a big one. Inside and outside were candles, stuck right into the beach. Wax was melting on the sand. The candles were all sizes, all colours. Some looked as if they had been burning a long time, from the amount of wax pooled beneath them and the way they had slumped. Every flame was dancing in the slight breeze.

Inside the circle were the members of the Club. Cassie's frightened mind registered glimpses of faces and no more, like flashes seen in lightning. The same faces she had seen gathered around the table in the back room that afternoon. Proud. Beautiful. Alien.

Faye was one of them. She was dressed all in black. And if Diana's hair seemed to be woven of moonlight, hers was woven of gloom.

Diana walked past Cassie and stepped into the circle. Suddenly Cassie realised that the ring drawn in the sand was not complete. There was a gap in its north-east corner, directly in front of her feet.

She was standing just outside the threshold.

Startled, her eyes came up to seek Diana's. Diana's expression revealed nothing; her face was pale and distant. Cassie's heart, which had been thudding dully, now picked up speed.

Diana spoke, her voice clear and musical, but she was not speaking to Cassie.

'Who challenges her?'

Faye's throaty voice rose in answer. 'I do.'

Cassie didn't see the dagger until Faye held it at her throat. It pricked, pressing slightly into the hollow, and she felt her eyes widen. She tried to hold completely still. Faye's hooded, enigmatic eyes were gazing straight into hers. There was a sort of fierce pleasure in their depths, and the same heat Cassie had seen in the science building when Faye had threatened her with fire.

Faye smiled her slow, scary smile, and the pressure of the blade against Cassie's throat increased. 'I challenge you,' Faye said directly to Cassie. 'If there is any fear in your heart, it would be better for you to throw yourself forward on this dagger than to continue. So what is it, Cassie?' she added, her voice dropping to a lazy, intimate murmur that could scarcely have been heard by the others. '*Is* there fear in your heart? Careful how you answer.'

Dumbfounded, Cassie only stared. Fear in her heart? How could there *not* be fear in her heart? They had done everything they could to terrify her – *of course* there was fear in her heart.

Then, moving only her eyes, she looked at Diana.

Cassie remembered Laurel in the back room today, after Faye had implied Diana might have had something to do with Kori's death. Laurel had looked confused for a moment, then her face had cleared and she'd said, 'I don't care what you say; you're never going to make me believe Diana would hurt Kori.'

That was faith, Cassie thought. Believing no matter what. Did she have that kind of faith in Diana?

Yes, she thought, still looking into Diana's steady green eyes. I do.

Then can I trust her no matter what? Enough not to be afraid any more?

The answer had to come from inside. Cassie searched through her mind, trying to find the truth. Everything that had happened tonight – them dragging her out of bed, carrying her down here without any explanation, the knife, the strangeness of this whole ceremony – it all looked bad. And someone *had* killed Kori...

I trust you, Diana.

That was the answer she found at the bottom of her mind. I trust you. Despite all this, no matter how it looks, I trust you.

She looked back at Faye, who was still wearing a little catlike smile. Gazing straight into those honey-coloured eyes, Cassie said clearly, 'Go on. There's no fear in my heart.'

Even as she said it, she felt the symptoms of terror drop away from her. The weakness, the giddiness, the thudding of her heart. She stood straight even though her hands were still tied behind her back and the dagger point was still at her throat.

Something flared in Faye's eyes. Something like grim respect. Her smile changed, and she nodded almost imperceptibly. The next instant her black eyebrows were raised ironically as she spoke.

'Then step inside,' she invited.

Straight forward? Into the dagger blade? Cassie refused to let her eyes drop from the golden ones in front of her. She hesitated an instant, then stepped straight forward.

The blade yielded before her. Cassie could feel a tiny trickle of wetness on her throat as it withdrew and Faye stepped back.

Then she looked down. She was inside the circle.

Diana took the dagger from Faye and went to the break in the circle behind Cassie. Drawing the knife through the sand, she bridged the gap, making the circle complete. Cassie had an odd sensation of closure, of something sealing. As if a door had been locked behind her. And as if what was inside the circle was different from anything outside.

'Come to the centre,' Diana said.

Cassie tried to walk tall as she did. Diana's shift, she

could see now, was slit all the way up to the hip on one side. There was something on Diana's long, well-made upper leg. A garter? That was what it looked like. Like the ornamental bands of lace and ribbon that a bride wears to throw at a wedding. Except that this was made of something like green suede and lined with blue silk. It had a silver buckle.

'Turn around,' Diana ordered.

Cassie hoped the cord binding her wrists was going to be cut. But instead she felt hands on her shoulders, spinning her faster and faster. She was being whirled around and pushed from side to side, from person to person. For an instant panic surged through her again. She was dizzy, disoriented. With her hands tied she couldn't catch herself if she fell. And that knife was somewhere...

Just go with it. Relax, she told herself. And magically, her fear dissolved. She let herself be bounced from one person to another. If she fell, she fell.

Hands steadied her, stood her facing Diana again. She was slightly breathless and the world was reeling, but she tried to draw herself up straight.

'You've been challenged and you've passed the tests,' Diana informed her, and now there was a little smile in Diana's green eyes, although her lips were grave. 'Now are you willing to swear?'

Swear what? But Cassie nodded.

'Will you swear to be loyal to the Circle? Never to harm anyone who stands inside it? Will you protect and defend those who do, even if it costs you your life?'

Cassie swallowed. Then, trying to keep her voice level, she said, 'Yes.'

'Will you swear never to reveal the secrets you will learn, except to a proper person, within a properly prepared Circle like the one we stand in now? Will you swear to keep these secrets from all outsiders, friends and enemies, even if it costs you your life?'

'Yes,' Cassie whispered.

'By the ocean, by the moon, by your own blood, will you so swear?'

'Yes.'

'Say, "I will so swear."'

'I will so swear.'

'She has been challenged and tested, and she has been sworn,' Diana said, stepping back and speaking to the others. 'And now, since all of us in the Circle agree, I call on the Powers to look at her.'

Diana raised the dagger above her head, pointing the blade at the sky. Then she pointed it to the east, towards the ocean, then to the south, then towards the western cliff, then towards the north. Finally, she pointed it at Cassie. The words she spoke as she did sent shock waves running down Cassie's spine:

> *Earth and water, fire and air,*
> *See your daughter standing there.*
> *By dark of moon and light of sun,*
> *As I will, let it be done.*
>
> *By challenge, trial, and sacred vow,*
> *Let her join the Circle now.*
> *Flesh and sinew, blood and bone,*
> *Cassie now becomes—*

'But we *don't* all agree,' an angry voice broke in. 'I still don't think she's one of us. I don't think she ever can be.'

CHAPTER
12

Diana turned sharply to face Deborah. 'You can't interrupt the ritual!'

'There shouldn't *be* a ritual,' Deborah blazed back, her face dark and intense.

'You agreed in the meeting—'

'I agreed we had to do whatever it took to make us strong. But—' Deborah stopped and scowled.

'But some of us may not have believed she'd pass the tests,' Faye interpreted, smiling.

Diana's face was pale and angry. The diadem she wore seemed to give her added stature, so that she looked taller even than Faye. Moonlight shimmered in her hair as it had off the blade of the knife.

'But she *did* pass the tests,' she said coldly. 'And now you've interrupted a ritual – broken it – while I was calling down the Powers. I hope you have a better reason than that.'

'*I'll* give you a reason,' Deborah said. 'She's not really one of us. Her mother married an outsider.'

'Then what do you want?' Diana said. 'Do you want us never to have a real Circle? You know we need twelve to get anything done. What are we supposed to do, wait until your parents – or the Hendersons – have another baby? None of the rest of us even has both parents alive. No.' Diana turned to face the others in the group, who were standing around the inside perimeter of the circle. 'We're the last,' she told them. 'The last generation in the New World. And if we can't complete our Circle, then it all ends here. With us.'

Melanie spoke up. She was wearing ordinary clothes under a pale green fringed shawl that looked both tattered and fragile, as if it were very old. 'Our parents and grandparents would like that,' she said. 'They want us to leave it all in the past, the way they did and *their* parents did. They don't want us digging up the old traditions and waking the Old Powers.'

'They're scared,' Deborah said scornfully.

'They'll be happy if we can't complete the Circle,' Melanie said. 'But is that what *we* want?' She looked at Faye.

Faye murmured coolly, 'Individuals can do quite a lot on their own.'

'Oh, come on,' Laurel put in. 'Not like a real Circle. Not unless,' she added, '*somebody* was planning to get hold of the Master Tools and use them all by herself.'

Faye gave her a slow, dazzling smile. '*I'm* not the one searching for the lost tools,' she said.

'This is all off the point,' said Diana sharply. 'The question is, do we want a complete Circle or don't we?'

'*We* do,' one of the Henderson brothers said. No, Chris, Cassie corrected herself. Suddenly she could tell them apart. Both the brothers looked white and strained in the moonlight, but Chris's eyes were less savage. 'We're going to do whatever it takes to find out who killed Kori,' Chris finished.

'And then take care of them,' Doug put in. He made a gesture of stabbing.

'Then we need a full Circle,' said Melanie. 'A twelfth person and a seventh girl. Cassie is both.'

'And she's passed the tests,' Diana repeated. 'Her mother was one of us. She went away, yes, but now she's come back. And she brought her daughter to us just when we need her. Just exactly when we need her.'

Stubbornness still lingered in Deborah's eyes. 'Who says she can even use the Powers?' she demanded.

'I do,' Diana replied steadily. 'I can sense it in her.'

'And so do I,' Faye said unexpectedly. Deborah turned to stare at her, and she smiled ingenuously.

'I'd say she can call on Earth and Fire, at least,' Faye continued, maddeningly bland. 'She might even prove to have quite a talent.'

And why, Cassie wondered dazedly, did that make hairs on the back of her neck stand up?

Diana's brows were drawn together as she gave Faye a long, searching look. But then she turned to Deborah.

'Does that satisfy your objection?'

There was a beat. Then Deborah nodded, sullenly, and stepped back.

'Then,' said Diana, with a quiet politeness that seemed to overlay an icy anger, 'can we please get on with it?'

Everyone stood away as she returned to her position. Once again she lifted the dagger to the sky, then to the cardinal points of the compass, then to Cassie. Once again she spoke the words that had sent chills down Cassie's spine, but this time she finished them uninterrupted.

> *Earth and water, fire and air,*
> *See your daughter standing there.*
> *By dark of moon and light of sun,*
> *As I will, let it be done.*

> *By challenge, trial, and sacred vow,*
> *Let her join the Circle now.*
> *Flesh and sinew, blood and bone,*
> *Cassie now becomes our own.*

'That's it,' Laurel said softly from behind Cassie. 'You're in.'

In. I'm in. Cassie knew, with a feeling of wild exhilaration, that nothing would ever be the same again.

'Cassie.'

Diana was unclasping the silver necklace she was wearing. Cassie's eyes were drawn to the crescent moon pendant that hung from it. It was like the one on the diadem, Cassie realised – and like Deborah's tattoo.

'This is a token,' Diana said, fastening the chain around Cassie's neck, 'of your membership in the Circle.'

Then she hugged Cassie. It wasn't a spontaneous gesture; it had more the feeling of a ritual. Next she turned Cassie around to face the others and said, 'The Powers have accepted her. I've accepted her. Now each of you has to.'

Laurel was the first to step up. Her face was serious, but there was a genuine warmth and friendliness in the depths of her brown eyes. She hugged Cassie, then kissed her lightly on the cheek. 'I'm glad you're one of us,' she whispered, and stepped back, her long, light-brown hair fluttering slightly in the breeze. 'Thanks,' Cassie whispered.

Melanie was next. Her embrace was more formal, and her cool, intellectual grey eyes still intimidated Cassie. But when she said, 'Welcome to the Club,' she sounded as if she meant it.

Deborah, by contrast, was scowling as she stepped forward, and she hugged Cassie as if she were trying to crack a rib or two. She didn't say anything.

Sean hurried up, looking eager. His hug was a little too long and too close for Cassie's taste, and she ended up having to extricate herself. He said, 'Glad you're in,' with his eyes fixed on her nightgown in a way that made Cassie wish it were flannel instead of light cotton.

'I can tell,' she said under her breath as he stepped back, and Diana, standing beside her, had to bite her lip.

Under normal circumstances the Henderson brothers might have been even worse. But tonight they didn't seem to care if it was a girl or a block of wood they were embracing. They hugged her mechanically and stepped back to watch again with their angry, faraway eyes.

And then it was Nick's turn.

Cassie felt something inside her tighten. It wasn't that she was attracted to him, exactly, but ... she couldn't help feeling a slight inner tremor when she looked up at him. He was so handsome, and the coldness that surrounded him like a thin layer of dark ice seemed only to enhance his looks. He'd stood back and observed the entire ceremony tonight with such detachment, as if none of it affected him one way or another.

Even his embrace was noncommittal. Sexless. As if he were merely going through the motions while thinking of something else. His arms were strong, though – well, of course, thought Cassie. Any guy who had an – arrangement – with Faye would have to be strong.

Suzan smelled of perfume, and when she kissed Cassie's cheek, Cassie felt sure she left a smudge of cherry-coloured lipstick. Hugging her was like hugging a scented pillow.

Finally, Faye came. Her heavy-lidded eyes were gleaming enigmatically, as if she were aware of Cassie's discomfiture and enjoying it. All Cassie was aware of was Faye's height and how much she herself wanted to run.

She had a panicked conviction that Faye was going to do something awful...

But Faye simply murmured, as she stepped back, 'So the little white mouse is tougher than she looks. I was betting you wouldn't even last through the ceremony.'

'I'm not sure I did,' Cassie muttered. She desperately wanted to sit down and gather her thoughts. So much had happened so fast... but she was in. Even Faye had accepted her. That fact could not be changed.

'All right,' Diana said quietly. 'That's it for the initiation ritual. Normally after this we'd have a party or something, but...' She looked at Cassie and lifted her hands. Cassie nodded. Tonight, a party could hardly be less appropriate. 'So I think we should formally dispel the Circle, but go on and have a regular meeting. That way we can get Cassie caught up on what she needs to know.'

There were nods around the circle and a collective breath released. Diana picked up a handful of sand and poured it over the line drawn on the beach. The others followed suit, each pouring a handful and smoothing it down so that the circle's outline was blurred, erased. Then they distributed themselves among the still-lighted candles, some sitting on the sand, others on outthrusts of rock. Nick remained standing, a cigarette in his mouth.

Diana waited until everyone was quiet, looking at her, then she turned to Cassie. Her face was grave and her green eyes were earnest. 'Now that you're one of us,' she said simply, 'I think it's time to tell you what we are.'

Cassie's breath caught. So many bizarre things had happened to her since she'd come to New Salem, and now she was about to hear the explanation. But strangely, she wasn't sure she needed to be told. Ever since they'd brought her here tonight, all sorts of things had been arranging themselves in her mind. A hundred little oddities that she'd noticed about New Salem, a hundred little mysteries that she'd been unable to solve. Somehow, her brain had begun putting them together, and now...

She looked at the faces around her, lit by moonlight and flickering candlelight.

'I think,' she said slowly, 'that I already know.' Honesty compelled her to add, 'Some of it, at least.'

'Oh, yes?' Faye raised her eyebrows. 'Why don't *you* tell *us*, then?'

Cassie looked at Diana, who nodded. 'Well, for one thing,' she said slowly, 'I know you're not the Mickey Mouse Club.'

Chuckles. 'You'd better believe it,' Deborah muttered. 'We're not the Girl Scouts, either.'

'I know...' Cassie paused. 'I know that you can light fires without matches. And that you don't use feverfew just in salads.'

Faye examined her nails, looking innocent, and Laurel smiled ruefully.

'I know that you can make things move when they're not alive.'

This time it was Faye who smiled. Deborah and Suzan exchanged smug glances, and Suzan murmured, 'Sssssss...'

'I know everybody's afraid of you at school, even the adults. They're afraid of anyone who lives on Crowhaven Road.'

'They're going to be more afraid,' said Doug Henderson.

'I know you use rocks for spot remover—'

'Crystals,' murmured Diana.

'—and there's something more than tea leaves in your tea. And I know' – Cassie swallowed and then went on, deliberately – 'that you can push somebody without touching them, and make them fall.'

There was a silence at this. Several people looked at Faye. Faye tilted her chin back and looked at the ocean with narrowed eyes.

'You're right,' Diana said. 'You've learned a lot from just watching – and we've been a little lax with security. But I think you should hear the entire story from the beginning.'

'*I'll* tell it,' said Faye. And when Diana looked at her doubtfully, she added, 'Why not? I like a good story. And I certainly know this one.'

'All right,' said Diana. 'But could you please try to stick to the point? I know your stories, Faye.'

'Certainly,' Faye said blandly. 'Now, let me see, where shall I start?' She considered a moment, head tilted, and then smiled. 'Once upon a time,' she said, 'there was a quaint little village called Salem. And it was just filled with quaint little Puritans – all-American, hardworking, honest, brave, and true—'

'Faye—'

'Just like some people here we all know,' Faye said, undisturbed by the interruption. She stood, switching her glorious black mane behind her, clearly enjoying being the centre of attention. The ocean, with its endlessly breaking waves, formed a perfect background as she began to pace back and forth, her black silk blouse sliding down just far enough to leave one shoulder bare.

'These Puritans were filled with pure little thoughts – most of them. A few just *may* have been unhappy with their boring little Puritan lives, all work, no play, dresses up to *here*' – she indicated her neck – 'and six hours of church on Sundays...'

'Faye,' said Diana.

Faye ignored her. 'And the *neighbours*,' she said. 'All

those neighbours who watched you, gossiped about you, *monitored* you to make sure you weren't wearing an extra button on your dress or smiling on your way to meeting. You had to be meek in those days, and keep your eyes down, and do as you were told without asking questions. If you were a girl, anyway. You weren't even allowed to play with dolls because they were things of the devil.'

Cassie, fascinated despite herself, watched Faye pacing and thought again of jungle cats. Caged ones. If Faye had lived in those days, Cassie thought, she would have been quite a handful.

'And maybe some of those young girls weren't so happy,' Faye said. 'Who knows? But anyway, one winter a few of them got together to tell fortunes. They shouldn't have, of course. It was *wicked*. But they did it anyway. One of them had a slave who came from the West Indies and knew about fortune-telling. It helped to while away those long, dull winter nights.' She glanced sideways under black lashes towards Nick, as if to say that she could have suggested a better way herself.

'But it preyed on their poor little Puritan minds,' Faye went on, looking sorrowful. 'They felt *guilty*. And eventually one of them had a nervous collapse. She got sick, delirious, and she confessed. Then the secret was out. And all the other young girls were on the hot seat. It wasn't *good* in those days to get caught fooling around with the supernatural. The grown-ups didn't *like* it. So the poor little Puritan girls had to point the finger at somebody else.'

Faye held up her own long, tapering, scarlet-tipped finger, trailing it across the seated group like a gun. She stopped in front of Cassie.

Cassie looked at it, then up into Faye's eyes.

'And they did,' Faye said pleasantly. She withdrew the finger as if sheathing a sword, and went on. 'They pointed at the West Indian slave, and then at a couple of other old women they didn't like. Women with a bad reputation around the village. And when they pointed, they said...' She paused for dramatic effect, and tipped her face up to the crescent moon hanging in the sky. Then she looked back at Cassie. 'They said... *witch.*'

A ripple went through the group, of agitation, bitter amusement, exasperation. Heads were shaking in disgust. Cassie felt the hairs at the back of her neck tingle.

'And do you know what?' Faye looked over her audience, holding them all spellbound. Then she smiled, slowly, and whispered, 'It worked. Nobody blamed them for their little fortune-telling games. Everyone was too busy hunting out the *witches* in their midst. The only problem,' Faye continued, her black eyebrows now raised in scorn, 'was that those Puritans couldn't recognise a witch if they fell over one. They looked for women who were offbeat, or too independent, or... rich. Convicted witches forfeited their worldly goods, so it could be quite a *profitable* business to accuse them. But all the while the real witches were right there under their noses.

'Because, you see,' Faye said softly, 'there really were witches at Salem. Not the poor women – and men – they accused. They didn't even get *one* right. But the witches were there, and they didn't like what was happening. It hit a little too close to home. A few of them even tried to stop the witch trials – but that only tended to arouse suspicion. It was too dangerous even to be a friend of one of the prisoners.'

She stopped, and there was a silence. The faces

surrounding Cassie now were not amused, but cold and angry. As if this story was something thing that resonated in their bones; not a cobwebby tale from the dead past, but a living warning.

'What happened?' Cassie asked at last, her own voice subdued.

'To the accused witches? They died. The unlucky ones, at least, the ones who wouldn't confess. Nineteen were hanged before the governor put a stop to it. The last public executions took place exactly three hundred years ago... September 22, the fall equinox, 1692. No, the poor accused witches didn't have much luck. But the real witches... well...' Faye smiled.

'The real witches got away. Discreetly, of course. After the fuss was over. They quietly packed up and moved north to start their own little village, where no one would point fingers because everyone would be the same. And they called their little village...' She looked at Cassie.

'New Salem,' Cassie said. In her mind, she was seeing the crest on the high school building. 'Incorporated 1693,' she added softly.

'Yes. Just one year after the trials ended. So you see, that's how our little town was founded. With just the twelve members of that coven, and their families. We' – Faye gestured gracefully around the group – 'are what's left of the descendants of those twelve families. Their only descendants. While the rest of the riffraff you see around the school and the town—'

'Like Sally Waltman,' Deborah put in.

'—are the descendants of the servants. The *help*,' Faye said sweetly. 'Or of outsiders who drifted in and were allowed to settle here. But those twelve houses on Crowhaven Road are the houses of the original families. Our families. They intermarried and kept their blood pure – most of them, anyway. And eventually they produced *us*.'

'You have to understand,' Diana said quietly from Cassie's side. 'Some of what Faye has told you is speculation. We don't really know what caused the witch hunts in 1692. But we *do* know what happened with our own ancestors because we have their journals, their old records, their spell books. Their Books of Shadows.' She turned and picked something up off the sand, and Cassie recognised the book that had been on the window seat the day Diana cleaned her sweater.

'This,' Diana said, holding it up, 'was my great-great-grandmother's. She got it from her mother, who got it from *her* mother, and so on. Each of them wrote in it; they recorded the spells they did, the rituals, the important events in their lives. Each of them passed it on to the next generation.'

'Until our great-grandmothers' time, anyway,' said Deborah. 'Maybe eighty, ninety years ago. *They* decided the whole thing was too scary.'

'Too *wicked*,' Faye put in, her golden eyes gleaming.

'They hid the books and tried to forget the old knowledge,' said Diana. 'They taught their kids it was wrong to be different. They tried to be normal, to be like the outsiders.'

'They were *wrong*,' Chris said. He leaned forward, his jaw set, his face etched with pain. 'We can't be like them. Kori knew that. She—' He broke off and shook his head.

'It's okay, Chris,' Laurel said softly. 'We know.'

Sean spoke up eagerly, his thin chest puffing out. 'They hid the old stuff, but we found it,' he said. 'We wouldn't take no for an answer.'

'No, *we* wouldn't,' said Melanie, casting an amused

glance at him. 'Of course, some of us were busy playing Batman while the older ones were rediscovering our heritage.'

'And some of us had a little more natural talent than others,' Faye added. She spread out her fingers, admiring the long red nails. 'A little more natural – flair – for calling on the Powers.'

'That's right,' said Laurel. She raised her eyebrows and then looked significantly at Diana. '*Some* of us do.'

'We all have talent,' Diana said. 'We started discovering that when we were really young – babies, practically. Even our parents couldn't ignore it. They did try to keep us from using it for a while, but most of them have given up.'

'Some of them even help us,' Laurel said. 'Like my grandmother. But we still get most of what we need from the old books.' Cassie thought about her own grandmother. Had she been trying to help Cassie? Cassie felt sure she had.

'Or from our own heads,' said Doug. He grinned a wild and handsome grin and for an instant looked again like the boy who'd gone racing through the hallways on roller blades. 'It's instinct, you know? Pure instinct. *Primal.*'

'Our parents hate it,' said Suzan. 'My father says we'll only make trouble with the outsiders. He says the outsiders will *get* us.'

Doug's teeth showed white in the moonlight. 'We'll get them,' he said.

'They don't understand,' Diana said softly. 'Even among ourselves not everybody realises that the Powers can be used for good. But we're the ones who can call on the Powers, and *we* know. That's what's important.'

Laurel nodded. 'My grandmother says there will always be outsiders who hate us. There's nothing we can do but try and keep away from them.'

Cassie thought suddenly of the principal holding the hanged doll by the back of its dress. *How apt*, he'd said. Well, no wonder... if he thought she was one of them already. Then her mind drew up short. 'Do you mean,' she said, 'that even adults know what you – what *we* are? Outsider adults?'

'Only the ones around here,' Diana said. 'The ones who grew up on the island. They've known for centuries – but they've always kept quiet. If they want to live here, they have to. That's just the way it is.'

'For the last few generations, relations have been very good between our people and the outsiders,' Melanie said. 'That's what our grandparents say, anyhow. But now we've stirred things up. The outsiders may not keep quiet forever. They might try to do something to stop us—'

'Might? They already have,' Deborah said. 'What do you think happened to Kori?'

Instantly voices rose in a babble as the Henderson brothers, Sean, Suzan, and Deborah burst into argument. Diana raised her hand.

'That's enough! This isn't the time,' she said. 'What happened to Kori is one of the things our Circle is going to find out. Now that we're complete, we should be able to do it. But not tonight. And as long as I'm leader—'

'*Temporary* leader. Until November,' Faye put in sharply.

'As long as I'm *temporary* leader, we'll do things when I say and not jump to any conclusions. All right?' Diana looked around at them. Some faces were shuttered, expressionless; others, like Deborah's, openly hostile. But most of the members nodded or gave some sign of acquiescence.

'All right. And tonight is for initiating Cassie.' She looked at Cassie. 'Do you have any questions?'

'Well...' Cassie had the nagging feeling that there was something she *should* be asking, something important, but she couldn't think of what. 'The guys in the Circle – what do you call them? I mean, are they wizards or warlocks or something?'

'No,' said Diana. ' "Wizard" is an old-fashioned word – it means a wise man who usually worked alone. And "warlock" comes from a word meaning traitor, deceiver. "Witch" is the proper term for all of us, even guys. Anything else?'

Cassie shook her head.

'Well, then,' Faye said. 'Now that you've heard our story, we have just one question to ask *you*.' She fixed Cassie with an odd half smile and said in a sweet, false voice, 'Are you planning to be a good witch or a bad witch?'

CHAPTER
13

Very funny, Cassie thought. But actually it wasn't funny at all. She guessed that there was a deadly serious side to Faye's question. Somehow she didn't see Faye wanting to use the Powers – whatever those were – for good. And she didn't see Diana wanting to use them for anything else.

'Does anybody have anything more to say? Questions, comments, club business?' Diana was looking around the group. 'Then I'm declaring the meeting over. You can all go or stay as you like. We'll have another meeting tomorrow afternoon to honour Kori and talk about a plan of action.'

There was a murmur of voices as people turned to one another and got up. The electric tension that had held the group together had dissipated, but there was an unfinished feeling in the air, as if nobody really wanted to leave yet.

Suzan went over behind a rock and pulled out several wet six-packs of diet soft drinks. Laurel promptly went behind another rock and returned with a large thermos.

'It's rose-hip tea,' she said, pouring a cup of fragrant, dark red liquid and smiling at Cassie. 'No tea leaves at all, but it'll warm you up and make you feel better. Roses are soothing and purifying.'

'Thanks,' said Cassie, taking it gratefully. Her head was spinning. Information overload, she thought.

I'm a witch, she thought then, wonderingly. Half a witch, anyway. And Mom and Grandma – they're both hereditary witches. It was a bizarre and almost impossible notion to swallow.

She took another gulp of the hot, sweet drink, shivering in spite of herself.

'Here,' Melanie said. She removed the pale green shawl and put it around Cassie's shoulders. 'We're used to the cold; you're not. If you want, we can make a fire.'

'No, I'm fine with the shawl,' Cassie said, tucking her bare feet under her. 'It's beautiful – is it very old?'

'It was my great-grandmother's great-grandmother's – if you can believe the old stories,' Melanie said. 'We usually get more dressed up for Circles – we can wear anything we feel like, and sometimes it gets outrageous. But tonight...'

'Yes.' Cassie nodded in understanding. Melanie was being nicer than usual, she thought. More like Laurel or Diana. It puzzled Cassie for a moment – and then she got it.

I'm one of them, she thought, and for the first time the full import of this struck her. Not a puppy off the street any more. I'm a full member of the Club.

She felt the bubbles of excitement, of exhilaration in her bloodstream again. And there was a deeper feeling, too, of recognition. As if something at her core was nodding, saying *Yes, I knew all along*.

Cassie looked at Melanie quietly sipping her tea, and at Laurel straightening a pink candle that was slumping over. Then she looked at Diana, standing a little distance up the beach with the Henderson brothers, the three blond heads close together. Diana seemed to feel no self-consciousness about wearing the thin white shift and the fancy jewellery. It seemed a natural costume for her.

My people, Cassie thought. The sudden sense of belonging – of loving – was so intense that tears came to her eyes. Then she looked at Deborah and Suzan, deep in conversation, and at Faye, who was listening with a bland smile to something Sean was excitedly saying, and at Nick, who was staring silently out at the ocean, a can of something that wasn't soda in his hand.

Even them, she thought. She was willing to try and get along with all the other members, with everyone who shared her blood. Even the ones who'd tried to keep her out.

She looked back at Laurel, to find the slim, brown-haired girl watching her with the hint of a sympathetic smile.

'A lot to deal with at once,' Laurel said knowingly.

'Yes. But it's exciting, too.'

Laurel smiled. 'So now that you're a witch,' she said, 'what's the first thing you're going to do?'

Cassie laughed, feeling something almost like intoxication. Power, she thought. There's so much Power out there – and now I can take it. She shook her head and lifted the hand that wasn't holding rose-hip tea. 'What *can* we do?' she said. 'I mean, what sorts of things?'

Laurel and Melanie exchanged glances. 'Basically, you name it,' Melanie said. She picked up the book that Diana had shown Cassie earlier and riffled through it, showing Cassie the pages. They were yellowing and brittle and covered with cramped, illegible writing. They were also covered with pink Post-it notes and plastic tape flags. Almost every page had one and some had several.

'This is the first Book of Shadows we got hold of,' said Melanie. 'We found it in Diana's attic. Since then we've found others – every family is supposed to have one. We've been working on this one for maybe five years, deciphering the spells and copying them out in modern language. I'm even putting it on my computer for easier cross-reference.'

'Sort of a Floppy Disk of Shadows,' Cassie said.

Laurel grinned. 'Right. And it's funny, you know, but once you start learning spells and rituals, it seems to wake up something inside you – and you start coming up with your own.'

'Instinct,' Cassie murmured.

'Right,' said Laurel. 'We all have it, some more than others. And some of us are better than others at certain things, like calling on the different Powers. I work best with Earth.' Laurel took a handful of sand and let it trickle through her fingers.

'Three guesses as to what Faye works best with,' Melanie said dryly.

'But anyway, to answer your question, there's lots we can do,' Laurel said. 'It all depends on your taste. Spells of protection, of defence—'

'Or attack,' put in Melanie, with a glance towards Deborah and Suzan.

'—spells for little things, like lighting fires, and for big ones, like – well, you'll find out. Charms for healing, and for finding things out – scrying and divining. Love potions...' She smiled as Cassie looked up quickly. 'That interest you?'

'Oh, a little, maybe.' Cassie blushed. God, she wished she could just gather her thoughts properly. She still had that nagging feeling that there was something she was missing, something obvious that she was overlooking and should be asking about. But what?

'There's a certain amount of debate over the ethics of love potions and love spells,' Melanie was saying, her grey eyes not entirely approving. 'Some people feel it violates a person's free will, you know. And a spell misused can rebound on the person who casts it – threefold. Some people don't feel it's worth the risk.'

'And other people,' Laurel said mock solemnly, her brown eyes sparkling, 'say that all's fair in love and war. If you know what I mean.'

Cassie bit her lip. No matter how hard she tried to concentrate on that nagging worry, another thought was pushing it out of her mind. Or, not a thought so much as a *hope*, the sudden glimpse of a possibility.

Love potions. And finding things out. Something to find *him* and bring him to her. Was there such a spell? She seemed to feel in her bones that there was.

To find *him* ... the boy with the blue-grey eyes. Warmth pooled in Cassie's stomach and her palms tingled. The very possibility seemed to lift her on wings. Oh, please, if she could only ask one thing...

'Supposing,' she said, and was relieved to hear her voice sound normal, 'you wanted to, say, find somebody you'd met and lost track of. Somebody you – liked, and wanted to see again. Would there be any kind of a spell for that?'

Laurel's brown eyes sparkled again. 'Now, is this a boy-type person we're supposing about here?' she said.

'Yes.' Cassie knew she was blushing again.

'Well . . .' Laurel glanced at Melanie, who was shaking her head in a resigned way, then turned back to Cassie. 'I'd say something like a simple tree spell. Trees are attuned to things like love and friendship, anything that grows and brings life. And fall is a good time to use things you harvest, like apples. So I'd do an apple spell. In one, you take an apple and split it. Then you take two needles – ordinary sewing needles – and put one through the eye of the other and bind them together with thread. Then put them inside the apple and close it up again. Tie it so it stays closed. Then tie it back on the tree and say some words to tell the tree what you want.'

'What kind of words?'

'Oh, a poem or something,' Laurel said. 'Something to invoke the power of the tree and help you visualise what you're asking for. It's best to make it rhyme. I'm not good at making up that kind of thing, but, like: "Friendly tree, friendly tree, bring my special friend to me." '

No. Not quite, Cassie thought, a thrill going through her. Laurel's words were changing in her mind, transforming, expanding. She seemed to hear a voice, bell clear and yet remote.

> *Bud and blossom, leaf and tree,*
> *Find him, bind him, now to me.*
> *Shoot and seedling, root and bough,*
> *Threads of love entwine us now.*

Her lips moved soundlessly with the words. Yes, she knew somehow in the very core of her that that was right. That was the spell... but would she really dare to use it?

Yes. For *him*, I'd risk anything, she thought. She stared down at her fingers as they absently combed through the sand. *Tomorrow*, she decided. Tomorrow I'll do it. And then afterwards I'll spend every minute of every day watching and hoping. Waiting for the time when I see a shadow and look up and it's him, or when I hear footsteps and turn and see him coming. Or when—

What happened next was so startling and unexpected that Cassie almost screamed.

A wet nose thrust under her hand.

What stopped her from screaming was something like heart failure; the shriek got to her throat, and then she actually *saw* the dog and everything went fuzzy. Her recoiling hand fell limply back. Her lips opened and closed silently. Through a blur and a mist she stared at the liquid brown eyes and the short, silky-bristly hairs on the muzzle. The dog stared back at her, mouth open and laughing, as if to say, 'Aren't you happy to see me?'

Then Cassie raised her eyes to look at the dog's master.

He was looking down at her, as he had that day on the beach in Cape Cod. The moonlight tangled in his red hair, turning some strands to flame while others were dark as wine. His blue-grey eyes looked silver.

He'd found her.

Everything was motionless. The ocean's roar seemed hushed and distant, and Cassie was aware of no other sound. Even the breeze had died. It was as if the entire world was waiting.

Slowly, Cassie got to her feet.

The green shawl fell behind her, discarded. She could feel the cold, but only because it made her aware of her own body, of every part of it, tingling like electricity. Yet strangely, although she was keenly aware of her body, she also seemed to be floating above it. Just like the first time, she seemed to see herself – and him – standing there on the beach.

She could see herself in her thin white nightgown and bare feet, her hair loose on her shoulders, looking up at him. Like Clara in the *Nutcracker* ballet, she thought, when she wakes up in the middle of the night and looks at the Nutcracker Prince who's come to take her away into a world of magic. She *felt* like Clara. As if the moonlight had transformed her into something delicate and beautiful, something enchanted. As if he might take her in his arms right then and dance with her. As if in the moonlight they could dance forever.

They *were* gazing at each other. From the moment their eyes had met, neither of them had looked away. She could see the wonder in his face. As if he were as surprised to see her as she was to see him – but how could he be? He had found her; he must have been looking for her.

The silver cord, she thought. She couldn't see it now, but she could feel it, feel the vibrations of its power. She could feel it connecting them, heart to heart. The trembling went from her chest into her stomach, and then all over.

The cord was tightening, drawing them together. It was pulling her closer to him. Slowly, his hand came up and he reached out to her. She raised her own hand, to put it in his—

And there was a cry from behind her. The tall boy looked over her shoulder, distracted. And then his hand fell away.

Something came between them, something bright. Bright like sunlight, shattering Cassie's trance. It was Diana, and she was embracing the tall red-haired boy. She was holding him. No – they were holding each other. Cassie stared, stunned, at the sight of *him* with his arms around someone else. She was barely able to comprehend the words she heard next.

'Oh, Adam – I'm *so* glad you're back.'

Cassie stood like a pillar of ice.

She hadn't seen Diana break down before, but Diana was breaking down now. She was crying. Cassie could see her shaking and could see how the tall boy – how *Adam* – held her to try and stop it.

Held her. He was holding Diana. And his name was Adam.

'You mean she hasn't told you about Adam yet? Diana, there's such a thing as carrying modesty too far...' 'Who is he? Is he your boyfriend?...' 'He's nice. I think you'll like him...'

Cassie fell to her knees and buried her face in Raj's fur, clinging to the big dog. She couldn't bear for anyone to see her face right now, and she was grateful for Raj's warm solidity as she leaned against him. Oh, God; oh, *God*...

Vaguely, she could hear Adam's voice. 'What's wrong? I tried to get back for Kori's initiation, but where is she? What's going on?' He looked at Cassie. 'And—'

'Her name is Cassie Blake,' Diana said. 'She's Mrs Howard's granddaughter, and she's just moved here.'

'Yes, I—'

But Diana, her voice distracted by grief, was still speaking. 'And we just initiated her instead of Kori.'

'*What?*' Adam demanded. 'Why?'

There was a silence. Finally, it was Melanie who spoke up, her voice as quiet and detached as a newscaster's making an announcement. 'Because this morning – or yesterday morning, rather, since it's really Wednesday now – Kori's body was found at the bottom of the school hill. Her neck was broken.'

'Oh, God.' Cassie looked up to see Adam's grip on Diana tighten. He shut his eyes briefly as she leaned against him, shaking again. Then he looked at the Henderson brothers. 'Chris... Doug...'

Doug's teeth were clenched. 'Outsiders did it,' he said.

'*Sally* did it,' snarled Deborah.

'*We don't know who did it*,' Diana said. She spoke with

passionate force. 'And we're not going to do anything until we find out.'

Adam nodded. 'And you,' he said, looking towards the back of the group. 'What have you been doing to help while all this was going on?'

'Not a damn thing,' Nick said. He had been standing with his arms folded over his chest, watching impassively. Now his defiant gaze met Adam's and locked with it. It was clear there was no love lost between the two.

'He has been helping, Adam,' Diana said, forestalling whatever Adam was about to say next. 'He's come to meetings, and he's here tonight. That's all we can ask.'

'It's not all *I* can ask,' Adam said.

'Ask away. You're not going to get anything more.' Nick turned around. 'I'm out of here.'

'Oh, don't go...' Laurel began, but Nick was already leaving.

'I've been showing up because Diana asked, but I'm through now. I've had enough for tonight,' he said over his shoulder. Then he was gone.

Faye turned to Adam and smiled her slowest, most dazzling smile. She put her hands together and clapped. 'Beautiful job, Adam. Here Diana has spent the last three weeks slaving to keep the troops together and you undo it all in the first three minutes. I couldn't have done better myself.'

'Oh, get stuffed, Faye,' said Laurel.

Cassie, meanwhile, was still kneeling. Although she was clinging to Raj, she could see, sense, think of only one thing. Adam's arm – *his* arm – around Diana's shoulders.

His name is Adam. And he's hers. Not mine; hers. He always has been.

It couldn't be. It was not possible. Beyond all hope, she had found him again; he had come to her. Without a love spell, as if drawn by the very intensity of her need for him, he had come – and she couldn't have him.

How could she have been so stupid? How could she not have realised? They'd all talked tonight about completing the Circle, about twelve members, always twelve. But if she'd stopped to count, she'd have seen that there were only eleven. Diana and Melanie and Laurel, that was three; and Faye and Suzan and Deborah, that was six. Plus the boys, the Henderson brothers and Nick and Sean – that was ten. And Cassie made eleven. All along something at the back of her mind had known that it didn't add up, and had been trying to tell her. But she hadn't listened.

And how could I have not known *anyway*? she thought. How could I have not realised the boy I'd met had to be one of them? The clues were all here, right in front of me. He has Powers – I saw that on the beach with Portia. He read my mind. He told me he was from somewhere else; he told me he was different. Portia even said the word.

Witch.

And tonight I found out that the Club is a coven of witches. The last generation of witches in the New World. I should have realised *then* that he must be one of them.

I even knew Diana had a boyfriend, a boyfriend who's been away 'visiting'. The pieces of the puzzle were all there. I just didn't want to put it together.

Because I'm in love with him. I didn't know how much until I saw him again tonight. And he belongs to my best friend. My 'sister'.

I hate her.

The thought was terrifying in its intensity, making her

fists clench in the big dog's fur. It was a raw, primal wash of emotion, a feeling so strong that for a moment it even wiped out the pain. A murderous hatred, red as blood, rushing out from her towards the girl with the hair like moonlight...

Like moonlight and sunlight woven together. Staring at it now, with that acid violence still raging inside her, another picture flashed into Cassie's mind. That same impossibly shining hair falling across the emergency brake in Diana's car. After Diana had rescued her from Faye.

When she was taking you home to take care of you, a voice whispered. And then she cleaned you up and fed you, introduced you to her friends. Protected you, gave you a place to belong. Made you her sister.

Now what was that you were saying about hating her?

Cassie felt the murderous red fury slipping away. She couldn't hold on to it, and she didn't want to try. She couldn't hate Diana... because she loved Diana. And she loved Adam. She loved them both and she wanted them to be happy.

So where does that leave *you*? the voice inside her asked.

It was all very simple, really. The two of them were so obviously perfect for each other. Both tall – Diana was just the right height to look into his eyes. Both seniors – Diana was mature enough for him, and how could Cassie ever have imagined that an older guy would go for her? Both strikingly attractive, both confident, both leaders.

And both full-blooded witches, Cassie reminded herself. I'll bet he's incredibly talented – of course he's talented. Diana wouldn't have anything but the best. Because she's the best herself.

And don't forget they're childhood sweethearts. They've

been together forever; they don't even see anybody else. Clearly they were made for each other.

So it was all very obvious and very simple – except then why did she feel as if there were razor blades shredding her guts? All she had to do was wish them happiness and put aside any thoughts of Adam and her together. Just resign herself to what was going to happen anyway. Just wish them luck.

That was when, clear and cold, the resolve came to her. No matter what happens, she promised, Diana will never know.

And neither will he.

If Diana found out how Cassie felt, it would upset her. She was so unselfish, she might even feel she had to *do* something – like give Adam up so Cassie wouldn't be hurt. And even if she didn't, she would feel awful.

So Cassie wouldn't let her know. It was as simple as that.

Not by word or look or deed, she promised herself fiercely. No matter what happens, I won't make Diana unhappy. I swear it.

A wet nose was poking at her, and soft whines sounded in her ears. Raj was complaining about the lack of attention.

'Cassie?'

And Diana was talking to her. Cassie realised what she must look like, clinging to the big dog in a daze.

'What?' she said, trying to keep her lips from trembling.

'I said, are you all right?'

Diana was looking at her, those clear green eyes full of concern. There were recent tears on the heavy lashes. Looking into those eyes, Cassie did the bravest thing she had ever done in her life. Braver than standing up to Jordan Bainbridge and his gun, far braver than throwing herself out to rescue Sally on the hill.

She smiled.

'I'm fine,' she said, giving Raj a final pat and getting to her feet. Her voice sounded like somebody else's, incredibly false and stupid. But Diana wasn't expecting her to be false, and Diana relaxed. 'I'm just – so much has happened tonight,' Cassie went on, 'I guess I'm a little overwhelmed.'

Adam was opening his mouth. He was going to tell everyone, Cassie realised. He was going to tell them how he and Cassie had met and everything that happened. And then Faye, who wasn't stupid, was going to put two and two together. She was going to realise he was the boy in Cassie's poem.

And that couldn't happen. She wouldn't let it. No one must ever know.

'And you didn't introduce me yet,' she blurted out desperately to Diana. 'You know I've been wanting to meet your boyfriend ever since you told me about him.'

There. It was said. Your boyfriend. Adam was looking puzzled, but Diana, innocent Diana, was looking chagrined.

'I'm sorry; I didn't, did I? Cassie, this is Adam – I know you two will like each other. He's been away—'

'Visiting,' Cassie put in feverishly as Adam opened his mouth again.

'No, not visiting. I know I told you that before, but now I can tell you the truth. He's been looking for certain – objects – that belonged to the old coven, the original one. From their records, we can tell that they had some powerful tools that somehow got lost. The Master Tools. Ever since Adam heard about them, he's been searching for them.'

'And coming back empty-handed,' Faye commented in her husky voice, amused. 'I don't suppose this time is any different.'

Adam's attention was distracted. He looked at the tall black-haired girl and smiled. It was a mischievous smile, full of the promise of secrets.

'What?' said Faye cynically, and then, as he simply kept smiling at her, 'What? You don't expect us to believe...'

'Adam,' Diana said, her voice changing, 'are you saying that...?'

Adam just grinned at them, then he jerked his head towards a duffel bag lying a little way down the beach. 'Sean, go get that.'

Sean scuttled to get it and came back saying, 'It's *heavy.*'

'Adam...' whispered Diana, her eyes wide.

Adam took the duffel bag from Sean and put it on the ground. 'It's too bad Nick was in such a hurry to get away,' he said. 'If he'd stayed, he might have seen this.' He reached inside with both hands and pulled out a skull.

CHAPTER

14

It was the size and shape of a human skull, but it seemed to be made entirely of crystal. The moonlight reflected through it, inside it. It had grinning crystal teeth, and its hollow eye sockets seemed to be staring directly at Cassie.

There was a frozen instant, and then Faye grabbed for it.

'Uh-uh,' Adam said, holding it away from her. 'No.'

'*Where did you get that?*' said Faye. Her voice was no longer lazy, but full of barely contained excitement.

Even through her numbness Cassie felt a twinge of apprehension at her tone, and she saw the swift glance Adam exchanged with Diana. Then he turned to Faye. 'On an island.'

'*Which* island?'

'I didn't know you were so interested. You never seemed to be before.'

Faye glared. 'One way or another I'll find out, Adam.'

'There's nothing else where I found it. Believe me, this was the only one of the Master Tools hidden there.'

Faye took a breath and then relaxed and smiled. 'Well,

the least you can do is give us all a chance to look at it.'

'*No*,' said Diana. 'Nobody even touches it yet. We don't know anything about this except that it was used by the old coven – by Black John himself. That means it's dangerous.'

'Do we know for sure this *is* the crystal skull Black John wrote about?' Melanie asked, her voice quiet and rational.

'Yes,' Adam said. 'At least, it fits the description in the old records exactly. And I found it in a place just like the place Black John described. I think it's the real thing.'

'Then it needs to be cleared and purified and studied before *any* of us work with it,' Diana said. She turned to Cassie. 'Black John was one of the leaders of the original coven,' she said. 'He died not long after New Salem was founded, but before that he took the coven's most powerful tools and hid them. For safe-keeping, he said – but really because he wanted them for himself. For personal gain and revenge,' she said, looking at Faye meaningfully. 'He was an evil man, and anything he touched is going to be full of negative influences. We're not going to use it until we're sure it's safe.'

If Black John had had anything to do with this skull, he *must* have been bad, Cassie thought. In some way she couldn't explain, she could *feel* darkness emanating from it. If she hadn't been so heartsick and dizzy, she would have said so – but surely everyone else could see for themselves.

'The old coven never found the lost Master Tools,' Laurel was saying. 'They searched, because Black John had left some clues about where he might have hidden them, but they didn't have any luck. They made new tools, but none were ever as powerful as the originals.'

'And now we've found one,' Adam said, with a flash

of excitement in his blue-grey eyes.

Diana lightly touched the back of his hand as it held the skull. She smiled up at him, and the message between them was clearer than words: pride and triumph shared. This was *their* project, something they'd been working on for years, and now they had succeeded at last.

Cassie clenched her teeth against the pain in her breastbone. They deserve a chance to be alone and enjoy it, she thought. With brittle, forced cheerfulness she said, 'You know, I'm getting tired. I think maybe it's time...'

'Of course,' Diana said, instantly concerned. 'You must be exhausted. We all are. We can talk more about this at the meeting tomorrow.'

Cassie nodded, and nobody else made any objections. Not even Faye. But as Diana was instructing Melanie and Laurel to walk Cassie up the beach to her house, Cassie accidentally met Faye's gaze. There was an odd, calculating expression in those golden eyes that would have bothered her if she hadn't been beyond caring by now.

At home, every light was blazing, even though the first streaks of dawn hadn't yet appeared over the ocean. Melanie and Laurel walked Cassie inside, and they found her mother and grandmother both sitting up in the parlour – a stiff old-fashioned room at the front of the house. The two women were wearing nightgowns and robes. Cassie's mother's hair was loose down her back.

Cassie saw at once by their faces that they knew.

Is this what I was brought here for? she thought. To join the Circle? There was no longer any doubt in her mind that she'd been *brought* here, deliberately, and for a very specific reason.

She got no answer from the voices inside her, not even from the deepest voice. And that was disturbing.

But she didn't have time to worry about it. Not now. She looked at her mother's face, drawn and anxious, but also full of a kind of half-concealed pride and hope. Like a mother watching her daughter high-dive in the Olympics, and waiting for the judges' scores. Her grandmother looked the same.

Suddenly, despite the aching pain in her chest, Cassie was filled with a surge of protective love for them. Both of them. She managed a smile as she and Melanie and Laurel stood in the doorway.

'So, Grandma,' she said, 'does our family have a Book of Shadows?'

The tension broke into laughter as the two women rose.

'Not that I know of,' her grandmother said. 'But any time you like, we'll take another look through the attic.'

The meeting on Wednesday afternoon was tense. Everyone was on edge. And Faye clearly had a hidden agenda.

All she wanted to talk about was the skull. They should use it, she said, and immediately. All right, then, if not *use* it, at least check it out. Try to activate it, see what imprints had been left on it.

Diana kept saying no. No checking it out. No activating it. They needed to purify it first. Ground it. Clear it. Which Faye knew would take weeks, if done properly. As long as Diana was in charge—

Faye said that at this rate Diana might not be in charge for long. In fact, if Diana kept refusing to test out the skull, Faye just might call for a leadership vote right now instead of waiting until November. Was that what Diana wanted?

Cassie didn't understand any of it. How do you check

out a skull? Or ground it or clear it? But this time the argument was too heated for anyone to remember to explain to her.

She spent the entire meeting *not* watching Adam, who had tried to speak to her beforehand, but whom she'd managed to evade. She clung grimly to her resolve all the way through, even though the energy it took to ignore him exhausted her. She made herself not look at his hair, which had grown a little longer since she'd seen him, or at his mouth, which was as handsome and humorous as ever. She refused to let herself think about his body as she'd seen it on the beach in Cape Cod, with its flat, sinewy muscles and bare long legs. And most of all, she forced herself not to look into his eyes.

The one thing Cassie did glean from the meeting was that Diana was in a precarious position. 'Temporary' leader meant that the coven could call a vote at any time and depose her, although the official vote was in November for some reason. And Faye was obviously looking for support so that *she* could take over.

She'd gotten the Henderson brothers on her side by saying they should use the skull right away to find Kori's killer. And she'd gotten Sean on her side simply by terrorising him, it looked like. Deborah and Suzan, of course, had supported her from the beginning.

That was six. It would have been six on Diana's side too, but Nick refused to voice an opinion. He showed up at the meeting, but sat through it smoking and looking as if he were somewhere else. When asked, he said it didn't matter to him whether they used the skull or not.

'So you see, you're overruled,' Faye told Diana, her honey-coloured eyes hot with triumph. 'Either you let us use the skull – or I call for a vote right now and we see if you still come out leader.'

Diana's jaw was set. 'All right,' she said flatly, at last. 'We'll try to activate it – just activate it and no more – on Saturday. Is that soon enough for you?'

Faye nodded graciously. She'd won, and she knew it.

'Saturday night,' she said, and smiled.

Kori's funeral was on Friday. Cassie stood with the other members of the Club and cried along with them during the service. Afterwards, at the cemetery, a fight broke out between Doug Henderson and Jimmy Clark, the boy Kori had gone with that summer. It took the entire Club to get them apart. The adults seemed scared to touch them.

Saturday dawned clear and cool. Cassie went over to Diana's in the evening after spending most of the day staring at a book, pretending to read it. She was worried about the skull ceremony, but she was even more worried about Adam. No matter what happens, she told herself, no matter *what*, I won't let anyone know how I feel. I'll keep it a secret forever if it kills me.

Diana looked tired, as if she hadn't been getting enough sleep. It was the first time the two of them had been alone together since the initiation – since Adam came. Sitting in Diana's pretty room, looking at the prism in the window, Cassie could almost pretend that Adam hadn't come, that he didn't exist. Things had been so simple then; she'd been happy just to be with Diana.

She noticed, for the first time, another wall of art prints like the ones she'd seen the first day.

'Are these goddesses too?' she asked.

'Yes. That's Persephone, daughter of the goddess of growing things.' Diana's voice was soft with tiredness, but she smiled at the picture. It showed a slender girl laughing as she picked an armful of flowers. All around her it was springtime, and her face was filled with the joy of being young and alive.

'And who's that?'

'Athena. She was the goddess of wisdom. She never married either, like Artemis, the goddess of the hunt. All the other gods used to go to her for advice.'

It was a tall goddess with a wide brow and clear, calm grey eyes. Well, of course they're grey; it's a black-and-white print, Cassie told herself. But somehow she felt they'd be grey anyway, and full of cool, thoughtful intelligence.

Cassie turned to the next print. 'And who's—'

Just then there was the sound of voices downstairs. 'Hello? Anybody up there? The front door was unlocked.'

'Come on up,' Diana called. 'My dad's at work – as usual.'

'Here' Laurel said, appearing in the doorway. 'I thought you might like these. I got them along the way.' She held out an armful of mixed flowers to Diana.

'Oh, Bouncing Bet! They're such a pretty pink, and I can dry them for soap later. And wild snapdragon and sweet melilot. I'll go get a vase.'

'I would have brought some roses from the garden, but we used them all for purifying the skull.'

Melanie smiled at Cassie. 'So how's our newest witch?' she said, her cool grey eyes not unsympathetic. 'Totally confused?'

'Well… a little confused. I mean' – Cassie picked at random one of the things she didn't understand – 'how do you purify a skull with roses?'

'You'd better ask Laurel that; she's the expert on plants.'

'And Melanie,' said Laurel, 'is the expert on stones and crystals, and this is a crystal skull.'

'But just what *is* a crystal, exactly?' Cassie said. 'I don't think I even know that.'

'Well.' Melanie sat down at Diana's desk as Diana came back and began to arrange the flowers. Laurel and Cassie sat on the bed. Cassie really did want to know about the things the Circle used to do magic. Even if she could never do the one spell she wanted to, she was still a witch.

'Well, some people call crystals "fossilised water",' Melanie said, her voice taking on a mock-lecturing tone. 'Water combines with an element to make them grow. But I like to think of them as a beach.'

Laurel snorted and Cassie blinked. 'A beach?'

Melanie smiled. 'Yes. A beach is sand and water, right? And sand is silicon. When you put silicon with water, under the right conditions, it forms silicon dioxide – quartz crystal. So water plus sand plus heat plus pressure equals a crystal. The remains of an ancient beach.'

Cassie was fascinated. 'And that's what the skull is made of?'

'Yes. It's clear quartz. There are other kinds of quartz too; other colours. Amethyst is purple. Laurel, are you wearing any?'

'What a question. Especially with a ceremony tonight.' Laurel pushed her long, light-brown hair back to show Cassie her ears. In each she was wearing a dangling crystal of a deep violet colour. 'I like amethysts,' she explained. 'They're soothing and balancing. If you wear them along with rose quartz, it helps draw love to you.'

Cassie's stomach clenched. As long as they could stay off subjects like love she'd be all right. 'What other stones are there?' she asked Melanie.

'Oh, lots. In the quartz family there's citrine – Deborah wears a lot of that. It's yellow and it's good for physical activity. Energy. Fitness. That sort of thing.'

175

'Deborah needs a little *less* energy,' Laurel muttered.

'I like to wear jade,' Melanie went on, twisting her left wrist to show Cassie a beautiful bracelet. It was set with a pale green, translucent oval stone. 'Jade is peaceful, calming. And it sharpens mental clarity.'

Cassie spoke hesitantly. 'But . . . do these things really work? I mean, I know all the New Agers are into crystals, but—'

'Crystals are not New Age,' Melanie said with a quelling glance at Laurel, who seemed about to argue the point. 'Gemstones have been used since the beginning by ancient peoples – and sometimes even for the right things. The problem is that they're only as good as the person using them. They can store energy and help you call on the Powers, but only if you have the talent for it in the first place. So for most people they're pretty useless.'

'But not for *us*,' said Laurel. 'Although they don't always work the way you'd expect. Things can get out of control. Remember when Suzan simply *covered* herself in carnelians and almost got mobbed at the football game? I thought there was going to be a riot.'

Melanie laughed. 'Carnelians are orange and very – stimulating,' she said to Cassie. 'You can get people overexcited if you use them wrong. Suzan was trying to attract the quarterback, but she nearly wound up with the entire team. I'll never forget her in the bathroom, pulling all those carnelians out of her clothes.' Cassie burst into laughter at the picture.

'You're not supposed to wear orange or red stones all the time,' Laurel added, grinning. 'But of course Suzan won't listen. Neither will Faye.'

'That's right,' Cassie said, remembering. 'Faye does wear a red stone on her necklace.'

'It's a star ruby,' Melanie said. 'They're rare, and that one's very powerful. It can amplify passion – or anger – very quickly.'

There was something else Cassie wanted to ask. Or rather, that she *had* to ask, whether she wanted to or not. 'What about a stone like – chalcedony?' she said casually. 'Is that good for anything?'

'Oh, yes. It has a protective influence – it can guard you against the harshness of the world. In fact, Diana, didn't you give...?'

'Yes,' said Diana, who had been sitting quietly on the window seat, listening. Now she smiled faintly in reminiscence. 'I gave Adam a chalcedony rose when he left this summer. That's a special kind of chalcedony piece,' she explained to Cassie. 'It's flat and round and it has a sort of swirling spiral pattern in it, like a rose's petals. It has little quartz crystals sprinkled over it.'

And tiny black shell things on the back, Cassie thought. She felt sick. Even the present he had given her was Diana's.

'Cassie?' They were all looking at her.

'Sorry,' she said, opening her eyes and faking a smile. 'I'm okay. I – I guess I'm a little wound up about this thing tonight. Whatever it is.'

They were immediately sympathetic. Diana nodded grimly, showing more animation than she had since Cassie had arrived that evening. 'I'm worried myself,' she said. 'It's way too soon. We shouldn't be doing this yet – but we don't have any choice.'

Melanie said to Cassie, 'You see, the skull absorbed energies from whoever used it last. Like an imprint of what was done, and who did it. We want to see what those are. So we'll all concentrate on it, and see what it will show us. Of course, we might not be able to activate it at all. Sometimes only a certain person can do that, or a certain code of sounds or lights or movements. But if we *can*, and if it's safe, we can eventually use its energy to show us things – like maybe who killed Kori.'

'The larger the crystal, the more energy in it,' Diana said bleakly. 'And this is a *big* crystal.'

'But why did the old coven carve it into a skull?' Cassie asked.

'They didn't,' Melanie said. 'We don't know who did, but it's much older than three hundred years. There are other crystal skulls out there in the world – nobody really knows how many. Most of them are in museums and things – there's one, the British Skull, that's in the Museum of Mankind in England. And the Templar Skull belongs to some secret society in France. Our old coven just got hold of this one somehow and used it.'

'Black John used it,' Diana corrected. 'I wish Adam had found any of the other Master Tools instead of this one. This one was *his*, Black John's favourite, and I think he might have used it to get rid of people. I'm afraid that tonight – I don't know. But I'm afraid something awful is going to happen.'

'We won't let it,' said a new voice at the door. Cassie's heart began to pound dully and blood rushed to her face.

'Adam,' said Diana. She relaxed visibly as he came over to the window seat to kiss her and sit beside her. She always seemed both more tranquil and more radiant whenever he was around.

'We'll keep the ceremony under strict control tonight,' he said. 'And if anything dangerous starts to happen, we'll just stop it cold. Did you get the garage ready?'

'No, I was waiting for you. We can take it down now.' Diana unlocked the large cabinet, and Cassie saw the crystal skull resting in a Pyrex baking dish full of pink rose petals.

'Looks like John the Baptist's head,' she murmured.

'I've used salt and rainwater to try and clear it,' Diana said. 'But what it really needs is a full course of crystals and flower essences, and then to be buried in moist sand for a few weeks.'

'We'll take every precaution,' Adam said. 'A triple circle of protection. It'll be all right.' He picked up the skull, with a few rose petals still clinging to it, and he and Diana left for the garage. Cassie watched him go.

'Don't be nervous,' Melanie told her. 'You won't really have to do anything at the ceremony. You won't be *able* to; it takes a long time to get the hang of scrying – years, usually. All you have to do is sit there and not break the Circle.'

Cassie tried not to mind the condescending note in her voice. 'Listen, do we have time for anybody to drive me over to my house?' she said. 'There's something there I'd like to pick up.'

Diana's garage was empty – of cars, at least. The floor was clean and bare, except for a circle drawn in white chalk.

'I'm sorry to make us all sit on concrete,' Diana said, 'but I wanted to do this inside – where I can be sure the wind won't blow out one of the candles.'

There were a number of white candles lying at the centre of the circle. They formed a smaller ring. In the very centre of that, something draped with a piece of black cloth sat on a shoe box.

'All right,' Diana said to the rest of the group, who had arrived in small clusters and were now standing in the garage. 'Let's get this thing over with.'

She had changed into her white shift and jewellery.

Looking at them now, Cassie suspected that the diadem and cuff bracelet – and maybe even the garter – had some mystic significance. She watched Diana 'cast' the circle, going around it with the dagger and then with water and then incense and then a lit candle. Earth, water, air, and fire. There were also some incantations, which Cassie tried to follow. But when they all filed into the circle and sat down knee to knee as Diana instructed, any interest in the actual ceremony flew right out of her mind.

She had ended up between Faye and Adam. She didn't know how it had happened. She had been in line to sit next to Sean, but somehow Faye had gotten in front of her. Maybe Faye didn't want to sit by Adam. Well, neither did Cassie, although for a very different reason.

Adam's knee was pressing against hers. That was how Diana had told them to sit. She could feel the warmth of it, the solidity. She could think of nothing else.

On her other side, Faye smelled of some heady, tropical perfume. It made her slightly dizzy.

Then all the lights went out.

Cassie didn't see how it was done; she was sure no one left the seated circle. But the overhead fluorescent panels had abruptly gone off.

It was pitch-black in the garage. The only light now was the flame of the single candle Diana held. Cassie could see her face illuminated by it, but nothing else.

'All right,' Diana said quietly. 'We're just going to be looking for the last imprints left. Nothing more than that; nobody goes in really deep until we know what we're dealing with. And I don't have to tell anybody that whatever happens, we don't break the circle.' She didn't look at Cassie as she said it, but several of the others did, as if to imply that maybe she *did* have to say it.

Diana touched the candle flame to the candle Melanie

held out to her. The flame doubled. Then Melanie leaned over to light Deborah's candle, and there were three flames.

The fire went around the circle until Laurel gave it to Adam. Cassie's hand was trembling as she held up her candle to receive the flame from him. She hoped everyone would assume it was just general nervousness.

At last all twelve candles were lit and stuck in their own wax to the concrete floor. Each shed a pool of radiance and cast huge dark shadows of the seated figures on the walls.

Diana reached into the ring of candles and pulled off the black cloth.

Cassie gasped.

The skull was facing her directly, its empty eye sockets staring at her. But that wasn't the most alarming thing. The skull was *glowing*. The candle flames around it played on it, and the crystal in turn reflected and refracted the light. It almost looked – alive.

Around the circle the others had straightened, tensed.

'Now,' said Diana. 'Find someplace inside the skull that interests you. Concentrate on it, look at the details. Then look for more details. Keep looking until you find yourself drawn into the crystal.'

Someplace that interests you? Cassie thought blankly. But when she looked carefully at the glowing skull, she saw that the crystal wasn't completely clear. There were gossamer webs and what looked like wisps of smoke inside it. There were internal fractures that seemed to be acting as prisms to form miniature landscapes. The closer Cassie looked, the more detail she saw.

That looks like a spiral or tornado, she thought. And that – that looks almost like a door. And a face . . .

She jerked her eyes away, stomach lurching. Don't

be silly; it's just imperfections in the crystal, she told herself.

She was almost afraid to look again. But no one else seemed disturbed. Their shadows loomed and flickered on the walls, but all eyes were turned towards the skull.

Look at it! *Now*, she commanded.

When she looked back at the skull, she couldn't find the misty face again. There, that proves it was just a trick of the light, she thought. But the skull had developed another disturbing quality. Things seemed to be moving inside it. It was almost as if the skull were made of water, contained inside a thin skin, and things were drifting slowly around.

Oh, stop it and pick one detail to focus on, she ordered herself. The doorway, look at that. It isn't moving.

She stared at the little prismatic fracture in the left eye socket, just where the pupil of a real eye would be. It looked like a half-open door with light spilling out.

Look at it. Notice the detail.

Dizziness from Faye's perfume swept over her. She was looking – just looking. She could see the door. The more carefully she looked, the larger it seemed. Or perhaps she was coming closer.

Yes, closer... closer. She was losing her sense of space. The skull was so large now; it seemed to have no boundaries, no shape. It was all around her. It had become the world. The door was right in front of her.

She was inside the skull.

CHAPTER

15

The door was no longer tiny but life-size, large enough to go in. It was ajar, and coloured light streamed from the other side.

Inside the skull, Cassie gazed at the door, her scalp tingling. If it opened, could I go inside? she wondered. But how could it open?

Maybe if she just imagined it opening... but that didn't seem to do any good. What had Melanie said? Crystals help us call on the Powers. What Powers would be connected with clear quartz? Earth and water? For sand and sea?

That sounded almost like the beginning of a poem.

> Earth and water, sand and sea
> As I will, so let it be...

She concentrated on the door, willing it to open. And as she stared, it did seem that there was more rainbow light spilling out. More... and more. Keep it opening. Let it draw you closer. She was floating in front of the door now. It was huge, like the door to a cathedral. Opening... opening... She was drowning in rainbow light.

Now! Go in!

But at that instant a scream tore through the room.

It was a scream of terror, high and wild, and it lanced through the utter silence. The door stopped opening, and Cassie felt herself being pulled backwards. The door was receding, faster, faster. Then, just before she found herself outside the skull, a face flashed before her eyes. The same face she'd seen before. But it wasn't receding; it was travelling towards her. Getting bigger. Bigger and bigger so fast – it would burst the crystal. It would—

'No!' cried Diana.

Cassie felt it at the same instant, an overwhelming sense of evil. Of something rushing towards them at incredible speed. Something that had to be stopped.

She never quite knew what happened next. Sean was sitting on the other side of Faye. Maybe he was the one who moved first; maybe he panicked and tried to bolt. In any case there was a commotion. Faye seemed to be trying to do something and Sean to stop her, or maybe it was the other way around. They were struggling. Diana was crying, 'No, no!' Cassie didn't know what to do.

She tried to check her instinctive flinching away from Faye, but it didn't matter. Faye lurched forward and Cassie felt the pressure of Faye's knee leave hers. The circle was broken, and Faye's candle went out.

Instantly all the other candles were snuffed out too, as if by a blast of wind. In the same instant Cassie felt the rushing thing reach the limits of the crystal. It burst out of the skull and past the dark, smoking candles. Cassie didn't know how she could tell this – everything was pitch-black. But she *felt* it. She could sense the rushing thing like an inkier blackness. It exploded past her, blowing her hair straight up and to the side. She threw out an arm to protect her face, but by that time it was gone.

There was a faint cry in the darkness.

Then everything was quiet again.

'Turn on the *lights*,' somebody gasped.

Suddenly Cassie could see. Adam was standing by the light switch. Diana was standing too, her face white and frightened. Around the circle every face reflected alarm and consternation – except Nick's. His was impassive as usual.

Faye was just sitting up. She looked as if she'd been blown backwards by some tremendous force. Fury blazing in her eyes, she turned on Sean. 'You pushed me!'

'No, I didn't!' Sean looked around the room for help. 'She was trying to get to the skull! She was lunging for it!'

'You lying little *worm*! *You* were trying to get away. You were going to break the circle.'

'She—'

'No, I *didn't*!'

'All right!' shouted Diana.

Adam came up beside her. 'It doesn't matter who did what,' he said, his voice tense. 'What matters is that – energy – that escaped.'

'What energy?' Faye said sullenly, examining her elbow for bruises.

'The energy that knocked you flat on your back,' Diana said grimly.

'I *fell*. Because this little snot *pushed* me.'

'No,' said Cassie before she could stop herself. She was beginning to shake in delayed reaction. 'I felt it too. Something came out.'

'Oh, *you* felt it. The expert.' Faye gave her a glance of scorn and disdain. Cassie looked around at the others, who were still sitting, and was surprised to see uncertainty in their expressions. Surely they had felt it too?

'I felt – something,' Melanie said. 'Something dark inside the skull. Some negative energy.'

'Whatever it was, it was released when we broke the circle,' Adam said. He looked at Diana. 'It's my fault. I shouldn't have let this happen.'

'You mean you should have kept the skull a secret from the rest of us,' Faye said sharply. 'For your own personal use.'

'What difference does it make?' Laurel cried from the other side of the circle. 'If something *was* released from the skull, it's out *there* right now. Doing God knows what.'

'It's – bad,' Cassie said. What she wanted to say was 'evil' but that seemed such a melodramatic word. Yet that was what she had sensed in the dark, rushing thing. Evil. The intent to destroy, to harm.

'We've got to stop it,' Adam said.

Suzan was fiddling with a button on her blouse. 'How?'

This silence was long and uncomfortable. Adam and Diana were looking at each other, seeming to have some grim unspoken conversation. The Henderson brothers were also telegraphing something to each other, but they didn't look as if they minded having something murderous and evil loose in the immediate community. In fact, on the whole they looked pleased.

'Maybe it'll get whoever got Kori,' Chris offered at last.

Diana stared at him. 'Is that what you think?' Then her face changed. 'Is that what you *were* thinking when we were reaching into it? Is that what you were *willing*?'

'We were supposed to just try and read the last imprints,' Melanie said, her voice as angry as Cassie had ever heard it.

The Henderson brothers looked at each other and shrugged. Deborah's expression was somewhere between a scowl and a grin. Suzan was still fiddling. Nick, face expressionless, stood up.

'Looks like that's all for tonight,' he said.

Diana exploded.

'You're damn right it is!' she cried, astounding Cassie. She snatched up the skull in her two hands. 'Now this is going to a safe place, where it belongs. Where it should have gone in the first place. I should have known you were all too irresponsible to deal with it.' Hugging the skull to her, she strode out of the garage.

Faye was instantly alert, like a cat who sees the flicker of a mouse's tail. 'I don't think that was a very nice way to talk to us,' she said throatily. 'I don't think she *trusts* us, do you? Hands up – how many people here want to be led by someone who doesn't trust them?'

If looks could maim, the one Melanie threw Faye would have left her a basket case. 'Oh, get *stuffed*, Faye,' she said in her classy accent. 'Come on, Laurel,' she added, and got up to follow Diana towards the house.

Cassie, not knowing what else to do, followed *them*. Behind her she heard Adam saying to Faye in a low, tightly controlled voice, 'I wish you were a guy.'

And Faye's laughing, husky answer: 'Why, Adam, I didn't know your tastes ran that way!'

Diana was putting the skull back in the Pyrex dish when Adam came in behind Cassie. He went to Diana and put his arms around her.

She leaned against him a moment, eyes shut, but didn't hold him in return. And after that moment she moved away.

'I'm all right. I'm just angry with them, and I've got to think.'

Adam sat on the bed, running a hand through his hair. 'I *should* have kept it a secret from them,' he said. 'It was my own stupid pride—'

'Don't,' said Diana. 'It would have been wrong to keep something from the Circle that belongs to them.'

'More wrong than to let them use it for stupid, malicious reasons?'

Diana turned away and leaned against the cabinet.

'Sometimes,' Adam said quietly, 'I wonder about what we're doing. May be the Old Powers should just be left asleep. Maybe we're wrong to think we can handle them.'

'Power is only Power,' Diana said tiredly, not turning. 'It's not good or bad. Only the way we use it is good or bad.'

'But maybe nobody can use it without ending up using it badly.'

Cassie stood and listened, wishing she were anywhere else. She was aware that in some terribly civilised way, Diana and Adam were having a fight. She met Laurel's eyes and saw that the other girl was just as uncomfortable.

'I don't believe that,' Diana said finally, softly. 'I don't believe that people are that hopeless. That *evil*.'

Adam's expression was bleak and longing, as if he wished he could share her belief.

Cassie, watching his face, felt a stab of pain, and then a wave of dizziness. She shifted, looking for a place to sit down.

Diana immediately turned around. 'Are you all right? You're white as a ghost.'

Cassie nodded and shrugged. 'Just a little dizzy – I guess maybe I should go home ...'

The anger had drained out of Diana's eyes. 'All right,' she said. 'But I don't want you out there by yourself.

Adam, would you walk her back? The beach way is faster.'

Cassie opened her mouth in reflexive horror. But Adam nodded quickly.

'Sure,' he said. 'Although I don't want to leave *you* alone...'

'I want Melanie and Laurel to stay,' Diana said. 'I want to start to purify this skull properly, with flower essences' – she looked at Laurel – 'and other crystals.' She looked at Melanie. 'I don't care if it takes all night; I want to get it set up. And I want to start now. This minute.'

The two girls nodded. So did Adam. 'All right,' he said.

And Cassie, who had been standing with her mouth open, suddenly thought of something and nodded too. Her hand automatically patted her front jeans pocket to feel the hard little lump there.

So that was how she found herself walking on the beach alone with Adam.

There was no moon that night. The stars shone with a fierce, icy brilliance. The waves roared and hissed on the shore.

Not romantic. Raw. Primitive. Except for the faint lights of houses above on the cliff, they might have been a thousand miles from civilisation.

They were almost all the way to the narrow path up the bluff to Number Twelve when he asked her. She'd known in her heart that she couldn't avoid it forever.

'Why didn't you want anyone to know that we'd met before?' he said simply.

Cassie took a deep breath. Now was the time to see what kind of actress she was. She was very calm; she knew what had to be done, and somehow, she would do

189

it. She *had* to do it, for Diana's sake – and his.

'Oh, I don't know,' she said, and marvelled to hear how casual her voice sounded. 'I just didn't want anybody – like Suzan or Faye – to get the wrong impression. You don't mind, do you? It didn't seem very important.'

Adam was looking at her in an odd way, hesitating, but then he nodded. 'If that's what you want, I won't mention it,' he said.

Relief washed over Cassie, but she kept her voice light. 'Okay, thanks. *Oh*, by the way,' she went on, fishing in her pocket. 'I've been meaning to give this back to you. Here.' It was strange how her fingers seemed to cling to the chalcedony rose, but she managed to open them and drop it into his hand. It lay on his palm, the quartz crystals seeming to capture a little of the starlight.

'Thanks for loaning it to me,' she said. 'But now that I'm an official witch, I'll probably be finding my own stones to work with. And besides' – she curved her lips in a teasing smile – 'we don't want anybody to get the wrong impression about *that* either, do we?'

She had never in her life acted like this with a boy, teasing and carefree and confident. Almost flirtatious while making it clear that she meant nothing by it. And it was so *easy* – she'd never imagined it could be this easy. It came, she supposed, from the fact that she was playing a role. It wasn't Cassie standing here; it was someone else, someone who wasn't afraid because the worst had already happened and there was nothing left to fear any more.

A wry smile had touched Adam's lips, as if he were responding automatically to her tone, but it disappeared almost instantly. He was looking at her hard, and she forced herself to return his gaze blandly and innocently, the way she had returned Jordan's on the beach that day in August. *Believe me*, she thought, and this time she knew the power of her own thoughts, the power she could draw on to enforce her will. *Sky and water, sand and sea; As I will, so let it be*. Believe me, Adam. Believe me. Believe me.

He looked away from her suddenly, turning sharply toward the ocean. It reminded Cassie, to her surprise, of the way she had broken free of Faye's mesmerising gaze.

'You've changed,' he said, and there was wonder in his voice. Then he turned back to look at her with that hard, unrelenting gaze again. 'You've really changed.'

'Of course. I'm a witch now,' she said reasonably. 'You should have told me that in the beginning – it would have saved a lot of trouble,' she added in a scolding tone.

'I didn't know. I could sense – something – in you, but I never thought of you being one of us.'

'Oh, well, it all turned out okay,' Cassie said quickly. She didn't like him talking about what he sensed in her. It was too dangerous. 'Anyway, thanks for walking me home. This is where I go up.'

With a final smile, she turned away and quickly climbed the narrow path. She couldn't believe it. She'd pulled it off! The relief that flooded her was actually painful, and when she reached the top of the path and saw her house, her knees felt weak. Oh, thank you, she thought, and started for it.

'Wait,' a ringing, authoritative voice behind her said.

I should have known it wouldn't be that easy, Cassie thought. Slowly, keeping her face expressionless, she swivelled to look at him.

The faint light from above reflected off the planes of his face as he stood on the bluff with the ocean behind him. Those high cheekbones, those humorous, expressive lips. There was no humour now. His eyes were as keen and piercing as when he had stared after Jordan and Logan that day on the beach, radiating a power she didn't understand, frightening her. They frightened her now.

'You're good,' he said. 'But I'm not completely stupid. There's something you're not telling me, and I want to know what it is.'

'No, you don't.' The words escaped her lips before she could stop them, but their flat sincerity was unmistakable. 'I mean – there's nothing I'm not telling you.'

'Listen to me,' he said, and to her dismay he stepped closer. 'When I first met you,' he said, 'I had no idea you were one of us. How could I? But I knew that you were different than that phony friend of yours. Not just another pretty girl, but somebody special.'

Pretty? He thought I was pretty? Cassie was thinking wildly. The clear, despairing calm was leaving her, and she clung to it desperately. Look cool and blank, she ordered herself. Politely inquiring. Let *nothing* show.

Adam's blue-grey eyes were flashing now, his odd, proud face clearly revealing his anger. But it was the hurt in the depths of those eyes that confused Cassie most.

'You weren't like any girl I'd met on the outside – you could accept mysterious things – even mystical things – without being afraid of them or trying to destroy them on sight. You were... open. Tolerant. You didn't automatically hate and reject anything different.'

'Not as tolerant as Diana. Diana's the most—'

'This hasn't got anything to do with Diana!' he said, and Cassie realised that he meant it. He was so completely honest and straightforward that betrayal had never even entered his mind.

'I *thought*,' he went on, 'that you were someone I could trust. With my life, even. And when I saw you hold out against Jordan – a guy practically twice your size – I knew I was right. It was one of the bravest things I'd ever seen – and all for a stranger. You let him *hurt* you for my sake, and you didn't even know me.'

Show *nothing*, Cassie thought. Nothing.

'And afterwards, I felt something special with you. A special understanding. I can't explain it. But I've thought about it ever since. I've thought about you a lot Cassie, and I was just waiting to tell Diana about you. I wanted her to know that she was right, that there were some outsiders who could deal with us, who could be trusted. Who might be friends of magic. She's been trying for a long time to get the Club to believe that. I wanted to tell her that you'd opened my eyes – in a lot of ways. After I left you, I even seemed to *see* more when I went out on fishing boats looking for the Master Tools. I'd look for islands while we were out laying the lines, and all of a sudden I felt like I could see clearer – or as if the ocean was revealing things. Helping me. I wanted to tell Diana that too, and see if she could explain it.

'And in all that time,' Adam finished, turning the full power of his blue-grey gaze on Cassie, 'I was never sorry I'd given you the chalcedony rose – even though we never do that with outsiders. I hoped you'd never be in enough trouble to need it, but I wanted to be there for you if you were. If you'd ever done what I told you, held it tight in your fist and thought of me, I'd have known, and I'd have tracked it down, no matter where you were. I thought you were that special.'

Was it true? Cassie wondered dizzily. All those times she'd held the stone – but she'd never held it clenched in her fist and thought only of him. She'd never followed his instructions because she'd never believed in magic.

'And now I get back – and find you're not an outsider after all. Or only half. I was *glad* to see you here, and to hear you'd joined the Circle. And from what Diana's said, she saw how special you were right away too. But I couldn't tell her I knew you – because for some reason you didn't want people to know. I respected that; I kept my mouth shut and figured you'd explain when you could. And instead—' He gestured all-inclusively. 'This. You've been giving me the brush-off all week, and now you act as if nothing ever happened between us. You even call on the Powers against me, to make me believe a lie. And now I want to know *why*.'

There was a silence. Cassie could hear the waves below, like soft, rhythmic thunder. She could smell the clear, cold night air. And finally, as if compelled, she raised her eyes to his face. He was right; she couldn't lie to him. Even if he laughed at her, even if he *pitied* her, she had to give him the truth.

'Because I'm in love with you,' she said, simply and quietly. And then she wouldn't let herself look away.

He didn't laugh.

He was staring, though, as if in disbelief. Not understanding what he thought he'd heard her say.

'That day on the beach, I felt something special too,' she said. 'But I felt – more. I felt as if we were... connected somehow. As if we were being pulled together. As if we belonged together.'

She could see the confusion in Adam's eyes – like the whirling, spinning confusion she'd felt when she'd discovered Kori's body.

'I know it sounds stupid,' she said. 'I can't even believe I'm saying this to you – but you asked for the truth. Everything I felt that day on the beach was wrong, I know that now. You've got *Diana*. Nobody in their right mind would want anything more. But that day – I had all sorts of stupid ideas. I actually thought I could see something connecting us, like a silver cord. And I felt so close to you, as if we understood each other. As if we were *born* for each other, and there was no point resisting it...'

'Cassie,' he said. His eyes were black with emotion. A look of – what? Utter disbelief? Revulsion?

'I *know* it's not true now,' she said helplessly. 'But then I didn't realise. And when you were standing so close to me, looking down at me, I thought you were going to—'

'Cassie.' It was as if her words had conjured something magical out of the air, or as if her own perceptions had been sharpened. Her breath caught in her throat as she saw *it* again. The silver cord. It hummed and shimmered, more powerful and vibrant than ever, linking them. It was as if her heart was directly connected to his. Her breath was coming faster and faster, and she lifted her eyes to his face in bewilderment.

Their gaze held. And in that instant Cassie recognised the emotion that had darkened those blue-grey eyes before.

Not disbelief, but realisation. A dawning understanding, and a wonder that made Cassie's knees feel weak.

He was... remembering, she thought. And seeing what had happened between them in a new light. Realising on a conscious level just what he had actually felt that day.

She knew this as clearly as if he had told her in words. She knew *him*. She could feel every beat of his heart, she could sense the world through his eyes. She could even see herself as he saw her. A fragile, shy creature of half-hidden beauty, like a wildflower in the shadow of a tree, but with a core of shining steel. And just as she could see herself, she could feel his feelings about her...

Oh, what was *happening?* The world had gone still,

and it contained only the two of them. Adam's eyes were wide and dazed, the pupils enormous, and she felt she was falling into them as he looked down at her. A lock of his hair had fallen onto his forehead, that marvellous, tangled wavy hair that was all the colours of autumn in New England. He was like some woodland god who'd come out in the starlight to court a shy tree nymph, and he was irresistible.

'Adam,' she said. 'We...'

But she never got to finish. He was too close to her now; she could feel his warmth, feel their electrical fields merging. She felt his hands cupping the backs of her elbows. Then slowly, slowly, she felt herself being drawn towards him until his arms were around her, embracing her fully. The silver cord could not be denied any longer.

CHAPTER

16

Cassie should have pushed him away, should have run from him. Instead, with a gasp, she buried her head in his shoulder, in the comfort of his thick Irish sweater. She could feel his warmth all around her now, anchoring her, keeping her safe. Protecting her. He smelled so good – like autumn leaves and wood fires and ocean wind. Her heart was pounding.

It was then that Cassie knew what *forbidden love* meant. It meant this, wanting this much, and feeling this wonderful, and knowing it was *wrong*. She felt Adam pull away from her slightly. She looked up at him and knew that he was as overwhelmed as she was.

'We can't,' he said in a thick voice. 'We *can't*...'

Gazing up at him, seeing only his eyes, the colour of the ocean that night when it had whispered to her to drown in it, Cassie's lips moved to form a soundless 'No.' That was when he kissed her.

And in that instant all coherent thought was lost. She was swept away by a salty wave of sheer *feeling*. It was like being caught in a riptide, sucked under, tumbling helplessly head over heels with no way to stop. She was dying, but so sweetly.

She was trembling, boneless. If he hadn't been holding her, she would have fallen. No boy had ever made her feel this way. In the wild and raging confusion there was nothing to do but surrender, to give herself up to it entirely.

Each shock of sweetness was greater than the last. She was almost senseless with delight, and she no longer even wanted to resist. Despite the wildness, the abandon of it, she wasn't afraid. Because she could trust him. He was leading her, wide-eyed and wondering, into a world she'd never known existed.

And still he was kissing her and kissing her – they were both intoxicated, dizzy with the madness of this. She knew her cheeks and throat were wildly flushed; she could feel the heat they made together.

She never knew how long they stood that way, locked in an embrace that should have melted the rock around them. She only knew sometime later that without letting go of her, he was guiding her to sit on a granite outcrop. Her breath slowing, she buried her face again in his shoulder.

And found peace there. The uncontrollable passion had given way at last to a warm and languorous drowsiness. She was safe, she belonged. And it was so simple, so beautiful.

'Cassie,' he said, in a voice she'd never heard him use before, and at the sound of it her heart dissolved and went out of her body, evaporating through the soles of her feet and her palms and her fingertips. She would never be the same again.

'I love you,' he said.

She shut her eyes without speaking. She could feel him rest his parted lips against her hair.

The silver cord had wrapped them in a shining cocoon, like still, moonlit water all around them. The wildness was over. Everything was so peaceful, so hushed. Cassie felt that she could float here forever.

My destiny, she thought. She'd found it at last. Every moment of her life had been leading to *this*. Why had she been so afraid of it, why had she ever wanted to escape it? There was nothing here but joy. She would never have to feel afraid again...

And then she remembered.

A shock of pure horror lashed through her. Oh, God, what have we *done?* she thought.

She pulled away so sharply that he had to catch her to keep her from falling backwards. 'Oh, *God*,' she said, feeling the horror sweep away everything else inside her. 'Oh, God, Adam, how could we?' she whispered.

For a moment his eyes were unfocussed, open but unseeing, as if he didn't understand why she had broken into their beautiful trance. But then she saw realisation come, and his silver-blue gaze shattered. Raw anguish shone out of his eyes.

Still in his arms, still looking up at him, Cassie began to cry.

How could they have let this happen? How could she have done this to Diana? Diana, who had rescued her, who had befriended her, who *trusted* her. Diana, whom she loved.

Adam belonged to Diana. Cassie knew that Diana had never thought of life without Adam, that all Diana's plans and hopes and dreams involved him. Diana and Adam were meant to be together...

She thought suddenly of the way Diana's haunting green eyes brightened when she saw Adam, of the tender, radiant look Diana got even talking about him.

And Adam loved Diana too. Cassie knew that as surely as she knew her own feelings. Adam idolised Diana; he adored her with a love as pure and strong and indestructible as Diana's for him.

But Cassie knew now that Adam loved her as well. How could you love two people? How could you be in love with two at the same time? Still, there was no way to deny it. The chemistry between herself and Adam; the empathy, the bond that drew them together, couldn't be ignored. Clearly, it *was* possible to love two different people at once.

And Diana had the first claim.

'You still love her,' Cassie whispered, needing to confirm it. An ache was beginning deep inside her.

He shut his eyes. 'Yes.' His voice was ragged. 'God, Cassie – I'm sorry...'

'No, that's good,' she said. She knew the ache now. It was the pain of loss, of emptiness, and it was growing. 'Because I do, too. And I don't want to hurt her. I never wanted to hurt her. That's why I promised myself I'd never let either of you know...'

'It's my fault,' he said, and she could hear the self-condemnation in his voice. 'I should have realised sooner. I should have recognised how I felt and dealt with it. Instead, I forced you into exactly what you were trying to prevent.'

'You didn't force me,' Cassie said softly, honestly. Her voice was quiet and steady; everything was simple and clear again, and she knew what she had to do. 'It was both our faults. But that doesn't matter; the only thing that matters is that it can never happen again. We have to make sure of that, somehow.'

'But how?' he said bleakly. 'We can be sorry all we want – I can hate myself – but if we're ever alone again...

I don't know what will happen.'

'Then we can't be alone. Ever. And we can't sit near each other, or touch, or even let ourselves think about it.' She was telling him what to do, but she wasn't afraid. She felt only the certainty of what she was saying.

His eyes were dark. 'I admire your self-control,' he said, even more bleakly.

'Adam,' she said, and she felt the melting inside her just at saying his name. 'We *have* to. When you came back Tuesday night after my initiation, when I realised that you and Diana... Well, that night I swore I would never let Diana be hurt because of how I felt about you. I swore I'd never betray her. Do *you* want to betray her?'

There was a silence, and she felt the involuntary heave of his lungs. And with her inner senses she felt his agony. Then he let his breath out and shut his eyes again. When he opened them, she saw his answer before he spoke it, and felt it as his arms released her and he sat back, the cold air rushing in between their bodies, separating them at last.

'No,' he said, and there was new strength in his voice. And in his face a new resolution.

They looked at each other then, not like lovers, but like soldiers. Like comrades-in-arms utterly determined to reach some common goal. Their passion held down and locked away, so deep that no one else would ever see it. It was a new closeness, maybe even more intimate than the trust of boyfriend and girlfriend. Whatever happened, whatever it cost them, they would not betray the girl they both loved.

Looking right into her eyes, he said, 'What oath was it you swore that night? Was it one you got from somebody's Book of Shadows?'

'No,' Cassie said, and then she stopped. 'I don't know,' she qualified. 'I thought I was making it up, but now it seems like it might have come from something longer. It just went, "Not by word or look or deed..."'

He was nodding. 'I've read one with those lines. It's old – and it's powerful. You call on the four Powers to witness you, and if you ever break the oath, they're free to rise against you. Do you want to swear it again now? With me?'

The abruptness of his question took her breath away. But she was eternally proud of herself that with scarcely any hesitation she spoke clearly. 'Yes.'

'We need blood.' He stood and took a knife out of his back pocket. Cassie thought she was surprised, then decided she wasn't. However nice a guy Adam might be, he was used to taking care of himself.

Without any particular flourish, he cut his palm. The blood showed black in the dim silvery light. Then he handed the knife to her.

Cassie sucked in her breath. She wasn't brave, she hated pain... But she gritted her teeth and put the knife against her palm. Just think of the pain you could have caused *Diana*, she thought, and with a quick motion she brought the knife downwards. It hurt, but she didn't make any noise.

She looked up at Adam.

'Now, say after me,' he said. He held his palm up to the star-filled sky. 'Fire, Air, Earth, Water.'

'Fire, Air, Earth, Water...'

'Listen and witness.'

'Listen and witness.' Despite the simple words, Cassie felt that the elements had indeed been evoked and were listening. The night had a sudden feeling of electricity, and the stars overhead seemed to burn colder and brighter.

Gooseflesh broke out on her skin.

Adam turned his hand sideways so that the black drops fell onto the scraggly beach grass and the sandy earth. Cassie watched, mesmerised. 'I, Adam, swear not to betray my trust – not to betray Diana,' he said.

'I, Cassie, swear not to betray my trust...' she whispered, and watched her own blood trickle off the side of her hand.

'Not by word, or look, or deed, waking or sleeping, by speech or by silence...'

She repeated it in a whisper.

'...in this land or any other. If I do, may fire burn me, air smother me, earth swallow me, and water cover my grave.'

She repeated it. As she spoke the last words, 'and water cover my grave,' she felt a *snapping*, as if something had been set in motion. As if the fabric of space and time right here had been plucked, once, and was resonating back into place. Breath held, she listened to it a moment.

Then she looked at Adam. 'It's over,' she whispered, and she didn't just mean the oath.

His eyes were like silver-edged darkness. 'It's over,' he said, and reached his bloodstained palm out to her. She hesitated, then took his hand with her own. She felt, or imagined she felt, their blood mingling, falling to the ground together. A symbol of what could never be.

Then, slowly, he released her.

'You'll give the rose back to Diana?' she asked steadily.

He took the chalcedony piece out of his pocket, held it in the palm that was still wet. 'I'll give it to her.'

Cassie nodded. She couldn't say what she meant, which was that where the stone belonged, Adam belonged.

'Good night, Adam,' she said softly instead, looking at

him standing there on the bluff with the night sky behind him. Then she turned and walked towards the lighted windows of her grandmother's house. And this time he didn't call her back.

'Oh, yes,' Cassie's grandmother said. 'This was in the front hall this morning. Someone must have put it through the letter slot.' She handed Cassie an envelope.

They were sitting at the breakfast table, the Sunday morning sun shining through the windows. Cassie was astonished at how normal everything was.

But one look at the envelope and her heart plummeted. Her name was written on the front in a large, careless hand. The ink was red.

She tore it open and stared at the note inside while her Raisin Bran got soggy. It read:

Cassie—
You see I'm using my own name this time. Come over to my house (Number Six) sometime today. I have something special I want to talk to you about. Believe me, you don't want to miss this.

Love and kisses,
Faye
P.S. Don't tell anyone in the Club you're coming to see me. You'll understand when you get here.

Cassie was tingling with alarm. Her first impulse was to call Diana, but if Diana had been up all night purifying the skull, she was probably exhausted. Faye was the last thing she needed to deal with.

All right, I won't disturb her, Cassie thought grimly. I'll go and see what Faye's up to first. Something about the ceremony, I'll bet. Or maybe she's going to call for a leadership vote.

Faye's house was one of the nicest on the street. A housekeeper let Cassie in, and she remembered Diana saying that Faye's mother was dead. There were a lot of single-parent families on Crowhaven Road.

Faye's room was a rich girl's room. Cordless phone, PC, TV and VCR, tons of CDs. Huge, lush sprawling flowers patterned everything, including a bed heaped with soft cushions and embroidered pillows. Cassie sat down on the window seat, waiting for Faye to appear. There were red candles, not lit, on the nightstand.

Suddenly the dust ruffle on the bed stirred, and out poked the face of a little orange kitten. It was followed almost immediately by a little grey one.

'Oh, you darling,' Cassie said, enchanted in spite of herself. She would never have guessed Faye was the type to keep kittens. She sat very still, and to her delight the two little creatures came all the way out. They jumped up on the window seat and ranged over her, purring like motorboats.

Cassie giggled and squirmed as one climbed her sweater and perched, precariously, on her shoulder. They were adorable kittens, the orange fluffy and spiky with baby fur, the grey sleek and tidy. Their tiny needle claws pricked her as they climbed all over her. The orange one got in her hair and poked bluntly behind her ear, and she laughed again.

He was trying to nurse, kneading his little paws against her neck. She could feel his cold little nose. The grey one was doing the same thing from the other side. Oh, what darling, darling little ...

'Ouch!' she cried. 'Ow – oh, don't! Get off, you! Get off!'

She pulled at the tiny bodies, trying to detach them. They were tangled in her hair and they hung on with claws – and teeth. When Cassie finally managed to pry them away, she almost threw them to the ground. Then her hands flew to her neck.

Her fingers came away wet. She stared in shock at the redness.

They'd *bitten* her, the little monsters. And now they were sitting on the floor and composedly licking the blood off their chops. A surge of violent revulsion passed through Cassie.

From the doorway, Faye chuckled.

'Maybe they're not getting all their vitamins and minerals from the kitten chow,' she said.

She was looking stunning this morning. Her tangled pitch-black hair was still wet and cascaded down in yards of natural curls. Her skin was damp and glowing against her burgundy robe.

I shouldn't have come, Cassie thought, feeling a wave of irrational fear. But Faye wouldn't dare to hurt her now. Diana would find out, the Circle would find out. Faye must know she couldn't get away with it.

Faye seated herself on the bed. 'So how did you like the ceremony last night?' she asked casually.

I knew it. 'It was fine until *something* went wrong,' said Cassie. Then she just looked at Faye again.

Faye laughed her rich, slow laugh. 'Oh, Cassie. I like you. I really do. I saw that there was something special about you from the beginning. I know we didn't exactly get the best start, but I think that's going to change now. I think we're going to be good friends.'

Cassie was speechless a moment. Then she managed to say, 'I don't think so, Faye.'

'But *I* think so, Cassie. And that's what counts.'

'Faye...' Somehow, after last night Cassie found she had the courage to say things she wouldn't even have dreamed of saying before. 'Faye, I don't think you and I have much in common. And I don't think I even *want* to be good friends with you.'

Faye only smiled.

'That's too bad,' she said. 'Because, you see, I know something, Cassie. And I think it's the sort of thing you'd want only a very good friend to know.'

The world rocked under Cassie's feet.

Faye couldn't be saying – oh, she couldn't be saying what Cassie thought she was. Cassie stared at the older girl, feeling something like ice congeal in her stomach.

'You see,' Faye went on, 'I happen to have a lot of other friends. And they tell me things, interesting things they see and hear around the neighbourhood. And you know what? Last night one of those friends saw something very, very interesting on the bluff.'

Cassie sat, her vision blurring.

'They saw two people on the bluff out near Number Twelve. And those two people were... well, shall we say they were getting very friendly themselves? Very friendly. It was pretty hot, the way I heard it.'

Cassie tried to speak, but nothing came out.

'And you'll never believe who those two people were! I wouldn't have believed it myself, except that it reminded me of a poem I'd read somewhere. Now, how did it go? *Each night I lie and dream about the one—*'

'Faye!' Cassie was on her feet.

Faye smiled. 'I think you get the point. Diana hasn't read that particular little poem, has she? I didn't think so. Well, Cassie, if you don't want her to hear it, or to know about what happened on the bluff last night, I'd say you'd better start being my friend and fast, don't you think?'

'It wasn't like that,' Cassie said. She was hot and shaking with fury, with fear. 'You don't understand at all—'

'Of course I understand. Adam is very attractive. And I always suspected that "eternal fidelity" routine of theirs was just an act. I don't blame you, Cassie. It's very natural...'

'That isn't what happened. There's nothing between us—'

Faye smirked. 'From what I hear, there *was* very little between you last night – sorry. No, really, I'd like to believe you, Cassie, but I wonder if Diana will see it the same way. Especially after she learns how you conveniently forgot to mention that you'd met her boyfriend over the summer – when he *awakened* you, I believe. How did that poem go again?'

'No...' Cassie whispered.

'And then the way you looked at him when he appeared after the initiation ceremony – well, Diana didn't see that, but I must admit that my suspicions were aroused. The little scene on the bluff only clinched it. When I tell Diana—'

'You *can't*,' Cassie said desperately. 'You can't tell her. Please, Faye. She won't understand. It's not that way at all, but she won't *understand*.'

Faye clucked her tongue. 'But Cassie, Diana is my cousin. My blood relation. I *have* to tell her.'

Cassie felt like a rat running frantically in a maze, searching for a way out that didn't exist. Panic was pounding in her ears. Faye *couldn't* tell Diana. It couldn't happen. The thought of how Diana would look – of how she would look at Cassie...

And at Adam. That was almost worse. She would think they had betrayed her, that Cassie and Adam had truly betrayed her. And how she would look then... how Adam would look...

Cassie could stand anything but that.

'You can't,' she whispered. 'You can't.'

'Well, Cassie, I told you before. If we were *friends*, really good friends, I might be able to keep your secret. Diana and I may be cousins, but I'd do anything for my friends. And,' Faye said deliberately, her honey-coloured eyes never leaving Cassie's face, 'I expect them to do anything for me.'

It was then, at last, that Cassie realised what this was all about. Everything went still around her, too still. Her heart gave one great thump and seemed to sink like lead. Down and down and down.

From the bottom of a pit, she asked Faye emptily, 'What kind of thing?'

Faye smiled. She leaned back against the bed, relaxed, the robe parting to reveal one bare shapely leg.

'Well, let me see,' she said slowly, drawing the moment out, relishing it. 'I know there was something... oh, yes. I'd really like to have that crystal skull Adam found. I'm sure you know where Diana's keeping it. And if not, I'm sure you could find out.'

'*No,*' Cassie said, horrified.

'Yes,' Faye said, and smiled again. 'That's what I want, Cassie. To show what a good friend you are. Nothing else will do.'

'Faye, you *saw* what happened last night. That skull is evil. There's already something awful on the loose because of it – if you use it again, who knows what might happen?' And, Cassie's numbed mind suddenly suggested, who knew what Faye might be planning to use it *for*? 'Why do you want it?' she blurted out.

Faye shook her head tolerantly. 'That's *my* little secret. Maybe, if we become good enough friends, I'll show you later.'

'I won't do it. I *can't.* I can't, Faye.'

'Well, that's too bad.' Faye's eyebrows lifted, and she pursed her full lips. 'Because that means I'm going to have to call Diana. I think my cousin has a right to know what her boyfriend is doing.'

She reached for the phone and pushed buttons with an elegant, scarlet-tipped finger.

'Hello, Diana? Is that you?'

'No!' Cassie cried, and grabbed Faye's arm. Faye pushed the mute button.

'Does this mean,' she said to Cassie, 'that we have a deal?'

Cassie couldn't form a yes or no.

Faye reached out and caught Cassie's chin in her hand, as she had that first day on the school steps. Cassie could feel the hardness of long nails, the coolness and strength of Faye's fingers. Faye was staring at her with those eyes, those strange honey-coloured eyes. Falcons have yellow eyes, Cassie thought suddenly, wildly. And Faye's fingers gripped her like talons. There was no escape. She was trapped... caught... like a white mouse caught by a bird of prey.

The golden eyes were still staring at her... into her. She was so lightheaded, so afraid. And this time there was no rock beneath her feet to steady her. She was in Faye's second-floor bedroom, trapped away from any help.

'Do we have a deal?' Faye said again.

No escape. No hope. Cassie's vision was blurring, going dim; she could barely hear Faye over the rushing in her ears.

She felt the last drops of resistance, of will, drain out of her.

'Well,' said Faye in her throaty, mocking voice.

Blindly, scarcely knowing what she was doing, Cassie nodded.

Faye released her.

Then she pushed the mute button again. 'Sorry, Diana, I got the wrong number. I meant to call the Maytag repairman. Bye now!' And with that she hung up.

She stretched like a giant cat, replacing the phone on the nightstand as she lay back. Then she put her arms behind her head and looked at Cassie, smiling.

'All right,' she said. 'The first thing is, you get me that skull. And after that... well, after that I'll think of what else I want. You realise that from now on I own you, Cassie.'

'I thought,' Cassie whispered, still unable to see for the grey mist, 'that we were friends.'

'That was just a euphemism. The truth is that you're my captive from now on. I own you now, Cassie Blake. I own you body and soul.'

THE
CAPTIVE

PART I

CHAPTER

1

Fire, Cassie thought. All around her she saw blazing autumn colours. The yellow-orange of sugar maple, the brilliant red of sassafras, the crimson of sumac bushes. It was as if the entire world was flaming with Faye's element.

And I'm trapped in the middle of it.

The sick feeling in the pit of Cassie's stomach got worse with every step she took down Crowhaven Road.

The yellow Victorian house at the bottom of the road looked as pretty as ever. Sunlight was striking rainbow sparks off a prism that hung in the highest tower window. A girl with long, light-brown hair called out from the porch.

'Hurry up, Cassie! You're late!'

'Sorry,' Cassie called back, trying to hurry when what she really wanted to do was turn around and run the other way. She had the sudden, inexplicable conviction that her private thoughts must show in her face. Laurel would take one look at her and know all about what had happened with Adam last night, and all about the bargain with Faye.

But Laurel just grabbed her by the waist and hustled her inside and upstairs to Diana's bedroom. Diana was standing in front of the large walnut cabinet; Melanie was sitting on the bed. Sean was perched uneasily in the window seat, rubbing his knees with his palms.

Adam was standing beside him.

He looked up as Cassie came in.

Cassie met those blue-grey eyes for only an instant, but it was long enough. They were the colour of the ocean at its most mysterious, sunlit on the surface but with incomprehensible depths underneath. The rest of his face was the same as ever: arresting and intriguing, pride showing in the high cheekbones and determined mouth, but sensitivity and humour showing there too. His face looked different only because last night Cassie had seen those eyes midnight blue with passion, and had felt that mouth...

Not by word or look or deed, she told herself fiercely, staring down at the ground because she didn't dare look up again. But her heart was pounding so hard she expected to see the front of her sweater fluttering. Oh, God, how was she ever going to be able to carry this off and keep her vow? It took an incredible amount of energy to sit down by Melanie and not look at him, to block the charismatic heat of his presence out of her mind.

You'd better get used to it, she told herself. Because you're going to be doing a lot of it from now on.

'Good; we're all here,' Diana said. She went over and shut the door. 'This is a closed meeting,' she went on, turning back to the group. 'The others weren't invited because I'm not sure they have the same interests at heart as we do.'

'That's putting it mildly,' Laurel said under her breath.

'They're going to be upset if they find out,' Sean said, his black eyes darting between Adam and Diana.

'Then let them be,' Melanie said unemotionally. Her own cool grey eyes fixed on Sean and he flushed. 'This is much more important than any fit Faye can throw. We have to find out what happened to that dark energy... and now.'

'I think I know a way,' said Diana. Out of a white velvet pouch she took a delicate green stone on a silver chain.

'A pendulum,' Melanie said at once.

'Yes. This is peridot,' Diana said to Cassie. 'It's a visionary stone – right, Melanie? Usually we use clear quartz as a pendulum, but this time I think the peridot is better – more likely to pick up traces of the dark energy. We'll take it down to the place where the dark energy escaped and it'll align itself in the direction the energy went and start swinging.'

'We hope,' Laurel murmured.

'Well, that's the theory,' Melanie said.

Diana looked at Adam, who had been unusually quiet. 'What do you think?'

'I think it's worth a try. It'll take a lot of mental power to back it up, though. We'll all have to concentrate – especially since we're not a full Circle.' His voice was calm and even, and Cassie admired him for it. She kept her face turned in Diana's direction, though as a matter of fact her eyes were fixed on the walnut cabinet.

Diana turned to Cassie. 'What about you?'

'Me?' Cassie said, startled, tearing her eyes away from the cabinet door. She hadn't expected to be asked; she didn't know anything about pendulums or peridot. To her horror, she felt her face redden.

'Yes, you. You might be new to the methods we use, but a lot of the time you have *feelings* about things.'

'Oh. Well...' Cassie tried to search her feelings, scrabbling to get beyond the guilt and terror that were uppermost. 'I think... it's a good idea,' she said finally, knowing how lame that sounded. 'It seems fine to me.'

Melanie rolled her eyes, but Diana nodded as seriously as she had at Adam. 'All right, then, the only thing to do is try,' she said, dropping the peridot and its silver chain into the palm of her left hand and clasping it tightly. 'Let's go.'

Cassie couldn't breathe; she was still reeling from the impact of Diana's clear green eyes, slightly darker than the peridot, but with that same delicate transparency, as if there were light shining behind them.

I can't do it, she thought. She was surprised at how stark and simple everything was now that she had actually looked Diana in the eyes. I *can't* do it. I'll have to tell Faye – no, I'll tell Diana. That's it. I'll tell Diana myself before Faye can, and I'll *make* her believe me. She'll understand; Diana is so good, she'll have to understand.

Everyone had gotten up. Cassie got up too, turning towards the door to hide her agitation – *should I tell her right now? Ask her to stay back a minute?* – when the door flew open in her face.

Faye was standing in the doorway.

Suzan and Deborah were behind her. The strawberry-blonde looked mean, and the biker's habitual scowl was even darker than usual. Behind *them* were the Henderson brothers, Chris frowning and Doug grinning in a wild way that was disturbing.

'Going somewhere without us?' Faye said. She was speaking to Diana, but her eyes remained fixed on Cassie.

'Not now,' Laurel muttered.

Diana let out a deep breath. 'I didn't think you'd be interested,' she said. 'We're going to trace the dark energy.'

'Not *interested*? When all the rest of you are so busy? Of course, I can only speak for myself, but I'm interested in everything the Circle does. What about you, Deborah?'

The biker girl's scowl changed briefly into a malicious grin. 'I'm interested,' she said.

'And what about you, Suzan?'

'*I'm* interested,' Suzan chimed in.

'And what about you, Chris?'

'*I'm*—'

'All *right*,' Diana said. Her cheeks were flushed; Adam had come to stand at her side. 'We get the point. We're better off with a full Circle, anyway – but where's Nick?'

'I have no idea,' Faye said coolly. 'He's not at home.'

Diana hesitated, then shrugged. 'We'll do our best with what we have,' she said. 'Let's go down to the garage.'

She gestured at Melanie and Laurel and they went first, elbowing past Faye's group, who looked as if they wanted to stay and argue some more. Adam took charge of Sean and got him out the door, then began herding the Hendersons. Deborah and Suzan looked at Faye, then followed the guys.

Cassie had been hanging back, hoping for the chance to speak to Diana alone. But Diana seemed to have forgotten her; she was engaged in a staredown with Faye. Finally, head high, she walked past the tall girl who was still semi-blocking the doorway.

'Diana...' Faye called. Diana didn't look back, but her shoulders tensed: she was listening.

'You're going to lose them all,' Faye said, and

she chuckled her lazy chuckle as Diana went on to the staircase.

Biting her lip, Cassie stepped forward furiously. One good shove in Faye's middle, she was thinking. But Faye rounded smoothly on her, blocking the doorway completely.

'Oh, no, you don't. We need to talk,' she said.

'I don't want to talk to you.'

Faye ignored her. 'Is it in here?' She moved quickly to the walnut cabinet and pulled at a handle, but the drawer was locked. They all were. 'Damn. But you can find out where she keeps the key. I want it as soon as possible, do you understand?'

'Faye, you're not listening to me! I've changed my mind. I'm not going to do it after all.'

Faye, who had been prowling around the room like a panther, taking advantage of this unique opportunity to examine Diana's things, stopped in her tracks. Then she turned slowly to Cassie, and smiled.

'Oh, Cassie,' she said. 'You really kill me.'

'I'm *serious*. I've changed my mind.' Faye just smiled at her, leaning back against the wall and shaking her head. Her heavy-lidded golden eyes were glowing with amusement, her mane of pitch-black hair fell across her shoulders as her head moved. She had never looked more beautiful – or more dangerous.

'Cassie, come here.' Faye's voice was just slightly edged with impatience, like a teacher who's put up with a lot from a backward student. 'Let me show you something,' Faye went on, catching Cassie's elbow and dragging her to the window. 'Now, look down there. What do you see?'

Cassie stopped fighting and looked. She saw the Club, the in-crowd at New Salem high school, the kids who awed – and terrorised – students and teachers alike. She saw them gathered in Diana's driveway, their heads gleaming in the first rays of sunset: Suzan's strawberry blonde turned to red, Deborah's dark curls touched with ruby, Laurel's long, light-brown hair and Melanie's short auburn and the Henderson brothers' dishevelled yellow all highlighted by the ruddy glow in the sky.

And she saw Adam and Diana, standing close, Diana's silvery head drooping to Adam's shoulder. He was holding her protectively, his own hair dark as wine.

Faye's voice came from behind Cassie. 'If you tell her, you'll kill her. You'll destroy her faith in everything she's ever believed in. And you'll take away the only thing she has to trust, to rely on. Is that what you want?'

'Faye...' Cassie seethed.

'And, incidentally, you'll get yourself banished from the Club. You know that, don't you? How do you think Melanie and Laurel are going to feel when they hear that you messed around with Diana's boyfriend? None of them will ever speak to you again, not even to make a full Circle. The coven will be destroyed too.'

Cassie's teeth were clenched. She wanted to hit Faye, but it wouldn't do any good. Because Faye was right. And Cassie thought she could stand being blackballed, being a pariah at school again; she even thought she could stand to destroy the coven. But the picture of Diana's face...

It *would* kill Diana. By the time Faye got finished telling it her way, it would. Cassie's fantasy of confessing to Diana and having Diana understand vanished like a pricked soap bubble.

'And what I want is so reasonable,' Faye was going on, almost crooning. 'I just want to look at the skull for a little while. I know what I'm doing. You'll get it for me, won't you, Cassie? Won't you? Today?'

Cassie shut her eyes. Against her closed eyelids the light was red as fire.

CHAPTER
2

Somewhere on the way downstairs Cassie stopped feeling guilty.

She didn't know exactly how it happened. But it was *necessary*, if she was going to survive this. She was doing everything she could to protect Diana – and Adam, too, in a way. Adam must never know about Faye's blackmail. So Cassie would do whatever it took to protect them both, but by God, she wasn't going to feel guilty on top of it.

And she had to handle Faye somehow as well, she thought, marching behind the tall girl, past Diana's father's study. She had to keep Faye from doing anything too radical with the skull. She didn't know how; she'd have to think about that later. But somehow she would do it.

If Faye had looked back just then, Cassie thought, she might have been surprised to see the face of the girl behind her. For the first time in her life Cassie felt as if her eyes were hard, like the blue steel of a revolver instead of the soft blue of wildflowers.

But right now she had to look neutral – composed. The

group on the driveway looked up as she and Faye came out the door.

'What took you so long?' Laurel asked.

'We were plotting to kill you all,' Faye said breezily. 'Shall we?' She gestured towards the garage.

There were only traces of yesterday's chalk circle left on the floor. Once again the garage was empty of cars – they were lucky Diana's father worked so much at his law firm.

Diana, her left fist still closed, went over to the wall of the garage, directly behind the place Cassie had been sitting when they had performed the skull ceremony. Cassie followed her and then drew in her breath sharply.

'It's *burned*.' She hadn't noticed that last night. Well, of course not; it had been too dark.

Diana was nodding. 'I hope nobody is going to keep arguing about whether there was any dark energy or not,' she said, with a glance back at Deborah and Suzan.

The wood and plaster of the garage wall was charred in a circle perhaps a foot and a half in diameter. Cassie looked at it, and then at the remnants of the chalk circle on the floor. She had been sitting there, but part of her had been inside the skull. Diana had told them all to look into it, to concentrate, and suddenly Cassie had found herself inside it. That was where she'd seen – felt – the dark power. It had begun rushing outwards, getting bigger, determined to break out of the crystal. And she'd seen a face...

She was grateful, suddenly, for Adam's calm voice. 'Well, we know what direction it started in, anyway. Let's see if the crystal agrees.'

They were all standing around Diana. She looked at them, then held her left fist out, palm up, and unclasped her fingers. She took the top of the silver chain with her right hand and drew it up taut, so that the peridot just rested on her palm.

'Concentrate,' she said. 'Earth and Air, help us see what we need to see. Show the traces of the dark energy to us. Everybody concentrate on the crystal.'

Earth and Air, wind and tree, show us what we need to see, Cassie thought, her mind automatically setting the simple concept in a rhyme. The wood of the wall, the air outside; those were what they needed to help them. She found herself murmuring the words under her breath and quickly stopped, but Diana's green eyes flashed at her.

'Go on,' Diana said tensely in a low voice, and Cassie started up again, feeling self-conscious.

Diana removed the hand that was supporting the crystal.

It spun on the chain, twirling until the chain was kinked tightly, and then twirling the other way. Cassie watched the pale green blur, murmuring the couplet faster and faster. *Earth and Air* ... no, it was useless. The peridot was just spinning madly like a top gone wild.

Suddenly, with broad, sweeping strokes, the crystal began swinging back and forth.

Someone's breath hissed on the other side of the circle.

The peridot had straightened out; it was no longer twirling, but swinging steadily and hard. Like a pendulum, Cassie realised. Diana wasn't doing it; the hand that held the chain remained steady. But the peridot was swinging hard, back towards the centre of the chalk circle on the floor, and forwards towards the burned place on the wall.

'Bingo,' Adam said softly.

'We've got it,' Melanie whispered. 'All right, now you're

going to have to move it out of alignment to get outside. Walk – carefully – to the door, and then try to come back to this exact place on the other side of the wall.'

Diana wet her lips and nodded, then, holding the silver chain always at the same distance from her body, she turned smoothly and did as Melanie said. The coven broke up to give her room and regrouped around her outside. Finding the right place wasn't hard; there was another burned circle on the outer wall, somewhat fainter than the one inside.

As Diana brought the crystal into alignment once more, it began to swing again. Straight towards the burned place, straight out. Down Crowhaven Road, towards the town.

A shudder went up Cassie's spine.

Everyone looked at everyone else.

Holding the crystal away from her, Diana followed the direction of the swinging. They all fell in behind her, although Cassie noticed that Faye's group kept to the rear. Cassie herself was still fighting every second to *not* watch Adam.

Trees rustled overhead. Red maple, beech, slippery elm – Cassie could identify many of them now. But she tried to keep her eyes on the rapid swish of the pendulum.

They walked and walked, following the curve of Crowhaven Road down towards the water. Now grasses and hedges grew poorly in the sandy soil. The pale green stone was swinging at an angle, and Diana turned to follow it.

They were heading west now, along a deeply rutted dirt road. Cassie had never been this way before, but the other members of the Circle obviously had – they were exchanging guarded glances. Cassie saw a chain-link fence ahead, and then an irregular line of headstones.

'Oh, great,' Laurel muttered from beside Cassie,

and from somewhere in back Suzan said, 'I don't believe this. First we have to walk for miles, and now...'

'What's the problem? Just gonna visit some of our ancestors underground,' Doug Henderson said, his blue-green eyes glittering oddly.

'Shut up,' Adam said.

Cassie didn't want to go inside. She'd seen many cemeteries in New England – it seemed there was one on every other street in Massachusetts, and she'd been to Kori's funeral down in the town. This one didn't look any different from the others: it was a small, square plot of land cluttered with modest gravestones, many of them worn almost completely smooth with time. But Cassie could hardly make herself follow the others onto the sparse, browning grass between the graves.

Diana led them straight down the middle of the cemetery. Most of the stones were small, scarcely reaching higher than Cassie's knees. They were shaped like arches, with two smaller arches on either side.

'Whoever carved these had a gruesome sense of humour,' she breathed. Many of the stones were etched with crude skulls, some of them winged, others in front of crossbones. One had an entire skeleton, holding a sun and moon in its hands.

'Death's victory,' Faye said softly, so close that Cassie felt warmth on the nape of her neck. Cassie jumped, but refused to look back.

'Oh, *terrific*,' said Laurel as Diana slowed.

The light was dying from the sky. They were in the centre of the graveyard, and a cool breeze blew over the stunted grass, bringing a faint tang of salt with it. The hairs on the back of Cassie's neck were tingling.

You're a witch, she reminded herself. You should

love cemeteries. They're probably your natural habitat.

The thought didn't really make her feel less frightened, but now her fear was mingled with something else – a sort of strange excitement. The darkness gathering in the sky and in the corners of the graveyard seemed closer. She was part of it, part of a whole new world of shadows and power.

Diana stopped.

The silver chain was a thin line in the gloom, with a pale blob below it. But Cassie could see that the peridot was no longer swinging like a pendulum. Instead it was moving erratically, round and round in circles. It would swing a few times one way, then slow and swing back the other way.

Cassie looked at it, then up at Diana's face. Diana was frowning. Everyone was watching the circling stone in dead silence.

Cassie couldn't stand the suspense any longer. 'What does it *mean*?' she hissed to Laurel, who just shook her head. Diana, though, looked up.

'Something's wrong with it. It led here – and then it just stopped. But if we've found the place, it shouldn't be moving at all. The stone should just sort of point and quiver – right, Melanie?'

'Like a good hound dog,' Doug said, with his wild grin.

Melanie ignored him. 'That's the theory,' she said. 'But we've never really tried this before. Maybe it means...' Her voice trailed off as she looked around the graveyard, then she shrugged. 'I don't know what it means.'

The tingling at the back of Cassie's neck was getting stronger. The dark energy had come here – and done what? Disappeared? Dissipated? Or...

Laurel was breathing quickly, her elfin face

unusually tense. Cassie instinctively moved a little closer to her. She and Laurel and Sean were the juniors, the youngest members of the Circle, and witch or not, Cassie's arms had broken out in gooseflesh.

'What if it's still here, somewhere... *waiting*?' she said.

'I doubt it,' Melanie said, her voice as level and uninflected as usual. 'It couldn't hang around without being stored somehow; it would just evaporate. It either came here and *did* something, or...' Again, though, she could only finish her sentence with a shrug.

'But what could it do here? I don't see any signs of damage, and I feel...' Still frowning, Diana caught the circling peridot in her left hand and held it. 'This place feels confused – strange – but I don't sense any harm the dark energy has done. Cassie?'

Cassie tried to search her own feelings. Confusion – as Diana said. And she felt dread and anger and all sorts of churned-up emotions – but maybe that was just *her*. She was in no state to get a clear reading on anything.

'I don't know,' she had to say to Diana. 'I don't like it here.'

'Maybe, but that's not the point. The point is that we don't see any burns the dark energy could have left, or sense anything it's destroyed or hurt,' Diana said.

Deborah's voice was impatient. 'Why are you asking *her*, anyway?' she said with a jerk of her dark head towards Cassie. 'She's hardly even one of us—'

'Cassie's as much a part of the Circle as you are,' Adam interrupted, unusually curt. Cassie saw the arch, amused glance Faye threw him and wanted to intervene, but Diana was agreeing heatedly with Adam, and Deborah was bridling, glaring at both of them. It looked as if an argument would break out.

'Be quiet!' Laurel said sharply. 'Listen!'

Cassie heard it as soon as the voices died down; the quiet crunch of gravel at the roadside. It was noticeable only against the deathly quiet of the autumn twilight.

'Somebody's coming,' Chris Henderson said. He and Doug were poised for a fight.

They were all hideously on edge, Cassie realised. The crunch of footsteps sounded as loud as firecrackers now, grating against her taut nerves. She saw a dim shape beside the road, and then saw Adam move forward, so that he was in front of both Diana and her. I'm going to have to talk to him about that, she thought irrelevantly.

There was a pause in the footsteps, and the dim shape came towards them. Adam and the Henderson brothers looked ready to rush it. Quarrel forgotten, Deborah looked ready too. Sean was cowering behind Faye. Cassie's heart began to pound.

Then she noticed a spot of red like a tiny burning coal floating near the figure, and she heard a familiar voice.

'If you want me, you got me. Four against one ought to be about fair.'

With a whoop, Chris Henderson rushed forward. 'Nick!'

Doug grinned, while still managing to look as if he might jump the approaching figure. Adam relaxed and stepped back.

'You sure, Adam? We can settle this right here,' Nick said as he reached the group, the end of his cigarette glowing as he inhaled. Adam's eyes narrowed, and then Cassie saw the daredevil smile he'd worn at Cape Cod, when four guys with a gun had been chasing him. What was wrong with him, what was wrong with everybody tonight? she wondered. They were all acting crazy.

Diana put a restraining hand on Adam's arm. 'No fighting,' she said quietly.

Nick looked at her, then shrugged. 'Kind of nervous, aren't you?' he said, surveying the group.

Sean emerged from behind Faye. 'I'm just high-strung.'

'Yes, you ought to be – from a tree,' Faye said contemptuously.

Nick didn't smile, but then Nick never smiled. As always, his face was handsome but cold. 'Well, maybe you have a reason to be nervous – at least some of you,' he said.

'What's that supposed to mean? We came here looking for the dark energy that escaped last night,' said Adam.

Nick went still, as if struck by a new idea, then his cigarette glowed again. 'Maybe you're looking in the wrong place,' he said expressionlessly.

Diana's voice was quiet. 'Nick, will you please just tell us what you mean?'

Nick looked around at them all. 'I mean,' he said deliberately, 'that while you've been scurrying around here, a crew's been up at Devil's Cove, pulling rocks off old Fogle.'

Fogle? Cassie couldn't place the name. And then suddenly she saw it in her mind's eye – on a brass plate in a wood-panelled office. 'Our principal?' she gasped.

'You got it. They say he got caught in an *avalanche*.'

'An avalanche?' demanded Laurel in disbelief. 'Around here?'

'How else do you explain the two-ton chunk of granite that was on top of him? Not to mention all the smaller stuff.'

There was a moment of shocked silence.

'Is he ...' Cassie couldn't finish the question.

'He wasn't looking too good when they got that chunk off him,' Nick said, and then, with less sarcasm, 'He's been dead since last night.'

'Oh, God,' Laurel whispered. There was another silence, just as shocked and even longer this time. Cassie knew they were all seeing the same thing: a crystal skull surrounded by a protective ring of candles – and one of the candles going out.

'It was Faye's fault,' Sean began in a whine, but Faye interrupted without looking at him. 'It was *his* fault.'

'Wait, wait,' said Diana. 'We don't know the dark energy had anything to do with it. How *could* it have, when we know it came here and then stopped?'

'I don't think that's much comfort,' Melanie said in a low voice. 'Because if it wasn't the dark energy, who was it?'

There was a sort of strange shifting in the group, as if everyone was standing back and looking at all the others. Cassie felt a void in the pit of her stomach again. The principal was – had been – an outsider, who hated witches. And that meant they all had a motive – especially anybody who blamed the outsides for Kori Henderson's death. Cassie looked at Deborah, and then at Chris and Doug.

Most of the rest of the coven was doing the same. Doug glared back, then gave a wild, defiant grin.

'Maybe we did do it,' he said, eyes glittering.

'Did we?' said Chris, looking confused.

Deborah just looked scornful.

There was another silence, then Suzan spoke in a petulant voice. 'Look, it's too bad about Fogle, but do we have to stand here forever? My feet are killing me.'

Adam seemed to shake himself. 'She's right; we should get out of this place. There's nothing we can do here.' He put an arm around Diana, and gestured everybody else ahead. Cassie lingered. There was something she wanted to say to Diana.

But Diana was moving now, and Cassie didn't have a chance. With the Henderson brothers in the lead, the group was taking a different route than the one they had taken in, cutting towards the north-east corner of the cemetery. As they approached the road, Cassie noticed the ground sloped up. There was a strange mound of grassy earth near the chain-link fence on this side; she almost tripped when she reached it. But even stranger was what she saw when they had passed it and she looked back.

The front of the mound was faced with stone slabs, and there was an iron door, maybe two feet square, set between them. The door had an iron hinge and a padlock on it, but it couldn't have opened anyway. Pushed right up against it was a large, irregular hunk of cement. Grass was growing up around the cement, showing it had been there a while.

Cassie's hands were icy cold, her heart was thudding, and she was dizzy. She tried to think, noticing with only part of her mind that she was passing by newer gravestones now, marble slabs with writing not worn smooth by time. She was trying to figure out what was wrong with her – was it just reaction to all the events of the past day and night? Was that why she was shaking?

'Cassie, are you okay?' Diana and Adam had turned around. Cassie was grateful for the growing darkness as she faced both of them and tried to get her mind clear.

'Yeah. I just – felt weird for a minute. But wait, Diana.' Cassie remembered what she had wanted to say. 'You know how you were asking me about my feelings before ... well, I have a feeling about Mr Fogle. I think the dark energy did have something to do with it, somehow.

But...' She stopped. 'But I don't know. There's something else strange going on.'

'You can say that again,' Adam said, and he reached for her arm to get her moving once more. Cassie evaded him and shot him a reproachful glance while Diana was staring into the distance. He looked at his own hand, startled.

There *was* something strange going on, something stranger than any of them realised, Cassie thought. 'What is that thing back there, with the iron door?' she asked.

'It's been there for as long as I can remember,' Diana said absently. 'Something to do with storage, I think.'

Cassie glanced back, but by now the mound was lost in darkness. She hugged herself, tucking her hands under her clasping arms to warm them. Her heart was still thudding.

I'll ask Grandma Howard about it, she decided. Whatever it was, it wasn't a storage shed, she knew that.

Then she noticed that Diana was toying with something around her neck as she walked lost in thought. It was a fine golden chain, and at the end of it dangled a key.

CHAPTER

3

'I think,' Melanie said quietly, 'that it's time to talk about the skull. Adam's never told us exactly how he found it—'

'No, you've been very secretive about that,' Faye put in.

'—but maybe now is the time.'

Diana and Adam looked at each other, and then Diana nodded slightly. 'All right, then, tell it. Try not to leave anything out.'

After the walk back from the cemetery they had crowded, all twelve of them, into Diana's room. Cassie looked around at the group and realised that it was divided. Suzan, Deborah, and the Henderson brothers were sitting on one side, near Faye, while Laurel, Melanie, Adam, and Sean were on the other side, near Diana.

At least, Cassie thought, watching Sean's uneasily shifting eyes, Sean was sitting on Diana's side for the moment. He could change any time. And so could Nick – Nick could vote with Diana one day, and then for no apparent reason vote with Faye the next. Nick was always an unknown factor.

And so, a voice inside her whispered, are you.

But *that* was ridiculous. Nothing – not even Faye – could make Cassie vote against Diana. Not when it really counted.

Adam was talking in a low, thoughtful voice, as if he were trying to remember precisely. 'It wasn't off Cape Cod, it was farther north, closer to Boston. Everybody knows there are seventeen islands off Boston Bay; they're all deserted and covered with weeds. Well, I found an eighteenth. It wasn't like the others; it was flat and sandy and there was no sign that people had ever been there. And there was something strange about it... I'd been to the place before, but I'd never seen it. It was as if my eyes had suddenly been opened after—' He stopped.

Cassie, looking at the lamp's reflection on Diana's gleaming pine-board floor, felt as if she were smothering. She didn't dare breathe until Adam went on, '—after working on the fishing boats all summer. But when I tried to head for the island, the tiller bucked, trying to keep me away or run me aground on the rocks. I had to wrestle with it to bring the boat in – and I had to call on Earth and Water or I'd never have made it. When I was finally safe I looked at the rocks and saw the wreckage of other boats. Anybody that had made it there before didn't make it away again alive.' He took a deep, slow breath.

'As soon as I stepped on the sand I could *feel* that the whole island was electric. I knew it was the place even before I saw the circle of stones in the middle. It was just the way Black John described it. Sea heather had grown up around the rocks, but the centre was clear and that's where I dug. About a minute later my shovel hit something hard.'

'And then?' said Diana.

'And then I pulled it out. I felt – I don't know, dizzy, when I saw it. The sun was glittering on the sand and it sort of blinded me. Then I wrapped the skull up in my shirt and left. The island didn't fight when I went; it was like a trap that had been sprung. That was – let's see, September twenty-first. As soon as I got back to the Bay, I wanted to start up to New Salem, but I had some things to take care of. I couldn't get started until the next day, and I knew I was going to be late for Kori's initiation.' He paused and threw an apologetic glance towards Doug and Chris.

They said nothing, but Cassie felt eyes flicker towards her. Kori's initiation had become Cassie's initiation, because on that morning Kori had been found dead at the bottom of the high-school steps.

'Just what is the point of all this storytelling?' Faye asked, her husky voice bored. 'Unless' – she straightened up, looking more interested – 'you think the rest of the Master Tools may be on that island.'

'I told you before,' Adam said. 'There was nothing else there, Faye. Just the skull.'

'And the point is that we need to know more about the skull,' Diana put in. 'For better or worse, we're stuck with it now. I don't think we should put it back on the island—'

'Put it *back*!' Faye exclaimed.

'—where anybody might find it, now that the protective spell is broken. It's not safe there. I don't know if it will be safe anywhere.'

'Well, now,' Faye murmured, looking sleepy. 'If it's too much trouble for you, *I'll* be glad to take care of it.'

Diana just shot her a look that said Faye was the last person she'd ask to take care of the skull. But, Cassie noticed with a sinking feeling, Faye's heavy-lidded amber eyes were not fixed on Diana's face. They were trained on the little gold key at Diana's throat.

There was a knock at the door.

Cassie started, hard enough that Laurel turned around and looked at her in surprise. But it was only Diana's father, who'd come home with a bulging briefcase in his hand.

Mr Meade looked around the crowded room in mild surprise, as if he didn't quite know who all these people were. Cassie wondered suddenly how much he knew about the Circle.

'Is everyone staying for dinner?' he asked Diana.

'Oh – no,' Diana said, looking at a dainty white and gold clock on the nightstand. 'I didn't realise it was after seven, Dad. I'll fix something quick.'

He nodded, and after one more quick, uncertain glance around the room, left. Bedsprings creaked and clothing rustled as everyone else got up.

'Tomorrow we can meet at school,' Melanie said. 'But I've *got* to study tonight; this whole last week has been shot and I've got a biology test.'

'Me too,' said Laurel.

'I've got algebra homework,' Suzan offered, and Deborah muttered, 'Meaning you've got a week's worth of soap tapes in the VCR.'

'All right, we'll meet tomorrow,' Diana said. She walked downstairs with them. Faye managed to catch Cassie's arm as the others were leaving, and she breathed in her ear, 'Get it tonight. Call me and I'll come and pick it up; then we'll put it back before morning so she won't notice it's gone.'

Cassie pulled her arm away rebelliously. But at the door, Faye gave her a meaningful look, and the flash in those amber eyes alarmed her. She stared at Faye a long moment, then nodded slightly.

'Do you want me to stay?' Adam was saying to Diana.

'No,' Cassie said quickly, before Diana could answer. They looked at her, startled, and she said, 'I'll stay and help make dinner, if it's all right, Diana. I told my grandma and my mom I'd be gone and they've probably already eaten by now.'

Diana's graciousness rose to the fore. 'Oh – of course you can stay, then,' she said. 'We'll be fine, Adam.'

'Okay.' Adam gave Cassie a keen glance, which she returned woodenly. He went out, following Chris and Doug into the darkness. The flicker of a match up ahead showed where Nick was. Cassie looked up at the night sky, which glittered brashly with stars but not a trace of moon, and then stepped back as Diana shut the door.

Dinner was quiet, with Mr Meade sitting there, leafing through a newspaper, occasionally glancing up over his reading glasses at the two girls. Afterwards they went back up to Diana's room. Cassie realised she needed to stall.

'You know, you never told me about that print,' she said, pointing. Decorating Diana's walls were six art prints. Five of them were very similar, black and white with a slightly old-fashioned look. Diana had told her they were pictures of Greek goddesses: Aphrodite, the beautiful but fickle goddess of love; Artemis, the fierce virgin huntress; Hera, the imperious queen of the gods; Athena, the calm grey-eyed goddess of wisdom; and Persephone, who loved flowers and all growing things.

But the last print was different. It was in colour, and the style was more abstract, more modern. It showed a young woman standing beneath a starry sky, while a crescent moon shone silver down on her flowing hair. She was wearing a simple white garment, cut high to show a garter on her thigh. On her upper arm was a silver cuff-bracelet, and on her head was a thin circlet with a crescent moon, horns upwards.

It was the outfit Diana wore at meetings of the Circle.

'Who is she?' Cassie said, staring at the beautiful girl in the print.

'Diana,' Diana said wryly. Cassie turned to her, and she smiled. 'The goddess Diana,' she added. 'Not the Roman Diana; another one. She's older than all the Greek goddesses, and she was different from them. She was a Great Goddess; she ruled everything. She was goddess of the night and the moon and the stars – there's a story that once she turned all the stars into mice to impress the witches on earth. So they made her Queen of the Witches.'

Cassie grinned. 'I think it would take more than that to impress Faye.'

'Probably. Some people say that her legend was based on an actual person, who taught magic and was a champion of poor women. Other people say she was first a Sun Goddess, but then she got chased out by male Sun Gods and turned to the night. The Romans got her confused with the Greek goddess Artemis – you know, the huntress – but she was much more than that. Anyway, she's always been Queen of the Witches.'

'Like you,' Cassie said.

Diana laughed and shook her head. 'I may not *always* be leader,' she said. 'It all depends on what happens between now and November tenth. That's the day of the leadership vote.'

'Why November tenth?'

'It's my birthday – Faye's too, coincidentally. You have to be seventeen to be permanent leader, and that's when we both will be.'

Cassie was surprised. Diana was still only sixteen, like her? She always seemed so mature, and she was a senior. But it was even stranger that Faye was so young, and that the cousins had the same birthday.

She looked at Diana, sitting there on the bed. As beautiful as the girl in the last print was, Diana was more beautiful. With hair that indescribable colour, like sunlight and moonlight woven together, and a face like a flower, and eyes like green jewels, Diana resembled something from a fairy tale or legend more than a real person. But the goodness and – well, *purity* that shone out of Diana's eyes were very real indeed, Cassie thought. Cassie was proud to be her friend.

Then the light flashed on the gold key around Diana's neck and she remembered what she was there to do.

I can't, Cassie thought, as her stomach plummeted giddily. She could feel the slow, sick pounding of her heart. Right this minute around her own neck was hanging the crescent-moon necklace that Diana had given her at her initiation. How could she steal from Diana, deceive Diana?

But she'd been through all that before. There was no way out. Faye would do exactly what she had threatened – Cassie knew that. The only way to save Diana was to deceive her.

It's for her own good, Cassie told herself. So just stop thinking about it. Do what you have to and get it over with.

'Cassie? You look upset.'

'I—' Cassie started to say, no, of course not, and change the subject the way she usually did when somebody caught her daydreaming. But then she had an idea. 'I don't really feel like going home alone,' she said, grimacing. 'It's not just the walk – it's that house. It creaks and rattles all night long and sometimes I can't even get to sleep. Especially if I'm thinking about... about...'

'Is that all?' Diana said, smiling. 'Well, that's easy to take care of. Sleep here.' Cassie was stricken at how easily Diana made the offer. 'And if you're worried about the skull,' Diana went on, 'you can stop. It's not going anywhere, and it's not going to do anything more to hurt people. I promise.'

Cassie's face flamed and she had to struggle not to look at the cabinet. She would never have mentioned the skull herself: she couldn't have gotten the word out. 'Okay,' she said, trying to keep her voice normal. 'Thanks. I'll call my mom and tell her I'm staying over.'

'We can drive to your house so you can get dressed in the morning – I'll check on the guest room.' As Diana left, the voices in Cassie's mind were rioting. *You little sneak*, they shouted at her. *You nasty, weaselly, lying little traitor—*

Shut up! Cassie shouted back at them, with such force that they actually did shut up.

She called her mother.

'The guest room's ready,' Diana said, reappearing as Cassie hung up the phone. 'But if you get scared in the night you can come in here.'

'Thanks,' Cassie said, genuinely grateful.

'What are big sisters for?'

They sat up and talked for a while, but neither of them had had much sleep the night before, and as the clock's hands edged closer to ten they were both yawning.

'I'll take my bath tonight so you can have one in the morning,' Diana said. 'The hot water doesn't last long around here.'

'Isn't there a spell to take care of that?'

Diana laughed and tossed a book to her. 'Here, see if you can find one.'

It was the Book of Shadows Diana had brought to Cassie's initiation, the one that had been in Diana's family since the first witches came to New Salem. The brittle yellow pages had a mildewy smell that made Cassie wrinkle her nose, but she was glad to have this chance to look at it. Towards the beginning of the book the writing was small and almost illegible, but further on it became stylised and beautiful, like copperplate. Different authors, Cassie thought, different generations. The Post-it notes and plastic flags on almost every page were the work of the current generation.

It was full of spells, descriptions of coven meetings, rituals, and stories. Cassie pored over it, her eyes moving in fascination from one title to the next. Some of the spells seemed quaint and archaic; others were like something out of a modern pop-psychology book. Some were just timeless.

A Charm to Cure a Sickly Child, she read. *To Make Hens Lay. For Protection Against Fire and Water. To Overcome a Bad Habit. To Cast Out Fear and Malignant Emotions. To Find Treasure. To Change Your Luck. To Turn Aside Evil.*

A Talisman For Strength caught her eye.

Take a smooth and shapely rock, and upon one face carve the rising sun and a crescent moon, horns up. Upon the reverse, the words:

Strength of stone
Be in my bone
Power of light
Sustain my fight

I could use that, Cassie thought. She continued flipping through the pages. *A Spell Against Contagious Disease. To Hold Evil Harmless. To Cause Dreams.*

And then, as if her guilty conscience had summoned it up, another spell appeared before her eyes. *For an Untrue Lover.*

Standing in the light of a full moon, take a strand of the lover's hair and tie knots in it, saying:

No peace find
No friend keep
No lover bind
No harvest reap

No repose take
No hunger feed
No thirst slake
No sorrow speed

No debt pay
No fear flee
Rue the day
You wronged me.

Cassie's pulse was fluttering in her wrists. Would anyone really put a curse like that on someone they loved, no matter how unfaithful?

She was still staring at the page when there was a movement at the door. She shut the book hastily as Diana came in, hair wrapped in a towel turban. But her eyes were drawn instantly to the gold chain Diana was dropping on the nightstand. It lay there next to a round stone with a spiral pattern in it, grey swirled with pale blue and sprinkled with quartz crystals. The chalcedony rose that Diana had given to Adam, and that Adam had given to Cassie. Now it was back where it belonged, Cassie thought, and something around her heart went numb.

'The bathroom's all yours,' said Diana. 'Here's a nightgown – or do you want a T-shirt?'

'A nightgown's fine,' Cassie said. All the time she was washing up and changing she kept seeing the key. If only Diana would leave it there...

It was still on the nightstand when she popped her head back in Diana's room. Diana was already in bed.

'Want me to shut the door?'

'No,' Diana said, reaching up to turn out the light. 'Just leave it open a bit. Good night.'

'Good night, Diana.'

But once in the guest room next door Cassie propped herself up on two pillows and lay staring at the ceiling. Strangely, it was almost peaceful, lying there and knowing that for the moment there was nothing she could do but wait. She could hear the sound of the ocean behind Diana's house, now louder, now softer.

She waited a long time, listening to the quiet sounds. She felt relaxed, until she thought about getting up – then her heart started to pound.

At last she was sure Diana must be asleep. Now, she thought. If you don't move now, you never will.

Breath held, she shifted her weight in the bed and let her legs down. The hardwood floor creaked slightly as she crossed it, and she froze each time.

Outside Diana's door, she stood straining her ears. She could hear nothing. She put her hand on the door and slowly, by infinitesimal degrees, she pushed it open.

Carefully, lungs burning because she was afraid to breathe too loud, she placed one foot inside the threshold and let her weight down on it.

Diana was a dim shape on the bed. Please don't let her

eyes be open, Cassie thought. She had the horrible fantasy that Diana was just lying there staring at her. But as she took another slow, careful step inside, and another, she could see that Diana's eyes were shut.

Oh, God, Cassie thought. I have to breathe. She opened her mouth and exhaled and inhaled silently. Her heart was shaking her and she felt dizzy.

Take tiny steps, she thought. She crept farther into the room until she was standing directly beside Diana.

On the nightstand, just a few inches from Diana's sleeping face, was the key.

Feeling as if she was moving in slow motion, Cassie put her hand out, placed it flat on the key. She didn't want to make any noise, but as she slid the necklace towards her, the chain rattled. She closed her fingers over it and held it tightly.

Now to get away. She forced herself to creep, all the time looking over her shoulder at the bed – was Diana waking up?

She reached the cabinet, and the little brass keyhole.

Fit the key in. She was fumbling; her fingers felt clumsy as sausages. For a moment she panicked, thinking, what if it isn't the right key after all? But at last she got it in and turned it.

The lock clicked.

Hot relief swept over Cassie. She'd done it. Now she had to get the skull and call Faye – and what if Faye didn't answer? What if Diana's father caught her phoning in the middle of the night, or if Diana woke up and found the skull missing...?

But as she eased the cabinet door open the world blurred and went dark before her eyes.

The hall light was shining into the cabinet. It was dim, but it was clear enough to show that all Cassie's caution had been in vain, and all her fears about getting the skull to Faye were pointless.

The cabinet was empty.

Cassie never knew how long she stood there, unable to think or move. But at last she pushed the cabinet door shut with shaking hands and locked it.

If it's not here, then *where* is it? Where? she demanded frantically of herself.

Don't think about it now. Put the key back. Or do you want her to wake up while you're standing here holding it?

The journey back to Diana's nightstand seemed to take forever, and her stomach ached as if someone were grinding a boot there. The key clinked as she replaced it on the nightstand and the chain stuck to her sweaty hand. But Diana's breathing remained soft and even.

Now get *out*, she ordered herself. She needed to be alone, to try and think. In her hurry to get away she forgot to be careful about placing her feet. A board creaked.

Just keep going, never mind, she thought. Then she heard something that stopped her heart.

A rustling from the bed. And then Diana's voice.

'Cassie?'

CHAPTER
4

'Cassie? Is that you?'

Sick dismay tingled down Cassie's nerves. Then she heard her own voice saying, as she turned, 'I – I was scared... I didn't want to bother you...'

'Oh, don't be silly. Come lie down,' Diana said sleepily, patting the bed beside her and shutting her eyes again.

It had worked. Cassie had gambled that Diana had just woken up that instant, and she'd been right. But Cassie felt as if she were reeling as she went over to the other side of the bed and got in, facing away from Diana.

'No more nightmares,' Diana murmured.

'No,' Cassie whispered. She could never get up now and call Faye, but she didn't care. She was too tired of stress, of tension, of fear. And something deep inside her was glad that she hadn't been able to go through with it tonight. She shut her eyes and listened to the roaring in her own ears until she fell asleep.

In her dream she was on a ship. The deck was lifting and dropping beneath her, and waves rose up black over the sides. Lost, lost... What was lost? The ship? Yes, but something else, too. Lost forever... never find it now...

Then the dream changed. She was sitting in a bright and sunny room. Her chair was low to the ground, its spindly wood back so uncomfortable that she had to sit up straight. Her clothes were uncomfortable too; a bonnet as close-fitting as a swimming cap, and something tight around her waist that scarcely let her breathe. On her lap was a book.

Why, it was Diana's Book of Shadows! But no, the cover was different, red leather instead of brown. As she leafed through it, she saw that the writing in the beginning was very similar, and the titles of some of the spells were the same as in Diana's.

A Charm to Cure a Sickly Child. To Make Hens Lay. For Protection Against Fire and Water. To Hold Evil Harmless.

To Hold Evil Harmless!

Her eyes moved swiftly across the words after it.

Bury the evil object in good moist loam or sand, well covered. The healing power of the Earth will battle with the poison, and if the object be not too corrupt, it will be purified.

Of course, Cassie thought. Of course.

The dream was ebbing. She could feel Diana's bed beneath her. But she could also hear a fading voice, calling a name. 'Jacinth! Are you in there? Jacinth!'

Cassie was awake.

Diana's blue curtains were incandescent with the sunlight they held back. There were cheerful pottering noises in the room. But all Cassie could think about was the dream.

She must have read that spell in Diana's Book of Shadows last night, absorbed it unconsciously as she was flipping through. But why remember it in such a weird way?

It didn't matter. The problem was solved, and Cassie

was so happy that she felt like hugging her pillow. Of course, of course! Before the skull ceremony Diana had said the skull should be buried for purification – in moist sand. Adam had found it on the island buried in *sand*. Right below Diana's back door was a whole beach of sand. Cassie could hear the ocean breaking on it this minute.

The question was, could she find the exact *place* in the sand the skull was buried?

Faye was in writing class. And she was furious.

'I waited up all night,' she hissed, grabbing Cassie by the arm. 'What happened?'

'I couldn't get it. It wasn't there.'

Faye's golden eyes narrowed and the long red-tipped fingers on Cassie's arm tightened. 'You're lying.'

'No,' Cassie said. She cast an agonised glance around and then whispered, 'I think I know where it is, but you have to give me time.'

Faye was staring at her, those strange eyes raking hers. Then she relaxed slightly and smiled. 'Of course, Cassie. All the time you need. Until Saturday.'

'That may not be long enough—'

'It'll just have to be, won't it?' Faye drawled.

'Because after that I tell Diana.' She let go and Cassie walked to her own desk. There was nothing else to do.

They had a minute of silence at the beginning of class for Mr Fogle. Cassie spent the minute staring at her entwined fingers, thinking alternately of the dark rushing thing inside the skull and Doug Henderson's tip-tilted blue-green eyes.

At lunch there was a note taped on the glass door of the back room in the cafeteria. *Outside in front*, it said. Cassie turned from it and almost ran into Adam.

He was approaching with a loaded tray, and he lifted it

to stop her from knocking it all over him.

'Whoa,' he said.

Cassie flushed. But then, as they stood facing each other, she discovered a more serious problem. Adam's smile had faded, she couldn't stop flushing, and neither of them seemed to be going anywhere.

Eyes in the cafeteria were on them. Talk about déjà vu, Cassie thought. Every time I'm in here I'm the centre of attention.

Finally, Adam made an abortive attempt to catch her elbow, stopped himself, and gestured her forward courteously. Cassie didn't know how he did it, but Adam managed to carry off courtesy like no guy she had ever known. It seemed to come naturally to him.

Girls looked up as they went by, some of them casting sideways glances at Adam. But these were different than the sideways glances Cassie had seen on the beach at Cape Cod. There, he'd been dressed in his scruffy fishing-boat clothes, and Portia's girlfriends had averted their eyes in disdain. These glances were shy, or inviting, or hopeful. Adam just tossed an unruly strand of red hair off his forehead and smiled at them.

Outside, the members of the Club were gathered on the steps. Even Nick was there. Cassie started towards them, and then a large shape bounded up and planted its front feet on her shoulders.

'Raj, get down! What are you doing?' Adam yelled.

A wet, warm tongue was lapping Cassie's face. She tried to fend the dog off, grabbing for the fur at the back of his neck, and ended it by hugging him.

'I think he's just saying "hi",' she gasped.

'He's usually so good about waiting just off campus until I get out of school. I don't know why—' Adam broke off. 'Raj, get down,' he muttered in a changed voice. '*Now!*'

he said, and snapped his fingers.

The lapping tongue withdrew, but the German shepherd stayed by Cassie's side as she walked over to the steps. She patted the dog's head.

'Raj usually hates new people,' Sean observed as Cassie and Adam sat down. 'So how come he always likes you so much?'

Cassie could feel Faye's mocking eyes on her and she shrugged uncomfortably, staring down into her lunch sack. Then something occurred to her: one of those witty comebacks she usually only thought of the next day.

'Must be my new perfume. Eau de pot roast,' she said, and Laurel and Diana giggled. Even Suzan smirked.

'All right, let's get down to business,' Diana said then. 'I brought us out here to make sure nobody's listening. Anybody have any new ideas?'

'Any one of us *could* have done it,' Melanie said quietly.

'Only *some* of us had any reason to,' Adam replied.

'Why?' said Laurel. 'I mean, just because Mr Fogle was obnoxious wasn't a reason to murder him. And quit grinning like that, Doug, unless you really did do something.'

'Maybe Fogle knew too much,' Suzan said unexpectedly. Everyone turned to her, but she went on unwrapping a Hostess cupcake without looking up.

'So?' said Deborah at last. 'What's that supposed to mean?'

'Well...' Suzan raised china-blue eyes to look around at the group. 'Fogle always got here at the crack of dawn, didn't he? And his office is right up there, isn't it?' She nodded, and Cassie followed her gaze to a window on the second floor of the red-brick building. Then Cassie looked down the hill, to the bottom where Kori had been found.

There was a pause, and then Diana said, 'Oh, my God.'

'What?' Chris demanded, looking around. Deborah scowled and Laurel blinked. Faye was chuckling.

'She's saying he might have seen Kori's murderer,' Adam said. 'And then whoever killed her, killed him to keep him from talking. But do we *know* he was here that morning?'

Cassie was now staring from the second-storey window to the chimney that rose from the school. It had been cold the morning they found Kori dead, and the principal had a fireplace in his office. Had there been smoke rising from the chimney that morning?

'You know,' she said softly to Diana, 'I think he *was* here.'

'Then that could be it,' Laurel said excitedly. 'And it would mean it couldn't have been one of us who killed him – because whoever killed him killed Kori, too. And none of us would have done *that*.'

Diana was looking vastly relieved, and there were nods around the Circle. A little voice inside Cassie was trying to say something, but she pushed it down.

Nick, however, had his lip curled. 'And who besides one of us would have been able to drop an avalanche on somebody?'

'Anybody with a stick or a crowbar,' Deborah snapped. 'Those rocks on the cliff at Devil's Cove are just piled up any old way. An outsider could've done it easy. So it's back to the question of which of them did it – if we have to ask any more.' There was a hunting light in her face, and Chris and Doug were looking eager.

'You leave Sally alone until we figure this out,' Diana said flatly.

'And Jeffrey,' Faye added throatily, with a meaningful look. Deborah glared at her, then at last dropped her eyes.

'Now that we've got *that* solved, I have a real problem to talk about,' Suzan said, brushing crumbs off the front of her sweater, an interesting process which Sean and the Hendersons watched avidly. 'Homecoming is in less than two weeks, and I haven't figured out who to ask yet. And I haven't even got any *shoes* . . .'

The meeting degenerated, and shortly after that the bell rang.

'Who are you going to ask to Homecoming?' Laurel asked Cassie that afternoon. They were driving home from school with Diana and Melanie.

'Oh . . .' Cassie was taken aback. 'I haven't thought about it. I – I've never asked a guy to a dance in my life.'

'Well, now's the time to start,' Melanie said. 'Usually the outsiders don't ask us – they're a little scared. But you can have any guy you want; just pick him and tell him to show up.'

'Just like that?'

'Yep,' Laurel said cheerfully. 'Like that. Of course, Melanie and I don't usually ask guys who're together with somebody. But Faye and Suzan . . .' She rolled her eyes. 'They *like* picking guys who're taken.'

'I've noticed,' Cassie said. There was no question about whom Diana went to dances with. 'What about Deborah?'

'Oh, Deb usually just goes stag,' said Laurel. 'She and the Hendersons hang out, playing cards and stuff in the boiler room. And Sean just goes from girl to girl to girl; none of them like him, but they're all too scared not to dance with him. You'll see it there; it's funny.'

'I probably won't see it,' Cassie said. The idea of walking up to some guy and ordering him to escort her was simply unthinkable. Impossible, even if she was a witch. She might as well tell everybody now and let them get used to it. 'I probably won't go. I don't like dances much.'

'But you *have* to go,' Laurel said, dismayed, and Diana said, 'It's the most fun – really, Cassie. Look, let's go to my house right now and talk about guys you can ask.'

'No, I've got to go straight home,' Cassie said quickly. She had to go home because she had to look for the skull. Faye's words had been ringing in the back of her mind all day, and now they drowned out Diana's voice. *All the time you need – until Saturday.* 'Please just drop me off at my house.'

In silence that was bewildered and a little hurt, Diana complied.

All that week, Cassie looked for the skull.

She looked on the beach where her initiation had been held, where stumps of candles and pools of melted wax could still be seen half buried in the sand. She looked on the beach below Diana's house, among the eelgrass and driftwood. She looked up and down the bluffs, walking on the dunes each afternoon and evening. It made sense that Diana would have marked the place somehow, but with what kind of mark? Any bit of flotsam or jetsam on the sand could be it.

As each day went by she got more and more worried. She'd been so sure she could find it; it was just a matter of *looking*. But now it seemed she'd looked at every inch of beach for miles, and all she'd found was sea wrack and a few old beer bottles.

On Saturday morning she stepped out of the front door to see a bright red car circling in the cul-de-sac a little past her grandmother's house. There was no building at the very point of the headland where the road dead-ended, but the car was circling there. As Cassie stood in the doorway, it turned and cruised slowly by her house. It was Faye's Corvette ZR1, and Faye was in it, one languid arm drooping out of the window.

As she went by Cassie, Faye raised her hand and held up one finger, its long nail gleaming even redder than the car's paint job. Then she turned and mouthed a single word at Cassie.

Sunset.

She went cruising on without a backward look. Cassie stared after her.

Cassie knew what she meant. By sunset, either Cassie brought the skull to Faye, or Faye told Diana.

I *have* to find it, Cassie thought. I don't care if I have to sift through every square inch of sand from here to the mainland. I have to *find* it.

But that day was just like the others. She crawled on her knees over the beach near the initiation site, getting sand inside her jeans in her shoes. She found nothing.

The ocean rolled and roared beside her, the smell of salt and decaying seaweed filled her nostrils. As the sun slipped farther and farther down in the west, the crescent moon over the ocean glowed brighter. Cassie was exhausted and terrified, and she was giving up hope.

Then, as the sky was darkening, she saw the ring of stones.

She'd passed by them a dozen times before. They were bonfire stones, stained black with charcoal. But what were they doing so close to the waterline? At high tide, Cassie thought, they'd be covered. She knelt beside them and touched the sand in their centre.

Moist.

With fingers that trembled slightly, she dug there. Dug deeper and deeper until her fingertips touched something hard.

She dug around it, feeling the curve of its shape, until she had loosened enough sand to lift it out. It was shockingly heavy and covered with a thin white cloth. Cassie didn't need to remove the cloth to know what it was.

She felt like hugging it.

She'd done it! She'd found the skull, and now she could take it to Faye...

The feeling of triumph died inside her. Faye. Could she really take the skull to Faye?

All the time she'd been looking for it, *finding* it hadn't been real to her. She hadn't thought further than simply getting her hands on it.

Now that she was actually holding it, now that the possibility was before her... she couldn't do it.

The thought of those hooded golden eyes examining it, of those fingers with their long red nails gripping it, made Cassie feel sick. An image flitted through her mind, of a golden-eyed falcon with its talons extended. A bird of prey.

She couldn't go through with it.

But then what about Diana? Cassie's head bent in exhaustion, in defeat. She didn't know what to do about Diana. She didn't know how to solve anything. All she knew was that she couldn't hand the skull over to Faye.

There was a throat-clearing sound behind her.

'I knew you could do it,' Faye said in her husky voice as Cassie, still on her knees, spun around to look. 'I had complete faith in you, Cassie. And now my faith is justified.'

'How did you know?' Cassie was on her feet. 'How

did you know where I was?'

Faye smiled. 'I told you I have friends who see a lot. One of them just brought me the news.'

'It doesn't matter,' Cassie said, forcibly calming herself. 'You can't have it, Faye.'

'That's where you're wrong. I *do* have it. I'm stronger than you are, Cassie,' Faye said. And as she stood there on a little dune above Cassie, tall and stunning in black trousers and a loose-knit scarlet top, Cassie knew it was true. 'I'm taking the skull now. You can run to Diana if you want, but you'll be too late.'

Cassie stared at her a long minute, breathing quickly. Then she said, 'No. I'm coming with you.'

'What?'

'I'm coming with you.' In contrast to Faye, Cassie was small. And she was dirty and dishevelled, with sand in every crease of her clothes and under her fingernails, but she was relentless. 'You said you only wanted the skull to "look at it for a while". That was the reason I agreed to get it for you. Well, now I've found it, but I'm not going to leave you alone with it. I'm going with you. I want to watch.'

Faye's black eyebrows, curved like a raven's wings, lifted higher. 'So voyeurism's your idea of fun.'

'No, it's yours – or your *friends*', rather,' Cassie said.

Faye chuckled. 'You're not such a spineless mouse after all, are you?' she said. 'All right; come. You might find it's more fun to join in than to watch, anyway.'

Faye shut the bedroom door behind Cassie. Then she went and took something out of the closet. It was a comforter, not rose-patterned like the one on the bed, but red satin.

'My spare,' Faye said, with an arch smile. 'For special occasions.' She shook it out over the bed, then went around the room lighting candles that gave off pungent, heady scents. Then she opened a velvet-lined box.

Cassie stared. Inside was a jumble of loose stones, some polished, some uncut. They were dark green and amethyst, black, sulphur-yellow, pale pink and cloudy orange.

'Find the red ones,' Faye said.

Cassie's fingers were itching to get into them anyway. She began to sort through the rainbow clutter.

'Those garnets are good,' Faye said, approving some burgundy-coloured stones. 'And carnelians, too, if they're not too orange. Now let me see: fire opal for passion, red jasper for stability. And one black onyx for surrendering to your shadow self.' She smiled strangely at Cassie, who stiffened.

Undisturbed, Faye arranged the stones in a circle on the comforter. Then she turned off the lamp and the room was lit only by the candles.

'Now,' Faye said, 'for our guest.'

Cassie thought that was an odd way to put it, and there was a sinking in her stomach as Faye opened the backpack. She'd promised herself that she would keep Faye from doing anything too terrible with the skull – but how?

'Just what are you planning to do with it?' she asked, trying to keep her voice steady.

'Just scrying,' murmured Faye, but she wasn't paying much attention to Cassie. She was gazing down as she slowly peeled the wet, sandy white cloth away to reveal the glittering dome of the crystal skull. As Cassie watched, Faye lifted the skull up to eye level, cradling it in red-tipped fingers. Reflections of the candle flames danced in the depths of the crystal.

'Ah,' said Faye. 'Hello there.' She was gazing into the empty eyesockets as if looking at a lover. She bent forward and lightly kissed the grinning quartz teeth.

Then she put the skull in the centre of the ring of gems.

Cassie swallowed. The sinking feeling was getting worse and worse; she felt sicker and sicker. 'Faye, shouldn't you have a ring of candles, too? What if—'

'Don't be silly. Nothing's going to happen. I just want to see what this fellow's all about,' Faye murmured.

Cassie didn't believe it.

'Faye . . .' She was starting to panic. This was a bad idea, this had always been a bad idea. She wasn't strong enough to stop Faye from anything. She didn't even know what Faye was *doing*.

'Faye, don't you need to prepare—'

'Be quiet,' Faye said sharply. She was hovering over the skull, gazing down into it, half reclining on the bed.

It was all happening too fast. And it wasn't safe. Cassie felt sure of that now. She could feel a darkness welling up inside the skull.

'Faye, what are you *doing* with it?'

More darkness, rising up like the sea. How could Faye be this powerful, to raise it from the skull so quickly? And all by herself, without a coven to back her up?

The star ruby at Faye's throat winked, and for the first time Cassie noticed matching gems on Faye's fingers. All these red stones – to heighten the energy of the ritual? To enhance the power of the witch – or the skull?

'Faye!'

'Shut up!' said Faye. She leaned farther over the skull, lips parted, her breath coming quickly. Cassie could almost see the darkness in the skull, swirling, rising like smoke.

Don't look at it! Don't give it any more power! the voice in her head cried. Cassie stared instead at Faye, urgently.

'Faye, whatever you're doing – it's not what you think! It's not safe!'

'Leave me *alone*!'

Swirling, rising, higher and higher. The darkness had been thin and transparent at first, but now it was thick and oily. Cassie wouldn't look at it, but she could feel it. It was almost at the top of the skull, uncoiling, wheeling.

'Faye, look out!'

The black-haired girl was directly over the skull, directly in the way of the rising dark. Cassie grabbed her, pulling at her.

But Faye was strong. Snarling something incoherent, she tried to shake Cassie off. Cassie threw one glance at the skull. It seemed to be grinning wildly at her, the smoke corkscrewing inside it.

'*Faye*,' she screamed, and wrenched at the other girl's shoulders.

They both fell backwards. At the same instant, out of the corner of her eye, Cassie saw the darkness break free.

CHAPTER
5

'**Y**ou stupid *outsider*,' Faye screeched, twisting away from Cassie. 'It was just getting started – now you've ruined everything!'

Cassie lay on her back, gasping. Then she pointed shakily, sitting up.

'That's what I ruined,' she said, her voice soft from lack of breath, and from fear. Faye looked up at the ceiling, at the dark, charred circle on the white plaster.

'It was coming right at you,' Cassie said, too unnerved to yell, or even to be angry. 'Didn't you *see* it?'

Faye just looked at her, black lashes heavy over speculative golden eyes. Then she looked at the skull.

Cassie leaned over and covered the skull with the cloth.

'What are you doing?'

'I'm taking it back,' Cassie said, still breathless. 'Diana was right. *I* was right, if I'd listened to myself. It's too dangerous to handle.'

She expected Faye to explode, possibly even to fight her. But Faye looked up at the stain on the ceiling and said musingly, 'I think it's just a matter of more protection. If we could capture that energy – channel it…'

'You're crazy,' Cassie told her bluntly. 'And,' she added, 'our deal is finished. I did what you asked: I brought you the skull. You used it and you almost got killed. So now it's over.'

Faye's lazy expression disappeared. 'Oh, no, Cassie,' she said. The hint of a smile curved her lips, but her eyes were predatory. Ruthless. 'It's only starting. Don't you see?' She began to laugh. 'You're more my captive now than ever. It's not just Adam any more – now I can tell Diana about *this*. How do you think the Princess of Purity is going to feel when she finds out her "little sister" stole the skull? And then brought it to *me* to use?' Faye laughed harder, seeming delighted. 'Oh, Cassie, you should see your face.'

Cassie felt as if she were smothering. What Faye said was true. If Diana found out that Cassie had dug up the skull – that Cassie had lied to her – that the whole story last Sunday about being too scared to go home had been a trick…

Just as it had the last time she'd stood in this room, Cassie felt her spirit, her will, draining away. She was more trapped than ever. She was lost.

'You take the skull back now,' Faye said, as if it had been entirely her idea. 'And later – well, I'll think of something else I want from you. In the meanwhile, you just keep yourself available.'

I hate you, Cassie thought with impotent rage. But Faye was ignoring Cassie completely, bending to pick up the bristling kittens, one grey and one orange, which had crawled out from under the dust ruffle. The vampire kittens, Cassie remembered distractedly – the ones with a taste for human blood. Apparently even *they* hadn't liked this business with the skull.

'What about that?' Cassie said, pointing at the dark stain on Faye's ceiling. 'Don't you feel at all responsible about letting it loose? It could be out killing somebody—'

'I doubt it,' Faye said, and shrugged negligently. 'But we'll just have to wait and see, I suppose.' She stroked the orange kitten and its fur began to lie flat again.

Cassie could only stare at her, tears rising to her eyes. She'd thought she could control Faye, but she'd been wrong. And right now the new dark energy could be doing anything, and she was helpless to stop it.

You could tell Diana, an inner voice, the core voice, whispered, but Cassie didn't even pretend to listen. She could never tell Diana now; that chance was over. Things had gone far too far with Faye.

'Cassie, are you nervous about something?' Laurel had paused with the white-handled knife in her hand.

'Me? No. Why?' Cassie said, feeling every moment as if she might jump out of her skin.

'You just seem kind of jittery.' Laurel gently snicked the knife through the base of the small witch-hazel bush. 'Now, this won't hurt a bit... you've got plenty of roots down there to grow back from...' she murmured soothingly. 'It's not about Homecoming, is it?' she asked, looking up again.

'No, no,' Cassie said. She hadn't even thought about Homecoming this week. She couldn't think about anything except the dark energy. Each day she expected to hear about some new disaster.

But today was Thursday, and nothing had happened yet. No avalanches, no bodies found, nobody even missing. Oh, if only she could let herself believe that nothing *would* happen. The energy she and Faye had released had been small – she felt sure of that now – and maybe it had just evaporated. Cassie felt a delicious peace steal through her at the thought.

Laurel had moved over to a clump of thyme. 'It's not too late to change your mind about coming,' she said. 'And I wish you would. Dancing is very witchy – and it's *Nature*. It's like one of our incantations:

Man to woman, woman to man,
Ever since the world began.
Heart to heart, and hand to hand,
Ever since the world began.'

She added, looking up at Cassie thoughtfully, 'Wasn't there some guy you met over the summer that you were interested in? We could do a spell to pull him here—'

'No!' said Cassie. 'I mean, I really don't want to go to Homecoming, Laurel. I just – I wouldn't be comfortable.'

'Thank you,' Laurel said. For an instant Cassie thought it was addressed to her, but Laurel was now talking to the thyme. 'I'm sorry I needed part of the root, too, but I brought this to help you grow back,' she went on, tucking a pink crystal into the soil. 'That reminds me, have you found your working crystal yet?' she said to Cassie.

'No,' Cassie said. She thought of the jumble of crystals in Faye's box. She'd liked handling them, but none of them had stood out as *hers*, as the one she needed as a witch.

'Don't worry, you will,' Laurel assured her. 'It'll just turn up one day, and you'll *know*.' She stood up with the thyme plant in her hand. 'All right, let's go inside and I'll show you how to make an infusion. Nobody should fool around with herbs unless they know exactly what they're doing. And if you change your mind about Homecoming, thyme soup helps overcome shyness.'

Cassie cast a look around the great wide world, as she always did now, checking for the dark energy, then she followed Laurel.

The next day, in American history class, Diana sneezed.

Ms Lanning stopped talking and said, 'Bless you' absently. Cassie scarcely noticed it at the time. But then, at the end of class, Diana sneezed again, and kept sneezing. Cassie looked at her. Diana's eyes were pink and watery. Her nose was getting pink, too, as she rubbed it with a Kleenex.

That night, instead of going to the Homecoming game, Diana stayed at home in bed. Cassie, who knew nothing about football and was only yelling when everybody else yelled, worried about her in some back corner of her mind. It *couldn't* have anything to do with the dark energy, could it?

'Applaud,' Laurel said, nudging her. 'For the Homecoming Queen. Sally really looks almost pretty, doesn't she?'

'I guess,' Cassie said, applauding mechanically. 'Laurel, how come one of *us* isn't Homecoming Queen? Instead of an outsider?'

'Diana didn't want to be,' Laurel said succinctly. 'And Deb and the others think it's too goody-goody. But from the way Jeffrey Lovejoy's looking at Sally, I'd say Faye made a mistake. She told Jeff to come to the dance with her, but he'd already asked Sally and he's a fighter. It'll be interesting to see who gets him.'

'You can tell me all about it,' Cassie said. 'I saw the last fight between Faye and Sally; this one I can miss.'

But it didn't turn out that way.

* * *

Cassie was in the herb garden when the phone call came. She had to go through the kitchen and into the new wing of the house to get to the telephone.

'Hello, Cassie?' The voice was so muted and stuffed-up it was almost unrecognisable. 'It's Diana.'

Fear crinkled up Cassie's backbone. The dark energy... 'Oh, Diana, are you *all right*?'

There was a burst of muffled laughter. 'Don't panic. I'm not dying. It's just a bad cold.'

'You sound awful.'

'I know. I'm completely miserable, and I can't go to the dance tonight, and I called to ask you a favour.'

Cassie froze with a sudden intuition. Her mouth opened, and then shut again silently. But Diana was going on.

'Jeffrey called Faye to tell her he's going with Sally after all, and Faye is *livid*. So when she heard I was sick, she called to say she would go with Adam, because she knew I would want him to go even if I couldn't. And I do; I don't want him to miss it just because of me. So I told her she couldn't because I'd already asked you to go with him.'

'*Why?*' Cassie blurted, and then thought, Ask a stupid question...

'Because Faye is on the prowl,' Diana said patiently. 'And she likes Adam, and the mood she's in tonight, she'll try anything. That's the one thing I couldn't stand, Cassie, for her to get her hands on Adam. I just couldn't.'

Cassie looked around for something to sit down on.

'But Diana... I don't even have a dress. I'm all *muddy*...'

'You can go over to Suzan's. All the other girls are there. They'll take care of you.'

'But...' Cassie shut her eyes. 'Diana, you just don't understand. I *can't*. I—'

'Oh, Cassie, I know it's a lot to ask. But I don't know who else to turn to. And if Faye goes after Adam…'

It was the first time Cassie had ever heard such a forlorn note in Diana's voice. She sounded on the verge of tears. Cassie pressed a hand to her forehead. 'Okay. Okay, I'll do it. But—'

'Thank you, Cassie! Now go right to Suzan's – I've talked with her and Laurel and Melanie. They'll fix you up. I'm going to call Adam and tell him.'

And *that*, Cassie thought helplessly, was one conversation she thought she could miss too.

Maybe Adam would get them out of it somehow, she thought as she drove the Rabbit up Suzan's driveway. But she doubted it. When Diana made her mind up about something, she was immovable.

Suzan's house had columns. Cassie's mother said it was bad Greek Revival, but Cassie secretly thought it was impressive. The inside was imposing too, and Suzan's bedroom was in a class by itself.

It was all the colours of the sea: sand, shell, pearl, periwinkle. The headboard on Suzan's bed was shaped like a giant scalloped shell. But what caught Cassie's eye were the mirrors – she'd never seen so many mirrors in one place.

'Cassie!' Laurel burst in just behind her, making Cassie turn in surprise. 'I've got it!' Laurel announced triumphantly to the other girls, holding up a plastic-draped hanger. Inside Cassie glimpsed some pale, gleaming material.

'It's a dress Granny Quincey got me this summer – but I haven't worn it and I never will. It's not my style, but it'll be perfect on you, Cassie.'

'Oh, God,' was all Cassie could think of to say. She'd changed her mind; she couldn't do this after all.

'Laurel – thanks – but I might ruin it . . .'

'Don't let her talk,' Melanie ordered from the other side of the room. 'Stick her in a bath; she needs one.'

'That way,' Suzan said, gesturing with splayed fingers. 'I can't do anything until my nails are dry, but all the stuff's in there.'

'Beauty bath mix,' Laurel gloated, examining the assortment of bottles on the gilt shelves in Suzan's bathroom. There were all kinds of bottles, some with wide necks and some with long narrow necks, green and deep glowing blue. 'Here, this is great: thyme, mint, rosemary, and lavender. It smells wonderful, and it's tranquillising, too.' She scattered bright-coloured dried flowers in the steaming water. 'Now get in and scrub. Oh, *this* is good,' she went on, sniffing at another bottle. 'Chamomile hair rinse – it brightens hair, brings out the highlights. Use it!'

Cassie obeyed dazedly. She felt as if she'd just been inducted into boot camp.

When she got back to the bedroom, Melanie directed her to sit down and hold a hot washcloth on her face. 'It's "a fragrant resin redolent with the mysterious virtues of tropical balms",' Melanie said, reading from a Book of Shadows. 'It "renders the complexion clear and brilliant" – and it really does, too. So hold this on your face while I do your hair.'

'Melanie's wonderful with hair,' Laurel volunteered as Cassie gamely buried her face in the washcloth.

'Yes, but I'm not going to give her a *do*,' Melanie said critically. 'I'm just making it soft and natural, waving back from her face. Plug in those hot rollers, Suzan.'

While Melanie worked, Cassie could hear Laurel and Deborah arguing in the depths of Suzan's walk-in closet.

'Suzan,' Laurel shouted. 'I never saw so many pairs of shoes in my life. What do you *do* with them all?'

'I don't know. I just like buying them. Which is lucky for people who want to borrow them,' Suzan called back.

'Now, let's get you into the dress,' Melanie said, some time later. 'No, don't look, not yet. Come over to the vanity and Suzan will do your make-up.'

Feebly, Cassie tried to protest as Melanie whipped a towel around her neck. 'That's all right. I can do it myself—'

'No, you *want* Suzan to do it,' Laurel said, emerging from the closet. 'I promise, Cassie; just wait and see.'

'But I don't wear much make-up – I won't look like me...'

'Yes, you will. You'll look more like you.'

'Well, somebody decide, for heaven's sake,' Suzan said, standing by in a kimono and waving a powder puff impatiently. 'I've got myself to do, too, you know.'

Cassie yielded and sat on a stool, facing Suzan. 'Hm,' said Suzan, turning Cassie's face this way and that. 'Hmm.'

The next half hour was filled with bewildering instructions. 'Look up,' Suzan commanded, wielding a brown eyeliner pencil. 'Look down. See, this will give you doe eyes,' she went on, 'and nobody will even be able to tell you're wearing anything. Now a little almond shadow...' She dipped a small brush in powder and blew off the excess. 'Now just a little midnight blue in the crease to make you look mysterious...'

Eyes shut, Cassie relaxed. This was fun. She felt even more decadent and pampered when Laurel said, 'I'll take care of your nails.'

'What are you using?' Cassie asked trustingly.

'Witch-hazel infusion and Chanel Flamme Rose polish,' Laurel replied, and they both giggled.

'Don't jolt my hand,' Suzan said crossly. 'Now suck in your cheeks like a fish. Stop laughing. You've got great cheekbones, I'm just going to bring them out a little. Now go like this; I'm going to put Roseglow on your lips.'

When at last she sat back to survey her work, the other girls gathered around, even Deborah.

'And finally,' Suzan said, 'just a *drop* of magnet perfume here, and here, and here.' She touched the hollow of Cassie's throat, her earlobes, and her wrists with something that smelled wild and exotic and wonderful.

'What is it?' Cassie asked.

'Mignonette, tuberose, and ylang-ylang,' Suzan said. 'It makes you irresistible. And I should know.'

Alarm lanced through Cassie suddenly, but before she had time to think, Laurel was turning her, loosening the towel around her neck. 'Wait, don't look until you've got your shoes on... Now!' Laurel said jubilantly. 'Look at that!'

Cassie opened her eyes and drew in her breath. Then, scarcely knowing what she was doing, she moved closer to the full-length mirror, to the lovely stranger reflected there. She could hardly resist reaching out to touch the glass with her fingertips.

The girl in the mirror had fine, light-brown hair waving softly back from her face. The highlights shimmered when Cassie moved her head, so it must be her – but it *couldn't* be, Cassie thought. *Her* eyes didn't have that dreamy, mysterious aura. Her skin didn't have that dewy glow, and she didn't blush that way, to bring out her cheekbones. And her lips definitely didn't have that breathless ready-to-be-kissed look.

'It's the lipstick,' Suzan explained. 'Don't smudge it.'

'It's possible,' said Melanie, 'that you've gone too far, Suzan.'

'Do you like the dress?' Laurel asked. 'It's the perfect length, just short enough, but still romantic.'

The girl in the mirror, the one with the delicate bones and the swan's neck, turned from side to side. The dress was silvery and shimmering, like yards of starlight, and it made Cassie feel like a princess. Suzan's shoes, appropriately, looked like glass slippers.

'Oh, thank you!' Cassie said, whirling to look at the other girls. 'I mean – I don't know how to say thank you. I mean – I finally look like a witch!'

They burst into laughter, except Deborah, who threw a disgusted glance at the ceiling. Cassie hugged Laurel, and then, impulsively, hugged Suzan, too.

'Well, you are a witch,' Suzan said reasonably. 'I'll show you how to do it yourself if you want.'

Cassie felt something like humility. She'd thought Suzan was just an airhead, but it wasn't true. Suzan loved beauty and was generous about sharing it with other people. Cassie smiled into the china-blue eyes and felt as if she'd unexpectedly made a new friend.

'Wait, we almost forgot!' Melanie said. 'You can't go to a dance without a single crystal to your name.' She rummaged in her canvas bag, and then said, 'Here, this will be perfect; it was my great-grandmother's.' She held up a necklace: a thin chain with a teardrop of clear quartz. Cassie took it lovingly and fastened it around her neck, admiring the way it lay in the hollow of her throat. Then she hugged Melanie, too.

From downstairs a doorbell chimed faintly, and, closer, a male voice shouted, 'For crying out loud! Are you going to get that, Suzan?'

'It's one of the guys!' Suzan said, thrown into a tizzy. 'And we're not ready. You're the only one dressed, Cassie; run and get it before Dad has a fit.'

'Hello, Mr Whittier; sorry, Mr Whittier,' Cassie gasped as she hurried downstairs. It wasn't until she was at the door that she thought, Oh, please, please, please, let it be any one of the others. Don't let it be *him*. Please.

Adam was standing there when she opened the door.

He was wearing a wry smile, appropriate for a guy who's been commandeered at the last minute into escorting his girl's best friend to a dance. The smile disappeared instantly when he saw Cassie.

For a long moment he simply stared at her. Her own elated smile faded, and they stood gazing at each other.

Adam swallowed hard, started to say something, then gave up and stood silent again.

Cassie was hearing Suzan's words: *It'll make you irresistible*. Oh, what had she done?

'We'll call it off,' she said, and her voice was as soft as when she'd told Faye about the dark energy. 'We'll tell Diana I got sick too—'

'We can't,' he said, equally soft, but very intense. 'Nobody would believe it, and besides...' The wry smile made an attempt at reappearing. 'It would be a shame for you to miss Homecoming. You look...' He paused. 'Nice.'

'So do you,' Cassie said, and tried to come up with an ironic smile of her own. She had the feeling it turned out wobbly.

Cassie took another breath, but at that moment she heard a voice from the second floor.

'Here,' Laurel said, leaning over the balustrade to toss Cassie a tiny beaded purse. 'Get her to the dance, Adam; that way she'll have a chance at some guys who're available.' And, from the bedroom, Suzan called, 'But not too many, Cassie – leave some for us!'

'I'll try to fend a few of them off,' Adam called back, and Cassie felt her racing pulse calm a little. They had their parts down now. It was like acting in a play, and all Cassie had to do was remember her role. She felt sure Adam could handle his... well, almost sure. Something in his sea-dark eyes sent thin chills up her spine.

'Let's go,' Adam said, and Cassie took a deep breath and stepped with him outside into the night.

CHAPTER

6

They drove to the school. Despite the tension between them, the night seemed clear and cool and filled with magic, and the gym was transformed. It was so big that it seemed part of the night, and the twinkling lights woven around the pipes and girders overhead were like stars.

Cassie looked around for any other members of the Circle. She didn't see any. What she saw were outsiders looking in surprise at her and Adam. And in the boys' eyes there was something more than surprise, something Cassie wasn't at all used to. It was the kind of open-mouthed stare guys turned on Diana when Diana was looking particularly beautiful.

A sudden warmth and a glow that had nothing to do with Suzan's artistry swept over Cassie. She knew she was blushing. She felt conspicuous and overwhelmed – and at the same time thrilled and excited. But through the wild mixture of emotions, one thing remained clear and diamond-bright within her. She was here to play a part and to keep her oath to be true to Diana. That was what mattered, and she clung to it.

But she couldn't just stand here with everyone staring

at her any longer; it was too embarrassing. She turned to Adam.

It was an awkward moment. They couldn't sit down together in some dark corner – that would never do. Then Adam gave a crooked smile and said, 'Want to dance?'

Relieved, Cassie nodded, and they went out onto the dance floor. In a matter of seconds they were surrounded by other people.

And then the music started, soft and sweet.

They stared at each other, helplessly, in dismay. They were in the middle of the dance floor; to get out they would have to forge their way through the crowd. Cassie looked into Adam's eyes and saw he was as confused as she was.

Then Adam said under his breath, 'We'd better not be too conspicuous,' and he took her in his arms.

Cassie shut her eyes. She was trembling, and she didn't know what to do.

Slowly, almost as if compelled, Adam laid his cheek against her hair.

I won't think about anything, I won't think at all, Cassie told herself. I won't *feel*... But that was impossible. She couldn't help feeling. It was dark as twilight and Adam was holding her and she could smell his scent of autumn leaves and ocean wind.

Dancing is a very witchy thing – oh, Laurel had been right. Cassie could imagine witches in ages past dancing under the stars to wild sweet music, and then lying down on the soft green grass.

Maybe among Cassie's ancestors there had been some witch-girl who had danced like this in a moonlit glade. Maybe she had danced by herself until she noticed a shadow among the trees and heard the panpipes. And then maybe she and the forest god had danced together, while the moon shone silver all around them...

Cassie could feel the warmth, the course of life, in Adam's arms. The silver cord, she thought. The mysterious, invisible bond that had connected her to Adam from the beginning... just now she could feel it again. It joined them heart to heart, it was drawing them irresistibly together.

The music stopped. Adam moved back just slightly and she looked up at him, cheek and neck tingling with the loss of his warmth. His eyes were strange, darkness just edged with silver like a new moon. Slowly, he bent down so that his lips were barely touching hers – and stayed there. They stood that way for what seemed like an eternity and then Cassie turned her head away.

It wasn't a kiss, she thought as they moved out through the crowd. It didn't count. But there was no way that they could dance together again and they both knew it. Cassie's knees were shaking.

Find some people to join – fast, she thought. She looked around desperately. And to her vast relief she glimpsed a sleek auburn crop and a head of long, light-brown hair interwoven with tiny flowers. It was Melanie and Laurel, in animated conversation with two outsider boys. If they'd seen what happened on the dance floor a minute ago...

But Laurel swung around at Adam's 'hello' and said, 'Oh, there you are!' and Melanie's smile was quite normal. Cassie was grateful to talk with them while the boys talked about football. Her lightheartedness, inspired by the magic of the dance, began to return.

'There's Deborah. She always gets one dance in before heading off to the boiler room with the Hendersons,' Laurel murmured, smiling mischievously.

'What do they *do* there?' Cassie asked as she followed Laurel's gaze. Deborah was wearing a black micro-mini and a biker's hat decorated with a gold link bracelet. Her hair was mostly in her eyes. She looked great.

'Play cards and drink. But no, not what you're thinking. None of the guys would dare try anything with Deb – she can outwrestle them all. They're just in awe of her.'

Cassie smiled, then she spotted someone else, and her smile faded. 'Speaking of awesome . . .' she said softly.

Faye had on a flame-coloured dress, sexy and elegant, cut in her usual knockout style. Her hair was black and glossy, hanging untamed down her back. She was like some exotic creature that had wandered on to campus by accident.

Faye didn't see the three girls scrutinising her. Her entire attention seemed to be focussed on Nick.

Cassie was surprised Nick was even here; he wasn't the type to go to dances. He was standing by a blonde outsider girl who looked frankly spooked. As Cassie watched, Faye made her way over to him and placed a hand with red-tipped fingers on his arm.

Nick glanced down at the hand and stiffened. He threw a cold glance over his shoulder at Faye. Then, deliberately, he shrugged her hand off, bending over the little blonde, whose eyes widened. Throughout the whole incident his face remained as wintry and remote as ever.

'Uh-oh,' Laurel whispered. 'Faye's trying to hedge her bets, but Nick isn't cooperating.'

'It's her own fault,' Melanie said. 'She kept after Jeffrey until the last minute.'

'I think she's still after him now,' said Cassie.

Jeffrey was just coming off the dance floor with Sally. His expression was the exact opposite of wintry; he looked as if he was having a wonderful time, flashing his lady-killing smile in all directions. Proud, Cassie thought, to have the Homecoming Queen on his arm. But it was funny, she thought the next minute, how quickly people stopped smiling when they ran into Faye.

Jeffrey tried to hustle Sally back onto the dance floor, but Faye moved as quickly as a stalking panther and cut them off. Then she and Sally stood on either side of Jeff, like a big, glossy black dog and a little rust-coloured terrier fighting over a tall, slim bone.

'That's stupid,' Laurel said. 'Faye could have almost any guy here, but she only wants the ones who're a challenge.'

'Well, it's not our problem,' Melanie said sensibly. She turned to the outsider boy beside her and smiled, and they went together onto the dance floor. Laurel looked nettled for an instant, then smiled, shrugged at Cassie, and collected her own partner.

Cassie watched them go with a sinking heart.

She'd been able to block out Adam's presence for the last few minutes, but here they were alone again. Determinedly, she looked around for some distraction. There was Jeffrey – he was in real trouble now. The music had started, Faye was smiling a lazy, dangerous smile at him, and Sally was bristling and looking daggers. The three of them were standing in a perfect triangle, nobody moving. Cassie didn't see how Jeffrey was going to get out of it.

Then he looked up in her direction.

His reaction was startling. His eyes widened. He blinked. He stared at her as if he had never seen a girl before. Then he stepped away from Faye and Sally as if he'd forgotten their existence.

Cassie was dismayed, confused – but flattered. One thing – it certainly got her out of her present dilemma with Adam. When she turned and looked into Adam's eyes, she saw he understood, without even nodding.

Jeffrey was holding out his hand to her. She took it and let him lead her onto the dance floor. She cast one glance back at Adam and saw that his expression was a paradox: acceptance mixed with something darker, more disturbing.

It was another slow dance. Cassie held herself at a decent distance from Jeffrey, staring uncertainly down at his shoes. They were dark brown loafers with little tassels, the left one slightly scuffed. When she finally looked up at his face, her awkwardness vanished. That smile was not only blinding but openly admiring.

When we first met he was trying to impress me, Cassie thought dizzily. Now *he*'s impressed. She could see the appreciation in his eyes, feel it in the way he held her.

'We make a good couple,' he said.

She laughed. Trust Jeffrey to compliment himself in complimenting her. 'Thank you. I hope Sally isn't mad.'

'It's not Sally I'm worried about. It's *her*.'

'Faye. I know.' She wished she had some advice for him. But nobody knew how to deal with Faye.

'Maybe you'd better be worried too. What's Diana going to say when she finds out you were here with Adam?'

'Diana *asked* me to come with him, because she was sick,' Cassie said, flaring up in spite of herself. 'I didn't even want to, and—'

'Hey. Hey. I was just teasing. Everybody knows Di and her prince consort are practically married. Although maybe she wouldn't have asked you if she'd known how beautiful you were going to look.'

He was still teasing, but Cassie didn't like it. She looked around the dance floor and saw Laurel, who winked over her partner's shoulder. Suzan was dancing, too, very close with a muscular boy, her red-gold hair shining in the gloom.

And then it was over. Cassie looked up at Jeffrey and said, 'Good luck with Faye,' which was the best she could offer him. He flashed the smile again.

'I can handle it,' he said confidently. 'Don't you want to dance again? No? Are you sure?'

'Thanks, but I'd better get back,' Cassie murmured, worried about the way he was looking at her. She managed to escape his restraining hand and started towards the sidelines, but before she could get there another boy asked her to dance.

She couldn't see Adam anywhere. Maybe he was off enjoying himself – she hoped so. She said 'yes' to the boy.

It didn't stop with him. All sorts of guys, seniors and juniors, athletes and class officers, were coming up to her. She saw boys' eyes wander from their own dates to look at her as she danced.

I didn't know dances were like this. I didn't know *anything* was like this, she thought. For the moment she was entirely swept up in the magic of the night, and she pushed all troublesome reflection away. She let the music take her and let herself just be for a while.

Then she saw Sally's face on the sidelines.

Jeffrey wasn't with her. Cassie hadn't seen Jeffrey in a while. But Sally was focussed on Cassie specifically, and her expression was venomous.

When that dance was over, Cassie evaded the next boy who tried to intercept her, and headed for Laurel. Laurel greeted her with glee.

'You're the belle of the ball,' she said excitedly, tucking her arm through Cassie's and patting Cassie's hand. 'Sally's furious. Faye's furious. *Everybody's* furious.'

'It's the magnet perfume. I think Suzan used too much.'

'Don't be silly. It's you. You're a perfect little – gazelle. No, a little white unicorn, one of a kind. I think even Adam has noticed.'

Cassie went still. 'Oh, I doubt that,' she said lightly. 'He's just being polite. You know Adam.'

'Yes,' said Laurel. 'Sir Adam the Chivalrous. He turned around and asked Sally to dance after you left with Jeffrey, and Sally almost decked him.'

Cassie smiled, but her heart was still pounding. She and Adam had promised not to betray their feelings for each other, not by word or look or deed – but they were making a horrible mess of things tonight on all fronts. Now she was afraid to look for Adam, and she didn't want to dance any more. She didn't want to be the belle of the ball; she didn't want every girl here to be furious with her. She wanted to go to Diana.

Suzan arrived, her extraordinary chest heaving slightly in her low-cut dress. She directed an arch smile at Cassie.

'I told you I knew what I was talking about,' she said. 'Having a good time?'

'Wonderful,' Cassie said, digging her nails in one palm. She opened her mouth to say something else, but just then she glimpsed Sean making his way towards her. His face was eager, his usually slinking step purposeful.

'I should have warned you,' Laurel said in an undertone. 'Sean's been chasing you all night, but some other guy always got there first.'

'If he *does* catch you he'll be all over you like a rash,' Suzan added pleasantly, rummaging in her purse. 'Oh, damn, I gave my lipstick to Deborah. Where *is* she?'

'Hi there,' Sean said, reaching them. His small black eyes slid over Cassie. 'So you're free at last.'

'Not really,' Cassie blurted. 'I have to – go find Deborah for Suzan.' What she had to do was get away from all this for a while. 'I know where she is; I'll be right back,' she continued to the startled Suzan and Laurel.

'I'll come along,' Sean began instantly, and Laurel opened her mouth, but Cassie waved at both of them in dismissal.

'No, no – I'll go by myself. It won't take a minute,' she said. And then she was away from them, plunging through the crowd towards the double doors.

She knew where the boiler room was, or at least where the door that led to it was. She'd never actually been inside. By the time she reached C-wing she'd left the music of the dance far behind.

The door marked CUSTODIAN'S OFFICE opened onto a long narrow room with unidentifiable machinery all around. Generators were humming, drowning out any other noise. It was cool and dank... spooky, Cassie thought. There were NO SMOKING signs on the walls and it smelled of oil and gas.

A stairway descended into the school basement. Cassie slowly went down the steps, gripping the smooth metal handrail. God, it's like going down into a tomb, she thought. Who would want to spend their time here instead of in the light and music up in the gym?

The boiler room itself smelled of machine oil and beer. It wasn't just cool; it was *cold*. And it was silent, except for the steady dripping of water somewhere.

A terrible place, Cassie thought shakily. All around her were machines with giant dials, and overhead there were huge pipes of all kinds. It was like being in the bowels of a ship. And it was deserted.

'Hello? Deborah?'

No answer.

'Debby? Chris? It's Cassie.'

Maybe they couldn't hear her. There was another room behind the boiler room; she could glimpse it through an archway beyond the machines.

She edged towards it, worried about getting oil on Laurel's pristine dress. She looked through the archway and hesitated, gripped by a strange apprehension.

Drip. Drip.

'Is anybody there?'

A large machine was blocking her way. Uneasily, she poked her head around it.

At first she thought the room was empty, but then, at eye level, she saw something. Something wrong. And in that instant her throat closed and her mind fragmented, single thoughts flashing across it like explosions from a flashbulb.

Swinging feet.

Swinging feet where feet shouldn't be. Somebody walking on air. Flying like a witch. Only, the feet weren't flying. They were swinging, back and forth, in two dark brown loafers. Two dark brown loafers with little tassels.

Cassie looked up at the face.

The relentless dripping of water went on. The smell of oil and stale alcohol nauseated her.

Can't scream. Can't do anything but gasp.

Drip and swing.

That face, that horrible blue face. No more lady-killer smile. I have to do something to help him, but how can I help? Nobody's neck bends that way when they're alive.

Every horrible detail was so clear. The fraying rope. The

swinging shadow on the cinder-block wall. The machinery with its dials and switches. And the awful stillness.

Drip. Drip.

Swinging like a pendulum.

Hands covering her mouth, Cassie began to sob.

She backed away, trying not to see the curly brown hair on the head that was lolling sideways. He couldn't be dead when she'd just danced with him. He'd just had his arms around her, he'd flashed her that cocksure smile. And now—

She stepped back and hands fell on her shoulders.

She did try to scream then, but her throat was paralysed. Her vision went dark.

'Steady. Steady. Hang on there.'

It was Nick.

'Breathe slower. Put your head down.'

'Nine-one-one,' she gasped, and then, clearly and distinctly so that he would understand, 'Call nine-one-one, Nick. Jeffrey—'

He cast a hard glance at the swinging feet. 'He doesn't need a doctor. Do you?'

'I—' She was hanging on to his hand. 'I came down to get Deborah.'

'She's in the old science building. They got busted here.'

'And I saw him – Jeffrey—'

Nick's arm was comforting, solid. 'I get the picture,' he said. 'Do you want to sit down?'

'I can't. It's Laurel's dress.' She was completely irrational, she realised. She tried desperately to get a grip on herself. 'Nick, please let me go. I have to call an ambulance.'

'Cassie.' She couldn't remember him ever saying her name before, but now he was holding her shoulders and looking her directly in the face. 'No ambulance is going to do him any good. You got that? Now just calm down.'

Cassie stared into his polished-mahogany eyes, then slowly nodded. The gasping was easing up. She was grateful for his arm around her, although some part of her mind was standing back in disbelief – *Nick* was comforting her? Nick, who hated girls and was coldly polite to them at best?

'What's going on here?'

Cassie spun to see Adam in the archway. But when she tried to speak, her throat closed completely and hot tears flooded her eyes.

Nick said, 'She's a little upset. She just found Jeffrey Lovejoy hanging from a pipe.'

'*What?*' Adam moved swiftly to look around the machine. He came back looking grim and alert, his eyes glinting silver as they always did in times of trouble.

'How much do you know about this?' he asked Nick crisply.

'I came down to get something I left,' Nick said, equally short. 'I found *her* about ready to keel over. And that's all.'

Adam's expression had softened slightly. 'Are you okay?' he said to Cassie. 'I've been looking everywhere for you. I knew *something* was wrong, but I didn't know what. Then Suzan said you'd gone to look for Deborah, but that you were looking in the wrong place.' As if it were the most natural thing in the world, he reached out to take her from Nick – and Nick resisted. For a moment there was tension between the two boys and Cassie looked from one to the other with dawning surprise and alarm.

She moved away from both. 'I'm all right,' she said. And, strangely, saying so made it almost true. It was partly necessity and partly something else – her witch senses were telling her something. She had a feeling of malice, of evil. Of darkness.

'The dark energy,' she whispered.

Adam looked more keen and alert. 'You think—?'

'*Yes,*' she said. 'Yes, I do. But if only we could tell for sure...' Her mind was racing. Jeffrey. Jeffrey's body swinging like a pendulum. *'Usually we use clear quartz as a pendulum...'*

She snatched Melanie's necklace off and held it up, looking at the teardrop of quartz crystal.

'If the dark energy *was* here, maybe we can trace it,' she said, fired with the idea. 'See where it came from – or where it went. If you guys will help.'

Nick was looking sceptical, but Adam cut in before he could speak. 'Of course we'll help. But it's dangerous; we've got to be careful.' His fingers gripped her arm reassuringly.

'Then – we have to go back in there,' Cassie said, and before she could change her mind she moved, darting into the far room where the feet still swung. Nick and Adam were close behind her. Without letting herself think, she held the crystal up high, watching it shimmer in the light.

At first it just spun in circles. But then it began to seesaw violently, pointing out a direction.

CHAPTER
7

Cassie followed the motion of the crystal. It was pointing upstairs, she decided – the opposite direction led into a wall.

'We'd better get out in the open, anyway,' Adam said. 'Otherwise we might not be able to follow it.'

Cassie nodded. She and Adam were speaking quickly, tensely – but calmly. Their violent agitation was held just under the surface, kept down by sheer willpower. Having something to *do* was what made the difference, she thought as they climbed the stairs. She couldn't afford to have hysterics now; she had to keep her mind clear to trace Jeffrey's killer.

In the hallway outside the custodian's office they ran into Deborah and the Henderson brothers.

'Adam, dude, what's goin' on?' Chris said. Cassie saw that he'd been drinking. 'We were just comin' down for a little liquid refreshment, you know—'

'Not down there,' Adam said shortly. He looked at Doug, who seemed less inebriated. 'Go get Melanie,' he said, 'and tell her to call the police. Jeffrey Lovejoy's been murdered.'

'Are you serious?' Deborah demanded. The fierce light was in her face again. 'All right!'

'*Don't*,' said Cassie before she could stop herself. 'You haven't seen him. It's terrible – and it's nothing to joke about.'

Adam's arm shot out as Deborah started towards her. 'Why don't you help us instead of picking fights with our side? We're trying to trace the dark energy that killed him.'

'The dark energy,' Deborah repeated scornfully.

Cassie took a quick breath, but Nick was speaking. 'I think it's garbage too,' he said calmly. 'But if it *wasn't* the dark energy, that means a *person* did it – like somebody who had a grudge against Jeffrey.' He stared at Deborah, his eyes hard.

Deborah stared back arrogantly. Cassie looked at her as she stood there in her short black tank dress – more like a sleeveless top than a dress – and her suede boots. Deborah was belligerent, antagonistic, hostile – and strong. For the first time in a long while Cassie noticed the crescent-moon tattoo on Deborah's collarbone.

'Why *don't* you help us, Deborah?' she said. 'This crystal is picking something up – or it was before we all started talking. Help us find what it's tracing.' And then she added, inspired by some instinct below the level of consciousness, 'Of course, it's probably dangerous—'

'So what? You think I'm scared?' Deborah demanded. 'All right, I'm coming. You guys get out of here,' she told the Hendersons.

Somewhat to Cassie's surprise, Chris and Doug did, presumably going off to tell Melanie.

'All right,' Cassie said, holding the crystal up again. She was afraid that it wouldn't do anything now that their concentration had been broken. And at first it simply hung at the end of the chain, swaying very slightly. But then, as the four of them stared at it, the swaying slowly became more pronounced. Cassie held her breath, trying to keep her hand from trembling. She didn't want to influence the crystal in any way.

It was definitely swinging now. In towards the boiler room and out towards the front of the school.

'Due east,' Adam said in a low voice.

Holding the crystal high in her left hand, Cassie followed the direction of the swing, down the hallway.

Outside, the moon was almost full, high in the sky, dropping west behind them.

'The Blood Moon,' Adam said quietly. Cassie remembered Diana saying that witches counted their year by moons, not months. The name of this one was hideously appropriate, but she didn't look back at it again. She was focussing on the crystal.

At first they walked through town, with closed stores and empty buildings on either side of them. Nothing stayed open past midnight in New Salem. Then the stores became less frequent, and there were a few clustered houses. Finally they were walking down a road which got lonelier and lonelier with every step, and all that surrounded them were the night noises.

There was no human habitation out here, but the moon was bright enough to see by. Their shadows stretched in front of them as they went. The air was cold, and Cassie shivered without taking her eyes off the crystal.

She felt something slip over her shoulders. Adam's jacket. She glanced at him gratefully, then quickly looked at the crystal again; if she faltered in her concentration it seemed to falter too, losing decisiveness and slowing almost to a random bobbing. It never swung as vigorously as the peridot had done for Diana – but then, Cassie *wasn't* Diana, and she didn't have a nearly-full coven to back her.

Behind her, she heard Adam say sharply, 'Nick?' And then Deborah's derisive snort, 'I wouldn't take it, anyway. I never get cold.'

They were on a narrow dirt road now, still heading east. Suddenly Cassie had a terrible thought.

Oh, my God – *Faye's house*. That's where we set it loose and that's where we're going. We're going to trace this stuff all the way back to Faye's bedroom... and then what?

The coldness that went through her now was deeper and more numbing than the night wind. If the dark energy that had exploded through Faye's ceiling had killed Jeffrey, Cassie was as guilty as Faye was. She was a murderer.

Then stop tracing it, a thin voice inside her whispered. You're controlling the crystal; give it a twirl in the wrong direction.

But she didn't. She kept her eyes on the quartz teardrop, which seemed to shine with a milky light in the darkness, and she let it swing the way it wanted to.

If the truth comes out, it comes out, she told herself coldly. And if she was a murderer, she deserved to be caught. She was going to follow this trail wherever it led.

But it didn't seem to be leading to Crowhaven Road. They were still going east, not north-east. And suddenly the narrow, rutted road they were on began to seem familiar.

Up ahead she glimpsed a chain-link fence.

'The cemetery,' Adam said softly.

'Wait,' said Deborah. 'Did you see – there, look!'

'At what, the cemetery?' Adam asked.

'No! At that thing – there it is again! Up there on the road.'

'I don't see anything,' Nick said.

'You have to. See, it's moving—'

'I see a shadow,' Adam said. 'Or maybe a possum or something...'

'No, it's big,' Deborah insisted. '*There!* Can't you see that?'

Cassie looked up at last; she couldn't help it. The lonely road in front of her seemed dark and still at first, but then she saw – something. A shadow, she thought... but a shadow of what? It didn't lie along the road as a shadow ought to. It seemed to be standing high, and it was moving.

'I don't see anything,' Nick said again, curtly.

'Then you're blind,' Deborah snapped. 'It's like a person.'

Under Adam's jacket, Cassie's skin was rising in goose pimples. It *did* look like a person – except that it seemed to change every minute, now taller, now shorter, now wider, now thinner. At times it disappeared completely.

'It's heading for the cemetery,' Deborah said.

'No – look! It's veering off towards the shed,' Adam cried. 'Nick, come on!'

Beside the road was an abandoned shed. Even in the moonlight it was clear that it was falling to pieces. The dim shape seemed to whisk towards it, merging with the darkness behind it.

Adam and Nick were running, Nick snarling, 'We're chasing after nothing!' Deborah was standing poised, tense and alert, scanning the roadside. Cassie looked at the chain in dismay. Everyone's concentration had been shattered, the crystal was gyrating aimlessly. She looked up to say something – and drew in a quick breath.

'There it is!'

It had reappeared beside the shed, and it was moving fast. It went *through* the chain-link fence.

Deborah was after it in an instant, running like a deer. And Cassie, without any idea of what she was doing, was right behind her.

'Adam!' she shouted. 'Nick! This way!'

Deborah reached the waist-high fence and went over it, her tank dress not hindering her at all. Cassie reached it a second later, hesitated, then got a foothold in a chain link, flicking her skirts out of the way as she boosted herself over. She came down with a jolt that hurt her ankle, but there was no time to worry about it. Deborah was racing ahead.

'I've got it,' Deborah shouted, suddenly pulling up short. 'I've got it!'

Cassie could see it just in front of Deborah. It had stopped in its straight-line flight and was darting from side to side as if looking for escape. Deborah was darting, too, blocking it as if she were a guard on a basketball team.

We must be crazy, Cassie thought, as she reached the other girl. She couldn't leave Deborah to face the shadowy thing alone – but what were they going to do with it?

'Is there a spell or something to hold it?' she panted.

Deborah threw her a startled glance, and Cassie saw that she hadn't realised Cassie was behind her. 'What?'

'We've got to trap it somehow! Is there a spell—'

'*Down!*' Deborah shouted.

Cassie dived for the ground. The shadow-thing had swelled suddenly to twice its size, like an infuriated cat, and then it had lunged at them. Straight at them. Cassie felt it rush over her head, colder than ice and blacker than the night sky.

And then it was gone.

Deborah and Cassie sat up and looked at each other.

Adam and Nick appeared, running. 'Are you all right?' Adam demanded.

'Yes,' Cassie said shakily.

'What were you two doing?' Nick said, looking at them in disbelief. And even Adam asked, 'How did you get over the fence?'

Deborah gave him a scornful look. 'I didn't mean *you*,' he said.

Cassie gave him a scornful look. 'Girls can climb,' she said. She and Deborah stood up and began brushing each other off, exchanging a glance of complicity.

'It's gone now,' Adam said, wisely dropping the subject of fences. 'But at least we know what it looks like.'

Nick made a derisive sound. 'What *what* looks like?'

'You can't still say you didn't see it,' Deborah said impatiently. 'It was here. It went for Cassie and me.'

'I saw something – but what makes you think it was this so-called dark energy?'

'We were tracing it,' said Adam.

'How do we know what we were tracing?' Nick rapped back. 'Something that was around the place Lovejoy was killed, that's all. It could be the "dark energy" – or just some garden-variety ghost.'

'A *ghost*?' Cassie said, startled.

'Sure. If you believe in them at all, some of them like to hang out where murders are committed.'

Deborah spoke up eagerly. 'Yeah, like the Wailing Woman of Beverly, that lady in black that appears when somebody is going to die by violence.'

'Or that phantom ship in Kennybunk – the *Isidore*. The

one that comes and shows you your coffin if you're going to die at sea,' Adam said, looking thoughtful.

Cassie was confused. She'd assumed it was the dark energy they were tracking – but who could tell? 'It did end up in the cemetery,' she said slowly. 'Which seems like a logical place for a ghost. But if it wasn't the dark energy that killed Jeffrey, who was it? Who would *want* to kill him?'

Even as she asked, she knew the answer. Vividly, in her mind, she saw Jeffrey standing between two girls: one tall, dark, and disturbingly beautiful; the other small and wiry, with rusty hair and a pugnacious face.

'Faye or Sally,' she whispered. 'They were both jealous tonight. But – oh, look, even if they were mad enough to kill him, neither of them could have actually done it! Jeffrey was an athlete.'

'A witch could have done it,' Deborah said matter-of-factly. 'Faye could've made him do it to himself.'

'And Sally's got friends on the football team,' Nick added dryly. 'That's how she got herself voted Homecoming Queen. If they strangled him first, and then strung him up...'

Adam was looking disturbed at this cold-blooded discussion. 'You don't actually believe that.'

'Hey, a woman scorned, you know?' Nick said. 'I'm not saying either of them did it. I'm saying either of them *could* have.'

'Well, we won't figure it out by standing here,' Cassie said, shivering. Adam's jacket had slipped off when she went over the fence. 'Maybe if we could try to trace it again—'

It was then she realised she wasn't holding the crystal.

'It's gone,' she said. 'Melanie's crystal. I must have

dropped it when that thing rushed us. It should be right here on the ground, then. It's *got* to be,' she said.

But it wasn't. They all stooped to look, and Cassie combed through the sparse, withered grass with her fingers, but none of them could find it.

Somehow, this final disaster, incredibly tiny in comparison to everything that had happened that night, brought Cassie close to tears.

'It's been in Melanie's family for generations,' she said, blinking hard.

'Melanie will understand,' Adam told her gently. He put a hand on her shoulder, not easily but carefully, as if keenly aware that they were in front of witnesses.

'It's true, though; there's no point in standing around here,' he said to the others. 'Let's get back to school. Maybe they've found out something about Jeffrey there.'

As Cassie walked, the Cinderella shoes hurting her feet and Laurel's silvery dress streaked with dirt, she found herself looking straight into the Blood Moon. It was hovering over New Salem like the Angel of Death, she thought.

Normally, on the night of the full moon, the Circle would meet and celebrate. But on the day after Jeffrey's murder Diana was still sick, Faye was refusing to speak to anyone, and no one else had the heart to call a meeting.

Cassie spent the day feeling wretched. Last night at the high school the police had found no leads as to Jeffrey's killer. They hadn't said if he'd been strangled first and then hung, or if he'd just been hung. They weren't saying much of anything, and they didn't like questions.

Melanie had been kind about the necklace, but Cassie still felt guilty. She'd used it to go off on what turned out to be a wild-goose chase, and then she'd lost it. But far worse was the feeling of guilt over Jeffrey.

If she hadn't danced with him, maybe Faye and Sally wouldn't have been so angry. If she hadn't let Faye have the skull, then the dark energy wouldn't have been released. However she looked at it, she felt responsible, and she hadn't slept all night for thinking about it.

'Do you want to talk?' her grandmother said, looking up from the table where she was cutting ginger root. The archaic kitchen which had seemed so bewildering to Cassie when she'd first come to New Salem was now a sort of haven. There was always something to do here, cutting or drying or preserving the herbs from her grandmother's garden, and there was often a fire in the hearth. It was a cheerful, homey place.

'Oh, Grandma,' Cassie said, then stopped. She *wanted* to talk, yes, but how could she? She stared at her grandmother's wrinkled hands spreading the root in a wooden rack for drying.

'You know, Cassie, that I'm always here for you – and so is your mother,' her grandmother went on. She threw a sudden sharp glance up at the kitchen doorway, and Cassie saw that her mother was standing there.

Mrs Blake's large dark eyes were fixed on Cassie, and Cassie thought there was something sad in them. Ever since they'd come on this 'vacation' to Massachusetts, her mother had looked troubled, but these days there was a kind of tired wistfulness in her face that puzzled Cassie. Her mother was so beautiful, and so young-looking, and the new helplessness in her expression made her seem even younger than ever.

'And you know, Cassie, that if you're truly unhappy here—' her mother began, with a kind of defiance in her gaze.

Cassie's grandmother had stiffened, and her hands stopped spreading the root.

'—we don't have to stay,' her mother finished.

Cassie was astounded. After all she'd been through those first weeks in New Salem, after all those nights she'd wanted to die from homesickness – *now* her mother said they could go? But even stranger was the way Cassie's grandmother was glaring.

'Running away has never solved anything,' the older woman said. 'Haven't you learned that yet? Haven't we all...'

'There are two children dead,' Cassie's mother said. 'And if Cassie wants to leave here, we will.'

Cassie looked from one to the other in bewilderment. What were they talking about? 'Mom,' she said abruptly, 'why did you bring me here?'

Her mother and grandmother were still looking at each other – a battle of wills, Cassie thought. Then Cassie's mother looked away.

'I'll see you at dinner,' she said, and just as suddenly as she'd appeared, she slipped out of the room.

Cassie's grandmother let out a long sigh. Her old hands trembled slightly as she picked up another root.

'There are some things you can only understand later,' she said to Cassie, after a moment. 'You'll have to trust us for that, Cassie.'

'Does this have something to do with why you and Mom were estranged for so long? *Does* it?'

A pause. Then her grandmother said softly, 'You'll just have to trust us...'

Cassie opened her mouth, then shut it again. There was no use in pressing it any further. As she'd already learned, her family was very good at keeping secrets.

She'd go to the cemetery, she decided. She could use

the fresh air, and maybe if she found Melanie's crystal she would feel a little better.

Once there, she wished she'd asked Laurel to go along. Even though the October sun was bright, the air was nippy, and something about the dispirited graveyard made Cassie uneasy.

I wonder if ghosts come out in the daytime, she thought, as she located the place where she and Deborah had had to throw themselves face down. But no ghosts appeared. Nothing moved except the tips of the grass which rippled in the breeze.

Cassie's eyes scanned the ground, looking for any glint of bright silver chain or clear quartz. She went over the area inch by inch. The chain *had* to be right here . . . but it wasn't. At last she gave up and sat back on her heels.

That was when she noticed the mound again.

She'd forgotten to ask her grandmother about it. She'd have to remember tonight. She got up and walked over to it, looking at it curiously.

By daylight, she could see that the iron door was rusty. The padlock was rusty too, but it looked fairly modern. The cement chunk in front of the door was large; she didn't see how it could have gotten there. It was certainly too heavy for a person to carry.

And why would somebody *want* to carry it there?

Cassie turned away from the mound. The graves on this side of the cemetery were modern too; she'd seen them before. The writing on the tombstones was actually legible. Eve Dulany, 1955–1976, she read. Dulany was Sean's last name; this must be his mother.

The next stone had two names: David Quincey, 1955–1976, and Melissa B. Quincey, 1955–1976. Laurel's parents, Cassie thought. God, it must be awful to have both your parents dead. But Laurel wasn't the only kid on Crowhaven Road who did. Right here beside the Quincey headstone was another marker: Nicholas Armstrong, 1951–1976; Sharon Armstrong, 1953–1976. Nick's mom and dad. It must be.

When she saw the third headstone, the hairs on Cassie's arms began to prickle.

Linda Whittier, she read. Born 1954, died 1976. Suzan's mother.

Died 1976.

Sharply, Cassie turned to look at the Armstrong headstone again. She'd been right – both of Nick's parents had died in 1976. And the Quinceys... she was walking faster now. Yes. 1976 again. And Eve Dulany, too: died 1976.

Something rippled up Cassie's spine and she almost ran to the headstones on the far side of the mound. Mary Meade – Diana's mother – died 1976. Marshall Glaser and Sophia Burke Glaser. Melanie's parents. Died 1976. Grant Chamberlain. Faye's father. Died 1976. Adrian and Elizabeth Conant. Adam's parents. Died 1976.

Nineteen seventy-six. Nineteen seventy-six! There was a terrible shaking in Cassie's stomach and the hairs on the back of her neck were quivering.

What in God's name had happened in New Salem in 1976?

CHAPTER

8

'It was a hurricane,' Diana said.

It was Monday, and Diana was back in school, still a bit sniffly, but otherwise well. They were talking before American history class; it was the first chance Cassie had had to speak to Diana alone. She hadn't wanted to bring the question up in front of the others.

'A hurricane?' she said now.

Diana nodded. 'We get them every so often. That year it hit with practically no warning, and the bridge to the mainland was flooded. A lot of people got caught on the island, and a lot of people got killed.'

'I'm so sorry,' Cassie said. Well, you see; there's a perfectly reasonable explanation after all, she was thinking. How could she have been so stupid as to have freaked out over this? A natural disaster explained everything. And when Cassie had asked her grandmother about the mound at the cemetery last night, the old woman had looked at her, blinking, and finally said, *was* there a mound at the old burying ground? If there was, it might be some sort of bunker – a place for storing ammunition in one of the old wars. Again, a simple explanation.

Laurel and Melanie came in and took seats in front of Cassie and Diana. Cassie took a deep breath.

'Melanie, I went back to the cemetery yesterday to look for your crystal – but I still couldn't find it. I'm sorry; I guess it's gone for good,' she said.

Melanie's grey eyes were thoughtful and serious. 'Cassie, I told you that night it didn't matter. The only thing I wish is that you and Adam and Nick and Deborah hadn't run off without the rest of us. It was dangerous.'

'I know,' Cassie said softly. 'But right then it didn't *seem* dangerous – or at least, it did, but I didn't have time to think about how dangerous it really was. I just wanted to find whatever killed Jeffrey.' She saw Melanie and Diana trade a glance; Melanie surprised and Diana rather smug.

Cassie felt vaguely uncomfortable. 'Did Adam tell you anything about what we were talking about out in the cemetery?' she asked Diana. 'About Faye and Sally?'

Diana sobered. 'Yes. But it's all ridiculous, you know. Sally would never do anything like that, and as for Faye . . . well, she may be difficult at times, but she certainly isn't capable of killing anybody.'

Cassie opened her mouth, and found herself looking at Melanie, whose grey eyes now reflected something like head-shaking cynicism. She looked back at Diana quickly and said, 'No, I'm sure you're right,' but she wasn't. Melanie was right; Diana was too trusting, too naive. Nobody knew better than Cassie just what Faye was capable of.

Ms Lanning was starting class. Laurel and Melanie

turned around, and Cassie opened her book and tried to keep her mind on history.

That entire school week was strange. Jeffrey's death had done something to the outsider students; it was different than the other deaths. Kori had been a Club member, or practically, and the principal hadn't been very popular. But Jeffrey was a football hero, one of their own, a guy just about everyone liked and admired. His death upset people in a different way.

The whispers started quietly. But by Wednesday Sally was saying openly that Faye and the Club had killed Jeffrey. Tension was building between Club members and the rest of the school. Only Diana seemed unaware of it, looking shocked when Melanie suggested that the Circle might not be welcome at Jeffrey's funeral. 'We have to go,' she said, and they did go, except Faye.

As for Faye... Faye spent the week quietly seething. She hadn't forgiven Suzan and Deborah for helping to get Cassie ready for the dance, she hadn't forgiven Nick for snubbing her, and she hadn't forgiven the rest of them for witnessing her humiliation. The only people she wasn't furious with were the Henderson brothers. When Jeffrey's death was mentioned, she looked hard and secretive.

Every day Cassie expected to get a phone call with some bizarre new demand, some new blackmail. But, for the moment, Faye seemed to be leaving her alone.

It was Friday afternoon, car-pooling home after school, that Laurel mentioned the Halloween dance.

'Of course you're coming, Cassie,' she said as they dropped Cassie off at Number Twelve. 'You *have* to. And you've got plenty of time, two weeks, to think of somebody to ask.'

Cassie walked into the house with her legs feeling weak. *Another* dance? She couldn't believe it.

One thing she knew: it couldn't be anything like the last one. She wouldn't let it be. She'd do what Laurel said, she'd find somebody to go with – and then she'd just stick with him the entire time. Somebody, anybody. Sean, maybe.

Cassie winced. Well, maybe not *anybody*. Starved for attention as he was, Sean might end up being a problem himself. She might never get rid of him.

No, Cassie needed some guy to be an escort and nothing else. Some guy who would absolutely not get interested in her, under any circumstances. Some guy who'd be completely indifferent...

A vision flashed through her mind, of mahogany eyes, rich and deep and absolutely dispassionate. Nick. Nick didn't even like girls. And Faye wouldn't care; Faye wasn't even speaking to Nick any more. Nick would be safe – but would he ever want to go with her to a dance?

Only one way to find out, she thought.

Nick was Deborah's cousin, and lived with her parents at Number Two Crowhaven Road. The peach-coloured house was run-down, and the garage was usually open, showing the car Nick was continually working on.

Adam had said it was a '69 Mustang coupe, which was something special. Right at the moment, though, it looked like a skeleton up on blocks.

When Cassie walked in late that afternoon, Nick was bent over the workbench, his dark hair shining faintly in the light of the naked bulb hanging from the rafters. He was doing something with a screwdriver to a part.

'Hi,' Cassie said.

Nick straightened up. He didn't look surprised to see

her, but then Nick never looked surprised. He didn't look particularly happy to see her either. He was wearing a T-shirt so covered with grease stains that it was difficult to read the slogan underneath, but faintly Cassie could make out the odd words *Friends don't let friends drive Chevys*.

Cassie cleared her throat. Just walk in and ask him, she'd thought – but now that was proving to be impossible. After a moment or two of staring at her, waiting, Nick looked back down at the workbench.

'I was just walking to Diana's,' Cassie said brightly. 'And I thought I'd stop by and say hi.'

'Hi,' Nick said, without looking up.

Cassie's mouth was dry. What had ever made her think she *could* ask a guy to a dance? So what if lots of guys had wanted to dance with her last time; that had probably just been a fluke. And *Nick* certainly hadn't been hanging around her.

She tried to make her voice sound casual. 'So what are you doing...' She had meant to ask 'for the Halloween dance' but her throat closed up and she panicked. Instead she finished in a squeak, '... right now?'

'Rebuilding the carburettor,' Nick replied briefly.

'Oh,' Cassie said. She searched her mind desperately for some other topic of conversation. 'Um...' She picked up a little metal ball from the workbench. 'So – what's this for?'

'The carburettor.'

'Oh.' Cassie looked at the little ball. 'Uh, Nick, you know, I was just wondering' – she started to set the ball back down – 'whether you might, um, want to – *oops*.'

The ball had shot out of her sweaty fingers like a watermelon seed, landing with a *ping* somewhere under the workbench and disappearing. Cassie looked up, horrified, and Nick slammed down the screwdriver and swore.

'I'm sorry – honest, Nick, I'm sorry—'

'What the hell did you have to touch it for? What are you *doing* here, anyway?'

'I…' Cassie looked at his wrathful face and the last of her courage left her. 'I'm sorry, Nick,' she gasped again, and she fled.

Out of the garage and down the driveway. Without thinking she turned right when she got to the street, heading back for her own house. She didn't want to go to Diana's, anyway – Adam was probably there. She walked up Crowhaven Road, her cheeks still burning and her heart thumping.

It had been a stupid idea from the beginning. Suzan was right; Nick was an iguana. He didn't have any normal human emotions. Cassie hadn't expected him to *want* to go to the dance with her in the first place; she'd just thought maybe he wouldn't mind, because he'd been nice to her in the boiler room that night. But now he'd shown his true colours. She was just glad she hadn't actually asked him before she'd dropped the ball – that would have been the ultimate embarrassment.

Even as it was, though, her chest felt tight and hot and her eyes felt sore. She kept her head carefully high as she passed Melanie's house, and then Laurel's. She didn't want to see either of them.

The sun had just set and the colour was draining out of everything. It gets dark so early these days, she was thinking, when the roar of a motor caught her attention.

It was a black Suzuki Samurai with the licence plate FLIP ME. The Henderson brothers were in it, Doug driving too fast. As soon as they spotted her they pulled over and stuck their heads out the windows, shouting comments.

'Hey, what's a nice girl like you doing in a neighbourhood like this?'

'You wanna party, Cassie?'

'C'mon, baby, we can show you a good time!'

They were just harassing her for the fun of it, but something made Cassie look up into Doug's tilted blue-green eyes and say nervily, 'Sure.'

They stared at her, nonplussed. Then Chris burst into laughter.

'Cool; get in,' he said, and opened the passenger side door.

'Wait a minute,' Doug began, frowning, but Cassie was already getting in, Chris helping her up the high step. She didn't know what had possessed her. But she was feeling wild and irresponsible, which she guessed was the best way to be feeling when you were with the Henderson brothers.

'Where are we going?' she asked as they roared off. Chris and Doug looked at each other cagily.

'Gonna buy some pumpkins for Halloween,' Chris said.

'Buy pumpkins?'

'Well, not *buy*, exactly,' Chris temporised.

For some reason, at this particular moment, that struck Cassie as funny. She began to giggle. Chris grinned.

'We're goin' down to Salem,' he explained. 'They have the best pumpkin patches to raid. And if we get done early enough we can hide in the Witch Dungeon and scare the tourists.'

The Witch Dungeon? thought Cassie, but all she said was, 'Okay.'

The floor of the minijeep was littered with bottles, bits of pipe, rags, Dunkin' Donut bags, unravelling cassette tapes, and raunchy magazines. Chris was explaining to Cassie about how to construct a pipe bomb when they reached the pumpkin patch.

'Okay, now, shut up,' Doug said. 'We've gotta go around back.' He turned the lights and engine off and cruised.

The pumpkin patch was a huge fenced enclosure full of pumpkins, some piled up, some scattered across the ground. Doug stopped the Samurai just behind a large pile by the booth where you paid for the pumpkins. It was fully dark now, and the light from the enclosure didn't quite reach them.

'Over the fence,' Doug mouthed, and to Cassie: 'Stay here.' Cassie was glad he didn't want her to climb it; there was barbed wire at the top. Chris laid his jacket on it and the two boys swarmed over easily.

Then they calmly started handing pumpkins over the fence. Chris gave them to Doug, who stood on the pile and dropped them to Cassie on the other side, motioning her to put them in the back seat of the jeep.

What on earth do they *want* with all of these, anyway? Cassie wondered dizzily as she staggered back with armload after armload. Can you make a bomb out of a pumpkin?

'Okay,' Doug hissed at last. 'That's enough.' He swarmed back over the fence. Chris started to climb over too, but just at that moment there was a frenzied barking and a large black dog with wiry legs appeared.

'Help!' squawked Chris. He was caught hanging over the top of the fence. The Doberman had him by the boot and was worrying it furiously, snarling. A man exploded out of the booth and began yelling at them and shaking his fist.

'Help! Help!' Chris shouted. He started to giggle and then yelped, 'Ow! He's takin' my foot off! Ow! Help!'

Doug, his strange slanted eyes glittering wildly, rushed back to the jeep. 'Gonna *kill* that dog,' he said breathlessly. 'Where's that army pistol?'

'Hold on, Max! Hold him till I get my shotgun!' the man was yelling.

'Ow! He's chewin' on me! It hurts, man!' Chris bellowed.

'Don't kill him,' Cassie pleaded frantically, catching Doug by the arm. All she needed was for him and the pumpkin man to start shooting at each other. Doug continued ransacking the litter on the jeep's floor. 'Don't kill the dog! We can just give him this,' Cassie said, suddenly inspired. She snatched up a Dunkin' Donuts bag with several stale doughnuts in it. While Doug was still looking for a gun, she ran back to the fence.

'Here, doggy, nice doggy,' she gasped. The dog snarled. Chris continued bellowing; the pumpkin man continued yelling. '*Good* dog,' Cassie told the Doberman desperately. 'Good boy, here, look, doughnuts, see? Want a doughnut?' And then, surprising herself completely, she shouted, '*Come here! NOW!*'

At the same time, she did – she didn't know what. She did… something… with her mind. She could feel it going out of her like a blast of heat. It hit the dog and the dog let go of Chris's foot, hind legs collapsing. Belly almost on the ground, it slunk over to the fence and crouched.

Cassie felt tall and terrible. She said, 'Good dog,' and tossed the doughnut bag over the fence. Chris was scrambling over in the other direction, almost falling on his head. The dog lay down and whined pitifully, ignoring the doughnuts.

'Let's go,' Chris yelled. 'Come on, Doug! We don't need to kill anybody!'

Between them, he and Cassie bundled the protesting Doug into the jeep and Chris drove off. The pumpkin-seller ran after them with his shotgun, but when they reached the road he gave up the chase.

'Ow,' Chris said, shaking his foot and causing the jeep to veer.

Doug muttered to himself.

Cassie leaned back and sighed.

'Okay,' Chris said cheerfully, 'now let's go to the Witch Dungeon.'

The Salem Witch Dungeon Museum looked like a house from the outside. Chris and Doug seemed to know the layout well, and Cassie followed them around the house, where they slipped in a back entrance.

Through a doorway Cassie glimpsed what seemed to be a small theatre. 'That's where they do the witch trials,' Chris said. 'You know, like a play for the tourists. Then they take 'em down here.'

A flight of narrow stairs plunged down into darkness.

'*Why?*' Cassie said.

'It's the dungeon. They give 'em a tour. We hide in the corners and jump up and yell when they get close. Some of 'em practically have heart attacks,' Doug said, with his mad grin.

Cassie could see how that might happen. As they made their way down the stairs it got darker and darker. A dank, musty odour assaulted her nostrils and the air felt very cool.

A narrow corridor stretched forward into the blackness, which was broken only by tiny lights at long intervals. Small cells opened out from either side of the corridor. The whole place had a heavy, underground feel to it.

It's like the boiler room, Cassie thought. Her feet stopped moving.

'Come on, what's wrong?' Doug whispered, turning around. She could barely see him.

Chris came back to the foot of the stairs and looked into her face. 'We don't have to go in there yet,' he said. 'We can wait here till they start to come down.'

Cassie nodded at him gratefully. It was bad enough standing on the edge of this terrible place. She didn't want to go in until she absolutely had to.

'Or...' Chris seemed to be engaging in some prodigious feat of thought. 'Or... we could just *leave*, you know.'

'Leave now? Why?' Doug demanded, running back.

'Because...' Chris stared at him. 'Because... because I say so!'

'You? Who cares what you say?' Doug returned in a whispering shout and the two of them began to scuffle.

They're not really scary after all, Cassie thought, a little dazedly. They're more like the Lost Boys in *Peter Pan*. Peculiar, but sort of cute.

'It's all right,' she said, to stop their fighting. 'We can stay. I'll just sit down on the stairs.'

Out of breath, they sat down too, Chris massaging the toe of his boot.

Cassie leaned against the wall and shut her eyes. She could hear voices from above, someone talking about the Salem witch trials, but only snatches of the lecture got through to her. She was drained from everything that had happened today, and this dreadful place made her feel sick and fuzzy. As if she had cobwebs in her brain.

A woman's voice was saying, '... the royal governor, Sir William Phips, established a special court to deal with the cases. By now there were so many accused witches...'

So many fake witches, Cassie thought hazily, half listening. If that woman only knew about the real witches lurking in her dungeon.

'...on June tenth, the first of the convicted witches was publicly executed. Bridget Bishop was hanged on Gallows Hill, just outside of Salem...'

Poor Bridget Bishop, Cassie thought. She had a sudden vision of Jeffrey's swinging feet and a wave of nausea passed over her. Probably Bridget's feet had been swinging when they hanged her, too.

'...by the end of September eighteen other people had been hanged. Sarah Goode's last words...'

Eighteen. That's a lot of swinging feet. God, I don't feel well, thought Cassie.

'...and a nineteenth victim was pressed to death. Pressing was a form of Puritan torture in which a board was placed on the victim's chest, and then heavier and heavier rocks were piled on top of the board...'

Ugh. Now I *really* don't feel well. Wonder how it feels to have rocks piled on you till you die? Guess I'll never know since that doesn't happen much today. Unless you happen to be caught in a rockslide, or something...

With a jerk, Cassie sat up straight, the cobwebs swept out of her brain as if by a blast of icy wind.

Rockslide. Avalanche. Mr Fogle, the high-school principal, had found out what it was like to have rocks piled on you till you died.

Weird coincidence. That was all it was. But...

Oh, my God, Cassie thought suddenly.

She felt as if her entire body were plugged into something electric. Her thoughts were tumbling over each other.

Rockslide. Pressed to death. Same thing, really. And hanging. The witches were hanged... just like

Jeffrey Lovejoy. Oh, God, oh, God. There had to be a connection.

'. . . never know how many died in prison. In comparison to the conditions there, the swift oblivion of a broken neck may have been merciful. Our tour will now take you—'

Broken neck. A broken neck.

Kori's neck had been broken.

Cassie thought she was going to faint.

Read on for a taster of the thrilling conclusion to
The Secret Circle...

THE POWER

'Cassie!' Diana said, jumping up as she saw Cassie's face.
'What's the matter?'

Adam was sitting on the bed; he rose too, looking
alarmed.

'I know it's late – I'm sorry – but we have to talk. I was
in the WitchDungeon—'

'You were where? Here, take this; your hands are like
ice. Now start over again, slowly,' Diana said, sitting her
down and wrapping her in a sweater.

Slowly, stumbling sometimes, Cassie told them the
story: how Chris and Doug had picked her up and taken
her to Salem. She left out the part about the pumpkin
patch, but told how they'd gone to the Witch Dungeon,
and how, listening to the lecture, she had suddenly seen
the connection. Pressing to death – rockslides; hanging –
broken necks.

'But what does it mean?' Diana said when she'd
finished.

'I don't know, exactly,' Cassie admitted. 'But it looks
like there's some connection between the three deaths
and the way Puritans used to punish people.'

'The dark energy is the connection,' Adam said quietly.

'That skull was used by the original coven, which lived in the time of the witch trials.'

'But that wouldn't account for Kori,' Diana protested. 'We didn't activate the skull until after Kori was dead.'

Adam was pale. 'No. But I found the skull the day before Kori died. I took it out of the sand...' His eyes met Cassie's, and she had a terrible feeling of dismay.

'Sand. "To Hold Evil Harmless,"' she whispered. She looked at Diana. 'That's in your Book of Shadows. Burying an object in sand or earth to hold the evil in it harmless. just like—' She stopped abruptly and bit her tongue. God, she'd almost said, 'Just like you buried the skull on the beach to keep it safe.'

'Just like I found it,' Adam finished for her. 'Yes. And you think that when I took it out, that alone activated it. But that would mean the skull would have to be so strong, so powerful...' His voice trailed off. Cassie could see he was trying to fight the idea; he didn't want to believe it. 'I did feel *something* when I pulled it out of that hole,' he added quietly. 'I felt dizzy, strange. That could have been from dark energy escaping.' He looked at Cassie. 'So you think that energy came to New Salem and killed Kori.'

'I – don't know what to think,' Cassie said wretchedly. 'I don't know why it *would*. But it can't be coincidence that every single time we interact with the skull, somebody dies afterwards, in a way that the Puritans used to kill witches.'

'But don't you see,' Diana said excitedly, 'it isn't every time. Nobody used the skull right before Jeffrey died. It was absolutely safe—' She hesitated and then went on quickly. 'Well, of course I can tell *you* two – it was safe out on the beach. It's still buried there now. I've been checking it every few days. So there isn't a one-to-one correspondence.'

Cassie was speechless. Her first impulse was to blurt out, 'Somebody did too use the skull!' But that would be insane. She could never tell Diana that – and now she was utterly at a loss. A shaking was starting deep inside her. Oh, God, there was a one-to-one correspondence.

It was like that slogan, *Use a gun; go to jail*. Use the skull; kill somebody. And she, Cassie, was responsible for the last time the skull had been used. She was responsible for killing Jeffrey.

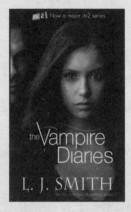
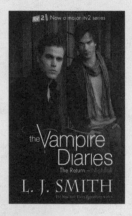
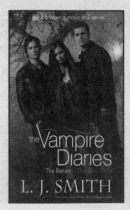
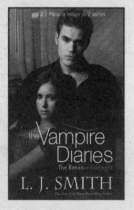

the Vampire Diaries

Stefan's Diaries

Stefan and Damon weren't always fighting or succumbing to their bloodlusts. Once they were loving siblings who enjoyed all the riches and happiness that their wealthy lifestyle afforded them; loyal brothers who happened to both fall for the same beautiful woman. Once they were alive...

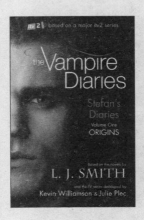

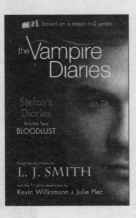

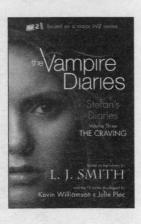

NIGHT WORLD

 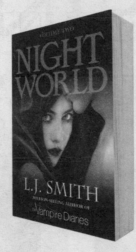 

Welcome to the Night World -
a secret world of vampires, werewolves,
witches, shapeshifters, and ancient souls
where humans are prey and relationships
with them forbidden. But we all know,
there's nothing like forbidden fruit ...

DARK
HEART
RISING

ENTER A WORLD WHERE ONE ENCHANTING
HEROINE MUST DECIDE BETWEEN TWO
DANGEROUSLY ENTICING CHOICES.

BEAUTIFUL DEAD

Not alive. Not dead. Somewhere in between
lie the Beautiful Dead.

A stunning series that will leave you restless.

Books 1-4
OUT NOW